Rapture

Rapture

David Sosnowski

Villard
New York

VILLARD BOOKS is a registered trademark of Random House, Inc.

Library of Congress Cataloging-in-Publication Data

Sosnowski, David.
Rapture / David Sosnowski.
p.   cm.
ISBN 0-679-45174-9
1. Virus diseases—Patients—Psychology—Fiction.   2. Angels—Fiction. I. Title.
PS3569.O716A8   1996
813'.54—dc20   96-7138

Random House website address: http://www.randomhouse.com/

Printed in the United States of America on acid-free paper

2   4   6   8   9   7   5   3

First Edition

Book design by Caroline Cunningham

For my parents,
Eugene and Florence

$\mathcal{A}cknowledgments$

$\mathcal{I}$ wish to thank the Arts Foundation of Michigan and the Michigan Council for the Arts and Cultural Affairs for the financial support that made completion of this work possible; the Ragdale Foundation, for a wonderful working space and atmosphere in which to begin a project that had scared me for over ten years; the *Alaska Quarterly Review,* for publishing "Fix," the short story upon which this novel is based; my agent, Linn Prentis, and editor, Craig Nelson, for making this particular dream come true; my copy editor, Amy Ryan, for making me look smarter than I am; my publicists, Brian McLendon and Kirsten Raymond; my family, for their love and understanding and all that family stuff; and the following friends, for their encouragement and support: Joe Matuzak, Mark Schemanske, Bob Hicok, Jay Pinka, Denise Brooks, Ken Cormier, Walter Meixner, Sheryl Pearson, Bob Haynes, Suzanne Brody, Danny Rendleman, Jan Worth, Pat Hardin, Carolyn Kraus, Kathy Weeks, Theresa Stoddard, Michelle Passino, Chris Dahl, Charles Baxter, M. L. Leibler, all the folks at the Writer's Center in Bethesda and the Ann Arbor Poetry Slam, as well as anybody else

Acknowledgments

who has ever published me, gotten me readings, been in writing workshops with me, or given me cuts in line; and, last but not least, I want to thank Josie Kearns, for being the only person other than myself to have read each of the many drafts it took to write this novel (and for not coming at me with a knife at any point in the process).

Part One

Hat Weather

$\mathcal{I}$t starts like this: with a hat. Precisely, a New Year's Eve party hat, molded from Styrofoam in the shape of a topper and swaddled in multi-colored cellophane. Why a New Year's hat, especially in mid-October, in the middle of the night, in the middle of a street running along the Detroit River? Who cares, and why not? Some things just *are*. What's important (maybe) is that it's there, tumbling end over end, clonking its prematurely festive way down the after-dark emptiness of West Jefferson. It darts into and out of cones of green-white mercury light, playing tag with scraps and tatters of urban excelsior, all blown by the same unseasonably warm breeze—perhaps the last good flying weather of the year.

That's what she thinks, at least, the She at whose feet the hat comes to rest. "Hello," she says, bending and tipping an imaginary counterpart. "What have we here?" She picks up the hat, checks for bugs or worse, and, finding none, scrunches it down over the scraggly red explosion of her hair. She pinches the flaps of her dark suit coat closed, switches from one profile to the next, admiring slivers of herself between the bars of a liquor store's window. Sharp, she thinks. The green matches her eyes, the rusty patches, her hair, and wings.

She understands about things just being. Like, for example, she's just an Angel—well, just a person with wings, actually. Why? Who cares, and why not? What's important (maybe) is that she's here.

The She is part of a pair—Angels, both—who will converge about two blocks from now. The other is a He, traveling from a different direction and without a party hat, but winged all the same. Each knows nothing about the other; each has chosen this place and time because of the unlikelihood of meeting anyone else of their kind.

Detroit doesn't get many Angels, even though, as cities go, it's actually Angel-friendly, if only by default. Its ledges, sills, and eaves, for example, sport no broken glass, no grease or barbed wire, unlike, say, New York, where an Angel can't find a safe roost to save his or her life. Still, the Angels have abandoned Detroit, leaving it the victim of its own bad-ass PR.

Leaving it, that is, a good choice for Angels looking for a little privacy.

Now, you might figure the two of them are heading toward St. Antoine's, a good, old-fashioned, Quasimodo-type church, made of rough-hewn stone blocks, complete with vaulting spires, rainspout-mouthed gargoyles, bloody Bible scenes in cartoon-vibrant stained glass—the works. You might guess that's where the pair are headed, but you'd be wrong. Angels—well, people with wings—generally stay away from churches for pretty much the same reason that Native Americans don't hang out with the wooden variety, and real jockeys refrain from posing on suburban lawns. Bad taste, feelings, memories and such. Of course, given the agenda of these two—their not wanting to be seen by other Angels—choosing a no-fly zone like St. Antoine's could make a perverse kind of sense. And it does, kind of, with one exception—point two on the pair's separate agendas—namely, height. Pure, simple, obnoxious, and anonymous—*height*.

Sure, St. Antoine's has its spires, stretching for all they're worth along the Detroit skyline, shooting up two times farther than Heaven by eighteenth-century standards, but dwarfed by its neighbor just a few blocks over—Wyandotte Steel. Wyandotte Steel, which rattled its last polluted breath back in the early eighties, is left now to rust and weeds, its windows shattered by kids with big-league ambitions, bad attitudes, or a belief in that urban voodoo that equates broken glass with granted wishes. Wyandotte Steel, abandoned and abused and standing, now, surrounded by NO TRESPASSING signs and orange barbed wire, torn open here and there because that's just how people are—here and there. Wyandotte Steel, with its laddered stacks—one, two, and three—sending their rippled reflections across the dark river toward Canada, waiting, stoically, for two Angels, coming from different directions, drawn by the same overlooked and Angel-free height.

And the funny thing is, neither notices the other—not, that is, until the party hat blows off the She-Angel's head just when she's halfway up stack one and he's almost to the top of stack three, and they're just a handful of yards apart. That's when she yells, "Shit!" lets go a hand to make a grab for the hat, swings out but misses, leaving her silhouette, wings and all, stamped for a split second against the crummy Detroit sky. He, hearing, reflexively says, "What?" and then scrunches tight against the rust of his own smokestack, trying to be small, trying to be invisible, trying to be what's impossible, now that he's opened his big, stupid mouth.

Time freezes. The She who said "Shit" looks at the He who said "What" and says nothing else. He, also, says nothing else. They're both found out, they know, their secret roost's exposed, but they're hoping to undo it by leaving the night air be, by holding their breaths, and forging on.

The wind is up and howling. Both of their hearts beat in their throats. Both their minds fix against the presence of the other, shutting like stubborn doors.

The feathers on either set of wings rustle.

The air, warm at ground level, is slightly cooler up here; both Angels can feel the flesh of their wings going goosebumpy, can feel the point where each quill meets skin, separately, like a stiffening nipple. And all these sensations are about life, about the simple animal joy of it, about the anticipation of flight, the spread and glide, the swoop and hover over the dark sparkling down-thereness of the Detroit River, the icy wind rushing in your hair and feathers . . .

Well, it's about that for at least one of them—for her, with her hand on the last rung now, pulling up to the mouth of the smokestack, to perch and think, to appreciate the sheerness of this height, the wildness of this wind. And God, could she ever use a cigarette just about now! She smiles at the thought—so Angelically incorrect—and notices her hat, a glitter, a speck, rocking on the surface of the river below.

For him, perched on the lip of his own smokestack, hands holding on, white-knuckled and backward, shoe toes wedged into the last rung—this, all of this, could be as much about death and getting it over with as it is anything else. For him, it's about a secret that's gotten too big, too heavy, and too embarrassing, goddammit, and why won't she just *go*? He sees her over there, rising now, standing on the edge, arms up like a swimmer ready to dive, wings spread, points up, knees crooked and ready for the spring and—*nothing*.

She waits.

Is she waiting for him?

Of course she is.

Get it over with, he thinks, first to her, and then, reluctantly, to him-self.

He rises, sticks his hands in his pockets, and looks up. He waits. Hopes.

But she's still there, waiting, too. It's like two pool players, he thinks, standing at adjacent tables, waiting for the other to take a shot, being po-lite—or not wanting the other to see how badly you play.

Screw it, he thinks. Just screw it.

He closes his eyes, works a shoe loose, and steps out into nothing. His wings do not spread so much as they are ripped open by the buffeting wind; they twist, turn cockeyed, whistle and shed. There is nothing graceful about his tumbling plummet; he shrieks without meaning to, all the long way down to the water, where his splash washes the party hat back to shore.

The She-Angel doesn't know what she's just seen, outside of its being all wrong. Angel suicides she knows about, has treated more than she cares to count, but they're always wrists or pills or gas—no jumpers. An Angel jumper is an oxymoron; it's like a fish trying to drown, or like trying to suffocate by holding your breath. Your body just won't let you do it; it's not natural. At some point, autopilot kicks in and . . .

His wings rise to the surface first, spread and float like twin lily pads. The She-Angel stops second-guessing the facts of the case and bolts from her perch. She banks a wing, turning her glide into a circle, dips the tip and begins wheeling herself downward in a steady spiral. She levels off a foot above the surface, beats her wings hummingbird-swift to maintain her hover and grabs his collar. Lifting him is out of the question; he's unconscious and weighs every bit of his hundred-ninety-plus pounds. So she glides him through the water, like a tugboat pulling a barge, floating him back to shore, where the party hat waits for both of them.

Pulling him up to land, she rolls him on his stomach. One wing is dislocated, and he's taken on water. Improvising, she pumps against his back, forcing out what she can of the river. She checks for a heartbeat and finds it—faint, but holding on. Shit, she really needs a cigarette now, something to calm her nerves, something to do with her hands, something to keep her company besides the pale, feathered thing lying next to her. She looks at him and sees the future. If he makes it, they'll send him to her—they send all the fucked-up Angels to her—and there goes her Wednesday after-lunch slot for the next couple of months.

Shit.

A girl goes out for a nice evening alone, wants to squeeze in a little night flying by the river, and what happens?

Shit.

She picks up the party hat and angles it jauntily on the back of his head. She could leave—she could just leave, but, of course, she can't. Help doesn't just *happen* in this part of Detroit; leaving and hoping for it to stumble by is as good as murder.

She remembers a convenience store a few blocks away, and though she's not fond of standing launches, she begins flapping, stirring up the dust and trash at her feet, steadily shinnying up the sky like an invisible rope. When she's high enough to clear the barbed wire, she begins pushing out, covering the distance in a fraction of the time it would take to walk.

Returning, she takes a seat on a rock next to the He-Angel, unwraps the cigarettes she bought to get change for the pay phone, and waits for the ambulance. She smokes down two Camels waiting, and then the rain starts.

Shit.

She removes her jacket and stretches it over her head, making a jury-rigged canopy by slipping the tips of either wing into the sleeves. Listening to the thrumming rain, she considers draping the coat over her silent partner but doesn't, realizing what a sheeted body might imply. Instead, she shifts the party hat to cover a bit more of his head and keeps on waiting.

She has begun thinking about going through his pockets when the ambulance finally arrives.

"Let me guess," the driver says. "It's party boy."

"No, it's me. He just got bored waiting."

Then, suddenly, and as if it's news: "Hey, you're an Angel," the driver says.

"Hey," she says back, "you're an ambulance guy."

"No," the driver says. "This ain't good. You're both Angels. You shoulda told the dispatcher . . ."

"I did. I told the operator."

"There's this whole special team for Angels, 'cause of how they are inside." He makes a swirling gesture around his heart.

"It's not *that* different," the She-Angel says, wasting her breath.

"Different enough, ma'am," the ambulance driver says. "Different cert level and everything. You need special training and my guys ain't got it."

"Listen, I work at the Medical Center in Ann Arbor . . ."

"Long way from A-square."

"That doesn't matter. What I'm trying to tell you is I've checked him out. He's got a dislocated wing. That's all. You're not going to break anything else."

"There's paperwork. There's liability insurance. There's chain of custody . . ."

"Here," she says, fishing a business card out of her wallet. "Have him sue me." She pauses as the driver reads the card, his lips moving. "Okay? Now, just lay him on his stomach so his head hangs off the gurney, and then have somebody hold it in a straight line with his body."

"You riding with him?" the driver asks.

"Me? No," the She-Angel says, raising her hands and turning to leave. "I'm just an innocent bystander."

"Hey!" an attendant shouts from the back of the ambulance.

She stops, turns around.

"What about this?" the attendant asks. He holds out the party hat, its cellophane blazing in the red and yellow moons of emergency light, rain steadily tapping on its emptiness.

"It's his," the She-Angel calls back, through the gusting rain, through the noise of the engine, idling. "It has sentimental value. He never goes anywhere without it."

The attendant says something like, "Okie-doke"—it's hard to tell through the rain—and slams the door, as the ambulance, the hat, the He-Angel who jumped, and the last good flying weather of the year first slowly, then quickly, sizzle away.

Part Two

The Son of Frankenstein

2

*A*s for him—the one who jumped—his name is Zander Wiles and he was the first Angel to go public, and live. He didn't start out as an Angel, of course, and of his wings and their coming, the first thing he remembers is this:

Plaid.

On the morning the wings happened—or began to happen—Zander woke up feeling, well, not very well and . . . plaid. Not that it was unusual for him to feel like a color; he'd felt blue, seen red, been green with envy and called yellow—he'd just never been all those colors at the same time.

Looking in the mirror as his face alternately flushed and drained, Zander tried to sort out the tangle of feelings inside. They seemed to be coming in stripes—nausea going from head to toe, a dull, pulsing numbness cutting across his chest, and a sort of free-floating terror lacing in and out. Waves of hot and cold ran from his solar plexus to his forehead, rolling like the lines on a broken TV screen. One arm started itching, deeply, as if ants were crawling around underneath the skin. Scratching was useless. They just got angry and ran away, up and over, out of reach between his shoulder blades—where they stayed, and grew.

Raised near the Detroit River, Zander had grown up thinking that formaldehyde was how summertime was supposed to smell, and that evacuations in the middle of the night were perfectly normal. Overcoats, bunny slippers, the crayons and coloring books for doodling till the all-clear—it was the same old song and dance, whenever this or that factory sprung a leak or caught fire. Everybody downriver knew the drill, and knew, too, that a good number of them would probably die from something weird. So waking up plaid wasn't completely unexpected. It was just part of the territory.

Of course, there were other things to blame. Zander had moved away, after all—and picked up a few stupid habits. Habits for which plaid might well be the payoff. As he sat on the edge of his bed that first morning, feeling messed up and motley, thinking about the life he'd led for the last several years, Zander realized that plaid was what he'd been flirting with, ever since his eighteenth birthday. It had been that long since he last felt terrified.

Terrified, that is, and parti-colored.

It was just three and something years earlier, and Zander was still living with his real mom and stepdad. Spring had sprung, windy and bright blue; maple trees rattled with helicopter seeds, shaking them free in a great, dry, spiraling rain. There'd been a solid week of warm, open-window weather, and Zander was looking forward to his impending adulthood. He'd begun collecting fetishes of emergence—the remnants of a blue egg, a shed snake's skin, the split carapace of a cicada.

Zander was a boy-man back then, about six foot three with barely enough pounds to keep him upright on his teetering skeleton, thick, black hair rolling to his shoulders and stubbling his chin, where he hoped it would make him look tougher. He wore olive green work shirts and blue jeans, Kmart bin tennis shoes, and Salvation Army suit coats pierced with buttons bearing the band names and slogans he believed in: SHIT HAPPENS; THEY MIGHT BE GIANTS; FUCK AUTHORITY. Over his brown eyes, he wore bottle green sunglasses, wire-rimmed and round. And despite the likelihood, given his appearance, no parts of his body were pierced or tattooed. After all, Zander hated needles with a passion, back then.

All told, he was a good kid, rebellious in all the socially sanctioned ways. He stashed *Playboys* under his mattress along with his copies of *Famous Monsters;* he read *Catcher in the Rye* and *On the Road,* smoked dope socially, and kept a video library of all the gangster and monster movies he could find. He'd been busted for shoplifting once—a lizard from a pet store, of all things. And he'd decided *not* to go to college (which was mainly bullshit), though he still went to church (which was bullshit, too, but something he did anyway, to please his mom).

But then his eighteenth birthday came and Zander got a chance he hadn't asked for—the chance to prove how tough he really was. It started with a twenty-dollar bill from Frank, his stepdad, who asked him to pick up some broasted chicken they'd ordered for his birthday party. Frank Smith was an almost-doctor who became a pharmacist when doctoring didn't pan out. He was the sort of wiry, knotty old man who marionettes about the house in an undershirt and dress pants, hoisted all the way up to his chest by suspenders. His mother, Karen, married Frank because . . . well, because she hurt badly after her real husband died and needed some bald gratitude to balloon her up, to keep her feet moving, one after the other. That, and she needed help with the mortgage. Problem was, Frank started thinking he deserved Karen; he also started ordering Zander around, right about the same time.

Frank saw himself as an up-by-the-bootstraps sort of guy; he also thoroughly believed in doing drastic things for the other guy's "own good." Thumbtacked to the corkboard next to the pharmacy counter, Frank displayed a few slogans of his own:

IF YOU'RE SO SMART, WHY AIN'T YOU RICH?

IT'S NOT ENOUGH TO BE GOOD; BE GOOD FOR SOMETHING.

Something. Become something. Those were Frank's marching orders the day Zander came home to say the Safeway hadn't gotten an order for broasted chicken or anything else from Frank. "Become something," he shouted from inside *his* house, while Zander stood outside, holding a key that didn't work anymore.

"Keep the twenty. Come back when you've made something of yourself."

It had begun raining, and the world went blurry as Zander stood there, sunglasses beading. He added up the situation, and kicked the door.

"Mom!" he shouted. "Frank's gone crazy. Let me in."

The venetian blinds fell closed with a clatter and Zander thought about heaving a brick through the front window, thought about howling at the top of his lungs for all the world—and the neighbors—to hear. Instead, he looked at his tennis shoes, standing in a puddle turned particolored by gasoline runoff from somewhere.

I'm surrounded by rainbows, he thought—no sarcasm, no irony intended.

He also thought of a few million other things he might say, might shout, but what was the point? They'd take too much time and he was getting wet.

Zander looked at his house and then the roofless sky.

He shrugged.

Through rainbows and oil, he sloshed away, toward whatever stupid future might have him.

Zander's first night on the street was spent thinking about cinematic, family-shaming suicides he might commit, and the burning ball of shittiness that would lodge in Frank's throat as he stared at his stepson's boxed and lifeless body.

Suicide, that is, and coffee.

Having just twenty dollars to his otherwise worthless name, and having no idea how long that would last, Zander had sold a pint to the local blood bank, and then went searching for the nearest bottomless coffee cup he could find—preferably a twenty-four-hour one. That's where he met Thom—cheap, burnt high school trash he hadn't noticed much before, except as a peripheral figure, leaning menacingly against the john's tiled wall, shaking down one loser or another. Thom was nearly a foot shorter than Zander, and angry in the way of little men. He wore a brown leather jacket, blond hair on the shortish side, and had a Jeffrey Dahmer–ish face that demanded a cigarette to go with it—and then wished the cancer back on *you,* just for looking, smartass.

Thom dealt—everyone who needed to know knew that much about him. He had a cool car and an apartment, no parents to speak of, except for some shadowy "hick losers down South" it wasn't a good idea to mention. He went to Zander's high school because that's where the business was, and what the hell good was a high school, anyway, without someone to get it high, and keep it there?

My, how times had changed . . .

Rain-soaked and homeless, down a pint of blood and up a pot of coffee, Zander saw things differently from the way they seemed when he could afford to look down on a guy like Thom. Now, Thom looked like an opportunity, like a last hope.

"Thom!" Zander said, slapping his leathered back with a lot of caffeine-induced heartiness.

Thom looked at him with his who-the-fuck-are-you face.

"Zander," Zander hinted.

"Zander," Thom said. "Nobody," he added, turning it into a last name.

"Alexander Wiles," Zander clarified. "Riverton High?"

"Oh," Thom said, stubbing out a cigarette and taking a sip from his own bottomless cup. He didn't elaborate.

"Can I talk to you?" Zander asked, knowing that his life was taking one of those changes of course that feels like forever.

Thom let out a long, thoughtful plume. "About?"

"Business," Zander said. He tapped out a cigarette from Thom's pack and tried to look cool lighting it. The flame shook out twice.

"Speak," Thom said, flicking open his own lighter—something gold, and stylish, and way out of Zander's league.

Zander helped Thom break into Frank's pharmacy, and was rewarded with a crash course in drug dealing. Among other things, Zander learned the importance of cutting smack with Similac, the infinite number of things that can be hollowed out, and how to start every conversation with "Are you a cop?" He got his own apartment and a cool car. He traveled. He met interesting people. As a courier, he got to swat flies in seedy California motels, baby-sitting illegals with balloons in their guts, waiting for the Ex-Lax to kick in. As a sometime user, he got precut stuff at cost. He saw at least one side of the world, met dangerous, feral women, and developed bad habits.

Then, suddenly, three and something years later, the glamour ran out and Zander found himself scared and confused.

And plaid.

Zander told Thom, of course, since Thom was the only friend he had in the world, and Thom said: "We'll get through this."

He clapped a hand to Zander's shoulder, squeezed, and added: "Together."

And then he disappeared without so much as a "See ya." The car and apartment—which were in one of Thom's many names—soon followed.

Zander hadn't gotten a proper diagnosis, of course. Or, more accurately, he hadn't succeeded in getting one. He'd gone as far as getting the blood test, but when he called for the results, the guy on the other end of the line got all flustered when he learned Zander's name.

"Could you wait a sec?" the phone guy asked, before covering the receiver with his hand. On his end, Zander could hear a muffled but excited exchange, during which he was sure he heard someone say, "It's him," and, less clearly, "the weird one," or "the wired one."

"I have to put you on hold," the phone guy said suddenly, coming back just long enough to click Zander into limbo.

When the line finally clicked back on, a new voice spoke. "I'm sorry, Mr. Wiles," it said, "but we don't give that information out over the phone."

"But when I came down, the clerk said you did," Zander said, already sensing the worst.

"The clerk was wrong," the new voice said. "Now, we know this is inconvenient, so we can send someone down to talk to you about the results. Do you still live at—"

Zander hung up the phone, realizing that the worst-case scenario wasn't having AIDS. The worst case was having AIDS in jail. The bastards had done a drug screen on him—he was sure of it—and now they were setting him up for a bust.

"Fuck," he muttered to himself, grabbing the suitcase he'd already packed, having been evicted just that morning.

. . .

A half hour later, while walking to the bus station with his suitcase in hand, Zander heard someone call out, "Alexander Wiles?" Turning out of reflex, he saw a great blue-and-white police cruiser, grinding to a halt behind him. The back doors opened and two men in lab coats got out.

"Mr. Wiles," one of them said, "may we have a word—"

"Fuck," Zander blurted, mainly to himself, before breaking into a run. He heard a clipboard clatter to the pavement behind him and turned just long enough to notice that the lab techs had begun running, too, their white coats fluttering like wings. The police cruiser followed behind, in low gear and with the siren on.

In three and something years of selling watered-down junk on the street, Zander had learned a few things about running away. And so, with his sneakers slapping down the pavement and his heart pounding in his throat, he ducked into an alleyway, found a Dumpster, and called it home. Once inside the sweaty, dank thing, he cursed himself for having been so naïve. He should have known better, should have known that his disease was like something criminal, and that getting it was like getting shot during a holdup. Nobody in their right mind took that sort of thing to a real doctor. No, that's what whiskey and switchblades were for. Plus, he didn't need a doctor to tell him what he had. AIDS is what he deserved for being bad, so AIDS is what he got. All those years of catechism had taught him that much about how God ran things.

Zander shooed a fly away from his face and fluffed up a garbage bag full of what smelled like leaves. He rested his head against the bag and pulled a sheet of cardboard over himself, trying to get some sleep. After a few hours of no sirens and no luck in the sleep department, Zander crawled out of the Dumpster, bent this time on throwing himself more comprehensively away.

Between hitchhiking and buses, Zander managed to get as far as the Upper Peninsula before stopping. There, he checked into the Saddlebag Motel and Grille, the name inscribed on a shingle swinging out front, over the picture of a horse and nursing colt. The neon sign in the office window flashed VACANCY next to a handwritten card listing the off-season rates by day and week. The rooms were actually separate cabins, surrounded by pines that sighed at the slightest breeze. With the skies already steel gray with winter, Zander felt like he'd exiled himself to the last place on earth. Which was good. That way, when he died, his parents wouldn't have to know about it—or any of the shadier details of his recent life.

That, at least, was the plan.

For some reason, Zander thought he knew who had given him the whatever-it-was he had. Through the blur and steam of all the possibilities, he could see a face and, searching, a name—Lizzy—followed by a nickname—Skreech—and . . . no last name he could remember. Skreech was some wigged-out junkie chick he'd met in San Fran during a courier gig. He called her what he called her because that was the sound she . . . well, didn't so much make as let out when she climaxed.

"Jesus Christ," he said, the first time she did it. "You some kind of bat?"

"Nope," she said, smiling. "Just batty." She crawled over his naked body, straddling his stomach with her legs. Making a thwipping sound with her tongue and lips, she bent forward and bit his neck.

"Jesus!" he said, clapping a hand to his throat and shooing her off. She'd drawn blood.

Prying his hand away, Lizzy licked his palm and the dribble of red at his neck. And Zander—a boy who'd loved monsters from the age of three—was hooked.

For the time being, at least.

He'd never meant it to last more than a weekend, but Skreech was fun and Zander's work schedule flexible. Plus, he needed a place to lie low, seeing as the latest balloon man had sprung a leak and seizured-out on him, midgig. And so he ended up spending three weeks with Lizzy, though he never quite learned her last name.

After two and a half weeks, Zander judged the coast clear and noticed he was getting bored with the bat chick. He began looking for an excuse to get out, and, on their three-week anniversary, he found it, while they celebrated in the shower.

He could still remember her, standing in front of him, her long body glistening, her head hung back, and her hair heavy with the shower's spray. She shut her eyes and began humming—some discordant, private tune that came in waves, tuning in and out of the rhythmic splashing. Zander had been talking, saying something stupid and lovey-dovey, figuring he'd wait for maybe three more days, and after that split—with or without an excuse. Then, all of a sudden, Lizzy doubled over and coughed out a blast of vomit.

"Jesus!" Zander blurted, backing away. And then, softer: "Are you okay?" he asked, toeing swirls of mess down the drain.

Skreech—Lizzy—filled her mouth from the shower head and spat. She was pale, wet, and naked, her arms and legs a junkie's highway map of black and blue knotted veins.

"I'm feeling better now," she said, her closed eyes turned toward the mildewed ceiling.

"You should've never tried eating that soap," Zander said, pulling her body into his, matching up bent spoons. She agreed, of course. The soap stunt had been one of those junk-inspired larks. Utterly impromptu. Utterly spontaneous. It had just occurred to her at the moment that eating soap was the quickest way to get at—and clean up—her act.

"I just wanna get *clean*," she said, tuning in to the rhythm of the shower again. "All the way. I wanna get clean and give up the gimmicks and move to the country. I wanna have a waterwheel and grind grain and open a mom-'n'-pop store. I wanna have calico in the windows. I—"

"Right," Zander said, cupping her breasts, kissing the back of her neck. "We'll open a goddamn five-and-dime already." He bit her flesh lightly, bringing a blush to the surface. "And we'll have a fucking shooting gallery in the back."

Lizzy broke away from him. "Go to hell!" she shouted. "I'm serious, dammit." She assumed the position against the tiled wall, arms spread-eagle, head sunk down, staring at her feet. "I'm sick," she said. "I'm sick to death and nobody cares."

"Hey, I care, kid," Zander said, smiling—pale, wet, and naked—a tasteless damp comedy. "I care lots."

"Lots?"

"Bunches," he said. "Three bags full." He tried taking her from behind again. "I care as much as I can—"

"Get off me, Wiles," Lizzy snapped, playing her trump; she did know *his* last name. "I don't need your shit. I need help."

Zander backed off, slowly, wondering what or who had gotten into her, and other stupid thoughts. He looked at her back. And he looked at her back. Her back spoke of backness and nothingness, of a reality that was just this flesh-covered bit of bone structure at the end of one junkie's tunnel vision.

Suddenly: "How'd you do this?" he asked, tracing what seemed to be two track marks down the center of her back.

"Do what?" she asked, still angry, still sick.

"This," Zander said, running his finger harder up and down the seam of flesh. "How the hell'd you get a needle back here?"

And then it occurred to Zander how she might get a needle back there.

"God *damn* you!" he shouted, grabbing a shoulder and spinning her around to face him. This was it—his excuse, his ticket out.

"That's it," he continued. "We're through."

"What?"

He stepped out of the shower and hastily wrapped a towel around his waist. "I'm outta here," he said, stalking about the apartment, packing his carry-on bag, leaving puddles.

"Wait," Lizzy called, bracing herself in the bathroom doorway, defiantly naked. "What the fuck is going on here?"

Zander zipped up the fly of his jeans. "You tell me," he said, shuffling on his leather jacket over his bare chest.

Lizzy had been through this before—flight mode—but had hoped Zander was going to be different. There was a sweetness inside him, somewhere underneath the gunk, a something shiny that wasn't all bullshit.

Of course, she'd been wrong before.

"What do you want me to say?" she finally asked, knowing nothing she said would matter.

"His name," Zander said, stepping into his boots.

"Whose name?" Lizzy asked, thinking, Straws. He's grasping at straws.

Zander gave her his I'm-not-a-fool look. "Who do you think?" he snapped, not giving her time to answer before slamming the door.

Once outside the apartment, Zander whistled an all-clear under his breath and took the steps two at a time. He didn't bother looking back.

Except now, of course. Except every couple of minutes, now, in desperate memory. It was her, he was sure of it. He'd gotten it from her. And why hadn't he learned her last name? Three weeks, for Christ sake! You'd think it would have come up *sometime* in three weeks. He hadn't asked, but . . . Jesus. If only he'd gotten her last name, maybe he could call her, confirm that whatever it was he had, *she* had. And that he'd caught it from her. And so *she* was to blame.

And what were those lines on her back, anyway? They looked like track marks, at first, but not really. They weren't bruise colored, but pink; they glistened from the shower spray and the bathroom light. They . . .

They looked exactly like the lines he'd found on his own back. Holding a small mirror in one hand and angling it over his shoulder to catch the reflection from the medicine cabinet, he'd found them, two distinct ridges running up his back, between his shoulder blades—back there, where the ants had grown into tarantulas.

Other things came back to him. He'd thought that Lizzy was pregnant—a thought that coincided, strangely enough, with his sudden need for more space. One morning into their second week together, she woke up and just began retching. Shortly after that, she got a really weird case of the munchies, wanting blue corn chips and Pepto-Bismol.

"Blue and pink," she'd said. "I've got this serious craving for something blue and something pink."

Cough drops and yogurt. Orange juice and Geritol. Lima beans, lima beans, lima beans! And liver—pork, chicken, calf's—not so much for the taste of it as the rusty-iron smell of it cooking.

Mint toothpaste on apple wedges.

"Are you . . . ?" Zander asked, after watching her dip a pizza slice into a shiny blue bowl of NyQuil.

"Nope," Lizzy said.

"But. I mean, how do you . . . ?"

"Pee test," she said, dipping another slice. "Nada."

"Oh."

He didn't believe her, not then. What else *could* she be, if not pregnant?

Now, of course, he found himself getting nostalgic for the sweet smell of burning liver. With some Formula-44 on the side, perhaps.

Zander stared out the cabin window, through the pale ghost of his own reflection. It had begun snowing, and he longed for that kind of simple purity, a blanket of white to hide under until this thing just went away and he could go back to not giving a shit. But he figured, too, that hiding was how this damn thing got you. He had to take the initiative. He had to fight. He had to *do* something, goddammit, and not just lie here and take it. There were things—there *had* to be things—he could do.

He decided to start by giving in to his whims. If he wanted it, he ate it. It was one of the things that he believed in, that the body, if you listened to it, would tell you what it needed. And food was a big factor in fighting this AIDS thing, he was sure, because all the pictures showed the victims whittled down to nothing, POWs at war with their own bodies. Maybe AIDS was as simple as that—a tapeworm that would leave the rest of your insides alone, if you only fed it enough. And so Zander ate. *Large quantities.* "Medium" and "small" dropped out of his vocabulary, replaced by "jumbo," "party-size," and "with everything."

Followed by Tums, and Pepcid, and Maalox—Zander cruising the aisles at the local pharmacy, tapping over-the-counter medications into his shopping basket. Selection was based on color, or bottle shape, or, once he hit the vitamin aisle, whatever words he could spell from their letters. And when all else failed, vibe would do.

Fem-Iron? Perhaps it was time he got in touch with that side of himself. Correctol? God, if it were only that easy . . .

And then, suddenly: "Son?" the pharmacist said behind his back as Zander knocked still more bottles into his basket, his eyes closed, one bottle for each note of the tune he was humming. His shoulders stiffened at the word "son," and the ridges on his back—they seemed to be gerbils today—flamed and clawed, trying, apparently, to eat their way out.

"Yes?" he answered, wincing.

"What *is* it you think you have?"

Zander turned his green-shaded eyes on the pharmacist like the headlights of a car, bent on running something or someone down.

"Rice-A-Roni," he said.

"What?"

"The San Francisco treat . . ."

"I'm sorry," the pharmacist said. "I don't follow you."

"Foot-in-mouth disease," Zander said, placing his basket at the pharmacist's feet. "Plague." He turned and headed for the door. "Everything," he said, breaking the beam of the electric eye.

"And nothing," he added, but mainly to himself, as the door whispered shut.

Fact was, Zander wanted to bite the pharmacist in the neck, wanted to feel his teeth go *click* through a little lump of warm flesh. Fact was, he'd begun eating rubber bands, and was thinking about wiper blades. Fact was, everything and everyone looked tempting—and pissed him off.

The ridges were getting bigger, and angrier. Without meaning to, he'd stopped sleeping, but kept the habit of dreams. With eyes wide, he had them, as if projected on a scrim strung across the real world. He saw himself approaching himself—one fat, one thin—the thin one shaking the hand of the fat one, the gesture broader and broader until the thin one was pulling the lever of a slot machine the fat one had become, his eyes rolling up into his head, becoming two bug-eyed black marbles and paying off, handsomely, the fat one's jaw open in a cartoon drop, releasing vitamins and rubies and *birds,* dozens of them, black and white, doves and crows, issuing out in an impossible torrent, his fat stomach rumbling with them, going pointy in spots underneath his tight shirt, meaning beaks, a congestion of beaks, and . . .

Zander was by himself again, washing dishes in the motel sink, staring at the mirror he'd broken the day before, during some rage or other.

Funny thing was, Zander didn't feel sick. He felt weird as hell, had these gerbils in his back, couldn't sleep, but . . . Oh, sure, he ate and ate and didn't put on a pound, even though he hadn't shit in a week or more, but . . . Oh, yeah, his heart raced like a bastard at the slightest anything, his temperature was running at something like a hundred and one, and he had fantasies about eating people, but . . .

He wasn't slowing down—that was the important thing. He didn't feel weak; in fact, he felt stronger than usual. Take the coffee mug. No way before he could have cracked a coffee mug just by squeezing it, just because somebody used the word "Wessonality" on TV.

Of course, that was Thursday.

By Saturday, he started dropping things. A coffee mug again, dropped, full and steaming—*crack-splash*—a big hot puddle running under Zander's bare feet where . . . he didn't feel a thing. Scalding hot coffee and . . . nothing, not even a flinch. Sitting on the bed, he looked at his feet, at the skin, which had gone green and hard, like a fingernail, or hoof—so hard that when he tapped it with a pencil, it clicked.

Trying to stand, Zander felt as if both feet had gone to sleep. They tingled but offered no real feedback, no sense of contact with the ground. His first step was wobbly, his second a failure that sent him thudding to the floor.

From his new vantage point, Zander surveyed the room. The bed was unmade, the covers bunched up like a condor's nest. Snowlight from the window bleached out the TV screen, which was showing either something about a war, or a rock video, judging from the explosions. On the nightstand, the telephone sat like Buddha, next to an open-mouthed pizza box. Wood paneling covered the bottom half of each of the four walls, followed by wallpaper running to the ceiling—something with horses and wagon wheels. And littering the floor where Zander lay were Twinkie and Snickers and Wonder bread wrappers, bottles and boxes of medicine, spent fifths and pints and dented cans, half bags of chips, the spatters of assorted sprayable, squeezable, and dippable condiments, the scattered, tented sections of some local newspaper . . . and a single fly, its proboscis checking the varnished wood for food.

Zander wondered about that fly, where it had come from, how it had lasted. It was winter; it was snowing; all good flies should be sleeping or hibernating or doing whatever the hell it is that flies do during the winter. He wondered if maybe it had snuck in, an egg in some food he'd lost under the bed. Was it possible the thing had been born and gone from maggot to fly, all, undetected—a whole goddamn life in this piss-poor dive?

Would it outlive him?

And so it was the fly that finally did it—made Zander decide to get up. And it was the getting up—the difficulty of it, the way it made his insides seem to come undone—that made Zander think: It.

This is It, he thought.

This is how the bad part starts.

3

*O*nce he stopped going outside, Zander was surprised by how many things he could order by phone. Take the gun, for instance. He'd found an ad in the local classifieds, dialed the number, and an hour later, a guy showed up at the door, wearing a leather jacket and a suspicious look.

"You a cop?" the man asked, after Zander answered the door on the fifth knock. He was still getting used to his dead feet, and had taken to using an umbrella as a cane.

"No," Zander said, and then remembered his own training. "Are you?" he asked.

"No."

"So?"

The man opened his jacket to reveal a silver-plated handgun, tucked into the waist of his pants. "Fifty bucks," he said. "No guarantees. No returns."

"Do I have to sign—" Zander began.

"You gonna kill anybody?"

"No."

"You gonna remember where you got this if you change your mind?"

Zander shifted his weight on the umbrella. "No."

"Consider yourself processed," the gun man said. He accepted Zander's money and dropped the gun and some ammo into a paper bag marked UNCLE JOHN'S FRESH FRUITS AND VEGETABLES. He crumpled the bag shut and handed it to Zander, who was surprised by the weight. Though it was probably foolish in his line of work, he'd never gotten around to arming himself.

Closing the door, Zander waited for the man to drive away. He set the grocery bag on the coffee table and settled into an overstuffed armchair. Resting his chin in his palm and his elbow on his knee, Zander stared at the bag, still crumpled shut.

He'd begun going downhill; the green skin was up to his knees and traces of it were showing on the ridges, his earlobes and fingertips. He'd gone from days of not sleeping to sleeping almost constantly—vast, dream-wild sleeps from which he was almost afraid to wake.

While he could still act on it, Zander had decided to buy a little something, a little just-in-case.

Now, however, with the just-in-case sitting in front of him in a grocery bag on his coffee table, all Zander could think was: I wasted my money.

I'm not going to do this.

This is stupid.

Zander blinked and hours passed. Time itself was turning green and crusting over. And still Zander sat, staring at the fluted goat's horn of the logo's cornucopia. He traced the letters in UNCLE JOHN until they became abstract geometrics, wholly separate from any language he knew. The folds and dents—the play of shadow and light where the bag was crumpled shut—held whole worlds.

And really, Zander was like that bag—just a fleshy sack full of weird, percolating chemicals, steaming off the muscles and tendons that held things in place . . .

Blink.

Another hour gone, and the green was spreading faster, crawling out from under the beige Cover Girl makeup he'd tried in an attempt to force normalcy. Now Zander imagined he could hear the green skin spread, crackling as it went. Both hands had already been overtaken, frozen into cups where they squeezed the armrests. They were no good anymore for squeezing triggers; he couldn't even use them to unbutton his shirt sleeves, to check what he already knew, that the green was tracking up his arms. His shoulders shook suddenly—the gerbils, fighting—and his umbrella crutch, propped next to the armchair, slid, its arc slow and painful, half-speed, quarter-speed, slicing the air with a drawn-out, mournful *whoop!* and cracking against the hard wood floor.

Getting up was pointless. Reaching, pointless. But Zander did, anyway, because he could still bend at the waist. And so he rose a bit, reaching, stretching toward the umbrella, just a bit too far and . . .

. . . and he tipped over—predictably—slamming to the floor once again, the umbrella crutch just an inch or two away from his fused fingers.

Zander looked at the umbrella like an opponent who had just won the last round. "Okay," he said, deciding to stay put for a while.

By the time the green sealed his eyes and lips, Zander had already fallen asleep and was dreaming.

Except it wasn't so much a dream, this time, as it was a flood of memories. His whole life was spinning backward, flashing memories like the cards in a Rolodex, settling, finally, on a memory of his father.

His *real* father.

The one who'd be waiting for him on the other side, once all this nonsense was through.

Zander's real father died when his son was only five years old. He died "under mysterious circumstances," which was also how he lived. The truth was, Zander didn't know much about his real dad, except that he was named Henry, worked as a janitor for Wyandotte Steel, and used to sing "Row, Row, Row Your Boat" in place of a lullaby.

That, and he was also a duck.

Henry had told him so himself—under mysterious circumstances.

It all began when Henry decided to show Zander where he worked, which meant staying up past midnight and everything. It was to be the event of the week, the one Zander counted off days till. It was also Henry's way of apologizing for having missed some father-and-son wingding because he was in the hospital again.

"It's no great shakes, kiddo," Henry had warned along the way, "but it pays for the roof."

Once inside the main building, Henry gave Zander a plastic bag to empty wastebaskets with while he powered up the industrial buffer used for polishing the block-long corridors of Wyandotte Steel. Before Zander got to the first office, however, he froze, watching as his father glided the great machine over the floor, buffing away the scuffs of careless soles, swirling out gleam in his wake. The bristled disk of the buffer ssssshhhhed across the floor like tires on wet pavement, spinning so fast it seemed to levitate. Henry's arms shone with the effort of keeping the thing in a straight line.

When his dad noticed Zander standing by the door of the janitor's closet, the bag empty and his eyes wide, it didn't take a psychic to read the boy's thoughts.

Henry switched off the machine and called to his son. "Hop on," he said.

"For real?" Zander asked.

Henry smiled and nodded his head yes before helping his son onto the machine's humped back.

"Hold on tight now," Henry warned. "And don't be scared."

He switched on the buffer and Zander started buzzing with the same giddiness that overtook him whenever they went to Kmart and he got to ride the mechanical horse. He laughed and said, "Wow!" which came out choppy, like when he shouted through a fan. The bouncing sound of his own voice made the boy laugh even more.

"Faster," Zander warbled, as Henry glided him down the hallway, the pilot of this magic carpet ride, the engineer of this particular brand of joy.

"Faster, faster, faster," Zander shouted, bouncing up and down on the machine, unable to contain himself. The sound, the vibrations, the forward momentum; being up past midnight, being with his dad, being this incredible flying thing . . .

It was wonderful.

It was beyond wonderful.

It could only last so long.

What happened next was not Henry's fault. The buffer just ran out of cord and yanked itself free of the outlet. The spinning disk stopped; the machine torqued and flipped over, pinning Zander underneath. His head hit the floor, opening a cut over his left eye. Stunned, Zander tried to get up, not realizing the fun had stopped until he noticed his own blood running out onto the freshly polished floor. That's when he began screaming, as Henry scooped him up and rushed to the car.

On the way to the emergency room, Henry drove fast and with one hand, while the other held a handkerchief to Zander's forehead. To calm the boy, and probably himself, too, he began singing "Row, Row, Row Your Boat," a little quietly, at first, almost ashamed to break the air with his voice, but then rising steadily to full volume. For a man with dirty fingernails, he had a beautiful singing voice, full of feeling, especially around the part about life's being but a dream. His had been one, after all—one of the bad kind, as the recent crisis just underlined.

As Henry sang, Zander quieted down and began listening. He always found it a bit strange that his dad would tear up over that stupid boat, but was reassured, too, by the lullaby tone of his father's voice. It was winter and the words came out as white curlicues of steam. Somehow, that made everything seem okay. Any father who could sing, drive, and make clouds all at the same time must know what he's doing. Zander closed his eyes and rested his head against the cool glass of the window.

At the hospital, the night nurse knew Henry's name, as if he were a regular. She handed him a clipboard and sent the two of them to the waiting room. As they waited, Henry looked at Zander's hands, which seemed just wrong—too small, pale, and still. He was quiet now and had been for some time—almost too quiet, meaning, maybe, shock. Henry didn't know much about treating such things but remembered that staying awake was important—perhaps vitally so. To keep Zander distracted, and conscious, Henry did the first thing that popped into his desperate brain.

He took off his shoe.

"Hey, sport," he said, nudging his son. "Stay with me." He paused long enough to make eye contact; his son's pupils were huge.

"Wanna see something neat?"

"Sure," Zander said, his voice half-asleep.

"Your father," he began, "unbeknownst to almost everyone is . . ." He paused; the waiting room was empty except for him and his son.

"What?" Zander asked groggily, struggling to stay awake for his father's secret.

". . . a duck," Henry said.

"No way," Zander said, slumping back into his chair.

"Way," Henry said, grabbing the toe of his sock and unmasking his foot with a flourish. "Ta-da!"

Zander leaned forward and carefully touched the web of flesh fanning between his father's toes. "How'd you do that?" he asked.

"Quack, quack," Henry said.

"Come on, Dad," Zander demanded, fully awake now. "Tell me."

"Quack, quack."

"Tell me, *please,*" he pleaded.

"I just *did,*" Henry said. "In Duck. A duck's secret's gotta be told in Duck."

"That ain't fair."

"Is so," Henry said, wriggling his weird, underwater toes. "Quack, quack, quack . . ."

Once the doctor was finished and had left the room, Henry congratulated Zander on joining a club that had just the two of them as members.

The monster club.

"You *do* like monsters, don't you?" Henry asked, just checking.

"Yeah?" Zander said, a little confused, knowing his father knew that he *loved* monsters.

"Good," Henry said, smiling, "because your dad, unbeknownst to almost everyone, is . . ."

"What?"

". . . a monster, of course," he said, smiling, rolling up his sleeves. He turned up his left wrist and traced the three pale, squiggly scars running up it, the rows of white dots flanking each zigzag, marking where the thread had gone in and come out.

"Wow!" Zander said, touching them. "Neat."

"That's where they sewed me back together," Henry said, "after I came apart. They even put electricity in my head, just like . . . like . . ."

"Frankenstein?"

"Yes," he said. "Just like Frankenstein." He raised both his hands and made monster fingers, clawing the air as they approached his already-giggling son. "Electricity," he said, "right . . . in . . . your . . . brain," punctuating the space between words with his vibrating fingers, his son giggling more with each new zap.

"And now you're a monster, too," Henry said, showing Zander his own brand-new stitches with a hand mirror. "You're the son of Franken-stein."

Zander beamed, admiring himself and the impossible coolness of his real monster stitches. Then he remembered something his father said.

"Are they gonna put 'lectricity in me, too?" he asked.

"No, kiddo," Henry said, patting his son's hand. "No, you got plenty of your own juice."

They were quiet for a moment; they'd already said more words to each other than they ever had before.

Overhead, the fluorescent lights hummed with plenty of juice of their own.

Suddenly: "Can we scare Mom when we get home?" Zander asked, breaking the silence the way five-year-olds will.

Henry smiled the best he could, coming back to the world where he'd placed his only son in the hospital.

"I think you can pretty much bet on it," he said.

And that was it—the last conversation between Zander and his real fa-ther. He fell asleep in the car on the ride home from the hospital, and Henry's work schedule meant he slept while Zander was awake, and vice versa. And then, just two nights later, a fire broke out at Wyandotte Steel, creating the "mysterious circumstances" under which Henry died. That night, the bullhorns directed Zander and his mom to the Big Boy on

West Jefferson, upwind of the plant. Standing in line, wearing pajamas along with their neighbors, they waited as the greeter smiled, and enquired of each party, "Are you with the evacuation?" The evacuees were then shown to tables in the back room and brought coffee or milk, and some pie, courtesy of Wyandotte Steel, "for the inconvenience."

When the telephone rang, Karen hung her head low. She was already shaking it no when one of the waitresses asked if there was a Mrs. Wiles in the place.

Later, at the emergency room, Zander recognized the night nurse.

"Remember me?" he asked.

"I'm a monster," he added, baring his little canine teeth. Zander stuck out his arms, Frankenstein-style. And the scare-job worked—it must have worked—because even his mom started crying.

The adult Zander—frozen and green on the floor of his motel room—drifts in and out for a while. While conscious, he knows only one thing: There is nothing whole left inside. Nothing but juice and the drained sacks of his organs, sloshing back and forth, back and forth like socks in a washing machine. What it is that's thinking this, he hasn't the faintest idea, except that it's inside, too, inside this hard case he's become, along with his wrung-out heart and these goddamn memories.

And then several weeks pass without even this much to cling to, while Zander's body begins digesting itself in earnest, converting tissue—bones, muscles, organs—into a simpler stuff. Chemically, it's a lot like what happens to Ebola victims, when they enter the phase just before death, known as meltdown. Which is exactly what happens to Zander. He liquefies and dies, alone, on the bare wood floor of his dingy little motel room.

Unlike an Ebola victim's death, however, Zander's doesn't last.

The funny thing about waking up once you've been dead already is that it takes a whole different sort of weirdness to make a decent impression. For example, when Zander woke up and found he'd shed his green skin—that pieces of it filled his clothes like crumbled potato chips, that the face part had come off, nearly complete, and was staring back at him, blank-eyed and green, with a slight tear down the center—his first thought was not about how weird this was but rather how the face looking back at him looked a lot like Henry and, being green and sunken-cheeked, a little like Boris Karloff in *Frankenstein*.

The weird part didn't come until he'd worked the word out of his cottoned throat—"Frankenstein"—putting it out there in the fetid air of wherever he was. That's when his body jerked without his meaning it to and the memory he had dreamed in his cocoon came back, whole for the first time, including the Frankenstein part he'd misplaced as a child—accidentally, on purpose. Until just that moment, the only thing he knew about his father's death was that nobody knew anything for sure. His father had died of dying. The wrist thing didn't necessarily change that, but it made him feel suddenly small, all the same.

Lying on the floor, Zander could feel his heartbeat moving his body, reminding him that he actually had a heart, despite his recent efforts to the contrary. He wondered if its beating was normal under the circumstances, whether it was working too hard, or if the floorboards were somehow magnifying it. He tried getting up, to break contact with the floor, to get away from the immediate noise of his heart, when he noticed the second weird thing. There was something on his back, pressing him down, stopping him. It felt like a little kid playing horsey, only not so little. More like a teenager, maybe.

And what happened to his shirt? The buttons, sprung, lay in a spray among the shed bits and pieces of himself, and the back was split in two, one half clinging with its sleeve on the left, and the other, a wrecked flag, tattered and surrendering to the right. His back was exposed, and cold, except for two points of incredible heat—one for each cheek where that big-assed kid was still riding him—and . . .

There was blood on the floor, just like at the end of the buffer ride, but different. It looked more like chocolate syrup, this time, thick and dark and gooey. Zander knew it was blood, though, if only from the rusty-iron stench of it, like when Lizzy was on her liver-burning jag. He'd been lying in a puddle of it for God only knows how long, and it was already dried in spots, gluing his new skin to the floor.

It wasn't suicide. Zander could just decide that, couldn't he? It was his memory. His past.

His father . . .

Zander closed his eyes and focused on regaining the use of his muscles. They came back gradually, but seemed funny and different, as if somebody had rewired them, taking shortcuts with some, rerouting others, and tossing in a whole new batch to get used to. Getting up on all fours took real time and real effort; rising to his feet was nearly a two-man job.

And the kid playing horsey, the memory of Henry, and the whole goddamn world were all still hanging on, pulling him down, and back, and . . .

Wobbly on his new legs, under the new weight of whatever it was clinging to his back, Zander made his slow, careful way to the bathroom. In the dark, the kid—a tall bastard—seemed to be standing behind him, silent, and careful, and judgmental.

Once Zander clicked on the light, however . . .

4

Zander leered at his reflection in the mirror, smiling with all his teeth like a lunatic, letting his eyes go blank and crazy. He was trying to feel like what he obviously was—nuts—trying to empty his head of whatever logic might be cluttering it up, denying what his eyes saw, had seen, were seeing. He forced a laugh and it came out like a bark: HA!

HA-HA!

Wings?

Wings, for Christ sake!

"I've sprouted *wings?*" he asked aloud.

Which was progress, actually—his admitting it. In the beginning, and for more than an hour, it had gone something like this:

Zander looks in the mirror.

The wings rustle.

He faints.

He dreams he's had a dream about growing wings.

He gets up.

He looks in the mirror.

He sees his wings, again.

They shrug and he feels the realness of them ripple through his muscles.

He faints again.

Et cetera.

Of course, Zander's wings *were* an especially dreadful sight—huge, crow black, the feathers all messed up and starched with dried blood. Luckily, however, he'd been spared the worst of it, the part when his wing stumps first poked through—naked, obscene little sprouts, like two impossibly long, twice-jointed index fingers. Starting at twenty-seven inches each—nine inches between each knuckle—their length doubled, and then doubled again over the next several weeks. And even the noise of their growing was horrible, like the skull-deep bone-splinter of a tooth being pulled.

The feathering began after the first day, covering Zander's still-growing wing stumps with a dingy gray down that looked like mold. When this disappeared it was replaced by spiky, hairlike filoplumes, which gradually lengthened and spread into Zander's mature plumage. By the time they were finally done, each wing ran to just under nine feet, with the tips starting slightly above Zander's calves and the arches cresting some two feet over the top of his head.

Staring at their absurd awfulness in the bathroom mirror, Zander turned, first to one side, and then the other.

"I look like a seagull," he said, out loud—something he'd been doing more of lately, seeing as he was crazy, anyway.

"I look like a fucking seagull," he repeated, "on the losing end of an oil spill."

It's funny, the things that will go through your head when you've just sprouted wings. For example: What was Zander now, exactly? Was he dead or alive? A human, or something else? If he wasn't dead and wasn't human, could he still . . . well, *die?* He looked like an angel, after all, and angels don't die. But that's because . . . because they're already dead, right? Why had he dreamed about his dead father, anyway? Why had it seemed so real? Had being plaid killed him? Had he died from it and become an angel, meaning that Heaven was just another room in the Saddlebag Motel?

And if he wasn't an angel, then what? Was this some kind of drug flashback? If he wasn't him, Zander might have thought so, but he knew his taste in drugs. The ones he did were things like pot, speed, coke, and heroin. He didn't do LSD or mushrooms. He didn't do the sorts of things that made you see things that weren't there. He could take the real world speeded up or slowed down, but he had no use for the shit that trashed reality completely.

Zander looked out the window for a distraction, only to wonder where the snow had gone, and how much time had gone with it. Beyond the pane, he could hear a bird trilling its little heart out. And then, suddenly, in the glass, he noticed the reflection of his wings, brooding behind him. He turned away from the window, and back to his thoughts.

So, were these things real, or what? They looked real, yes, but they'd looked real in the dream, too, and which was this, anyway? Zander knew about his dreams like he knew about his taste in drugs; neither pushed that reality thing very far. He wondered if he'd somehow developed the sort of imagination that would dream up wings and . . . He looked for something utterly mundane, something too trivial for his brain to include in any dream about wings. Which is when he noticed the slip of paper that had been wedged under his door.

He picked it up and read it. He was being evicted. Again.

"God *damn* it," Zander blurted, forgetting about his wings just long enough to fling open the door, step out onto his porch, and begin the angry march to the office to complain. Out in the fresh air and sunshine, his wings stirred. One tapped him on the shoulder, a gentle reminder.

"Shit," Zander said, as if he'd been caught naked. He bolted back inside and slammed the door. "Thanks," he said, breathing a sigh of relief.

And then he wondered whom—or what—he was thanking.

"Hey," Zander said, feeling safer now that he imagined his wings as somehow separate from the rest of himself. "Hey, Heckle and Jeckle. You guys for real?"

He opened up the pocketknife he'd used for most of his eating and

unfolded the corkscrew. "I said," he said, reaching back with his new con-
vincer, ready to jab, "are you . . ."

He didn't finish.

Instead, he found his head slammed into the bathroom mirror, jarring
loose a fragment from where he'd cracked it earlier. The wings fluttered
furiously, beating against his back—*Whack! Whack! Whack!*—scolding him
for his lack of faith.

And Zander found it all pretty fascinating—how much it *seemed* to
hurt whenever his wings *seemed* to hit him. Finally, stumbling back into
the living room, struggling against the contrary wind his wings made,
Zander grabbed on to the edge of the dresser to keep himself up, to give
himself an anchor against his new wildly pitching wings. He smiled in
spite of himself—in spite of the pain—at his wings' raw physicality, at
the way their twisting and flapping stretched new muscles he couldn't
imagine himself imagining.

"I'll take that as a yes," Zander said, as his wings, satisfied that they'd
made their point, folded back into place.

More thoughts, too many thoughts, all urgent, all vital, competing for
Zander's attention:

Was anything else going to sprout? Were things going to start falling
off? What was he going to do about that eviction notice? How was he
ever going to go outside again? What would people think? What would
Frank and his mom think? Would he tell them? Should he? Oh brother,
he could just see *that* little reunion.

Zander turned on the shower, trying to get away from his thoughts,
but they followed him anyway. Was the water too cold or too hot
for wings? Was water even okay? Jesus, he hoped it was, because he
didn't know what else to do with them, what with all that blood gunk-
ing them up. He stood, watching as the shower hissed, trying to feel if his
wings knew what was coming, and whether they had an opinion on the
matter.

"Ducks," he finally said, out loud. Ducks are okay with water, and he
was the son of a duck, so . . .

He shook his head, angry, and disgusted, and frustrated over the absurdity of—well, just everything. He stepped under the spray, muttering something about ducks and their secrets and what was and wasn't fair.

With soap in his eyes, shampoo in his hair, and nothing but plain old water beading up on his slowly unsoiling wings, Zander thought about Lizzy, and their parting. The wondering part of him wondered if . . . But no. No, he couldn't accept that. Something like this was weird enough happening once. No, he was plaid; she had AIDS. He got wings, and she was dead someplace. Or shacked up with that bastard who helped her shoot up back there. Or maybe she stuck with that cleaning-up-her-act act, and was getting ready to play mommy to some kid—*his* kid, maybe—the one she lied about when he asked if she was pregnant. But one thing was for sure: There was no Saint Skreech the Archangel running around out there.

After all, how could she keep something like this secret? How was Zander going to? And why should he hide these things in the first place? Was there money in this? What were the dangers, after all? Zander thought about it. He put himself in the world's place, imagined what he'd do if he ever got his hands on an honest-to-God angel. First, there'd be the *National Enquirer,* then the circus, TV, lab, morgue, dissection room, stuffing room, display case, Michael Jackson, the Smithsonian—the whole freak-show/tits-and-ass rag.

Thinking some more, Zander wondered if maybe it had begun already. "It's him," the lab guys had said—he heard it through their fingers.

"The weird one."

Stepping out of the shower, Zander entered the living room, toweling off his hair. His wings, taking their cue, snapped open to full display, once, twice, three times, shivered, and then did it all again, sending spray everywhere—spattering the drawn shade, stippling what was left of the mirror, sizzling on the lightbulb that flickered whenever he walked past it. He peeked out the window. If the lab guys knew anything, if they wanted to dissect him, they'd surely have found him by now, right?

And then, more questions:

Could he fly? Sure, Barnum and Bailey back there were big, but were they big enough? And how the hell do you fly, anyway? Do the wings know how, by instinct, and all you have to do is give them enough sky?

And who the hell was Zander, anyway, to get wings? Did he deserve them? How was he picked? Did junkie ex–drug dealers deserve wings? If all that shit didn't count against something like this, what did?

Zander walked around the living room where he'd—what?—hatched? kicking the shattered bits of his—what?—shell? cocoon? pod? into a little pile. And boy, if that didn't seem just about right. Kicking broken pieces of yourself, your busted-up, broken, gone-for-good old life. Jesus, he'd been through a lot of lives lately. Suburban son, moderately okay Catholic kid, turns eighteen and . . . gone. Drug dealer living the high life, wakes up feeling plaid and . . . gone. AIDS victim, been through the rage, done the denial, et ceteraed the et cetera, ready but not really ready to die in this fleabag motel and . . . gone. An angel—or at least a jerk with wings—sweeping up yet another life and waiting for the time when this one, too, would be . . .

And still, more questions, increasingly the same:

What do they mean? What do they mean? What do they mean?

And, occasionally, an answer. Like: Nothing. Like: Go with the flow. Like: Stop asking so goddamn many questions.

Zander stood in the middle of the room, his wings and hair drying, trying to think about how to think about nothing. Zooming in on a snowy field behind his eyelids, he managed to clear just enough room to notice that his legs were starting to get that steel-band feeling. Opening his eyes again, Zander realized that he'd been on his feet pretty much since the time he stopped fainting, meaning for hours, and with the wings' extra pounds on top of everything. He looked for a place to sit. The overstuffed armchair was still there in the corner, opposite the coffee table and looking like a damn fine idea. Zander took a step toward it and then stopped.

"Shit," he said, realizing there was plenty he hadn't thought about yet, in between all that God-Life-and-Death business. Like:

How was he going to sit down?

Or wear a shirt?

Or use the toilet?

Or sleep? Now that he thought of it, Zander realized he felt about as beat as he'd ever been. He looked at the bed, not knowing how to work it. Before, he'd always slept on his back, but now he had these built-in kickstands, preventing something as simple as that. Could he just lie on top of them? Would they break? Would they even let him?

Zander tried and regretted it immediately. The wings, feeling trapped, bucked and flapped and kicked wildly, popping the rest of his body up into the air for a moment, and then doing it again once he'd come crashing down.

"Okay, okay," Zander muttered. "I get the point." Sighing, he rolled over on his stomach and hugged his pillow. But the wings kept at it, flapping and shuddering and . . . and bawling like a child. Each down flap sent whatever wasn't nailed down in his room flying, while his wings kept at it, kept flopping about with no control at all, fueled by a pure, infantile rage. They banged into each other overhead, recoiled, and then clenched themselves like a baby's balled-up fists. And each time they did, Zander could feel it as a spasm in his back, as if wires in the wings went straight to a knot of muscles next to his kidneys.

"Fuck!" Zander shouted, less fascinated by this particular round of pain. And the wings responded to the tone of his voice just like a baby, too, seeming to get even more upset, making them flap, bang, clench, flap, bang, clench, again and again.

"I'm sorry," Zander tried. "Please stop," he pleaded, his voice warbled by the pumping wings.

And then, from nowhere, Zander remembered the buffer ride, and the way it ended. He remembered himself, in the car and screaming, with Henry white-knuckling the steering wheel. He remembered the steam-words and the easy calm they brought.

And he thought: What the fuck?

He thought: It's worth a shot.

"Row, row, row your boat," he began singing in a voice not nearly a match for his old man's. "Gently down the stream," he added, trying to imagine the wings as his child—a son—crying and in trouble. Putting himself in Henry's place, Zander thought about what a killer that stupid song could be, once the words meant something other than what the dictionary said.

And thinking that, Zander noticed his wings slowing down. By the time he'd gotten to the dream part, they were already folded back into place, sleeping like a couple of babies.

Twenty hours later, Zander woke up starving. His wings were still asleep, judging from the way they sagged on his back, the deadness of their weight, and Zander tried not to disturb them as he reached for the telephone. He'd memorized the number of the pizza place in town, back when his feet had gone dead. He looked at the old boxes, scattered about the room, the lids of some chattering like novelty-store teeth, under a draft coming from somewhere. If he were the paranoid sort, Zander thought, he'd think they were laughing at him—which wasn't to say they weren't.

With his hand on the receiver and his finger poised to dial, Zander jumped ahead to the exchange at the door. How would he handle it? Using the door to hide behind, he'd probably end up overtipping the delivery kid, just to keep the transaction short and sweet. "Sorry," he'd say, "I just stepped out of the shower. Keep the change."

"But it's a twenty, sir."

"I said, 'Keep the fucking change,' " he'd say, his fuse getting shorter by the second, his wings maybe rustling to get the attention he was denying them. And the delivery kid he swore at and overtipped? He'd go back with reports of something weird going on at the motel up the road. Cops would follow to check things out. They wouldn't appreciate being talked to from behind the door. They wouldn't give a fuck about the shower or his apologies. The lab guys would be called . . .

Zander growled, shook his head, and put down the receiver. He picked it up again and started from scratch.

Pressed to his ear, the receiver gave off a staticky gale, ebbing like the tide in some electronic seashell. "Now what?" he muttered. Hanging up, Zander tried disconnecting and reconnecting several times in rapid succession, but nothing seemed to clear it.

And then he noticed that the sound seemed familiar, its pattern of ebbs and flows matching . . . Did it? He placed a hand to his chest. Yes! Matching his heartbeat and, awake now, his wings, beating to the same time. Well, not *beating*, exactly—*puffing*, maybe, something gentle, slight, almost absentminded, like a cat's idling purr.

"Hello," he said, when the other side picked up, loud enough to be heard over the static. "Hello, I seem to have a bad connection. I want to get a pizza. No, PETE-ZAA. Yes. Can you call me back?" he asked, shouting out the number of the motel-room phone. "Thanks." He hung up, and the phone rang almost immediately. "Yes. Thank you. No, it doesn't seem to be any better, does it."

Shouting his order, Zander wondered if all angels had this kind of trouble communicating.

"Hail Mary, full of . . ." Pause. "I said, 'HAIL MARY . . .' "

Oh brother . . .

Later in the day, after the pizza, Zander discovered that the TV was like the telephone, the colors swirling and the picture rolling as he approached it. The lights, too, continued to flicker whenever he got near, their filaments rattling inside like the fairy-tinkling of some Christmas ornament. And his watch flashed 12:00 despite all efforts to reset it, and then went black altogether.

The bathroom door, when he walked past, seemed to snag on something and swung closed by itself. At first, he thought it was just the wind, a breeze stirred up by his passing wings. But no, something else was going on. He tried it again, opening the door and then standing before it as still as he could. First, nothing. A bit closer, and the knob quivered. An inch more, and the door swung shut, the knob pulled straight toward Zander's chest.

Tying his room key to a string and holding it at arm's length, Zander watched as the makeshift plumb line dangled diagonally, pointing once again toward his heart. He remembered Henry's answer when he asked if they were going to put electricity in him, too.

"No, you got plenty of your own juice."

Zander rubbed his temples, trying not to, but thinking anyway. Okay, he thought. Another lesson. Wing sufferers can't sleep on their backs; they can't use the telephone, TV, or even cohabitate very well with the modern world; they can't sit on anything with a back; and, apparently, they have something magnetic in their chests.

"No wonder they got kind of scarce," he said, and then corrected himself. " 'We,' I meant," he said, meaning the singular "we"—the one that only popes and kings and madmen use.

You can only keep wings a secret for so long before sharing them with somebody. Zander had ruled out his parents and most of the people he knew for various reasons, most having to do with their inability to cope with the physical fact of wings, or to keep that fact a secret. Eventually, he settled on his old boss, contact, and sort-of friend—Thom. Telling Thom had its advantages. First, Zander had something on Thom he could use against him if he needed to. Second, Thom had balls, and somehow, those seemed like they might come in handy. And third, Thom was an exuberant liar.

It was this last attribute that made him the intuitive choice for confessor. There was something mad and ballsy about just up and sprouting wings, then turning around and saying, "Okay, here they are; deal with 'em." Thom's life, what Zander knew of it, was pretty much made up as he went along. One day, his parents were double agents who'd sold him to get out of a bind; the next, he'd come to Michigan after escaping from a child pornography ring used to fuel the coffers of some Southern Methodist church in Georgia; and the next, his folks had been killed in a crash, when their car was broadsided by an EMS van, rushing to get some spare parts to the hospital for a double transplant. Clearly, reality wasn't as fixed for Thom as it was for most people—and wings required someone who could cope with reality when it played loose.

Despite his previous taste in drugs and dreams, Zander was growing to appreciate that particular attribute.

The first thing Thom did after Zander let him in and he got a glimpse of his ex-partner's new prides, new joys, was to . . . *laugh.* He burst out laughing, almost dangerously loud, grabbed a chair, and had to sit down. He tried to talk, but then laughed some more, finally breaking into a cough.

"What the fuck're you supposed to be?" he managed to wheeze. "Chicken Little?"

"What do you mean?" Zander said, crossing his arms, his wings hitching higher on his back as he did so.

"C'mon, c'mon, c'mon," he said, reaching for one of Zander's wings. "Let's see one of these."

"Don't, Thom."

"C'mon. Where'd you get 'em?"

Zander was about to say, "*God,* damn it," when one of the wings lashed out on its own and slashed across Thom's face. The feathers, surprisingly stiff, left little paper-cut scratches across one cheek and over the opposite eyebrow. The quickness of the wing surprised both of them; they both just stood there, quiet, while beads of blood rose along the scratches on Thom's face.

Once the blood ran together, snailed down his cheek and into the cloth of his collar, Thom snapped out of it. "Jesus," he said.

"They're for real," Zander said.

"Jesus," he repeated.

"Thom," Zander said.

"Huh? What?"

"I don't know what to do."

"Yeah. Uh-huh."

"Thom . . ."

"Yeah?"

"They're for real."

"Uh-huh."

"Thom?"

"Yeah?"

"I'm afraid."

Once Thom accepted what had happened, he was a little in awe of his ex-partner. Not worshipful, or anything religious and strange, just . . . careful. Here Zander was, a kid Thom had saved—well, not so much *from* the streets as *for* the streets—but saved him, nevertheless, pathetic, just-kicked-out-of-his-warm-suburban-home waif that he was, and then, boom, the geek drops a load of wings on him. Wasn't he supposed to be dying of the plague or something?

Thom stared at the wings, at the oil making them shine blue, and something dark fluttered in his chest. "You haven't told anyone *else* about this, have you?" he asked, suddenly.

"No, I—," Zander began.

"Good," he said. "Don't."

"Why?" Zander asked, and Thom clammed up.

"C'mon," Zander said.

Thom lowered his head, avoiding his ex-partner's eyes.

"Thom?" Zander repeated. "Tho-om . . ."

Finally: "I wanted to kill you, okay?" Thom said, barely a whisper. "Just now."

"Oh yeah?"

"Oh, yeah."

"Some bud," Zander said, though the confession wasn't a total surprise. Somewhere in the back of his head, he was still waiting for the lab guys to show up.

"Why?" Zander finally asked, partly to add some sound to the room, which had grown too quiet.

"It wasn't for long," Thom said. "I just had this image for a split second of me wringing your neck, and it felt like, yeah, right, that's what you deserve. I mean, why you? Why not me?" He paused. "We're, like, friends, right? Here I am, your friend, and I'm jealous enough to kill you." Another pause. "Shit, a stranger wouldn't think twice about it."

"I see," Zander said, recalling where he'd hidden his just-in-case gun, just in case.

The longer he lived with it—with them—the more Thom's attitude toward the wings changed. Unable to take his eyes off them, he grew steadily more excited, more energized, and as full of questions as Zander had been on his own first day. Did he, could he, should he, did he ever think about? Zander could see him getting high on the very concept, on its potential. "Man," he said a lot. "Man" this, and "Man" that. And "Jesus."

He began pacing the room, raking his fingers through his hair.

"There's something here," he said, tapping his head. "These things . . ."

"Wings?"

"Wings. Mean something. They're here—there—for some reason. I'm thinking like a talent—a talent you can turn into . . ."

"A career?"

"Well, not exactly, but . . ."

"A sideshow attraction?"

"No . . ."

"A . . . something?"

"Yes!"

And so it went, a first-joint, freshman-college-dorm kind of evening full of earnest discoveries about time and space and God and stuff.

And incredible, sudden, hollowed-out hunger.

In the middle of a thought, Zander stopped. "Pizza and beer," he said, presenting it conclusively, like Einstein ending with M and C and squared.

Thom slapped his forehead with the heel of his hand. "Of course!" he said. "It's all so simple!"

One of the things Zander was discovering was that the weird cravings of his prechange phase were just a warm-up act for the ravenous hunger that came during the postwing period. He no longer mixed foods and pharmaceuticals for aesthetic reasons, but the amount he needed just to meet the physical needs of the wings was considerable. After all, Zander's body weight had increased by 30 percent. Natural or not, though, his new needs embarrassed him—especially the way they tended to steamroll over hard-learned niceties like "Thank you" and "Please."

Which is why after he grabbed Thom up by the collar and shouted, "I'm serious, dammit," thumping him against the wall to emphasize his point, Zander immediately put him back down again and apologized. "I'm sorry," he said. "I'm just *really* hungry."

Thom looked at Zander with something new in his eyes—fear. It was a good look for him, Zander decided.

"Ah, okay," Thom said, finally finding his voice. "Pizza and beer, right? It's on me, okay? I'll . . . I'll be right back."

And it occurred to Zander as Thom left to fetch the food that he could stand this being-an-angel business. He could stand it just fine.

"You know," Thom said, upon his return, "this is a lot like Communion." He held the door open with one foot, navigating through the doorway with two extra-large pizzas, and a twenty-four-pack of Miller. "Bread and booze, right?"

Thom was a lapsed something, too, religionwise, and it occurred to Zander that he had mentioned more God things in the last few hours than he had in the entire rest of the time Zander had known him. Though Zander supposed that it was only natural after you've just met an angel face-to-face, still it was beginning to bug him. Then a phrase just popped into his head: It's only human, he thought. And after that, there came another thought: Being "human" no longer included someone called Zander Wiles.

Zander didn't *say* any of this, of course. Instead, he said that beer and pizza was as much like Communion as he was like Saint Peter, and Thom said that that had been his point.

"Exactly," he added.

So they had their little unholy mass, toasted Zander's sproutings, and got drunk, giggly, stupid, and then sleepy, eventually passing out. In the morning, Zander woke to find Thom already up, a slice of cold pizza in one hand and a warm beer in the other. He sat in the blue glow of the

cable TV, occasionally putting down his beer to channel-surf with the re-
mote control. He'd stop on the preacher stations, take a pull, take a bite,
make a thoughtful face, and surf on.

It was Thom who first saw the dark potential of being an angel. The thing
he'd been tapping at through his forehead had finally hatched during the
night. And it was with them there, now, in the motel room, along with
the pizza boxes, beer empties, and the channel changer. Zander stood in
front of the TV, causing the images to swim and swirl, while Thom
spelled out the details.

"If we pick the *right* people," Thom said, "your secret stays secret, and
we stand to make a little cash." It'd be a hoot, he said, a piece of cake. He
had the car, they could hide Zander's wings somehow and take I-75
South right into the heart of the New Age's *Paper Moon* country.

Thom was serious. *This* was the something Zander's wings meant, the
something they could be used for. If some asshole in a bad haircut and a
white suit could milk the faithful, they'd sure as hell listen to a bona fide
angel.

To his credit, Zander was not enthusiastic about Thom's proposal, but
he didn't have many alternatives. What he *did* have was a bill and an eviction notice from the Saddlebag Motel, not to mention a pair of bad-luck
wings spreading out from his shoulder blades. Thom, the businessman,
offered to put him—meaning Zander's bill—on his own MasterCard,
for which certain services would be exchanged. Meaning Thom and he
were partners, again—for better or worse, for richer, and richer, and
richer—so Thom predicted, as long as they played their cards right.

Zander was not the only one with something on his shoulders; Thom had
a chip on his. His chip was in the shape of Georgia, his home state, where
he'd lived with his parents and a few hundred other faithful in a small
community of clapboard houses, nice gardens, and brainwashed zom-
bies—all owned, more or less, by one New Age guru named Sam. Sam
did not have a title like Reverend or Father, though he sometimes accepted the prefix Doctor, and he didn't admit to any last name at all. Dr.

Sam was the leader of a millennially challenged group of individuals who called themselves "Longevites," a sort of bastardized enjambment of "longevity" and something else—"Muscovites," perhaps. Dr. Sam did the usual end-of-the-world song and dance, and promised his followers excellent good health, in this life and the next, provided they took his medicines. Dr. Sam's medicines—he called them "vaccines"—immunized people against things like fearfulness, bad karma, and pollution. They worked just like regular vaccines, he claimed, by introducing a manageable dose of the problem and letting the body build up an immunity. So: The antipollution pills were gelatin capsules full of ground charcoal Dr. Sam swore was "devil-black diesel dust straight from the rusty smoke-stacks of Pennsylvania." Fear was fought by swallowing the dried and ground thyroids of mice who had been scared to death (or black pepper and nutmeg, depending upon your viewpoint). Thom, who admired Dr. Sam while despising his followers, was turned out (or escaped—again, depending on your viewpoint) when, at thirteen, he packaged his own antireligion capsules, filled with scraps of the Bible and a few of Dr. Sam's pamphlets. Finding few takers but plenty of snitches, Thom was sent to his aunts in Michigan, to await the end of the world, unvaccinated.

And it was to Dr. Sam–land, Georgia, that Thom proposed to return—with a real angel, this time.

The first obstacle was hiding the wings. Zander had thought about it even before Thom showed up, and figured that part of the disguise would involve a backpack—one of the big ones, like mountaineers use, but with the bottom cut out. This took care of the arches, but there was still considerable overhang. Even though the wings were knuckled and could fold up to a certain extent, Zander knew there was no way he was squeezing them into the backpack—if they would be willing to go there in the first place. It was Thom who contributed the second half.

"A topcoat," he said, just like that. "We pick up a couple of topcoats from the Salvation Army, rip out the lining, and sew it back in like a couple of big-ass pockets. You slip your arms in the sleeves, the wings in the pockets, and then you hide the remaining hump with your backpack idea." He smiled. "Simple."

"A couple?" Zander asked.

"Huh?"

"You said, 'A couple,' " Zander repeated. " 'We pick up a couple of topcoats from the Salvation Army.' Why do we need a *couple* topcoats?"

"Well, we'll need a couple backpacks, too, I guess," Thom said, thinking his logic went without explanation, but then realizing it didn't. "You know. A set for you, and a set for me."

"Why a set for you?"

And that's when Thom explained to Zander his theory about weirdness. Singular weirdness was just that, he explained, and all the responsibility for being weird rested with the weirdo. Tandem weirdness, however, suggested a plan and a purpose and a group of like-minded individuals to whom this was anything but weird. Tandem weirdness suggested a regularness under the strangeness, which it was the observer's responsibility to divine. If you didn't know what these two jokers in trench coats and backpacks were up to, well that just showed how little you knew. And—if and when someone was brave enough to risk looking ignorant, brave enough to ask what the hell the deal was with these coats and backpacks, especially in Georgia, especially with the heat turned all the way up—Thom was ready for them.

" 'Spelunking,' we'll say. 'We're spelunkers, and the packs are for gear and the coats are for bat shit. All *experienced* cave divers know *that*.' "

"*Are* there any caves in Georgia?" Zander asked.

Thom gave him his best like-it-matters-you-asshole look.

"Sorry," Zander said, stung. "I'm overthinking it," he added, deciding not to question Thom's wisdom ever again—at least not when it came to weirdness.

"Good morning, Angel of Death," Thom greeted when he came around to pick Zander up, after paying his bill at the motel and agreeing to take it out of Zander's share of the golden fleece.

"Yeah, yeah. Right," Zander said, struggling with his backpack, trying not to bang it against the door well as he negotiated his way into Thom's Ferrari.

"You know this is a mile-down-the-road drug car, don't you?" Zander said, crawling into the backseat where he could stretch out. "Ain't no spelunking car, no way."

"Yeah, well," Thom said, anxious for the ride, anxious for his homecoming, and revenge. "Why don't you go spelunk yourself or something?"

"Yeah. I hear your mother spelunks goats."

"Motherspelunker."

"That's *bad* motherspelunker, to you."

And so on.

For the most part, Thom's plan was simple. They'd drive to his old stomping grounds in Georgia and park outside a little New Age shop, called Heaven on Earth. Along with Dr. Sam's pills, and lottery tickets, Heaven on Earth sold angel stuff—cards, and statues, and paintings, stained-glass ornaments, books, little wing pins, and your own set of wings for Halloween, made out of coat-hangers and cotton. Taped up at the cash register, along with the MasterCard and Visa decals, was a prayer for evoking your guardian angel in times of need. And they'd wait outside, Thom and Zander, a couple of vultures in their Salvation Army overcoats, and follow customers home. Preferably older customers. Preferably widowed.

Zander's job was to "appear" outside their kitchen windows, tapping, or outside their bedroom windows, a handful of pebbles for their attention. He'd spread his death-black wings, cast his awesome shadow, and tell them that he had some Good News, and some Bad News. The Good News was that the Bad News could be made to go away for the right amount of folding money, which he'd call an offering, or a donation, or a tithe. And the Bad News was . . . well, *very bad*. He'd let the shadow of his wings fall on them; let them shiver and come to their own conclusions.

For his part, Zander couldn't believe there were people that gullible. Thom asked him why not, said that last time he checked, people were *still* voting Republican, *still* listening to country music, and *still* sending money to the various Dr. Sams the world had to offer.

"And anyway, we'll have the demographics tied up," Thom said. "Question one: Are they gullible? Answer: Yes, they live in Dr. Sam–land. Question two: Do they believe in angels? Answer: Yes, enough to waste their money on 'em at Heaven on Earth. Question three: Do they have disposable income? See answer two."

"But is it right?" Zander asked.

Thom looked at him cross-eyed in the rearview mirror. "Of course it is," he said. "We're spelunkers."

There was another reason Zander was doing this, of course. It was an experiment. He wanted to see if he could. This was clearly not a good thing he was doing and he wanted to see if he could still do bad things. He wanted to see how much of him had turned angelic, wanted to see if he still had free will, where it counted. He wanted to know what the wings did when you did bad things. Did they protest when their own safety wasn't at issue? Did they intervene? Did bad deeds cost feathers? Make them wither, make them go away?

Childishness. Magic reasoning. Yes. But what was the alternative? The rational universe, as far as Zander knew, was broken. Without meaning to, he'd been the one to break it. And magic reasoning, God, and the rest of it had the coattails for this kind of thing, so Zander rode them, checking the sights and looking for signs for when it might be a good idea to jump off.

Experimentation was also the answer for what he was doing in the backseat, as they crossed into Georgia. The radio wasn't much good on the trip, what with Zander and his magnetic chest, so Thom and he tried talking. After talking was exhausted, they sought security in the structure of exchanged jokes. After that, nostalgia for their mutual childhoods, with Thom coming up decidedly short, having been raised without TV. Silence was the option they'd settled on, somewhere around Kentucky.

And so, in silence, having just entered Georgia, Zander kneeled on the backseat, facing the rear window, and poked his finger with his pocketknife. The sun was behind them and light filled the car, glistening off the red bead that rose to the surface of Zander's finger. Squeezing, pumping more out, Zander watched as the bead's surface tension broke and the drop snailed down his finger, following gravity, following the normal laws. Zander curved his hand, first one way, and then another, controlling the drop's descent, sketching a shiny red trail that flamed against his white skin in the bright sunshine.

Thom, having watched it all in the rearview mirror, finally spoke up. "What the fuck are you doing?" he asked.

"Huh?" Zander said, his concentration broken.

"What are you doing?"

"Nothing."

"Nothing," Thom repeated.

"Checking," Zander said. "Just checking."

A Georgia diner on a Sunday morning: Zander and Thom sit at the counter because Zander can't fit in a booth. Thom begins to take off his backpack and is halted by Zander. "Oh yeah," Thom says, hoisting the straps back around his shoulders. Zander can see the waitress eyeing him as she refills his coffee, wondering why they don't take off their backpacks, and wondering where Zander put the three breakfast specials he's had since getting here. Thom is checking through the yellow pages for addresses, shows Zander that between "Amusement Parks" and "Animal Cemeteries," there is a separate listing for "Angels—Paraphernalia." Zander silently taps the page and underlines the cross-reference—"See Religious Goods."

Finally, the waitress breaks the ice:

"You boys on your way to church?" she asks.

Zander: "No." Thom: "Yes."

"I was just joking," she says. "You ain't dressed for church. What y'all got up for, anyway?"

Zander: "Spelunking." Thom: "Peach inspector."

Zander looks at Thom and crosses his eyes. He sips his coffee, a sign that he has formally absented himself from the conversation.

"We're with the FDA," Thom explains. "Fruits Division. Spelunking's the code-name for the operation. It's a surprise inspection of this year's peach crop, which is why we're here on Sunday. Now, we need you to keep quiet about this, you understand"—Thom reads her name tag— "Betty?"

The waitress shakes her head. "I thought it was something special like that." She refills their coffee. "Can I ask you something, though?"

"Shoot," Thom says.

"What're the coats for?"

"Fruit flies," he says. "They carry disease. Worse than mosquitoes and rats, actually."

"Really?" she says. "I never knew that."

"We don't like to"—Thom pauses, drops it just a notch—"alarm the populace."

"Oh . . ."

She goes to tally up their bill, and draws a little smiley face under the bottom line. Thom pays the bill, and Zander leaves the tip, a little bit more than 15 percent, on account of her smile, and naïveté.

Making an excuse of getting a toothpick, Thom returns to the counter and pockets the tip, as well as a salt shaker.

Heaven on Earth was closed on Sundays. From across the street where Thom parked the Ferrari, the store looked dark, but it was impossible to tell for sure without leaving the car and walking right up to the door. Thom pulled the handle—nothing; he pushed—nothing. Looking up, he noticed a handwritten sign on a three-by-five card, in multicolored Magic Marker. In the upper left corner, a chubby cherub wiped a tear from the corner of his eye with his pudgy fist. His wings were dinky relative to the rest of him, and in comparison to Zander's real-live wings. The wings were white inside, left the same color as the index card, but were outlined in blue. Next to the cherub, a note:

"Dear Nice People," it said. "We're sorry to disappoint you, but our modest shoppe is closed today. Even God rested on the Sabbath, and we, His humble servants, but follow. If it is a sunny day, why not go for a picnic; if it's raining, rejoice for the lilies, who surely need it—and wait for the rainbows."

A felt-tip rainbow, drawn with a protractor, filled the lower right corner, next to the word itself, catercorner from the cherub.

"Goddammit to hell," Thom blurted, pressing up against the glass and hooding his eyes with his hands, trying to make out whether anyone was in there, in the dark, who might warrant a finger gesture or two. Finding no one, Thom trudged back to the car.

"Strike one," he said, flooring it and stirring up a cloud of dust big enough to hide the storefront of Heaven on Earth.

Pulling along an outside pay phone at a nearby gas station, Thom swiveled up the Yellow Pages, turned to the listing for "Angels—Paraphernalia" and pulled it out, as well as the page for "Religious Goods." He handed them to Zander and said, "Read."

"Christ Way Books," Zander read.

"Skip."

"Covenant Enterprises."

"Next."

"Good News God Stuff," Zander read. "Inc." Pause. "Holy Ghost Health Foods. Li'l Angels Used Religious Supplies. Mustard Seed Tapes, CDs 'n' More. The New Dawn Shoppe—"

"Go back," Thom said. "The God one. Is there an ad?"

"Yeah," Zander said. "Good News God Stuff, Inc. Serving all your spiritual needs since 1985. Incense. Statues. Bibles. Crystals, Angels, T-Shirts. Candles, Vestments, Holy Cards. Rosaries. Star Charts. Tarot. Wind Chimes. More." Pause. "That's cute. They even got their list in the shape of a cross." He lifted the fluttering sheet for Thom to see. "Open Sunday thru Friday. Closed Saturdays. Reader on Premises."

"Address?"

Zander read it aloud.

"Sounds like the mall," Thom said. "Oh, what the hell. At least they're open."

Thom thought that they should look for victims who were elderly and widowed. Partly, this was fallout from his readings in the field of scamology, *Paper Moon,* et al. Partly, it was what passed for common sense. Elderly, to make death a demographically viable subject area, and widowed because, well, two heads are more skeptical than one. Also, Thom had seen the pie charts in *USA Today* showing that the majority of U.S. wealth was held by citizens sixty-five and older. And, though he didn't tell Zander this, they were the least likely to be armed, had the slowest reflexes when they were, and were generally easier to beat up, if such became necessary. Thom preferred beating up to shooting, partly because it was more practical in the long run, especially in terms of prison sentences, which it was just plain amateurish not to factor in, as a business expense, up front. They did have backup, of course—what with Thom's .48 in the glove compartment and the suicide special Zander had stashed in his suitcase—but the plan was to go in, heavy on the bullshit, light on the ammo.

Pulling into a parking slot at the mall, Thom outlined the following candidate profile for Zander:

"Flag one: White hair," he said. "After that, look for some form of impairment. Hearing aids, walkers, canes, portable oxygen units—all these are good. Blind, to the point of having a red-and-white cane, a dog, or even Coke-bottle eyeglasses—these are a waste of our time and your obvious assets. The widowed part is the trickiest, but I'm gonna say that anyone meeting the other criteria, with a wedding band and nobody immediately beside them, counts." He paused. "Whoever sees one first, coughs. Wait until we've both confirmed it—a nod will do—and I run back to the car and start circling until you and the pigeon come out. I pick you up and then we follow them back to their car. Simple? Simple. I'm counting the cash already . . ."

Simple? Not quite.

The first likely victim was spotted by Thom after they had been waiting for nearly an hour at a food-court table within sight of Good News God Stuff, Inc. Most of the clientele were decidedly "off profile"—early to late thirties, Birkenstocked, tie-dyed, vegetarians (most likely), and filling their macraméed, carry-in shopping bags with crystals, whale-song CDs, and Tibetan anything, or otherwise just stopping in for a quick reading to see how Monday's board meeting would go. But when they struck, it had all the earmarks of pay dirt. An elderly gentleman in a dark suit wearing a hat with a bright red feather in the band, sprouting tufts of white from underneath the brim, clutching a rosewood cane like life itself.

"You follow him," Thom said. "I'm off to start circling."

"Like a vulture?" Zander added.

"Is there any other way?" Thom said, smiling with all his teeth—but especially the canines—showing.

Victim Number One proceeded to make his God Stuff purchases and then hobbled out, while Zander trailed at a safe distance. As he followed him to an ice cream parlor, and from there to a greeting card store, it occurred to Zander that this was not going to be as easy as he'd thought. It also occurred to him that by splitting up, they'd lost the security of tandem weirdness. Surely Zander stuck out like a sore thumb; surely the man, or somebody else, noticed Zander following him, in his backpack and trench coat. By the time they hit the ATM, bound, he was sure, to withdraw more fuel for a full-day spree, Zander was also convinced that security had been notified, and that some camera somewhere was watching his every move. When Victim Number One headed for the multiplex cinema, Zander broke off the trail and went to flag down his co-vulture.

"What happened?" Thom said, pulling up to the curb.

"Multiple pit stops," Zander said. "And then a movie."

"Shit," Thom muttered. "Well, get back in there and I'll meet you at the food court."

Once they'd gotten the hang of identifying worthwhile victims, the rest of the scam worked like a charm. It got so Zander didn't have to say anything at all during his visitations. The blackness of his wings said it; the coldness of his shadow. He was the Ghost of Christmases Yet to Come—dark, silent—while all his poor Scrooges raved, hitting him sometimes, but apologizing, and, eventually, pleading. Having experienced them himself when he was still dying of AIDS, Zander recognized all the Kübler-Ross stages—denial, rage, bargaining—and his victims went through them in lockstep, as if they were the essential items in a grocery list.

No.

Jesus.

No.

I still have so much to do.

Please.

I don't want to die.

I'm not ready.

There's been a mistake.

Yeah, yeah, yeah, Zander thought, realizing how a professional killer does it, how it's just a matter of having heard it all before. The predictability of the pleading steels you against any sympathy, makes you more determined to be heartless. Their woe was so . . . *pedestrian*. Gradually, Zander began seeing himself less and less as an Angel of Death, and more like the world's last Complaints Department clerk. And as they pleaded for "Just one more chance," he sat behind his Plexiglas, cool, deaf for the most part, and thinking about dinner, waiting for a break in the babble when he could call: "Next?"

And then, beyond this, past the sociopathic and psychopathic and apathetic, came the objective observer, curious about the emotional gears and cogs that made people's faces go all those different ways. Once he was through with this gig, Zander thought, it might be a kick to go into something mental health–ish, like psychology, or psychiatry—one of those high-paying, full-time scams.

Until then, of course . . .

"Next."

Zander will always remember his last victim with a certain degree of brittleness. Even more so than the wings, she (and her husband) were the wedge that split his old self from his new self—or so he liked to believe.

Thom and Zander had been waiting outside of one victim's house for an hour and a half, and were about to descend when a car pulled up outside and a flock of grandkids spilled out.

"Shit," Thom muttered, turning the key in the ignition and pulling away. The day was mostly done for, they still hadn't made their nut, and Thom was in no mood to go back to the mall, and square one. So they just began driving around the neighborhood, looking for clues, for potentials.

And that's how they found her house. It was March and she still had her Christmas lights strung in the branches of her tree out front, still had them framing her roof and windows. And not only were they out, but they were on, competing with the Georgia sun, the humming cicadas. Plaster wise men stood in plaster awe outside a plywood manger.

"Oh Jesus," Thom said, putting the car in park. "Bingo."

They waited to make sure the coast was clear, and then Zander slipped out of his overcoat and backpack. He went to the rear entrance and knocked on the screen door.

She comes to the door in a bright yellow party dress and high heels, clearly the best thing she has and she's been wearing it—judging from the stains, the smells—for weeks. Her hair is a dingy gray and loose about her head. Her eyes are fairly wild and Zander knows this is a loser, a bum choice. He's thinking about leaving when she throws open the door and pulls him inside.

"Finally," she says, "you've come."

The stench inside is unbelievable and flies are buzzing everywhere. She's jabbering away about how it might not seem like such a long time for an angel with forever on his calendar, but that months are a long time for humans and she's been waiting that long, and didn't really know what to do but wait. She's still tugging at Zander, holding on to one of his wings and pulling him deeper into the house, toward the door where the stink seems to be coming from.

And Zander is way ahead of the game on this one, because that smell can be only one thing—ripe death.

So, finding a rotting corpse behind that door doesn't surprise him, and neither does the tuxedo its flesh is mingling with, the bed it's lying in, or the dozen or so spent solid air fresheners ringing the body like long-dead votive candles. None of these things surprises, overmuch. No, it's the corpse's *wings* that throw Zander off his game, make him sag at the knees, and then catch himself.

All he knows is that he has to get out of there—fast. Prying away her fingers, he bolts out the screen door and runs back to the car. He pounds on the window and Thom rolls it down.

"What's wrong?" he asks.

"The jig's up," Zander says. "There's another one."

"Another what?"

"Another me," Zander says. "Another angel, except he's old and dead."

"No shit," Thom says, smacking a wad of gum, a real smart guy.

"No shit," Zander says. "Let's go."

"Hold your horses," Thom says. "This, I gotta see."

"Tho-om . . . ," Zander whines. "Let's not and say we did."

It's no use. He's already out of the car and walking toward the house. Zander thinks about driving away and leaving him there, except that he can't fit behind the steering wheel. Reluctantly, he follows Thom back to the house.

"He's dead alright," Thom says, as Zander reenters. "And she's kind of checked out of her skull for the moment. But they do seem to have some nice stuff here." He slides open a cabinet drawer containing the Sunday silver. That's when Zander notices that he's holding a pillowcase from the bedroom, and the stain of something rotten on the front of his shirt.

She's sitting at her yellow Formica kitchen table, smoking a cigarette, framed in a square of sunlight coming through the window. She doesn't acknowledge Thom's looting, instead focusing all her attention on Zander, the one who's come to take her dead husband home. Zander is split between the two of them, watching Thom out of the corner of his eye, and catching bits and pieces about her husband's change, about how she thought he was dead when he went all green, and was about to bury him out back—he'd told her beforehand not to "involve" anybody, and she took that to mean doctors, or, when the time came, morticians—but when she had him in a headlock and was dragging him out back, her watch crystal fogged, meaning he was still breathing, and still alive.

Once he came out with wings, she decided never to almost bury him again, no matter what. But then he'd gotten so much thinner after the wings. And the chest pain—he kept complaining about this pulling and stretching pain in his chest. And one day, he just stopped moving, and stopped breathing. She doesn't know what you call that when it happens to an angel. So she decided just to wait.

"For you," she says, staring at Zander with her crazy, no-nonsense eyes.

Zander turns around a chair and sits opposite her. Framed now in her square of sunlight, he traces the lightning branches of the veins on her hand. When she asks him, casually, who Thom is, he says: "The devil."

She says that's nice, and asks if Zander would like some tea.

. . .

What Zander did to Thom, he did because Thom was a selfish son of a bitch, and he'd convinced Zander that he was one, too. But Zander was changed, and what he did to Thom, he did to prove that he wasn't like him, that the two of them were as different as their anatomies suggested. He did it because Thom saw the tragedy of this last one as just another opportunity, and, God damn him, he didn't understand what that woman's husband *meant* to Zander. Up until the moment when he opened that door, as far as Zander knew, he was immortal and alone. Why not? He looked like an angel and everybody knows angels are immortal. It was easy to join in Thom's kind of cockiness when you saw yourself as being somehow, fundamentally, outside this world, untouchable by it.

Still, Zander wondered what Thom did, when he woke up naked in the backseat of his Ferrari, with a knot the size of a halved plum on the back of his head, and his once-again *ex*-partner having disappeared. Zander wondered if Thom had any idea how lucky he was, how close he'd come to being buried alongside that poor woman's angel husband, behind the house, under the tree she said he'd planted when they were first married. By the time Thom came to, of course, Zander was already history, having re-donned coat and backpack and hitched his way back to Michigan.

Though a part of him winced to admit it, Zander Wiles was a changed man.

And he was ridiculously happy—happier than he'd ever been before. Now that he'd found another, he knew that there would be more, and more, and that he wasn't alone. It was only a matter of time, now. All the danger was a matter of rarity. If there were others, he was safe; the lab guys wouldn't bother. Thom was right in that—tandem weirdness offered protection.

And the world was getting weirder every day.

6

On the morning their world—and everybody else's—changed, Jimmy and Pete stood in the surf of Half Moon Bay, eeling. Though neither would admit it to the other, they both liked the lullaby sound of the tide, the sight of the early morning sun reflecting off the water, and the fluttering green hair of the seaweed. They loved the crunch of the sand under their bare feet, and even the buck and squiggle of the eels they were pulling out of the bay and feeding into the burlap bags they carried over their shoulders. Jimmy, for his part, chalked it all up to God, and thanked Him at night in his prayers. Pete just thought it was cool, and left it at that.

Both had lived in Moss Beach all their lives and had seen dozens of weird things the water had left behind. So, when they heard the baby cries of seagulls fighting over food behind the outcropping just ahead, they knew it meant something big had washed up on shore again.

"A buck says it's a seal," Jimmy said.

"Two, and it's a dolphin," Pete said.

The two ran up the side of the outcropping and peered over the edge, to see if either had won.

Neither had.

"Jesus," Jimmy said, making a mental note to add one more to the Lord's-Name-in-Vain column for confession. "Jesus," he whispered again, before he'd even finished his tally.

Below them, surrounded by seagulls, lay the clearly dead body of a woman, clothed in nothing but seaweed and the spread wings of the gulls. Pete grabbed a rock and threw it toward the body, causing the whole scene to explode with bird shrieks and flapping. Wings scissored past them, puffing warm, salty air down on their skin, while beaks darted at their soft parts, dangerous yellow streaks. And as the racket carried itself away, the boys noticed that the biggest gull had stayed, a monstrous, impossible bird, still, patient, waiting apparently for some privacy before eating the whole body itself.

"Hey," Jimmy called, hefting and then tossing his own rock. "Beat it!" Followed by nothing. Nothing but the sick thud of a rock hitting a dead body. Afraid to look, but looking anyway, the boys again peeked over the edge, only to see the body still there, still dead, still still—and the second rock lying amid the feathers of the great gull's wings.

"Nuts, man," Pete said. "This is majorly nuts."

That said, there was nothing else to do about it, but what they did— namely scramble over the outcropping, down and around to where the body had washed up, to get a better view.

The closer they got, however, the clearer one thing became—whatever that was on her back, it wasn't a seagull. Or a bird of any kind. Or separate from the body of the woman herself.

Pete was the first one to touch the body, albeit just the wing, and with a piece of driftwood, roughly three feet long. With it, he worked up one wing, exposing where feather and flesh fused.

Jimmy, for his part, was all eyes, riveted on this miracle, and terror, all rolled into one. An angel. He was seeing an angel with his own two eyes. Something only God, and Jesus, and Mary, and saints could see. But a dead one. And a naked one. One that made his teenage prick get stiff, even though he tried to think it down, knowing that it meant hell for sure. Tunneling his vision, he concentrated on just that little bit of the back where Pete was working with the stick, the place where feathers and flesh met, where, when Pete lifted, Jimmy could see the strings of muscles, stiff and hard but still working under the pale dead skin . . .

And Jimmy lost it—his hard-on, and his breakfast.

"Oh, great," Pete called after his friend. "Like this ain't gross enough already." Pete dug his stick into the sand, angled under the body to act as a lever, to turn it over. Jimmy returned just as Pete succeeded, the body rolling over to reveal eyes, open, blank.

"It's an angel," Jimmy said, his voice full of awe, wiping the corner of his mouth with his bare arm.

"Yeah," Pete said. "So what else is new?"

After burying her body in the sand, marking it with a cross of pebbles, and swearing to keep the angel a secret, each boy left to break his promise in his own way. Jimmy, who was Catholic, went to confession to ask if it was a sin to poke a stick at a naked woman, if the naked woman had wings, and was dead, and was, you know, an angel? Pete, without half the baggage that Jimmy was carrying around, called the *National Enquirer* and was paid a twelve-thousand-dollar finder's fee.

Everybody assumed it was a hoax, of course, like the space aliens who doled out political advice to all sides during a recent presidential election; the sightings of Elvis, Hitler, and JFK; the miracle, eat-everything diets that not only shed the pounds but cured AIDS and cancer; the flesh-eating virus.

It was that last one, and the fact that it had been picked up by the regular press, that gave people justifiable pause, that made folks reserve judgment until they had time to check *The New York Times* the next morning, where the same photos appeared, albeit with smaller-point blurbs, and an even smaller slug line, crediting the photos to their original source.

It was the *Times*'s story that included the full details of the local coroner's autopsy report, and was tagged with actual quotes from said report. "The chest cavity," said one, "does not contain muscle fiber, but . . .

piano wire . . . like I'd cut into a steel-belted radial." Another explained that the "wire" in the chest cavity seemed to be magnetized, like the windings of a huge motor. Its field was cited as the explanation for the coroner's discovery that his digital wristwatch continually reset to 12:00 during the course of the autopsy, no matter how often he tried setting it to the actual time. The chest cavity's magnetic field was also blamed for erasing the cassette the coroner used to dictate his original notes.

Though both boys *could* be reached for comment, their quotes—peppered with "you knows" and "wows"—were not judged particularly illuminating.

Zander had just returned to Michigan and was staying in a cheerier hotel, thanks to his share of the take, which he'd kept despite claims of having changed. He'd walked to the local Kroger to get a few supplies to tide him over while he cleared his head and tried to figure out his next course of action. Standing in the 10-Items-or-Less line, Zander noticed the tabloid's full-page headline first, reading simply, and with a surprising degree of restraint: EARTH ANGEL, EARTH ANGEL! and promising STARTLING PIX INSIDE!

Zander felt dizzy, and suddenly naked. His wings began working in the pockets of his overcoat, spreading and closing the flaps like a flasher. The tops of his wings tried to rustle, pushing and pulling at the fabric of the backpack.

A fellow customer tapped Zander on the shoulder. "Excuse me, sir, but do you have something *alive* in there?"

Zander wasn't paying attention; instead, he held the paper in his hands, trembling, prepared to spread the tabloid open, to unfold its papery wings, thinking: Thom, what have you done? Because, of course, *that* was the story. Thom had come to, done something to the old woman—killed her, perhaps—exhumed the body of her angel husband, and cashed it all in at the nearest whorehouse. If such was the case, he'd probably already exposed Zander, and it was only a matter of time before he'd be dancing in the red and blue lights of a dozen squad cars. They'd have the lab guys with them—and a SWAT team.

"Excuse me, sir. Your baby . . . I don't think you're supposed to zip those things all the way up." Followed by a hand, reaching for the zipper of his backpack.

Zander wheeled around and barked: "LEAVE ME ALONE!" He was going to add: "You pervert," deflecting the attention away, when he opened the paper and saw her: Lizzy.

Winged.

Dead.

Filleted, and in full color.

"Hey, sport. Stay with me." It was Henry's voice from a million years ago, coaxing Zander out of shock. He blinked, and found himself still standing in the Kroger express line, holding an open copy of the *National Enquirer*. There was no one ahead of him, and the clerk was gesturing angrily for him to step forward. Zander felt like he'd been swallowed by a sea anemone, with fingers from behind, closing—all over his body, all over his coat, all over his backpack.

"Hey, buddy. Step lively," somebody called from behind.

Good idea, Zander thought, leaving his basket on the conveyor belt. Ignoring the Heys and Wait-a-minutes, he bolted straight for the front door.

The door, that is, with the turnstile.

Wired to the detector, and the alarm.

The one that locked up as soon as Zander crossed its electric beam, with his chest full of piano wire and magnets. Pitching forward, Zander's head slammed into the glass door, setting off a bowfront of transferred energy that expressed itself as a large, splintery circular crack, making a target of itself and the greasy bull's-eye left by Zander's forehead. Target, or halo—depending upon your perspective.

Envisioning the angry crowd that was surely surging his way, with their pitchforks and flaming torches, Zander pushed against the door with all the strength and adrenaline he could muster, which proved—the one lucky break in a shitty day—just enough. His tennis shoes slapping across the asphalt, Zander ran as fast as he could, his body describing impossible angles with the pavement, thanks to his new center of gravity. No doubt, he looked quite the sight, all tousle-haired, and coat a-flapping, a gangly, galloping hunchback, darting past the moth-haloed lamp-posts, careering off abandoned shopping carts, rolling over the hoods of cars, screeching to a halt—

Skreech!

Zander ran. As fast as he could. From as much as he could. Zander kept on running all the way back to his hotel room, where he slammed the door, barred it with his body, and waited for the tears that threatened, or the end of the world—whichever came first.

The tears won. Zander cried, and he kept on crying until the fists started banging on the walls, after which he sobbed, the pillow pressed to his face. It was a long-overdue cry, including Henry, and Lizzy, and that poor bastard in Georgia—*all* the poor bastards in Georgia, but especially the dead one with wings. He cried because of the drugs and his shittiness. He cried in apology for all the poor bastards he'd been a bastard to.

He cried because, of the three angels he knew, he was the only one who wasn't dead. Yet. Maybe the whatever-it-was was just taking longer in his case. Maybe it would take months, maybe years, maybe days, and it really didn't matter, because in many ways, he was already dead. The Zander who was innocent was dead; the Zander who slept with Lizzy was dead; the Zander who knew Thom was dead. And even though most of those models deserved to be discontinued, seeing them go still hurt.

It hurt because he didn't have a say in all of this. It hurt because he didn't know what was coming next. It hurt because there were going to be others, and they'd ask him, and he didn't know.

It hurt because he was afraid to go to sleep anymore, to close his eyes, because every time he opened them, something else had changed.

But by the morning, after sleeping fitfully, the only thing that had changed was Zander's mind. The world had its dead angel and had taken pictures of her insides. He was safe from that, at least. And this, these wings, were . . . *something*. Maybe not the something Frank had meant, all those years ago when he locked Zander out, but something, nevertheless.

Undeniably something.

And anyway, Zander wanted to see their faces—Frank's, his mom's, and everybody else's. He thought back to their victims—Thom's, and his—and remembered all the ways their faces went. He missed that— missed *inspiring* that. Fear. Awe. It was a kick, a goof. Zander liked it. He wanted more.

He called his parents, and got the ball rolling.

"Hello?" Karen answered faintly, at the end of a long, staticky corridor.

"Hello"—wait for the static to subside—"Mom?"

"Zander? Zander, is that you?"

"Yes, Mom," Zander said.

"Zander, where are you calling from? You sound terrible. You sound like you're calling from Brazil."

"I'm right in your backyard, Ma. It's just one area code over."

"Did you say you have a cold?"

"No, Ma."

"Zander?"

"Yes?"

"Can you call me back? This is a *terrible* connection."

"It won't get any better."

"What?"

"I said . . . ," Zander began. "Oh, never mind. It's on this side. It's in the phone."

"Oh."

"Ma?"

"Yes?"

"I got something very . . . *difficult* to tell you and Dad."

"It's okay."

"What's okay?"

"We know."

"Know what?"

"You know . . ."

"No. Know what?"

"You're gay."

83

"What?"

"Well, you are, aren't you?"

"No."

"No?"

"No. What made you think . . . ?"

"Oh. Never mind."

"Ma?"

"Yes?"

"It's real important that I see you and Frank, and that you guys prepare to be shocked, okay? If Frank's still on that heart medicine, you should have it nearby, and—"

"Zander?"

"Yes?"

"Have you killed someone?"

"No . . ."

And so it went.

By the time Zander showed up, Karen had him guilty of every atrocity she could imagine—though none of them were ones he'd actually committed. Zander supposed this was mainly his fault. He should have called earlier. For all they knew, he'd died years ago, fallen off the edge of the planet, or been reduced to a pile of ashes like those *Enquirer* people who just go up in flames for no good reason. And then he calls, a bolt from the blue, telling them he's got heart-attack-grade news and to just sit tight until he gets there. He should have told her it was good news, like winning the lottery. But Zander knew his mom. If he said it was *like* winning the lottery, she'd think he *had* won the lottery, and instead of mentally bailing him out of jail, she'd be halfway to thanking him for the new house he was going to buy them.

Still, Zander could have done without the sight of their hands as he walked through the front door. The hands that had once brushed bangs out of his eyes when he was a child had gotten clawlike and knobby. They twisted pointlessly at a dish towel, binding and unbinding themselves, while Frank's hands, the ones that had pushed him out the door, now dug into the Naugahyde of a La-Z-Boy's armrests.

Zander didn't know what to say. He took a crumpled-up copy of the *Enquirer* from his pocket. His wings were safely tucked into his overcoat and backpack.

"Oh, you saw that," Karen said. "Isn't that terrible?"

"You mean her dying?" Zander asked.

"Dying? Sally Dew's not dying. She's just a sick woman."

Sally Dew, who was on page three, was a TV soap opera star who had apparently become addicted to cosmetic surgery.

"No, not her," Zander said. He folded the tabloid around to its front cover. "Her," he said. "Skree . . . ah, the angel woman."

"Oh," Karen said nonchalantly. "It's a fake," she announced. "Airbrushed."

"Like *Playboy* used to do," Frank added, a bit too wistfully for his wife's liking.

"Ma . . . Dad," Zander pleaded.

"What?" they asked, together.

"It's not a fake," he said. "They're for real."

"Bullshit," Frank said.

"Yeah," Karen added. "What he said."

"Trust me," Zander said. "I know. They're real."

"So like what," Karen said, "you're a journalist, now?"

"No, I'm . . . ," he began, and stopped. "I'm . . ." He pointed at the picture of Lizzy, both longing for and dreading the revelation, the unzipping of his backpack. He knew the way their faces would go—like the faces of his Georgian victims. Not that he minded in Frank's case, but his mother—that was another matter.

"You're what?" she demanded of her son.

"An angel," Zander said, reaching with a nauseating sadness for his backpack.

"Like fun you are," Karen said.

"Yeah," Frank chipped in. "What she said."

Zander honestly didn't expect that both of them would faint. His mom was a possibility, but she was the willow in the family; she'd bend over, weep, rustle her leaves, but stay rooted. Frank, however, was his target, the one he'd been betting on. Frank was a pharmacist, after all, a man of science; he prided himself on being able to separate the truth from the bullshit. It was Frank's conviction that there were no more surprises that made him a sucker for the big ones. And wings definitely fell into the big category.

Too big, apparently, judging from the way Karen lay sprawled on the floor, while her husband lolled to one side in the La-Z-Boy, the TV clicker resting under his limp fingers, lying on its scan button. With channels skimming by and images swimming, Zander approached the TV and turned it off. Satisfied that they were both still breathing, he took a seat on the footstool, rested an elbow on a knee, his chin on his fist, and thought.

A psychiatrist, having a patient faced with such a decision—which of his parents to revive first—would probably make much of either choice. As the son making that choice, Zander picked his mother, because she was his *real* parent, not a step one, and hadn't been directly involved in his birthday eviction. Of that, Zander was relatively certain. Why had she baked a cake, after all, if she knew there wasn't going to be a party? And anyway, Zander knew how Frank worked—throw in a hand grenade, and then sweep up the pieces later. No consultations—just do it. Zander liked to think of this—these wings—as *his* little hand grenade. And these were the pieces he was staring at.

"Mom," he said, patting her cheek, tugging her into a sitting position. "C'mon. Rise and shine . . ."

"Wha . . . ," she said, coming to. Zander could see her focusing on his wings. He braced himself for it.

"Are we . . . ?" she began.

"No, Ma. We're not dead."

"But . . ."

He shrugged his shoulders, his wings followed, and she fainted again.

"I'm going to New York," Zander announced, once he'd gotten both of them to stop fainting, and after running through a sanitized version of his life since the lockout.

"New York?" Karen asked. "Why New York?"

"I need an agent," Zander said. "I don't know much about being an angel, but I know there's got to be some sort of money in this, at least while it's new, and—"

"New?" Frank asked.

"Yeah, well," Zander said. "There's me. And her. And at least one other I know about, also dead. There's gotta be others, and now that it's public, they'll be thinking about doing the same thing *I'm* doing. Trust me. If I don't strike now, it'll be cold in a year."

"Dead," Karen echoed. "What's this about another dead one? Is this— are these things . . . ?"

"I don't know," Zander said, because he didn't, and he didn't want to talk about it, figuring that if he kept busy, maybe—like when he'd eaten his way out of dying from AIDS. Celebrity would be a project—and a source of income—to keep him distracted from the questions that could kill him if he thought about them too much.

"So, anyway," he continued, moving on, "I've got to act fast."

"You'll take care of yourself, right?" Frank said. "That little boot out the door did ya some good, right? You learned how to take care of your-self, I mean."

"Right," Zander said, thinking of all the things he could say about what he'd learned, and how he'd taken care of himself.

"You'll call when you get in, right?"

"I'll send a telegram."

"And no surprises?" Karen asked.

Zander stopped himself from giving her one of Thom's don't-be-an-asshole faces. He'd closed the door on that life; he was going back to being the good son—just with wings, this time.

"Right," he said. "No surprises."

Frank clapped a hardy hand to his stepson's shoulder. "At least no new ones, eh?" He laughed.

In spite of himself, Zander laughed right along with his stepfather, the enemy—probably more out of relief than anything else.

"That's a good one, Dad," he added, for good measure, not knowing then that it was the happiest he'd ever see Frank, not knowing how badly he'd break his promise of no surprises.

. . .

After reaching New York, Zander learned that the Big Apple wasn't as bad as he'd heard. In fact, it was surprisingly easy to get a good New York agent using ingenuity, the Yellow Pages, a handgun, and a knapsack full of wings.

Zander was a veteran of the late-night talk-show horror story, knew from second and third hand how hard it was to get an agent, to get into the business, to get a break. And he didn't have time to waste; who knew who might be planning the same break, now that Lizzy had given away the game. Snippy secretaries with air-traffic-controller headsets, filing their nails and telling him to take a seat . . . these were not things he had the time or patience to deal with.

"Hello, Ms.—" he paused, reading her nameplate "—Shaffer. Can I see Mr. Larson?"

She paused, thought, took two shaves off the fingernail she was working on, and delivered her line: "Do you have an appointment?"

"Kind of," Zander said, reaching into his pocket and placing the gun on her appointment book.

"Is that for real?" Ms. Shaffer asked, looking at the gun with more curiosity than fear. "We had a guy in here last week, brings in some kiddie squirt gun. Security kicked out his spleen or something."

"It's real."

"Is it loaded?"

She had him there. Zander paused, thought Clint Eastwood, and pointed it at her. "Why don't we find out?"

"Okay, okay," she said. "Just a sec." She talked into the microphone floating in front of her mouth. "Mr. Larson, there's a Mister . . ."

"Zander Wiles."

She held her hand over the microphone. "What kind of name is that?" she asked.

"Alexander Wiles," Zander said. "Okay?" He moved the gun forward, to remind her it was there, was a participant in this conversation.

". . . a Mr. Alexander Wiles here, with a gun, and he wants to see you." She paused. "Well, it looks like one of those German thingies. A waddayacallit, Luger or something." Pause. "No, he won't tell me. He pulled that old 'You feel lucky?' bluff." Pause. "Yeah. Midwest, I'd say. Maybe even Iowa."

"Michigan," Zander said, feeling like a silly amateur. And then a thought occurred to him. "Detroit," he added.

"He says he's from Detroit," she said. "Oh, okay." Pause. "Mr. Larson says it's a good thing you come from a place with balls, otherwise . . ."

The door opened and Mr. Larson waved him in. Zander placed the gun back in his pocket as a sign of good faith, and walked into his office.

"What's in the knapsack?" Mr. Larson asked. "The thousand-page miniseries I've been waiting for all my life?"

"It's . . ." and Zander realized he didn't know how to say it, hadn't planned this part in the bathroom mirror. He gave him his well-worn copy of the *Enquirer*. He was reaching for the zipper on the knapsack when Ms. Shaffer's voice came over the intercom.

"They're here," she said.

"Send them in," Mr. Larson said.

"I've got wings!" Zander shouted, as the door blew open and three security guards followed, hands bracing wrists, guns leveled at his heart, head, and groin.

"Freeze!" said one.

"Drop it!" said another.

"Up in the air!" said the third.

Zander raised his hands over his head, his backpack only half unzipped, a few feathers poking out. "Honest," he said. He worked the muscles of his back, like Houdini in a straitjacket, trying to push one wing up and out of its topcoat pocket and the rest of the way out of the pack.

"Are you telling me . . . ," Mr. Larson began.

"Yes," Zander said. And he could feel it happening. He was almost there, could feel the opening widen as the zipper slipped down against his wings' persistent squirm. It was like sex, this strange little tableau, life and death holding their breath against the climax, this coming into or out of, this fundamental, deep muscle release . . .

"Yes," Zander repeated, timing it just right, the wings springing from his backpack like the petals of some sped-up flower on PBS.

"Well fuck me," Mr. Larson said, shooing security out the door and closing it.

"Fuck me and the horse I rode in on," he added, his way of saying—Zander later learned—that they had a deal.

Zander was booked for his first gig that afternoon, and for the next four weeks seemed to do nothing but run from studio to studio. He didn't complain, though, because he knew that this wasn't going to last. Zander told Bill—Mr. Larson—his concern about others and he agreed that a slash-and-burn, saturation-bombing approach was the best strategy. "The second another one of you guys shows up, expect your earnings to drop by half. Half again for Mr. or Ms. Three, and so on. And if any of them has a good smile and a sense of humor, consider yourself retired. We're talking good old-fashioned snatch-and-run. 'Cause frankly, Zander, Teri Garr you ain't."

Zander nodded to all of this. Bill was right. Zander even agreed to Bill's plan for how he—Zander—should be marketed.

It began with an innocent enough question: "What do you think about not talking?"

"What?" Zander asked.

"Not talking," Bill repeated. "As a gimmick. Or maybe we could have some fake language worked up for you." He paused, paced, arms folded, one hand absentmindedly stroking his chin. "I definitely see you onstage with an interpreter."

"A professional actor?" Zander asked.

"Yes."

"Someone to supply the personality I lack?"

"More or less," Bill said.

Truth was, nobody cared, at first. The producers on the first show didn't buy the interpreter routine, viewing it as a way of milking two appearance fees out of one act. And they were already familiar with Zander's "interpreter," a nephew of Bill's who handled the incontinent monkeys for whichever zoo person was making the rounds at the time. Truth was, wings were wings—there were no better tits, or asses, though Zander worked hard to make himself a big one of the latter.

He reacted to fame and fortune badly, with one thing: Fear. Zander didn't want to freeze on camera. He didn't want to be a country bumpkin, either, smiling and waving at mom and dad at home. And so, instead, he got angry—anger being his best emotion, the one that got him through when all else failed. He glared at the red light like he was challenging it to take a swipe at him. He'd answer the hosts' questions like they were the dumbest things he'd heard, got hot when they seemed to ask the same thing again and again. He suggested, on occasion, that Geraldo could kiss various unfeathered parts of his anatomy. And he flew off the handle when the subject turned, as it inevitably did, to flying. Zander had it in his contract, goddammit—film only, no videotape, because of the chest thing; no mikes within ten feet of the talent, again because of the chest thing; and absolutely *no questions about flying.* That last one was the hardest for all of them, the promise they usually broke after the first few minutes. Zander let it slide, but showed he was pissed, and mentally waited for any other slip-ups, which would justify anything he might choose to do. Like throw Jerry Springer into the audience, to see if he'd . . . *spring.* For example.

And contrary to Bill's predictions, the media ate it up. Personality wasn't an issue. Zander's lack of it only lent fodder to the columnists, who dubbed him "Hell's Angel," but who nevertheless devoted thousands of column inches to him, which was all that mattered, anyway.

Until, that is, they learned about the real Zander Wiles.

On the home front, things were not going well. Zander was in New York, being famous, which is what he thought Frank wanted—the something he was told to become. And, at first, both his parents claimed pride, but then it soured. What was there to be proud of, after all? Had he cured cancer? No. Had he even earned his wings? No. He was just lucky, and an exhibitionist, and, to be honest, a prick. It was no picnic being the parents of somebody the press called Hell's Angel. It took its toll.

Not that they ever mentioned it. No, the resentment came out in subtler ways. Zander would return home for a visit, and one of his parents would explain the obvious to him, as if he were a stranger. He'd say, "I *know* you have to jiggle the handle. We've *always* had to jiggle the handle," and Frank would yell at him not to yell at his mother. "I'm not yelling," Zander would yell, and Karen would say something about the old Zander, like he was some better brother the current version had killed. His stepfather would chime in with something about how Zander had changed, and that's when things would really blow up.

Change, and who had, and who hadn't—these were touchy subjects in those days.

Still are.

So they cued the slamming doors, followed by the angry stomping offs, and the wild blue tapestry of accusations and obscenities. Karen assumed the role of shuttle diplomat between Zander and his stepfather, relaying their assorted he-said-to-tell-yous, and providing polite translations where necessary. When that grew old, she'd remind Frank that Zander was at least *her* flesh and blood, while threatening Zander with Frank's bad heart. And then, one day, sooner than either of them expected, the heart threat came true.

The last straw was the Donahue show. Phil was running up and down the aisles with his white hair and microphone, and Zander was perched on a backless stool, shouting his answers through a megaphone to avoid the shrill feedback he caused whenever the mike got too close to his chest. They could have probably figured out a better arrangement, used shotgun mikes with parabolic collectors or something like that, but the show's producers liked the megaphone's theater. It made things more real, somehow, underlined Zander's essential difference from any other guest they'd ever had.

The show had a call-in segment, and was going out live, and the end of Zander's career began with the following words:

"Hello, this is Sarah, and I'm calling from Georgia . . ."

Sarah recognized Zander and his most recognizable appendages.

"You bastard!" she shouted. And the world agreed.

"Sarah," Zander began. "I'm sorry . . ."

"Bastard?" Phil said, in his Phil way. "Caller, why is Mr. Wiles a bastard?"

"I can explain," Zander lied.

"Sarah in Georgia?" Phil repeated. "Can you help us out here?"

"He . . ." and Zander could imagine that she was having as hard a time explaining what had happened between them as he was. "He stole from me . . ."

"Stole," Phil repeated. "What did he steal, Sarah?"

Dead air. Zander could feel the mike picking up his staticky heart, all the way from the audience. Floorboards. Poe. Beating and hideous and heart.

"My religion," Sarah finally said. "My faith in God."

"How'd he do that, Sarah?" Phil said, thinking he had the answer, and plowing along. "It's not his fault he looks like somebody's idea of religion. It just happened, right, Zander?"

"It just happened," Zander agreed, though they were talking about totally different Its.

"He came into my house," Sarah said. "He took advantage of me."

"When?" Phil asked. Two cameras swung into position, to catch Zander's reaction, full front and profile; he imagined the split screen mug shot the TV audience was watching, imagined them turning down the sound of his louder and louder heart. "Have you met our guest before?"

"Yes," Sarah said. "About a month ago. My husband had just died and . . ."

And Zander got up, walked toward the host, and grabbed the mike. It whistled and popped with the *lub-dub* of Zander's heart and finally blew out. Zander, the rapidly falling star, dropped the dead mike and walked to the back of the theater, pushed through the double doors and out of the public part of his life. Sarah from Georgia filled the breach he left in the media, her and a few of the others. They made back several times whatever Zander had taken from them.

With the possible exception of their faith, of course.

The door to his parents' home was locked, and the lock had been changed—a familiar motif by now. "Become something . . . *better*." That'd be Frank's new tune. And it'd be Zander and James Dean, walking down the glistening wet boulevard of broken dreams, once again—this time with wings to bead up in the rain. Of course, this time, Zander was in a really bad mood, had a chest full of piano wire and pulleys, and the door—well, the door didn't weather as well as it had when he was eighteen.

BOOM. BOOM. BOOM. *Splinter. Crack.* Reach through, twist, and:

"I'm home from the war," Zander announced.

Frank threw a bottle over Zander's head; it shattered and sprayed him with glass and foam.

"Why thanks, Stepdad," Zander said. "I think I *will* make myself at home."

"Zander . . . ," Karen said, entering at the sound of the commotion, backpedaling toward the kitchen, but then stopping. "We weren't expecting you."

"You weren't expecting me to get in," Zander clarified.

"Zander . . . ," she tried again.

"Listen," Zander said. "You saw it; I did it; it was stupid, but I didn't have a roof over my head at the time, just in case you've forgotten."

"Excuses," Frank said.

"Yes," Zander said. "They are that. I was wrong and there's no excuse, but I'm part of this family, and I need a little *support* right now."

"Jesus . . . ," Frank said.

"Can I stay?"

"No," his stepfather said. "You've humiliated—"

"Yes," his mother broke in. "Yes, Zander. You can stay."

"Karen . . . ," Frank protested.

"Shut up, Frank," Karen said. She cupped her hand to the back of Zander's neck and squeezed.

"It's like wires inside there," she said in a low voice, concerned and soothing. "Like a knot of steel bands."

"I know," Zander said.

In the weeks that followed, the rest of it came out. And the rest of the rest of it. Ex-clients from his drug-dealing days called in to radio talk shows; Thom resurfaced with stories to sell. News vans found his parents' home and pulled up on the lawn. The house was surrounded, and klieg-lit at night like a concentration camp. Nobody could leave without being swallowed up. To buy his parents a few moments out, to get groceries, to get away, Zander granted a last interview, the answers shouted from his upstairs bedroom window.

"Did you know the Angel-girl from California?"

"Yes."

"Were you lovers?"

"Yes."

"Did you use drugs together?"

"Yes."

"Did you shoot up together?"

"Yes."

And yes, Zander would regret those answers to those questions, given so his parents could take in a movie, away from all the chaos. He'd regret the answers, and all that came to follow from them—but first he had another domestic crisis to deal with.

Returning, Zander's parents had made a decision. Frank had, and he threatened to leave if Karen didn't agree. His point was simple: They— *he*—couldn't go on living like this. He didn't know how right he was.

Zander, it was clear, had to leave. For the good of his parents. He could do that, couldn't he? They deserved that, didn't they?

As Frank pulled on his wing, trying to show him the door, Zander exploded. "Get away from me, you jealous old man!" Zander shouted, pushing his stepfather away, slamming him into the plasterboard, sending a wide, creasing crack from floor to ceiling.

Frank went fish-eyed, gulping for breath. He grabbed his chest. And Zander didn't believe it. Poor acting. Zander was a professional; he made real money on the basis of much more convincing con jobs. He stepped over his stepfather's body and went downstairs.

He made himself a peanut butter and jelly sandwich and poured a glass of milk—comfort food to settle his nerves. His mother entered the kitchen and asked Zander where Frank was.

"Upstairs," Zander said. "Faking."

"Faking what?" Karen asked.

"A heart," Zander began, meaning to add "attack," but then deciding against it. "He's faking a heart. Like he's got one."

Karen blanched and ran out of the kitchen. She ran upstairs and then downstairs. All the phones were disconnected. She rushed back to the kitchen and saw Zander. She didn't trust him. Not with this. Not ever again. And so, instead, she threw open the front door. Into the klieg-lit chaos, she shouted:

"Someone call an ambulance! Please. It's an emergency."

There may have been a moment at Frank's funeral when Zander and his mother could have fixed things, but Zander screwed that up, like he seemed to be screwing everything up. His presence turned the service into a circus. The place was standing-room only, and the strangers were there, waiting, before Zander even arrived, a sea of curious bodies between him and the casket. It took Zander several minutes to find his mother in the crowd, and when she noticed him pushing through to her, she turned away. She hadn't talked to her son since the ambulance ride to the hospital.

"Mom!" Zander shouted at her retreating back. "I'm sorry."

She stopped and let Zander catch up with her. "Make them go away," she said. "Make them go home."

He began to say that he didn't know how. He began to say how sorry he was, and that he wished it had been him, instead, and Jesus, what was becoming of their family? All of these things were in his head, ready to say.

But Zander didn't say them.

What he did, out of reflex, was accept a magazine and pen, passed to him from behind. Instead of saying "Sorry," he said, "Who's this to?"

Karen—Zander's mother, Frank's wife, and now, widow—watched in horror, and when Zander clicked the pen, she slapped him across the face.

"You bastard," she said. She turned away.

"Right," Zander said, letting her be that way, letting her stew in her own sauce, as his face stung. He'd let her have the silent treatment right back, he thought. He'd finish this and apologize, in due time.

He returned to the matter at hand. "You were saying?" he said, looking over this latest groupie. She was petite and blond and would have looked good in wings.

"Angela," she said, smiling.

"No kidding?" he said, glancing down at the magazine she offered. They'd used the standard publicity shot of Zander, brooding. Above it, a headline read: HOW WINGS ARE SPREAD.

While he signed, his wings beat the air gently. It was summer and they were at least good at that—fanning. Despite the circumstances, it was actually a pretty nice day. One of those slow, dreamy summer ones.

And then Zander's world changed. Again.

Even today, he can't say where the guy came from. All Zander knew was that one minute he was signing autographs at his stepfather's funeral, and the next he was coughing and stars were going off behind his eyes. The stranger's head had hit him square in the breadbasket; Zander groaned and hit the floor, struggling for breath.

Still wheezing, he felt hands on his hand, and then a sharp pain flashing through it, radiating out to the fingers and shooting up his arm. Footsteps pounded away and out the funeral parlor door. Outside, the air split with whoops and laughter.

Chaos broke out. Flowers were spilled. Chairs were upset. Nobody knew anything about anything, especially about what had just happened. It just seemed like a good idea to get out of the way, and as quickly as possible.

And when Zander brought his throbbing hand into view, it was already swelling, the dark ring made by human teeth running free with his—maybe magical, maybe contagious— blood.

"Mom?" he called, light-headed, and desperate.

The world swirled around him like the colors on a TV screen scrambled by his magnetic heart.

"Mom?" he called again, afraid, and knowing he'd blown it—blown it worse than he'd ever blown it before.

Part Three

The Fraud

As for *her*—the Angel who watched Zander jump—her name is Cassie O'Connor. The *famous* Cassie O'Connor. She's a therapist, one of the few in the country to specialize in dysfunctional Angels. The thing she's famous for, though, is her book, *The Angel Blues,* a best-selling, pop-psych *Oprah*-ization of her case studies, complete with glaring generalizations and easy answers. Cassie is also a fraud—a fact she's waiting for her public to realize.

At the moment, she does her waiting—famously—standing by the famous window of her famous office, looking out at the patients she's made infamous. Yesterday, the city ran a hose from a fire hydrant to the courtyard just outside her office. The firemen, dressed in helmets and yellow slickers, cranked open the spigot for a happier task than usual. The water gushed and gurgled, making a pleasant background *ssshhhh* for most of the afternoon and forming a wonderfully huge puddle. It is late February, and winter is having its last fling. Yesterday's puddle is therefore frozen today, providing the season's last rink.

Some of the hospital staff have brought their children with their skates, and they are out there now, laughing, playing tag with mittened hands, starting at one end and building speed, twisting to stop and sending up rooster tails of shaved ice. Snow drifts across the glassy surface in their wake, gathering in lines and loops, spirals here and there, almost . . . *something,* almost someone's cursive script, almost saying something, before scattering, and almost writing something else.

Some of Cassie's clients are out there, too, among the half thoughts and squiggles, gliding with the rest, arms and wings spread happily, laughing. To look at them now, you'd think Cassie's critics were justified—those who referred to "Angel therapy" with the same arched eyebrows and quotes they usually reserved for "pet cemetery." She checks the time; the group session should have started five minutes ago. Cassie sighs fog onto the window and smears it away.

One little boy in a powder blue coat and black wool stocking cap seems to have invented a game, maybe called "Bowling for Angels." He starts by running full throttle at one of Cassie's clients, and pulls himself into a ball just before striking. The patients hop, cup their wings, and hang in the air for a second as the boy whizzes under their feet and into the snowbank surrounding the rink. The boy hits the bank again and again, each time sending up happy puffs of snow. And each time he gets up, giggling, loving this utterly and completely and almost as much as the patients do.

The boy is maybe three or four and has never known a world without Angels. They, and the rest of the world, are his friends, his playmates. Unlike Cassie, he doesn't know that the Angel in red he's just zipped by has rope burns underneath her scarf, that the one in green tried tranquilizers, or that the one in blue was found in a Neiman Marcus window display, crying inconsolably. All he knows is that when he smiles, they smile back—and they're really hard to catch!

Whizzz-puff.

More giggling, more smiles, more tugging on wings with mittened hands. "Let's do it again. C'mon, please, please, please . . ."

Cassie knows she should send an attendant to remind her truants about the group session, to bring them down to earth and the merciless slouching toward diagnosis. Should probably, but won't. If nothing else, that's one of the things Cassie has learned in her years as an Angel and a therapist: Respect joy. Joy is not something that happens instead of something else important; it isn't a waste of time; it is, really, what time was invented for. It happens almost never, and if you don't respect it, it happens less and less. Cassie should know, not being overjoyed—or overly joyous—by anyone's definition, especially lately.

So, no, she won't interfere. They'll come for her when they need her, she knows, and more's the pity. Till then, it's enough to leave them out there, where they can break her heart and do their own some good.

As Cassie waits for the world to notice what a fraud she is, she twists in her hands a perfect piece of evidence that it hasn't. It's a note, practically an apology, and an invitation. The first paragraph explains to her that she's famous and probably busy and that no one will think the worse of her if her answer is no. The next paragraph explains that the note-writers are the parents of a client of hers who's dead now and scheduled to be buried on such and such date, at such and such time. It goes on to say that he spoke of Cassie, liked her, that he knew and they knew she'd tried to help, and it would mean so much if she could please come—if it's not too much trouble; if it's not against the law.

"Against the law?" Cassie says aloud, her breath fogging her office window again. She guesses they must mean something about therapist-client relations, and ethics. She doesn't think they're commenting on the quality of treatment their son got under her care. They could, of course; they'd be justified, but the only witness to that fiasco was dead, and apparently too polite to tell his parents the truth.

When she's feeling defensive, Cassie will say that she wrote *The Angel Blues* as a plea for tolerance and understanding on both sides of the Angel Issue. She wrote it to show Pedestrians what Angels are like, and to remind Angels what they were like, before they grew wings. She wrote it to dispel mobilist myths on either side and to show that despite superficial differences in mobility styles, all people are really the same underneath.

When she's defensive, she says she wrote *The Angel Blues* to save the world.

The fraud in her, of course, wrote it to meet Oprah.

. . .

Cassie's office window is framed in icicles, fangs in a mouth threatening to swallow the world whole. Outside, the inevitable happens: One of the children throws himself backward in the snow, works his arms and legs. Steam comes out of his innocent mouth—steam, meaning words, words Cassie can predict. "Lookit me," he says, in the brittle chill of this Christmas card tableau. "Lookit me; I'm an angel!"

Every thing—and one—freezes. A parent, politically correct to the nth degree, bolts to the rescue, yanking the child up with one frightening tug, brushing off the snow with more force than is normally associated with a full-out thrashing. More steam from both their mouths—the child's sobs, the parent's hurried explanation about people of all kinds and their feelings, about all the things we just don't do anymore, like wear blackface, or make angels in the snow.

The mother turns to Cassie's patients, tries to blame this inadvertent mobilist faux pas on an ex-husband who still has visitation rights. More steam. None of it comes from the Angels. They have big lungs and can hold their breath for the duration of this ugliness. They get regular practice. When the red one starts crying, it's not for any slight, mobilist or otherwise. She's crying for the brittleness of everything nowadays, for all the breath-holding, and hand-holding, for the whole, general touchiness of the world. She's crying, mainly, for the moment that lies in pieces before her, for the memory of what and who she is, and where.

And one by one, they come back inside—to Cassie, and her real world.

The weatherpeople are predicting rising temperatures and rain. By mid-afternoon, the rink will be a puddle again. Cassie wonders for a moment whether she should turn the group around, send them back out, in search of a little more joy. Maybe she should put on her skates and join them.

Instead, she straightens chairs, listening to her Angels in the hallway, slurping off their skates, sshhing out of parkas, stamping feet, rubbing shoulders, rustling wings—doing whatever it takes to get warm.

8

Cassie O'Connor spent a good chunk of her growing up on a small farm in Cedar Run, Michigan—praying for a tornado to carry her house someplace (anyplace) else. Cedar Run wasn't much more than a speck on state maps, located somewhere Kalamazoo-ish between freeway exits. It was the sort of place that hardly existed between censuses, lacking, for example, such town-making staples as a Main Street, a hardware store, barbershop, church, or even a theater. Drake—which wasn't much to speak of, either—had all those things, plus the single school bus that drove from farm to farm, picking up the dozen or so students Cedar Run had to offer.

Another thing Cedar Run didn't seem to have was much patience with people like the O'Connors. There was, it seemed, a certain aura of okayness that came only with having a half-dozen generations live and die on the same scrap of dirt, and where anything less qualified you as "just passing through." Since Cassie and her mom, Mercedes, had inherited their farm from a bachelor uncle who had himself bought the place at a bank auction—well, they'd be packing up and moving any day now, surely.

"We're not *from* here," Mercy would say, trying to explain why the other kids treated Cassie the way they did. She'd pause and add: "Not exactly the worst sin in the world, considering."

Eventually, it became a game they'd play, whenever Cassie came home crying, stung by some local snub—the "People Not from Cedar Run" game.

"Albert Einstein," Mercy would call.

"President Kennedy," Cassie would say, wiping a tear from her eye.

"Picasso, Mahatma Gandhi, and Jesus Christ," her mother would add, the figures getting bigger and more important, depending upon the hurt they were called upon to heal.

The farm—and Cassie's and Mercy's living manless upon it—was part of the problem. That, and the fact that they didn't quite know what to do with the place to begin with. What type of farm went for whole years (sometimes) with nothing being planted? What type of farmer turned his fields into parking lots for BMWs and Cadillacs, full of wrong-haired types in suits and evening dresses, or army jackets and ponchos with safety pins stuck everywhere, including their faces? Whatever the hell this deal was about, the locals were pretty sure it *wasn't* about taking farming seriously.

Not that Mercy completely ignored the tilling and toiling and other *farm* things—she had chickens one year, pumpkins usually, and corn almost every year—it's just that farming wasn't what her heart was built for. What Mercy was, around the heart area, was an artist, a sculptor. She welded together pistons and rods, shovel and saw blades, hinges and old TV antennae into half-finished statements about longing she left out in the Michigan rain to rust, and complete. It was *this* crop—the rusting, rustic art crop—that paid the bills and brought in the Caddies and Beamers with their out-of-state plates. It was also the crop that gave Cassie the most joy, watching her mother at work, the fine muscles of Mercy's arms shifting underneath her shiny skin, her overalls spattered with silvery solder stars. Not making a peep—not daring to—Cassie sat in the barn, on the milking stool for the cow they didn't have, watching as her special mom pulled down her dark-dark goggles before sparking up the oxyacetylene torch, and lighting the shaggy Gauloise she'd fixed in the corner of her mouth.

"This is dangerous, Casper," she'd say, talking tough-guy around the loosely rolled stub and pulling down Cassie's junior pair of goggles. By "this," she meant both the flame *and* the cigarette. "It's just . . ." She paused. *"Très*—how you say?—*cool,* no?"

"Très cool, *oui,* mama," Cassie would say—four, maybe five—already well on her way to being the weirdo the local kids would torture.

As a mother, Mercedes O'Connor was only slightly dangerous. Dangerous, partly, because she drank a bit more than she should, smoked too much, and taught her daughter long words and foreign phrases to piss off the locals—but dangerous, mainly, because she was the most glamorous thing in a glamourless town. Cassie fell in love with her mother, utterly and exclusively, joining her in the "People Not from Cedar Run" club. Together, they took to calling the place they lived—the place they were *stuck*—Dry Run, something a little short of whatever real life had to offer.

"Remember when we went to that gallery in Chicago?" Mercy would say, sitting across the kitchen table from her pouting daughter. "How pretty it was? And remember how hot and crummy the train was?" She'd wait for Cassie to nod. "Well, honey, this is the train; it sucks, but it's going someplace pretty."

The only other specialness Cassie had in her Dry Run life was her bike, the one with all those *things* stuck on it, the gears and sparkles, the spray paint and doll arms raised palm up, holding rhinestones. It started small when Cassie was five, and she discovered the sound of power playing cards could make when you wedged them into the spokes; at six and seven, it was plastic streamers and metal sparkle handgrips. Pedestrian, still—average and derivative by most standards—but an important motif was introduced. The streamers! Cassie loved the streamers, the way the wind flagged them out whether she was riding or not, making her bike more than it was, making it something in motion all the time, and almost alive. Whatever form her bike-art took, there would always be something—flags or pinwheels, or Barbie-doll hair—*something* for the wind to play with.

Wind being what it was all about, after all. Wind, and power, and speed, and escape. Whenever Cedar Run became too much—or the too-little it usually was—Cassie could just hop on her bike and outrun the whole damn place. Standing all the way up on the pedals and pumping as fast as she could, nothing—not even her stupid life—could touch her.

By eleven, Cassie went baroque, dressing up her bike as well as herself for Halloween. With Mercy's help, she painted the metal parts flat black to make them invisible, and then painted an old straw broom from handle to bristles in phosphorescent paint, before wiring it to the cross-bar. Straddling the broomstick, she set off after dark, flying low, a peaked cap on her head, her missing father's overcoat fluttering. After that, Cassie found herself looking for things specifically for her bike—a bunch of varnished wildflowers, a racoon's tail, the busted-out insides of a radio. At thirteen, she went through a Barbie-doll phase, buying up every misused Barbie she could find at garage and barn sales and stringing their heads together into a voodoo Amazon necklace she slung from her handlebars. And the more the locals made fun of her—the more they started calling her, not even "O'Connor," but "Bike girl," or "that girl with the bike"—the more things Cassie glued on.

That is, until, almost suddenly, Cassie found herself eighteen—and the sort of girl the boys had stopped teasing.

If the dress had been anything but red, she might have forgiven him. But red meant he didn't understand, didn't appreciate the situation, didn't know that Cassie didn't need more red in her life, that red was so very much, and so very big a part of the whole problem. The only answer for red was doing what Cassie did, which was to hang the dress by its spaghetti straps from the scarecrow's broomstick crucifix, letting it flap in the breeze—a great red flag, signaling the opposite of surrender.

This all happened when she was eighteen, before the wings and before *Oprah,* and was the biggest thing in Cassie's life, next to those future things. She looked back at the dress—gaudy, red, and flagging—and figured he'd get the message. He didn't. Instead, he kept trying, kept giving her things she didn't want, things she had to figure out what to do with.

Like candy. (Puh-leeze . . .)

Or flowers. (Ditto.)

Or balloons. Silvery *heart* balloons—which were very close—but filled with helium, making them No's.

Or chicken soup—again, close—but *Campbell's,* and so, again, No.

What Cassie wanted was an apology, not things. Yes, she knew that things could talk—what was art, anyway, if not talking things?—but she knew, too, that some things are just too important for symbols.

But she couldn't come right out and tell him, either. Telling him, she knew, was like cheating on a test, the scores for which will follow you throughout your life. No, he had to figure it out for himself, had to understand that the only way to say you're sorry is to *say* you're sorry. Even folks from Cedar Run should be able to understand that.

Of course, Cassie realized, rape's a big thing to be sorry *for,* but that still doesn't mean you don't have to say it.

The boy who did it was named Jack Buchholz. He was in Cassie's high school homeroom, and decided that he had a lot in common with her, seeing as he customized cars, and seeing as Cassie was, well, "that girl with the bike."

When Jack first tried to impress her, he did it by telling her about his car, the painful restoration of the engine, the modification of the chassis, about how decals weren't good enough and how he hand-painted the dragon that curled across its body. Cassie said yes to that boy, the one who could get lost in a summer afternoon with a small brush, doing scales, each one separately in different shades of green to give it reptilian depth. For her, the story—the dragon—was about patience; for Jack, unfortunately, it was about things that breathe fire.

Afterward, Jack was totally confused. It was supposed to feel good, and be about love, and magic and stuff, and was something of a guy secret that guys had to let girls in on. It was a guy's job to show them what was out there and what they were missing, and once they got the hang of it, well, hell . . . you know. Jack . . . Jack was just doing his job, as a guy.

It was the way her *fists* kept coming back to him, to his back, that made him think (slowly)—that made him feel (eventually) bad. It was the bruises in the hand mirror, reflecting the bathroom mirror, reflecting his back that made him buy the dress, the one that cost so much, looked so pretty, she'd have to forgive him—if forgiving was what was called for—or thank him, if it wasn't.

Afterward, Cassie rode her bike faster and harder than she ever had, trying to clear her head, to get away, and to figure out what to do with the rape. That she had been was clear; she'd been forced against her will. The dictionary definition was nothing more complicated than that. She'd said, "No!" Beyond that, she'd resisted. As she ground through the gravel of the road to and past her house, Cassie ran it through her mind, trying to figure out if there was anything she had done, or could have done. The answer was wind, and the beating of her own heart as she worked at the pedals.

In her heartbeat, Cassie could still hear the stupid thuds of her fists on his back, remembered thinking how he must be hollow inside to make that kind of noise. She remembered his other noises, too, and how she couldn't place the animal they reminded her of.

As the muscles in her legs began feeling like steel bands, she remembered the other thing she couldn't place. Herself. She couldn't place herself *there,* at the scene of the crime, at the place *it* had happened. She was in the tree spreading its aloof and leafless branches over them. She was still in that tree, kept having to tell herself that it had happened in the first place, and that she was the person it had happened to. She thought of herself as forever modified: Cassie O'Connor—*raped woman.*

I am a *raped woman,* she thought, washing her hair.

I am a *raped woman,* fixing a flat.

On TV, raped women were always in shock, or outraged, or Lady Macbeths who showered and showered and couldn't quite get "clean." Cassie didn't feel dirty, just—she didn't know—*weird,* like there was a her-her and a mirror-her, and they'd switched places. Plus, there was the whole ending thing; this thing didn't seem to have one. And every time she tried to forget it, stupid Jack dumped off some other dumb thing, reminding her all over again.

In her head, Cassie knew how it should end. It would start with the sound of gravel, crunching. He'd turn around, nervous, and find . . . nothing. Cassie would smile from her safe distance, continue following, closing in on him slowly, until they'd made it to Drake, to civilization. She would close the distance between them, standing up to pedal faster, cut in front of him, say nothing when he stopped short, panicked. She'd wheel away to let him through, and when he passed, and looked back, she'd turn the front wheel in, and hold it there. She'd begin circling him, drive him to the center of town—silent in her strong way—as people left their safe houses, their shops, aproned, holding dishrags, half-shaved.

Surrounded by gawkers—and Cassie—Jack would realize the weakness behind his own silence, the cowardice behind his ventriloquism of things. Out of self-loathing and desperation, he'd cry, "Stop!"

Before God, Drake, and Cassie, he'd confess.

The police would be called. He'd be taken in.

She'd get on with her life.

What *really* happened was, for a month, the phone rang at odd hours, Cassie got it, and there was no one there. Well, Jack was there, she knew, on the other side, choosing a coward's silence. Cassie waited, silent, too, and growing less picky. Even a cleared throat, a sad "Um," might have worked. She got neither. She waited for the click. Sometimes it took several minutes.

And in the morning, there'd be some other new thing waiting on her porch, being useless, trying to say and not say at the same time.

Knitting yarn.

An electric can opener.

A twenty-dollar bill.

Cassie finally decided to sell Jack a clue and to end this thing, once and for all. It cost the twenty dollars and a bike trip to the hardware store in Drake, where Cassie bought a Kryptonite bike lock, the kind that nothing can cut through. From there, she rode to the Buchholz place, and found Jack's Corvette parked behind the barn.

The dragon gleamed in the sun, its fangs dissolving into the front grille. Cassie popped the hood and lifted her bike, placing it flat against the engine. She laced the lock through as much inside stuff as she could, fingering down into the guts of the car, looking for things that couldn't just be unplugged, and replugged, and gotten around. She looked for hard parts, with holes, found them and slipped the bolt through.

She thought about the names of things automotive, the violence.

Choke. Throttle. Brake.

Block. Shield.

Head.

She turned the key and the lock clicked, tying her bike to all that violence, inextricably. After lowering the hood on her gift to Jack, Cassie left on foot, hoping he'd get the message this time.

At first, Cassie didn't know why she couldn't tell her mother about the rape, just that she couldn't. By the time she finally named the reason—embarrassment—too much time had gone by, and there was no simple way to bring it up without also bringing up how long she'd waited to say anything. Still, each could feel the sea change, the unspokenness of something hanging there between them.

"What's wrong?" Mercy would ask.

"Nothing," Cassie would say.

"Where's your bike?" Mercy would try.

"Sold it."

Eventually, out of something like desperation, Mercy said, "Mother Teresa," as Cassie sat at the kitchen table, staring at the same page of poetry she'd been staring at for at least fifteen minutes.

"Huh?" Cassie said, looking up. "Oh," she said. It was a sad oh, an oh that said there's a million miles from here to there. "Um," she tried, playing along for her mother's sake. "Somebody else. Anne Boleyn . . ."

Mercy looked at her daughter, imagining what it might be, and how much worse it might be than she *could* imagine.

Not too long after that, Cassie and her mother had their first argument ever over Mercy's drinking. Drunk, Mercy was mostly harmless, a bit clumsier than usual, more easily amused or moved to tears, more verbal about her love of people and things, and that was about it. It had been going on for years, and was never viewed as much of a problem by either of them. So what if she broke stuff now and again—especially since it was generally bought used anyway? Mercy was "carefuller"—that was the broken word she used for it—carefuller about things she couldn't replace, like Cassie's love. Cassie, for her part, excused her mother's drinking because she *did* love Mercy, and figured her mom deserved something that made her happy, whatever it was. Cassie had her bike, after all; her mom had brandy and cigars after midnight. They were even-steven; they had an arrangement.

Now, however, Mercy's drinking suddenly became a "dysfunction," which is what the guidance counselor called it when Cassie'd been sent to see him, after swearing for five colorful minutes at her Home Ec teacher one afternoon. Cassie's acceptance of the drinking was "enabling," and "denial," and "codependent," plus a whole list of other words it was clearly a bad thing to be. Did she ever wonder about her missing father? the counselor asked. Did her mother ever . . . ? And didn't Cassie used to have a bike she rode to school? Whatever happened to that?

"No," Cassie said.

"No," she repeated.

And: "Sold it."

Afterward, after graduating, and after starting to feel like the Fifty-Foot Woman with everything seeming suddenly dinkier and so much easier to break, Cassie decided to apply to college, just to get out of the house, and Cedar Run, once and for all. When she was accepted by the University of Michigan with a full scholarship, Mercy—Cassie's mom—poured her her first drink.

"You don't want to seem like an amateur when it comes to those frat parties," Mercy said, standing on the porch with her daughter, the ice tinkling in their glasses.

"Moi?" Cassie said. "Heaven forbid."

It was a cool summer night and the two leaned, shoulder to shoulder, on the porch railing, watching as fireflies flew up among the cornstalks like pale green embers.

"Mom," Cassie said, the word having just popped out.

"Yes?" Mercy said, expectantly.

Cassie paused. She thought about telling her mother that she loved her, but that seemed weird, almost like a farewell and a kiss-off, like wishing someone a good life. Her mother knew she loved her, right? But what was she supposed to do about that word she'd let float out there, on the summer breeze, the one with its bags packed, full of so much stuff? Cassie looked down. She tapped her glass to her mother's glass.

"Cheers," she said.

Cassie was a college sophomore by the time the first symptoms appeared. The morning sickness, the lateness of her period, the weird cravings, the high sensitivity to smells, noises—hell, *any* sensory input—pointed one way, as far as she was concerned: She was pregnant. Problem was, Cassie was pretty sure she *wasn't* pregnant. Couldn't be, in fact. The last time she'd "been exposed" to that sort of thing was . . . *back then*. Sure, it *felt* like she was expecting, but barring a miracle . . .

Which, of course, she couldn't.

Not anymore.

Not since . . .

Well, not since things had started getting so *weird*. The old rules didn't apply anymore. All science was suddenly pseudoscience. Facts weren't facts; they were unfounded and embarrassing habits of thought. Rumors spread. In Poughkeepsie, they were having virgin births; in Dayton, children were being born with goat feet and horns; in Bethesda, the NIH and CIA ran an orphanage full of kidnapped freak babies they'd reported as dead to their mothers, and then hidden away to study their secret, freak genes . . .

So.

So Cassie reserved judgment until all five of the home pregnancy tests came up negative, after which she decided to get serious. By serious, she meant a search of symptoms through the School of Medicine's database. This was *not* something she looked forward to. Cassie had been taking a lot of premed courses lately, knowing in some vague way that her major, once she declared it, would have something to do with helping people in pain. As a result, she had become more than familiar with the medical school's library. As a result, she was also quite aware of the queuing situation in front of the Am-I-Terminal? terminal. Perhaps it was just a sign of the times, but the number of hypochondriacs seemed to have gone up exponentially within the last few years. And they all seemed to know about the med library, and its one public terminal.

When Cassie entered the library, she had second thoughts about join-ing—*seeming* to join—this particular herd. She was not a jumper-to of conclusions; the fact that she weighed the possibility of pregnancy and tested the hypothesis five times showed that, she thought. Plus, the line. Jesus! The line was just too damn long. If she didn't have much time left, why waste it here; if she was okay, who could say she wouldn't catch something from the one hypochondriac who *wasn't* a hypochondriac? Cassie eyeballed the line, trying to follow it from the back where she stood to the front, trying to calculate its length in terms of feet, bodies, and hours. She couldn't. It was just too long, snaking around the micro-fiche carousel, through Periodicals, and looping twice around the full-color copier where undergrads looked both ways before slipping their sheets of taped twenties under the lid. The line shuffled tennis-shod and army-booted feet, pressed fingers to throats and wrists, coughed, back-handed foreheads, checked glands, raised and lowered magnifying glasses over suspicious moles. Occasionally, it brushed up against the back of the person in front of it—a quick hand darting, checking—before coughing an apology, and making notes. Occasionally, an "Oh fuck!" sprang from the head of the line, was ssshhhed, and then ssshhhed back.

After three hours in line—during which she had to ask the person in front of her six times to save her space so she could run to the bathroom where she didn't quite throw up—Cassie finally reached the terminal. With her fingers poised over the gray-smudged keyboard, Cassie paused for a moment and wondered how many healthy hypochondriacs in line today would be back tomorrow, to check if they'd caught anything from this keyboard. She shook her head, grimaced, and entered her symp-toms. The CD-ROM engaged, hummed, and clicked, and told Cassie the statistical likelihood of her having either the flu, food poisoning, AIDS, or that new, weird one—Angelism.

Taking a stab at being levelheaded, Cassie decided that it was probably one of the first two. She'd rest, drink fluids, ride it out. When her symptoms persisted into the following weeks, however, Cassie gave up on levelheaded and dove into the deep end of panic.

AIDS.

She had AIDS.

Maybe Jack hadn't forced a baby on her, but he'd taken her life hostage, all the same. Fuck! Fuck and goddammit! Goddammit to hell. Cassie thought about the scarecrow back home, the one she'd given her rape-red dress to, the one with straw for guts, playing home to all manner of chirping and chittering insects. She identified. She could feel the bugs in her blood. Cassie reached for the telephone, got it out of its cradle and . . . put it back. She couldn't tell her mother this. Either. Her mother was an artist with a clumsiness problem, and bad news made her clumsier. So, instead, Cassie stopped caring about assignments and due dates, went to class when she went to class, late—and started thinking about things like revenge, and funeral arrangements.

And then the dorsal ridging began.

Hardly noticeable at first, a slight difference in skin temperature, not much else, the ridges-to-be woke up with an attitude, like cayenne-peppered fingers scratching down her back, making her skin flame, then swell, letting Cassie know her hijacked future had changed directions once again. And though there still wasn't a whole lot known about Angelism, Cassie knew enough to know she better hide.

And quick.

9

By the time Cassie changed, the world's attitude about Angels had also changed—thanks in large part to Angels like Zander Wiles. As Zander suspected, even as he was playing the winged clown on the talk-show circuit, there were other Angels underground, all over the place, and still deciding. Eventually, they began showing themselves—media groundhogs, checking for shadows in the spotlight Zander left on. There was Sheryl, for example—a kinder, gentler, more media-friendly Angel from Denver. Later, there was Mike from Pittsburgh, who was not only an Angel, but also played concert piano reasonably well. By the time there were enough to justify a Stupid Angel Tricks segment on *Letterman,* however, the math had gotten scary.

Newspapers started running body counts, as if it were a plague, or a war. And as the numbers grew, as Angels went from a mere curiosity to one of the world's fastest-growing minorities, the media's focus shifted. Angels became a topic of serious discussions and op-ed pieces; they became matters of social, economic, political, and public-health concern.

They went from guesting on *The Tonight Show* to being Issue Number One on *The McLaughlin Group*.

To do something—or at least to create the appearance—Congress passed legislation requiring that Angels be registered as such. Lengthy questionnaires became part of the process, including questions about an Angel's most personal habits. This information was collected, along with feather, saliva, stool, urine, semen, pap, vaginal-secretion, and blood samples. Databases were formed, checked, double-checked, and cross-checked, looking for the common thread that would tie all Angels together, that would point to a cause, a mode of transmission. But the analyses told the world nothing. There was no pattern. The plot of a disease looks like a stained tablecloth, with the darkest part of the stain—the greatest number of cases—occurring in the center where the outbreak started, and then radiating outward. The plot for Angelism was utterly random, looking more like a map of lightning-strike victims than any sort of disease.

And it was humiliating, really, to have this thing out there—this *wing* thing—widespread and spreading wider, and inexplicable despite the heroic efforts of smart people everywhere to explain it. Was that twinge of heartburn the pizza talking, or were you about to sprout a head from your chest—one with a whole different point of view, and, worse yet, different politics? Science, whose job it was to place such ideas into the Okay or Silly pile . . . well, science was having a hard time of it lately.

So people turned to religion, only to find that it was having trouble in the explanation department, too. What was it supposed to do, after all, with this new, dark-sided brand of miracles? Luckily, religion didn't have to *prove* whatever it came up with, just so long as it stuck by the story, once all the many Its agreed to what the story was going to be. The problem was, there were no points to be gained by claiming Angels as proof of any particular brand of religion—not with Angels out there like Zander Wiles. Not with homeless Angels pissing against walls in the Vatican. It was hard to feel all warm and . . . *ecclesiastical* about such things. Sure, it was one thing to debate how many angels could pass through the eye of a needle, but it was quite another to talk about Angels passing out with needles in their arms. And so the Ecumenical Council on Angels declared that the similarity between heavenly angels and this less glittery variety was just a coincidence. Angels were not *angels,* per se; they were just people with wings, as flawed as people without, or possibly more so.

And the general public? It just wanted to know what wings were all about. The Big What. Were they about good and evil, and if so, which, and what does it mean if you *don't* grow wings? And what about the economy? What about the transportation industry; what about airlines, oil refineries, car companies? Should we stop building roads? Would the "Rapture Dividend" offset the deficit? And what about Third World Angels? What if they just start flying over here, raiding our crops like a bunch of goddamn crows? Is this a depression, or a manic-depression? Wall Street's like a yo-yo, breaking records top and bottom. And what about Jack in accounting? He came down with it and that damn magnet thing fucked up his computer. Sure, sure, hire somebody else, but what if *they* get it? What if the president gets it and gives our jobs to a bunch of fuckin' Angel scabs?

And as the numbers grew, Angel words started clunking into the popular vocabulary. Technical words, like: Angelism, Human Wing Growth Syndrome, the Rapture, Penguinism, Post-Angelic Stress Disorder, Angelic Field Syndrome, the Halo Effect, Aerophobia, Aeromania, and Aviaholism. Street words for Angels, like: "The upwardly abled," "the upwardly mobile," Birds, Sparrows, Pigeons, Chickens, Chicken Shits, Crows, Featherbrains, Airheads, Aviators and Aviatrixes, Flyboys, Skycaps, Skyscrapers, Sky-shitters, God-shitters, Window Cleaners, Heavenly Hosts or Hostesses, Choir Boys, Glee Clubbers, Icari, and Lucky Bastards. And street words for non-Angels, like: Normals, Clodhoppers, Pedestrians, or Peds. And one word for the hate going in either direction: Mobilism.

Of course, some of the new words were really old ones, with new meanings. Words like "Angel," for example. Or "Vampire."

It was too bad Zander didn't take his agent's advice to keep his mouth shut. After all, it was that last interview that caused all the trouble, the one granted so his parents could see a movie. It started with the word "yes" in response to the question: "Did you know the Angel-girl from California?" With it, and the answers that followed, Zander painted a simple, but incomplete picture: Angelism spread like AIDS. Some Angels were murdered outright and drained—or "harvested," the polite, Vampire euphemism. Others became "fast food"—another euphemism, this one describing the random bite that left victims bleeding and scarred, but alive. And as Vampirism spread, so did hepatitis and AIDS, and slowly—too slowly—the caveats.

Like: It's only contagious *during* the ridge stage.

Like: It's never contagious *after* the wings show.

Like: Who knows *where* that food's been?

The handcuffs and blindfold were bad enough, but Cassie was pretty sure that being made to ride in the trunk was going too far and was just plain mean-spirited.

"We have to take precautions," her escort told her. "You don't know what those bloodsuckers would do to find a Coop."

"But I'm going to be one of you," Cassie protested, struggling against the hand that was pushing down her head, getting ready to close the hood. "You've felt the ridges. That's proof, right?"

"In El Paso," the escort said, calmly, explaining about Bad Men and Candy to a child, "a whole Coop got wiped out. A Vampire smoked 'em out by injecting silicone into his back."

"But . . ."

"But nothing," he said, adding before slamming the hood: "The only real proof has feathers on it."

From inside the trunk, Cassie heard the motor start up and worried about small holes in the chassis, about carbon monoxide poisoning, and whether or not the rest of her life was going to be just like this—a ritual of taking orders from people she couldn't see, and hiding from the teeth of strangers.

Code words are exchanged—shouted—to be heard over the rain, which began during the drive to the Coop. The voices stop, and rain closes over the breach. In the middle of nowhere, in the middle of a downpour, Cassie begins thinking about death—hers, or the bastards who decided

to treat her like this. She's soaked and shivering; she's been standing—
blindfolded and handcuffed and asking questions that draw no answers—
for the last ten minutes or more. Suddenly, in the distance, she can hear
the sucking sound of boots slogging through mud. New voices begin
talking about "packages" and "deliveries" and "invoices," followed by the
unmistakable sound of a shotgun being racked.

Cassie worries about peeing, even though she stopped doing that two
weeks ago. Expecting dueling banjos any second, she flinches as a hand
rests on her shoulder.

"Cassie?" a voice says, gentle and calm and altogether different from
what she's been subjected to up to this point.

"I thought I was 'the package,'" Cassie says. "Or was that 'inven-
tory'?"

"Sorry about the draconian precautions," the voice says, while the
hand nudges her to step forward. "My name's Bob. I'll be your tour guide
through this wonderful process called 'The Change.' I'm sure your escorts told you about El Paso. Mike—that was your driver—probably
didn't tell you that he had friends in El Paso. We're all still a little jumpy."

"No, he didn't mention that part."

"Mike's shy," Bob continues. "I suppose that doesn't come across too
well when you're blindfolded."

"Speaking of which," Cassie says, craning her head, trying to aim it
wherever the voice's eyes might be. "Would you mind?"

"Well, seeing as we're here—step up; that's good—I don't suppose it
could hurt."

Cassie feels hands—surprisingly warm despite the coldness of the
rain—carefully unknotting her blindfold. She feels the cloth fall away but
still can't see, realizing, sheepishly, that she's clenched her own eyes
tight, that she's been holding them shut for the better part of her trip.
Blinking them open, the first thing she sees is a flickering yellow window
ridged with lace curtains. Homey, she thinks. She looks at the floor of the
porch, by the front door; a rubber mat with daisies clustered in the top
left and bottom right corners says WELCOME. Very homey, Cassie cor-
rects herself. Homey with a vengeance.

"Aloha," Bob says, pushing the front door open with one hand and
guiding Cassie in with the other. Sitting on pillows on the hardwood

floors, a half-dozen Angels sit before a fireplace, toasting marshmallows. The fire sends their weird shadows over the walls and turns their faces golden. At the door's squeak, they turn and smile.

"Happy birthday, Cassie!" they shout, and begin singing the birthday song. Another Angel pushes in from the kitchen, bearing a thickly iced cake with a single candle in it. Cassie wonders if the Vampire got the same sort of treatment in El Paso, before betraying the lot. The thought makes her feel cold.

"You guys," she says, masking dread with embarrassment. She wants to cover her eyes and realizes she can't, because of the handcuffs.

"Bob?" she says; she rattles the cuffs.

"Oops," Bob says, producing the key and clicking the shackles open. "Sorry . . ."

"So let's try that again," Cassie says. "You *guys,*" she repeats, shielding her eyes, her blush. She digs a toe into the floor, pivots, pivots, embarrassed. "Gee, you guys are swell."

Cassie's "puberty" was decidedly different from Zander's. For one thing, she knew what she had and where it was going. What she didn't know about, she learned by reading the Coop's many pamphlets and handbooks, like *My New Wings: An Introduction; Molting: What Every Angel Should Know; A Wing and a Prayer: A New Angel's Guide to the Ethical Uses of Flight; Angelism vs. Penguinism—or, What Do I Do If My Wings Don't Work?;* and *Mommy, Where Do Wings Come From? The State of the Science So Far.* Cassie read through all of these with interest, practicing the imaging exercises they suggested, thinking happy thoughts, like:

"I *was* a cocoon; I *am* a butterfly" (or)

"My wings are my children, with needs and wants of their own" (or)

"To fly, I must throw myself at the ground—and miss" (and)

"I can't reach the right altitude with the wrong attitude."

She also did her best to ignore what every Angel feared most—even more than being harvested by Vampires—namely, Penguinism. Only one in five hundred Angels sprouted wings without the nerves and muscles needed to make them work, but the odds were still short enough to worry. As Cassie learned from her reading, Penguinism was more than just an inconvenience, some excess baggage you got saddled with, without the payoff of flight. Penguinism messed with the body's internal gyroscope—what the pamphlets called "proprioception," the thing that causes ghost limbs in amputees, and can make real limbs seem artificial after certain types of head injuries. In Penguinism, not only don't your wings work, but your body doesn't even recognize them as being there, so that Penguins are constantly disoriented and have to go around on all fours for fear of falling. Amputation—the obvious solution—is prohibited, due to the fear that the secondary traits of Angelism might just be dormant in the Penguin, and could self-correct at any inconvenient, post-op time.

Cassie also discovered how little science knew about Angelism. It knew, for instance, that the whatever-it-was insinuated itself into the host's DNA and turned on ancient, avian switches, causing the raptor gunk in our genes to take both paths this time, toward primate *and* pterodactyl. That much of the How, science had nailed down. It was the Why, however, where science hit a wall.

There were theories, of course. At the time of Cassie's change, the three leading contenders were the Magic, Locust, and Government theories.

The Magic Theory was just what it sounded like—no real theory at all. According to it, wings just happen. And while they may seem to follow some of the massaged laws of physics, biology, and aerodynamics, they don't *have* to. They're a random blessing for those who feel like viewing them that way, and a curse for the rest. They are here because no one can come up with a reason better than habit for why they shouldn't be. In short, they are their own reason, and a pox on those who say that's not good enough.

The Locust Theory, on the other hand, maintained that Angelism was a cyclic phenomenon, with Angels appearing in waves throughout history. This explained why Angels existed as an archetype in the popular psyche, and why they were so frequently featured in religious art. The phenomenon was likened to a human version of the seventeen-year locust, the triggering gene or mechanism being recessive to some nth degree, surfacing and flourishing once every millennium or so for a generation or so, and then receding back into the murky gene pool.

Somehow, when the planets were in the right configuration, comet X was in the house of Aquarius, or sunspot activity reached some important point, what was left of the raptor genome within our own was reawakened to manifest itself as best it could within the context of our otherwise human anatomy. Historically—according to the theory—Angels generally faded out of populations after a generation or two, dissolving from flesh and blood reality into hearsay, legend, and myth. The current outbreak, however, would be the first time that humans had both Angels *and* cameras—machines with sufficiently little imagination as to be trustworthy. Therefore, even when the Angels went away this time, they would be remembered, posing an ongoing problem for science—to be solved, perhaps, before the next time came.

On the third hand—since we're talking about extraneous limbs—there was the The-Government-Did-It Theory, which saw Angelism as the second in a class of "military viruses" that began with AIDS. The contractor charged with developing AIDS was in danger of losing its government funding because of the unacceptably long latency period of its product, making it useless for military application. Angelism was developed as an apology, the product being a sort of super ground-to-air soldier. Integration was the biggest obstacle, however, and it took exposure to three bioengineered retroviruses to produce the full complement of Angelism's many changes.

This last theory went as far as developing placeholder names for the viral agents, once they were discovered—Human Angeloproficiency Virus (HAV) I, II, and III. For a time, this caused the wittier paranoids to call Angels and Pedestrians the HAVs and the HAV-nots. Considering the world's proficiency with labels, of course, things could have been much worse.

When she wasn't reading, watching her portable TV, or listening to her Walkman, Cassie sewed. It was a survival skill, she learned quickly enough. As the commentators debated in their op-ed columns about how the Rapture fit into the big picture, Angel-gonnabes knew at least one thing that wings meant: None of their clothes would fit anymore. At the time Cassie changed, there weren't any specialty clothiers, yet, no chain of Big-n-Tall-(n-Winged) stores catering to the Angel with a killer sense of fashion. With the number of Angels per urban center still in the single digits, the market just wasn't there, and until it was, Cassie and her kind had to make do on their own, becoming the Jacks and Jills of any number of trades they'd taken wholly for granted before the change.

Cassie still remembers those make-do, ad hoc days with a certain strange fondness. Angels were a new world unto themselves—winged pilgrims, wandering about the unfriendly old world, improvising its remaking in their image. They'd see each other, haunting the aisles of this or that Salvation Army—making those places earn their names for once—their wings poking over the racks of plaid and lime green suit coats, rounding the tables piled with old shoes and jeans. They'd go to the counter with an armload of jackets, and shirts, and twice as many dresses, most fairly horrid.

The clerks never knew what to make of them, would invariably go quiet, or apologetic, or strangely angry, before stuffing the rumpled dresses into a brown paper bag and tossing the plastic hangers into a bin with a bony clatter. The Angels themselves, strangely angry, never bothered to explain their seeming mishmash of purchases, didn't mention that the dresses, horrible as they were, were good for their long zippers, which were cheaper than if bought new.

Cassie, of course, had her Coop-mates do her shopping before she sprouted, spending her time in her nest, slicing open her old shirts and jackets. Anything with a back, anything that left the back anything other than bare—these garments would be as worthless as straitjackets once she changed. Sharon, a longtime Angel and Bob's assistant, described the necessary alterations, and why hemming a simple pair of holes wasn't good enough.

"It's not like wings are an extra pair of arms poking out your back," she said. "They're a helluva lot bigger, and a helluva lot more difficult to manage. You can't work 'em like you were slipping your arms through sleeves. The holes would have to be big enough for the biggest part of the wing to pass through, which is right here, right around the crest joint. What you want is a couple of panels you can close around this smaller joint, this stumpy bit where the wing meets the back."

And so, using a borrowed seam ripper, Cassie did as she was instructed and removed the zippers from the latest batch of Salvation dresses. Then, after hemming the slits for the first eight inches from the top, she'd stitch in the zippers, all the while growing increasingly weary of her Coop-mates and their comments about her flies being undone, and about how that's really what they were, weren't they? Flies.

What she didn't weary of, though, was the therapeutic calm that came with this simple, concentrated act of preparation. She imagined this was the attraction of knitting booties for babies-to-be, could see Mercy, her belly big with the future, working needles and yarn, the clicking as steady as an old-fashioned clock. Even now, Cassie does her own alterations and frequents resale shops. They calm her, like grocery stores calm some people. They make her feel . . . she's not sure, exactly. Authentic, she guesses.

Of course, nowadays, Cassie's stitching has improved greatly over her early Coop attempts, and she's switched from zippers to Velcro. She remembers those early botch-ups, and smiles. They were the sort of thing that would have made Dr. Frankenstein proud—jagged and obvious. The hemming was done simply to prevent fraying, and she used whatever fabric or thread she happened to have on hand. Her early ensembles were patchwork, mainly, and works of general protest, the uniform of her latest alienation—her bike all over again, this time gutted out in cloth and thread. After all, she reasoned, if society insisted on underlining instead of assimilating her difference, she'd not bother protecting its sense of fashion. So a swatch of something floral hemmed the hole in a white shirt, laced up with the same black thread that held in a lime green zipper under one wing, and the baby blue one under the other. She was going to be an angry bag Angel, dressed for the Apocalypse, piecing together disparate scraps, just as she herself had been pieced together by God—or whomever.

Of course, before she could be an angry anything, she'd have to learn how to get dressed.

"It's not as easy as you might imagine," Sharon said, during what the Coop folks called "dress rehearsal." "Which is why we use these." She dipped into the hallway outside Cassie's nest and returned with a harness outfitted with two big-as-life wings, cut from bright red foam rubber.

"They're not as heavy as your real wings will be," Sharon said, "but for now, we're just dealing with the space issue." She helped Cassie put on her demo wings, tugging the tongue through the belt buckle and latching it down. She handed Cassie one of the altered shirts. "Okay," she said. "Show me."

Cassie worked her hands through the sleeves and buttoned up the front. She tugged at either shoulder until the free-hanging panels were situated to either side of her fake wings. Reaching around to work on the first zipper, she hit a wall of foam rubber. Trying to get below or around it, she realized that human arms just didn't quite bend that way. Finally, squishing the wing aside, Cassie grabbed hold of the zipper's tongue and . . . stopped.

Sharon was applauding.

"You've just broken your wing," she said. "Congratulations."

Cassie looked at her instructor, at a decided disadvantage, given the neon-colored absurdity of her Nerf appendages. She reddened and boiled down the smartass comments in her head to: "Well?"

"You got two options," Sharon said. "Either get your ass a husband, or get yourself a hook." She dipped into the hallway again and produced the latter. "I prefer this," she said, showing Cassie the homemade contraption, consisting of a fish hook attached to a length of bell wire. "Less demanding than a husband." She then proceeded to work the hook through the hole in the tongue of a zipper, grabbed the wire, pulled it over her shoulder, held down the tail of her shirt with one hand, and pulled the wire forward with the other. "Like so," she said, and then handed the hook to Cassie.

Cassie did her best, wiggling, working, pulling. Her heart sank when the zipper slowed down midway through its upward glide, but she toughed it out and completed the move. Sharon cleared her throat and Cassie looked down at the red crumbs and chunks of foam rubber littering the floor of her nest.

"After the first couple of mornings," Sharon said, "you'll probably only pinch off a few feathers at a time." She paused. "No feathers, and it's a good sign for the rest of the day."

. . .

Bob, the self-proclaimed tour guide to Cassie's metamorphosis, had a decidedly low-impact approach to his job. Once a day he'd tap on her door and ask if she needed anything. Usually, Cassie said no, and thank you, and went back to her books, TV, or wardrobe. On the day the first bit of green showed up, however, she changed her mind.

"Yes," she said. "A hug."

"Hmmm," Bob said. "I don't know if we've got one of those. Have you asked Sharon to check supplies?" He turned toward the hallway, "Sharon!" he shouted. "Hugs? We got any?"

"Fuck you," Cassie said.

"Oh now, that's a whole 'nother order."

"Fuck you and the Pegasus you flew in on," Cassie emphasized. "I'm scared, dammit."

"I know," Bob said, quietly. "I'm just trying to joke you out of it." He spread his arms and his wings. "Okay, okay," he said. "Give it a go."

Cassie stepped forward and realized, once she was next to him, she didn't know what to do with her arms. From every angle she looked at it, his wings seemed to be in the way. "Um," she said.

"Not as easy as it looks, eh?" Bob said. He stepped back. "Still, there's nothing that a little geometry and contortionism can't fix." He held his arms out and demonstrated, cocking one shoulder at a forty-five degree angle and aiming down, while the other arm pointed up, with the elbow sharply crooked. "You see, you have to—if you'll forgive the expression—'ride the crack,' working your arms in there, between my wings."

Cassie stepped forward again, angling her arms as directed. She'd gotten out of the habit of human contact and simple things like hugging, ever since . . . Now, feeling Bob's body next to hers, Cassie's skin contracted, as need and fear, her old life and new one, overlapped. "Everything changes, doesn't it, every bit of life?"

"Pretty much," Bob said, hugging her gently, noting the tightness of all her muscles. "You can't just go around adding wings to people and expect them not to change in other ways. It's like water and peroxide, you know?"

"Yes," Cassie said, and then she thought about it. "No," she said, backing up, the mood thankfully broken. "What are you talking about?"

"H₂O and H₂O₂," Bob said, happy to follow this detour around what could have become emotionally sticky terrain. Though he had no idea of her past, as a transformation counselor Bob was well aware of the vulnerability of changelings—as well as the many temptations those vulnerabilities posed. "Water and peroxide," he continued. "The difference is just one atom, but it changes everything from the ground up."

"Hmmmm," Cassie said. "Very . . . comforting."

"To a chemist, very likely," Bob said. He smiled. "You know what you need more than a hug?"

"What?"

"A back rub," Bob said. "Get 'em while they're hot," he said. " 'Cause they *are* going out of style, especially when you . . . you know . . . finish up here."

Cassie considered the invitation, wondering whether it was meant to be a proposition. She looked at Bob. He wore blue jeans and a plaid shirt; he was dull and practical and, she decided, safe.

"What the hell," she said. "A back rub sounds good."

Bob gestured toward her cot and Cassie lay down, resting her chin in the cradle of her fists. Bob placed his hands around her neck and shoulders, kneading them, rolling out the fear, the anxiety, the tension. It was exactly what she'd been needing for longer than she cared to remember. "My God, Bob," she said, turning to look up at him. "Where'd you learn to do that?"

"It's just a skill," he said. "Something I picked up."

Cassie paused. "You're holding out, Bob. There's something you're not telling me."

"You don't *really* want to know."

"Sure I do," Cassie said. "Unless you're like the Boston Strangler, or something."

"I used to work in a mortuary," Bob said. "Before I changed. It was my job to—excuse the expression—'unstick the stiffs.' You know, once rigor mortis had set in, to get them in the box . . ."

Cassie's skin went cold all over, except for where Bob's hands had been, where it burned. She sat up from the cot. "You don't get many dates, do you, Bob?"

"Nope," Bob said. "But I can fly." He got up and went to the door. "Just holler if you need anything else."

The green had taken over both hands, making it impossible for Cassie to sew, when Bob stopped by her room again. "It's Good-bye Day," he announced, smiling. He did a spot check of the various things in her room; Cassie looked at him in disbelief.

"What do you mean, Good-bye Day?" Cassie demanded. "I'm still contagious. You can't kick me out."

"Not you, my dear," Bob said. "The modern world. That," he said, pointing to her portable TV. "And that," her portable stereo. "You read about Angelic Field Syndrome in those pamphlets, right? AFS . . ."

Cassie looked at him strangely. "AFS?"

"The magnet thing," he said. "The Halo Effect."

"Oh," Cassie said. *"That."*

"Oh," Bob echoed. "That. Right. So anyway, when you change and get wings you also get this goosed-up electrical field for some reason, like a big ol' magnet in your chest. You get too close to electronic things and you tend to give 'em serious bad vibes. Let me demonstrate." He gestured for her to turn on the TV. "Observe." He approached the set and the image snowed over, began swirling, and throbbing. "Touch my neck," he said.

Cassie looked down at her hands, at the fingers green and hard. She used her elbow instead, and felt his pulse telegraphing up her funny bone.

"Watch the TV and count the flashes," Bob said.

She did as she was told; her eyes widened. "You're doing that," she said. "It's matching your heartbeat."

"Exactly."

"But why?"

"It's got something to do with how the muscles change, maxing out on dietary iron until they're like wire," Bob said. "The rest of it, I don't know. Except, it goes both ways. If you hang around electrical stuff too long, you start getting dizzy." Pause. "And then your head explodes."

"What?"

"Kidding," Bob said, tapping her on the shoulder playfully.

Cassie folded her arms. She wasn't laughing.

"So, anyway, it's Good-bye Day," he continued, switching off the TV and opening Cassie's window. "Would you do the honors?"

Cassie took the TV carefully in her hands, the fingers fused together and hard, imagining that this is what it would feel like to wear bronzed mittens. She looked out the window. One story down, rocks ringed the foundation, reining in a garden of daisies and weeds. Among the vegetation and rocks, plastic shards sprung up, shattered circuit boards and blasted cathode ray tubes; ruptured cassettes sent shiny plastic spaghetti flagging in the wind. Cassie ducked her head back in and looked at Bob.

"Really?" she said.

"Yup," he said. "But you get to fly."

Cassie heaved the set to the rocks below, turning away before it hit. Bob handed her the portable stereo, and she tried to drill holes in his brain with her eyes.

"Keep your eyes on the prize," he said, smiling. "Consider it a crash diet from electronics."

Cassie stepped toward the open window, holding her music like the last, best part of her heart.

Cassie's withdrawal from the modern world was not a pretty sight. With the spreading green shutting down her sense of touch, and nothing much to occupy her remaining senses other than the four walls of her room, Cassie took first to pacing. Five good strides could cover the room. To fill the silence, she began calling off the steps: "One," she started, "two, three, four, five," first in a low voice to herself, then gradually raising the volume, through conversational to shouting. She started adding "Mississippis" after a while, and "fucking Mississippis" not too long after that. For punctuation, she'd kick the wall when she reached it, turn around, count her steps, and kick again. Framed pictures shook off the walls, their glass shattering; shelves of books whose pages she could no longer turn unhooked themselves and dumped their cargo.

Bob and Sharon let her go, knew that this was the worst part of the change for many Angels. Cassie would feel stupid about it later, and that was reward enough for putting up with a little howling—"You stupid, miserable, motherfucking sons of bitches"—colorful though it might be.

Bob and Sharon, of course, also knew that it could only go on for so long. After Cassie went quiet, they'd check in on her, clean up whatever needed cleaning up, and make sure she was in as comfortable a position as possible. As it was, when Cassie stopped, Bob and Sharon found her at her window, her skin a reptilian emerald and hard from head to toe. The window was open and her lush red hair blew back like the hair of a mannequin, the only part of her currently animated. Her frozen gaze looked downward, at the TV graveyard; her shell, under her eyes, glistened.

"Another one," Bob said, nudging Sharon, before grabbing one of Cassie's elbows as Sharon grabbed the other. "On three," he said, and counted off. Lifting Cassie's frozen body into the air, they carried her to the cot. Bob worked the body into a reasonable position.

"Hey," he said, over the squeaking and splintering of Cassie's carapace. "You know what this reminds me of?"

"What it *always* reminds you of," Sharon said.

"The mortuary," they said together.

"Just like old times," Bob said, wiping his brow and then giving Cassie one last crack for good measure.

Once hatched, Cassie was a quick study. She learned to fly her first time out, launching from the roof of the Coop and seeing from a bird's-eye view her neighborhood of the past several months. "It's beautiful!" she shouted, though neither Bob nor Sharon could have possibly heard her from where they stood on the ground. Before she went up, both had assured her that she was lucky to change when she had, coming out in June, when the flying season was really just getting started. Some Angels came out in the dead of winter and had to sit and brood about the mechanics of flight, just long enough to realize the many hundreds of ways things could go wrong. It was best like this—hatch, and do it. Dry your wings on your first spin around the Coop.

Cassie couldn't believe she had gotten so nuts about having to give up TV. Flying—shit, flying was worth a hundred *Lettermans* and *Jeopardys*. Flying was like sex, but safer, Cassie thought, riding the rising thermals like the warm belly of a lover she could finally trust. Below her, circling back from the bright green treetops surrounding the Coop, returning to the clearing, Cassie looked down to see doll-sized versions of Bob and Sharon, flagging her over toward the north where, really, there just seemed to be more trees. They were the bosses, though, and so Cassie did it, straightening out her lazy circle into a straight line, over the tops of the trees to the north and . . .

A lake!

A great stretch of water beyond the trees, impossibly blue and still, and as Cassie crossed over, moving from flying over land to flying over water, she felt like she'd hit a speed bump. She tripped in the air, tumbled a bit, but managed to right herself and—oh God! The air over water, the quality of the thermals was completely different from those rising from the land. The land, with its different colors, textures, and structures, heated unevenly, making the air above bumpy, but over water—it was like a skating rink, smooth and slick and seeming like it could go on forever . . .

Cassie laughed. It was the first real laugh she'd had in over two years, ever since . . . that thing she decided not to think about anymore. Instead, she laughed, giving herself willingly to the wind. She laughed as hard as she ever had, and then came, even harder. Oh, this was madness and it was worth everything she'd been through, everything she'd given up, and more.

This would be her new birthday. Time started over from this point on and she'd celebrate it every year. She'd celebrate everything, every day—by flying.

To hell with her music.

To hell with her shows.

Fuck TV!

10

In The Angel Blues, Cassie called it the Rip Van Winkle Syndrome, and her own was the first case she studied. For three months, on average, Angels-to-be are severed from the world; for the last month, they're in what passes for a coma. Nothing comes in or goes out; no phone calls or letters, not even to best friends or family or lovers. No last words are allowed; no See-you-in-Septembers. You disappear. *Poof!* Anything less is the road that leads to El Paso. Relationships are strained, of course, sometimes broken. Things happen, sometimes, that you can't go back and fix. Important things are missed. Things the Angel has to forgive him- or herself for.

Take Cassie.

She was sprung from the Coop as happy and bright as a new dime—Mercury head, naturally. After all the things she couldn't tell her mom, she finally had something to write home about. Hell, she had something to *fly* home about, which she promised herself she'd do. Flying was—Jesus!—flying was the opposite of embarrassment, the opposite of Cedar Run, the opposite of all the shit and angst and shit she'd been through over the last two and something years and . . . Mercy was going to be beside herself with joy; she'd be stupid with pride. Cassie would come home flying, triumphant, wearing something diaphanous and flowing, her wings in full majestic spread, the sun backlighting her wherever she went, like Liberty on the back of some other old coin. Clouds would part; horns someplace offstage would blow and she and Mercy would get . . . they'd get clumsy together. They could get clumsy on their asses, so shitfaced clumsy their bladders would burst, but before Cassie's did, she'd fly over the Buchholz place; she'd call Jack's name at the top of her lungs and . . . She'd have to wear a skirt, not her favorite thing to wear, but . . .

God *damn,* but she was going to *love* being an Angel!

(This was the good news . . .)

The bad news was, by the time Cassie blew the Coop, Mercy had been dead for a month and a half.

Cassie hadn't phoned or written to her mother in months; it was part of the deal with the Coop. Nothing came in or went out that could give them away. But now that she was sprung, she couldn't wait to tell her mom, to catch up on old times, to swap girl stuff with her first, best, and only friend. In the Coop, Cassie had started feeling bad about the last two years between herself and Mercy. Ever since the rape, Cassie had grown reticent with her mother, on the premise, apparently, that no news was good news. So: No news was what Mercy got. Cassie's few letters home were dopey affairs, full of class schedules, weather reports, exam grades, and cafeteria menus. Still, as pathetic as these empty missives were, they triggered a torrent from Mercy—letters, postcards, and care packages full of Cassie's favorite snacks, recommended readings, and photos of the seasons' changes, taken from her old bedroom window. Every so often, Mercy would include a toy from Cassie's childhood with a note: "Remember this?"

Cassie was embarrassed by the emotional rate of exchange, how her few pennies came back as dollars. Embarrassing or not, however, the mail from her mother became a lifeline. During her stay at the Coop, Cassie imagined the hoard she'd have waiting for her when she returned and collected the months' mail from the post office. She'd take it all back to her dorm, getting a bottle of expensive brandy along the way. She'd stay up all night like her mother sometimes did, sipping brandy, opening each box or letter slowly, savoring. She'd let herself be loved uncompromisingly, and then she'd fly home and return that love properly for the first time in over two years.

At the post office, she asked the clerk to check twice to see if there wasn't more.

"Maybe it spilled over behind a shelf," she suggested.

The clerk returned on the second try with an, "Oh yeah; almost forgot," and a registered letter from some professional-looking, but non-mom source, probably announcing that she was being expelled for missing the better part of a semester. Cassie scribbled her signature and tossed it into the shopping bag along with the rest of her loot, promptly forgetting it.

Back at the dorm, Cassie arranged everything by postmark date and began with the oldest, noting that the last bit of real mom mail was a package sent two months earlier. The first few letters picked up where she and her mother had left off, before Cassie left for the Coop, but soon began ending with PSs, and PPSs, asking if anything was wrong, and why didn't Cassie write anymore. One included a postcard with return postage and two big check boxes: I 1) AM ____ 2) AM NOT ____ STILL ALIVE. Others asked, in slightly sloppier handwriting, where Cassie was whenever Mercy tried to call. Did she ever think of getting an answering machine or voice mail or something? Call collect. Please. This was followed by a package containing an answering machine, and a note that read: "That's just its name. I've never gotten any real answers from one of these damn things. Not even after the rubber hose. Love, Mom."

Cassie felt like a royal creep and wondered what sort of gifts prodigal daughters were buying their mothers nowadays.

And then Cassie came to the last package—a Remember This? box. Inside, she found her Barbie-headed Amazon necklace, some of the heads melted, their hair reduced to plastic, beady stubble. The letter enclosed had been misshuffled, so that the last page came first, bearing only the PPS.

"Of all things," it said, "this survived."

The trapped smell of burnt plastic the box released sent a panic through Cassie. With all appropriate dread mounting, she shuffled the first page up front. It was written in pencil, in longhand, on stationery from a hotel twenty miles outside of Cedar Run.

"Dear Casper," it began.

"I seem to have burned down the house. I hope you don't hate me. I've gotten clumsier lately. If it wasn't sewed on, I'd probably send you my head for safekeeping. Are you okay? I keep telling myself that college is a busy time and all that, but . . . I hope you're seeing three boys at once and making them all crazy. And getting straight A's!

"Those smoke detectors you made me buy really worked. I was up late reading *The Great Gatsby* in the family room and I guess I nodded off. That shriek got me going, though, and I woke up and there was smoke everywhere, some of it flashing with light, like a thunderstorm, and I knew that meant the flames were reflecting off of something and that the fire was getting ready to come into the living room. And so I rushed outside in nothing but my housecoat, tucking *GG* into my pocket and taking the cellphone with me. I didn't even have any slippers on, and it was cold and the grass was wet and I ended up waiting forever.

"The firepeople had to come all the way from Grover's Mill, seeing as Drake's gone bankrupt. Did I tell you about that? Mayor Pyles—poor man—killed himself over it. Bullet through the head.

"By the time the firepeople got here, I'd gotten so worked up watching the fire, I just couldn't anymore. So I turned my back to it and started reading about Jay and Daisy. Have you ever read it? I recommend it highly, though I think it's best read by the light of a burning house. Preferably one's own.

"Sorry if that's too glib. All my other emotions are a bit broken right now. The firepeople almost had me put away. Apparently, it's bad form to cuss and cry when your life goes up in smoke.

"I hope you're doing well. I miss you terribly, but I'm trying to improve.

"Love, Mom."

Cassie sat back and examined her feelings about the letter; she was surprised by the fact that she wasn't surprised. She wasn't mad, either, and she certainly didn't hate her mother. Even as a child, a part of her expected to wake up in the middle of the night, running from the flames of her mother's "clumsiness." It was just an eventuality that eventually happened.

She looked down and noticed a PS.

"I hope you're taking vitamins," it said. "There's some bug going around and I feel like I'm on the edge of something. My old-lady bones are all acting up. Serves me right, a woman my age, staying out all night in her bare feet and nightgown. Probably just a chill. Dress warm."

And, besides the PPS she'd already read, that was it. She rechecked the postmark. That was what worried her—the fact that this was the last letter, that there hadn't been any others in two months.

She rechecked the piles—real and junk—to see if she'd missed anything. That's when she rediscovered the registered letter, the one—she picked it up, read the logo—from Somebody, Somebody and Somebody Else, Attorneys-at-Law.

She tore open the envelope but couldn't keep her eyes traveling in lines from left to right. They darted, grabbing words like "decedent," "disposition," "estate." Cassie's new magnetic heart pounded with both its fists on the inside of her rib cage. Her breathing went short, inhaling "please," exhaling "no . . ." She locked her eyes and read.

Inside, the letter explained about what was gone (Cassie's mom, from pneumonia, the Jim Henson kind) and what was left (some dirt, some paperwork, some rust and charred twigs). But there were other things it explained about, too. Like . . .

Like.

Like astrophysics.

(This was all between the lines.)

It explained about the shrinking universe (between the lines). And absolute zero, and black holes. It explained about how everything in the world can come down to a point so grave with gravity, even light can't get out alive. It explained about big, final things—this letter from the three somebodies—all the opened-ended, unending, *ending* things.

And it hurt. Sort of.

It hurt. Kind of.

Like forever.

. . .

When she could feel at all, Cassie felt like she had a slow leak in her soul—each day going down a little more, a few pounds less per square inch. It was grief, she guessed. She had to. It was another one of those things that didn't seem quite real to her, like the rape. In her dreams, she was back at the farm, sleeping in her bed, with her mom outside in her nightgown, trying to find a door that hadn't been locked, a lock that hadn't been changed.

During the day, she sat on the painted boulder in the center of the quad, tossing croutons to the pigeons, making them work for it by tossing them as hard as she could, sometimes straight up, sometimes aiming at their tiny, bobbing heads. She was between semesters and unemployed and the money from the land she inherited and sold meant she didn't have much else to do but things like this. Oh, she could read, of course; she could fly, could get drunk or drink coffee at a sidewalk café, but she did none of these things because all of these things scrambled her thoughts, the darkness of which she was just now learning.

Plus, of course, she had her aim to work on.

11

By the time Cassie returned to the real world and started taking classes again, she found herself in a nearly nonstop state of being pissed. It was a good emotion—the strongest she had—and it kept grief and the other shit at bay. She found she was angry at the universe for playing trick-or-treat, for rolling out the red carpet, only to yank it from beneath her feet. She was angry at people in general because people in general were treating her like she was even more different than usual. She'd left Cedar Run to find a world that could cope with a little personal weirdness, and then she got even weirder, passing a point beyond the polite acceptance of even college-town types. Everywhere she went, her wings kept getting in the way. Returning to classes, she returned not as a student, but as an *Angel* student, frequently the only one in her class. Teachers learned her name first, called on her the most, couldn't seem to stop making eye contact with her as they lectured. Well, not so much *eye* contact as *wing* contact. They couldn't stop staring at her wings. It wasn't a new problem; before, she'd complained about men always staring at her breasts, but this was somehow worse, as if they were really staring at a prettier cousin who always stood behind her. It was worse, because the women did it as much as the men. On the first few occasions, Cassie asked, "What?" and turned around. "What is it?" she demanded.

"Nothing," they said, leaving her to put two and two together.

"Oh," she said.

Even now, she still has to stop herself from looking back. In the right mood, with men, she'll stare at their crotches; with women, their breasts. In the right mood, she'll ask both the same question:

"Real?"

And then there were the helpers, the ones who knew what she should be doing or studying better than she did. Take anatomy. Cassie was still doing some premed work, trying to make up her mind about how to help people in pain, and had been putting off gross anatomy for the last several semesters. In addition to all the blood and guts it promised, Cassie'd heard nothing but horror stories from fellow students about the professor. Of course, they'd always append their comments with the mysterious, "Well, maybe it won't be so bad for *you* . . ." not bothering to explain to Cassie what *that* was supposed to mean. When she'd ask, they'd only say, "Oh, Symanske's got your number. She's waiting for you, wing-chick . . ."

The course was taught by Dr. Rebecca Symanske, who'd been some whiz-bang whiz kid way back when and gotten her Ph.D. at the age of twenty. Now, in her late thirties, she'd returned to her alma mater and was considered one of the finest teachers in the School of Medicine. This, of course, only lent credence to the theory that she was also a little insane.

Once again, Cassie was the only Angel in the class and was, of course, Dr. Symanske's favorite. She particularly liked using Cassie's wings as the butt of some pun. Whereas most teachers were dreadfully polite on the subject, not mentioning them directly in class, Dr. Symanske positively reveled in bringing them up. For example, she'd taken to calling Cassie "Cad," which was short for "Caduceus," which is what Cassie reminded her of.

"A stick with wings," she clarified, taking a poke at Cassie's exaggeratedly straight posture.

"Cad," she'd say, after Cassie burst into class, late once again, "you don't have a prayer." She'd pause and add, "You have the wings, but no prayer . . ."

It was under Dr. Symanske's wing—so to speak—that Cassie experienced her first Angelic autopsy. It was autumn and the trees were on fire with fall colors—red, yellow, orange, some already burned down to brown—the wind crackling through their dryness like real flames. Devil's Night and Halloween were both fast approaching and people—students, faculty—seemed more mischievous than usual. Just the day before, the dissection group two tables down from Cassie's had lifted the sheet on their cadaver, only to find that someone had folded down all but the middle finger on either hand, while another group found that its body had one of its eyes superglued open, and the other glued shut, in a hellish, permanent wink. Rumor had it that Dr. Symanske herself was responsible for these rather gross anatomical greetings, and so Cassie had reason to be nervous when Rebecca entered the classroom one day, cracked all her knuckles at once like she usually did to get the class's attention, and then immediately said: "Good morning, Cad."

She continued: "Did you know that today is your lucky day?"

"No, Dr. Symanske, I—" Cassie began.

"Well, it is," she said. "You see, I have a little treat for you and your group." She smiled with a teacher's kind of evil, and placed both pinkies into her mouth. Inflating her cheeks, she blew a shrill, taxi-stopping whistle that bounced as hard as marbles off the lab's tiled walls. Suddenly, the double doors banged open as a couple of undergrads wheeled in a new cadaver, still sheeted.

"I hope you appreciate the trouble this was to get," she said. "A friend of mine at Ypsi General cued me in on this particular specimen's availability, and so, naturally, I thought of *you,* Cad." She pulled back the sheet with a flourish, revealing a nude Angel—dead, white, and male, perhaps in his late sixties.

"Cad," she said, "meet Max."

Cassie looked at Max like she was looking at her future. She knew his story in a flash, and wondered how much he'd gotten. She wondered if it was enough, was worth the fluorescent brutality of being here, now, like this. It was widely known that medical schools and research facilities actively courted still-living and elderly Angels, offering them money, free medical treatment, in-home care, or other sweetheart deals all for their signature on a contract that guaranteed that people like Max ended up in places like this. Cassie looked at Max's frozen-lined face, wondering what the going rate would be once Angel Boomers like her started dying.

A buck fifty? A buck twenty-five?

Cassie shook her head and forced her eyes away from the cadaver, as Dr. Symanske droned on in the background, explaining herself. Cassie— Dr. S. was in the process of suggesting—had managed to distance herself from the reality of the autopsy. For her, she continued, dissecting a Pedestrian was like a Pedestrian dissecting a chimp—close, but not as personally threatening as the real thing. If Cassie was feeling apprehensive, nauseous, was identifying a bit too strongly with Max and his cold-slabbed fate . . . well, *good*. That was the idea. There were certain realities, she said, and Cassie should get used to them. She might think she was free to choose a specialty, but the reality was Pedestrians weren't going to trust her, and Angels would. Cassie's patients would be Angels—expecting anything else was naïve.

Dr. Symanske continued preaching in this vein, while Cassie let her stare drift back to Max, and the sad, shrunken stem of his penis. She imagined him younger, joking with his lovers, maybe naming the thing, happily letting it pitch a tent under his sheets, bidding it, proudly, "Down, boy . . ." She saw him forcing it on women with black marble eyes, and closed her own. Behind her lids, tight like clenched teeth, she saw his lover in the morning, looking very much like Dr. Symanske, her leonine blond hair wet from a morning shower, her long body wrapped in a bathrobe, knees pulled to chest as she perched in a sunseat with winter behind her, both hands wrapped around a steaming cup of coffee . . .

She hadn't had such thoughts about her group's original cadaver. Its—she wouldn't even venture a "his"—its skin reminded her of the rubber skin on a Barbie doll; underneath, it was butcher-shop variations, steaks and cutlets, a bit too marbled from a long life of heart-clogging American cuisine, but nothing she couldn't take—a fact she'd been proud of, until now. So maybe Dr. S. was right. Maybe Cassie *had* stopped connecting to nonwinged humans; their deaths didn't particularly interest her; their maladies were the maladies of cats and dogs to a veterinarian. Reaching inside them, sloshing among their tubes and slippery bits was like fingering through the guts of Jack's car, and it felt like revenge.

She looked at her fellow students—all Pedestrians with Pedestrians on the slabs before them—and she wondered if there was a way their hearts felt, drawing their scalpels down the chests of their mirrors. Should she be wincing? Did *hers* tighten enough? When she was in Max's place, what would she want—what would she *demand*—of the Angel opening her?

Standing with a scalpel in her hand, in front of her dead Angel, Cassie wondered why it was she was here, now, in this position. What was she doing, taking gross anatomy? Hadn't Mercy's death been enough death for the year? Hadn't her own change been sufficiently gross and anatomical? What was she trying to prove, and why couldn't she just give Dr. S. the knife back, hang up her lab smock, and go throw pots or something?

She looked at Max's stiff body and thought of Bob's mortuary-trained hands burning against her skin. She looked at Dr. S., daring her to chicken out. She gritted her teeth and dove in. Placing the blade at the base of Max's throat, she unzipped him downward in one swift jerk, powered by anger, curiosity, and fear. She felt she had to do it this way, afraid to pause and look down, for fear of falling into the cut she was making. Swabbing away the blood and pinning back the flaps of chest skin, a thought came into her head: Wings, front and back.

Despite all her Coop reading, Cassie was unprepared for how weird Max was inside. She'd heard about the wire muscles, the jury-rigged pulley setup of their ligatures, the hypertrophied pineal gland, the reinforced bones, the mysteriously absent appendix—but she'd not seen any in their bloody glory. And Max was definitely *that*—bloody. Unlike her original cadaver, he hadn't been drained but had been left intact, pristine. Nothing was to be altered that might confuse the results, Dr. S. explained.

Only a handful of autopsies had been performed on Angels up to that time, and most medical textbooks didn't have much else to offer other than a few lurid photos with *National Enquirer* copyrights running along the edge. The texts on comparative human and Angelic anatomies were still being written, and as Cassie soon discovered, Dr. Symanske had uses for Max beyond his becoming just another training dummy for scalpel practice. She'd oversee the dissection personally, which was to be filmed by a couple of undergrads on work-study. Her piece was going to be different from other treatments of the subject—primarily because of Cassie, her Caduceus, the Angel at her shoulder.

At the time, there weren't many Angels in the medical field, practicing *or* training, and Dr. Symanske thought Max and Cassie would make an interesting pair. Perhaps her student could shed the light of personal experience on the possible uses and functions of otherwise inscrutable structures. Repeatedly throughout the procedure, she'd lean over Cassie's left wing, poke about in the viscera, and say, "There. That. What do you suppose *that* does?" With the same bloodied hand she'd palpate the muscles of Cassie's chest or back through her lab coat. "It's right about . . . *here,* isn't it? Move your right wing a bit. No. More . . . like this, a rotating motion."

Once, she laughed, in front of all the turning heads in class, her bloody hand—her hand, that is, covered with Max's blood—slipped between the wings of Cassie's lab coat and past the buttons of her blouse, pressing warm and wet against her skin. "You know what it feels like?" she asked.

Cassie's head exploded with a thousand humiliating thoughts, with emotions doing cartwheels past one another, leapfrogging over the backs of all the ones she thought she understood. She didn't dare speak, for fear that her voice would splinter like a boy's, going through some new kind of puberty. She knew one thing; one thing kept coming home: Dr. Symanske's touch thrilled her, electrically, and she saw her again as an early morning lover—*hers,* this time—risen and showered, warming her hands on a cup of coffee.

"It feels like a little mouse," Dr. Symanske said. "He's trapped and struggling under a sheet of something leathery, but soft. Buckskin, maybe."

"Hmmmm," Cassie managed, feigning only faint interest and distance.

Later, when Cassie washed, she dabbed carefully around the dried stain of her teacher's hand, clarifying the fingers where movement had blurred them. She was interested, but not lovesick. She didn't plan to go around with it there forever. She was just curious to see what it looked like to have Dr. Symanske's—Rebecca's—hand that close to her heart.

From the outside, the place looked like an abandoned artist's loft—something that Cassie should have taken as a warning. The door was painted a glossy shade of her unfavorite color—red—and bore at eye level a brass plate announcing, in flourishing script, CLUB GIGI. The club was located on the second floor of a building off Liberty Street in downtown Ann Arbor, over a shop that specialized in chandeliers, and another that sold feathers, baskets, wooden gods, and other trinkets stolen from Africa or South America. As Cassie scaled the squeaky staircase to the vestibule where she now stood, she'd grown increasingly apprehensive. There was no light in the stairwell, and what she could see of the carpeting convinced her it had only recently been rescued from the city dump. Flyers announcing concerts, poetry readings, and movie festivals rattled and shshed from where they were thumbtacked or stapled over one another, right into the wall. The handrail she'd touched by mistake groaned and leaked plaster dust.

Could Dr. Symanske really have meant *this* place? Cassie unfolded the note she'd found written on the back of her anatomy exam; she reread it by the pink glow of the lit doorbell. "Dear Cad," it said. "We have some talking to do. Meet me at," and it listed the address she now double checked, looking between the page and the wooden numbers screwed to the wall over the red door. The note said nothing about a Club Gigi, though there was a date and time—today, and a few minutes from now.

Not knowing what else to do, Cassie pressed the pink doorbell. A buzzer sounded and the door opened, apparently by itself.

"Yes?" a voice said from below; Cassie looked down and noticed a female dwarf peeking through the crack. Music and smoke snuck into the stairwell. "Can I help you?"

"I'm supposed to meet someone here," Cassie said, offering the crumpled scrap of paper, as if it were a passport.

"Been here before?" the miniature maître d' asked, accepting the slip of paper.

"No," Cassie said, sure of that—if nothing else.

"You a cop?" the diminutive doorperson asked, shining a penlight on the note.

Cassie began to explain that she wasn't, that she was just a student with the university and—when she was cut short.

"Oh," the dwarf said. "You're a friend of Becky's," she continued, as if that were a fully adequate explanation. "You should have said so right away."

Cassie entered Club Gigi and was shown to a corner table under a baby spot. A rotating filter in front of the light turned first red, then green, yellow, and then red again. In the center of the table, a candle dribbled its wax over a spent Perrier bottle, while another played bud vase to a single white rose. Both threw shadows across the tablecloth—yellow, red, green—caution, stop, go . . .

Cassie could relate.

Of course, her table was no different from any of the other tables at Club Gigi, with the possible exception that hers was one of the few without a couple seated across from each other, holding hands, stroking faces, the one laughing, the other twisting hair about a finger, nervous, maybe, coy, perhaps . . .

It was when she realized that the only men in the room were the teenage boys acting as waiters—and that all the couples were women with other women—that Cassie answered yes to her waiter's question about whether or not she'd like to start with a drink.

"A Long Island iced tea," she said, and paused. "Do you sell that by the carafe?" she added.

"Arts and carafes, yes," the waiter said—an old joke, apparently. That's when Cassie noticed that the tray he held was, in fact, an oversized artist's palette, that the general decor of the place was fifties beatnik art studio, the waiters, bereted, the walls, Pollocked.

When her drink arrived, Cassie drained half almost immediately, and then sat still as the warmth sank in and spread to her feathers. Before getting here, she'd thought Dr. Symanske wanted to talk about her grade, or maybe some sort of research assistantship to continue the work they'd begun. Now that the agenda had changed—and become obvious—she didn't know what she thought.

Mercy would approve—the thought just came to her—and Cassie ached all over again with the heavy work of missing her mom. She'd never really thought about her mother's sex life; it didn't seem a polite thing to do. There was Cassie's father, obviously, about whom she knew nothing. There were a few other men who came and went, who stayed a few weeks after one of Mercy's shows and then left, a tipped hat out the front door, "Sorry it didn't work out . . ." There was Aunt Rita, who wasn't an aunt, and who was so far back in Cassie's memory she wasn't entirely sure she was real. Aunt Rita wore suit coats and smoked those French cigarettes before Mercy picked up the habit. Cassie—was this a real memory?—had seen them . . . kissing . . . she was almost sure it was kissing . . . once in the kitchen, on the lips . . . she was almost sure it was the lips . . . and she hadn't thought of that, *ever,* until just now, and it hurt; it hurt like her mom's dying all over again, the thought that she could have not known Mercy at such a basic level.

Was that it? Did that explain the weirdness she was feeling inside about Dr. Symanske?

Were such feelings hereditary?

Oh, brother . . .

Cassie shook her head, and wondered about what it was she was thinking of doing. Was it wrong? It wasn't serious. If it wasn't serious, was that okay, or not okay? Because it wasn't—it definitely wasn't—a serious thing; it was just a *casual* fling, and providing it stayed that way . . . well, what harm could it do?

Cassie looked at the harm it could do—not to her, but to the other women of Club Gigi. Was it fair to them for her to dabble, to flirt with something other than a whole heart? There were no casual flings here. There was face touching, deep, longing glances, candle-lit eyes tearing with happiness; there were fingertips touching across the tabletops, a war-torn recognition of their shared otherness. There were legs, arms, throats, breasts; there were eyes, some on her, weighing her availability, perhaps. There were big women, and little women, ugly, pretty, tall, and short women, army-fatigued, leather-bound, and calicoed women . . .

And one woman with wings, seated at an otherwise empty table, with a candle, a flower, and a traffic light's indecisiveness.

Cassie was an outsider among outsiders of a wholly different sort, and it made her feel lonelier than when she was just alone. The fact of them and their otherness, their presence and numbers, compared to her singleness, subtracted something from her, making her smaller and less than she already was. Their happiness made her sad; their seriousness made her realize what she wasn't. This thing with Dr. S.—Rebecca— was a crush, pure and simple, and though it would probably happen, it wasn't about who Cassie was or her sexuality; it was about what she needed. It was about shared warmth, the pressure of fingertips, about someone else's arms holding her together so she could let go of that tight ball of pain in her chest without blowing apart.

It was about safety and not being hurt, this time.

Cassie looked about and wondered where her teacher was. Some of the women had left their tables and were dancing under the traffic light. She should just leave, should get out now. This was not her place. *Her* place—if there *was* such a thing—would feel like a revelation, like an arrival, like . . . like the bubble of pure joy that rose in her chest when she leaped from the roof of the Coop that first time. Her place wouldn't make her feel like a fraud-creep-peeping-Tom . . .

She'd tell Dr. Symanske that she had a cold. If she tried hard enough, she could almost feel something coming on. She'd leave a note in her box and . . .

Warm lips.

Pressing.

Against her cheek.

And a fingernail drawing itself down her spine.

Cassie flinched. A shudder worked its way through her bones and out her wings, beating in blind defense. The women of Club Gigi stopped dancing, hugging, touching, and stared, instead, at the room's only Angel and the commotion she'd made. Cassie held on to the table like an anchor as she tried to calm her bucking wings.

Dr. Symanske came around from behind her and pulled up a seat. Pinching her nose, she reached for Cassie's bar napkin, and then set it back down, pinkened with blood. "Hello to you, too," she said, tapping the back of Cassie's hand, and then, softer, "Remind me never to surprise you like that again."

"So, was this subtle enough?" Rebecca asked, once Club Gigi had returned to its own business.

Cassie didn't know how to respond, and so didn't. She drank some more of her Long Island iced tea and stared at her own fingers in the candlelight.

Rebecca reached across the tabletop like the other Club Gigi women and covered Cassie's hand. "I just wanted you to know that it's okay," Rebecca said. "There are others like us. You're not alone."

Cassie thrilled at the touch of her teacher's hand. This *would* happen. She should say something, though, she thought, should explain that actually, she *was* alone, and that this—her being here—was about loneliness and its cure, and she really wasn't *really* part of the "us" that included the rest of this room, and . . . shit! It was too complicated. It . . .

"Dr. Symanske . . . ," she tried.

"Becky."

"Becky," Cassie said. "How did . . . ?"

"I know?" Becky asked.

Cassie thought no, but shook her head yes.

"It's not that hard," Becky said. "The body's terrible at keeping secrets. Pupils dilate, breathing quickens, blood rushes to inappropriate places at inappropriate times, making us blush, and," she smiled, "worse. We're in a constant state of self-incrimination."

Cassie felt like a bug scrambling at the sides of a test tube; she could feel herself incriminating herself all over.

"Can we leave?" Cassie asked, suddenly, by which she meant, "Can we get out of here?" and, maybe, "Can I go back to my dorm and think about this?"

What Becky heard, of course, had nothing to do with letting Cassie go back to her dorm. "Of course," she said, her eyes brightening. "Let's blow this pop stand."

. . .

Back at her apartment, Becky poured the two of them some wine, apologizing for the Dixie riddle cups, which were the only drinking ware in her apartment that didn't need cleaning. "You know how it is," she said, in one swift stroke equalizing her student and herself. "You have school all day long, classes and office hours and meetings, and then you come home in the evening with a stack of papers to grade, and who can face the dishes?"

She'd changed into her street clothes. Here, in her nest, Becky wore wire-rimmed glasses instead of contacts. Her hair was loose like Cassie had imagined it—wild and a little leonine—and instead of her lab coat, she wore a loose-fitting T-shirt from a rock concert she'd attended when Cassie was just entering puberty. When she moved, stretching backward with her fingers knit over her head to crack her back, the cloth fell against her skin and brought out the shape of her breasts—small, slightly conical. Cassie noticed Becky's nipples pressing against the fabric, felt ashamed for looking, and lowered her eyes.

Becky wore torn jeans that zippered at the ankle, just above her tiny bare feet. Her gorgeous, *Pedestrian* bare feet.

"Make yourself comfortable," Becky said, handing a cup of wine to her guest.

Cassie looked about the apartment, trying to find some other distraction, and someplace to sit. She noticed that the room's only piece of furniture seemed to be a three-sectioned futon, folded into something resembling an upside-down square-root sign, and acting as a chaise lounge. Carrying her Dixie riddle cup, Becky took her place on the futon. Cassie, at a loss, kneeled behind it, letting her chest lean against its cushioned back, and resting her elbows along the top.

"Are you *comfortable* like that?" Becky asked.

"It's okay," Cassie lied. "There's not a lot of Angel-friendly furniture out there. Bar stools, some computer chairs . . . that's about it."

"What do you do?" she asked.

"I stand a lot," Cassie said.

"Do they hurt if you lean back on them?"

"Kinda, but not really," Cassie said. "It's more that they get . . . claustrophobic. They try to flap and if they find they can't, they panic and try harder and . . . well, you saw what they did at the club."

"Indeed," Becky said, mulling it over. "Is it different if they know what's coming?"

Cassie began to answer, and then felt Becky's hand cupping the back of her neck, pulling down. Becky craned back, and up, closed her eyes, and kissed Cassie's lips lightly, once, twice, and then a third time, harder, pushing past them with her tongue. Cassie kissed back with a need so raw and pure, Becky opened her eyes and thought about stopping.

Thought, but didn't, instead kissing back herself, harder still, as if it were a neediness marathon, and the winner won the whole world as her prize.

For a moment, they stopped kissing and looked at each other, breathing hard. Under the blunt light of Becky's apartment, Cassie noticed her teacher's nipples once again, hard and casting the slightest of shadows across the fabric of her T-shirt. They reminded Cassie of something, of apostrophes—no—of quote-within-a-quote marks, setting off some secondhand comment about her teacher's heart.

God, she hated this in men—their fracturing of whole women into parts, like cutlets and steaks in some butcher's textbook. But she couldn't help it, now, and wondered if Becky was seeing her the same way, acknowledging, for the sake of argument, the existence of some vague Cassie underneath that huge canopy of wings.

Suddenly, and saying nothing, Becky rose from the futon. She crossed to the other side of the apartment and switched off the lights. Cassie heard the slip of fabric passing over skin, the rustle of hair dropping free of Becky's T-shirt. Zippers sawed open, one, two, three followed by the thump and click of denim and rivet hitting hardwood floor. The naked padding of bare feet crossed in front of her, and then behind.

"Claustrophobia, huh?" Becky said, announcing her intention, warning the wings before slipping her arms under and around, hugging, and pressing her chest against Cassie's back, against her wings.

Shuddering, Cassie's wings brushed softly against Becky's breasts, her quills tingling like they did from warm breezes. Becky giggled, and then laughed, hugging Cassie tighter about the neck and raising her legs to wrap them around her student's waist.

"Cad," she said, in a breathy, new voice. "Have I ever told you how much you remind me of Cupid?"

. . .

Cassie was in love. Well, not Love, love, but Becky—this thing with Becky—was definitely going to be a hard drug to kick. Completely by accident, Cassie had stumbled upon the perfect reentry-to-the-real-world relationship, and, recognizing it, she decided to hold on with both hands. Becky—this thing with Becky—was convenient, fun, warm, and sexy, and held completely in check by Cassie because Cassie was not in love with Becky. Meaning, she was in control—an entirely satisfactory thing to be, when you've been run over by life a few times in a row.

Cassie remembered a snippet of poetry from someplace:

> *If loving equal cannot be*
> *Let the better-loved one be me.*

In the Becky-Cassie dynamic—Cassie was sure—she was the better-loved one. And she loved it.

Which is where the irony snuck in. Though Cassie could completely imagine coping with the loss of Becky, she had a harder time imagining life after losing the power the relationship with Becky gave her. Fortunately, of course, being the one in control, being the better-loved one, Cassie was calling the shots, could pick or choose the freshness date on this particular coupling.

And then . . .

Becky bit Cassie. It wasn't much of a bite, could have been the product of passion, but it did draw blood, and Becky's tongue flicked lightly over it before she apologized. But Cassie didn't hear the apology. Instead, she heard her own brain, yelling: Vampire!

But she's a doctor! the other side of her brain yelled back. And: It's not contagious after they sprout.

"Where'd you go?" Becky asked, afterward, toweling the sweat from her body.

"El Paso," Cassie said, winning a pair of crossed eyes, and a "You goof . . ." from Becky.

That night, Cassie dreamed of Becky in her lab, spitting out her blood onto a slide. Under the microscope, the cells swam magnified as Becky poked at them with a pipette, drawing off their nuclei. Behind her, sheets of celluloid were clipped to a light box, and smudged with the dark rungs of somebody's—Cassie's—DNA. In the dream, Cassie tried to see herself in the stretched, bar-coded stain. Instead, all she could see was the Giacomettis in her mother's coffee table book, the lumpy-atomed stick people, frozen in midstride, looking like the long shriek she could feel coming.

Among the corpses and test tubes, backlit by Cassie's DNA, Becky stood in silhouette—pregnant. Pregnant with Cassie's baby by cloning. And Cassie was there, placing her hand (her missing father's hand?) on the belly of Mercy (of Becky?) while the future growing there flinched, the wings inside beating a timpani, loud enough to wake the dead. And Cassie.

She'd started thinking too much. She'd started thinking about the relationship, and what it might be about from Becky's side, started thinking dangerous, dumb questions like: If I weren't a student . . . ?

If I weren't an Angel . . . ?

And with that, the expiration date arrived; the relationship was spoiling. Cassie would confront Becky, explain that it just wasn't working out. She'd do it in a restaurant. It would keep the chance of scenes to a minimum.

She'd . . .

And then she saw Becky with a man. Another student—a new one—an Angel. They were in an alley—how fitting—between buildings, and she was kissing him with all the black-hole wanting Cassie knew so well.

She couldn't breathe. She felt like a car that had just been traded in, like a car that had been sold for parts. Her heart hurt—and it shouldn't be doing that because this was what she was going to do anyway, but Becky had beat her to the punch and . . .

Trick-or-treat.

Cassie was a one-plus-one-equals-the-rest-of-your-life kind of thinker—at least back then, when she was still a student with an undecided major, a majorly broken heart, and an interest in stopping pain. This was like Jack, again, and in a way, worse, because she'd helped it happen, had let her neediness blind her to clues she should have seen. God, she felt like an idiot! The stupid, stupid romanticizing about women loving women, and how it would be different—*better*—because . . . she didn't know why. The statistical correlation of their parts? The higher-than-average percentage of the anatomy they shared? Of course, she'd conveniently left wings out of the equation—wings being the uncommon denominator that inverts every value, stacks the deck against every deal, left her forever the more-than-opposite sex to either variety or persuasion . . .

Betrayal. It was a human disease. You exposed yourself to it the second you let down your guard and were stupid enough to trust someone else, someone as needy and as greedy in their need as you.

Cassie wanted to scream and so she did, in her echoey stall in the dorm's group bathroom, scaring at least two back to their rooms. And after the scream, she cried, flushing the toilet again and again to hide the sound.

She was twenty-two and didn't need this kind of shit. She . . . she needed to *do* something, to make the pain stop, and to let Rebecca know that you just don't *do* this to people. She saw it all clearly now—saw Becky, and what she was about. She was . . . a sexual dilettante, an adventurer, and sampler. Love, and the making thereof, was a matter of quotas to be filled. One of each. She'd probably had the dwarf at Club Gigi; maybe Max had other uses. And Cassie—Cassie was the checked box next to "Red-haired, green-eyed, single, white, female Angel." She'd been had and done, and Becky was moving on, now, to the next variation on the feathered theme.

Bitch.

Cassie thought about Jack, again, and revenge and her bike, and about what she could padlock to what this time to make her point . . .

And then the answer came to her, the way it sometimes will.

Cassie's decision to kill herself focused her in an almost magical way. The emotions she thought she couldn't control anymore suddenly stood up, rolled over, did whatever she said. She smiled a lot, seeing things and people and judging them the last time for this, the last time for you. She'd send a note to Becky's department head, explaining why it was that her naked body was found in her teacher's apartment, and she'd make a point of *not* donating it to science. She'd run up her MasterCard to the limit, buying completely worthless but poignant shit and having it delivered to Becky's university box—stuff she'd have to explain but couldn't, like dildos big enough to embarrass the Washington monument, subscriptions to *Screw* and *The Watchtower,* inflatable sheep . . .

And on the day she was going to do it, Cassie woke up feeling great! Her head was clear, her joints didn't feel gummy, she felt—forgive her—more *alive* than she had in days. She looked at Becky, snoring away next to her. That was part of it; she decided they'd do it one more time, Cassie using her new knowledge, and Becky's heartlessness to fuel her into it, this last act.

Becky rolled onto her back—how she envied her that!—and assumed her Christ-crucified posture, one arm draped just below Cassie's neck, cradled in the notch of her wings.

Becky mumbled in her sleep, and Cassie nudged her hip into the hip of her soon-to-be *very* ex. When that didn't wake her, she placed a hand to her shoulder and gave it a gentle shake. "Becky," she said. "It's alive," she said, quoting Dr. Frankenstein.

"Huh?" Becky asked, groggy, eyes still closed.

"It's alive," Cassie repeated. It was one of their signals.

Becky smiled and inched up the oversized T-shirt she wore over her pajama pants. And afterward, they showered together—something they almost never did, given the space limitations. This time, however, Cassie pulled aside the shower curtain to make more room and covered the tiled floor with several layers of towels to catch the spray.

"What has gotten into you, Cad?" Becky asked as she entered the bathroom.

"Oh, you know," Cassie said, knowing that was no answer to her question, but kissing her before she could ask any others.

This would make her feel guiltier, she thought. Remembering this—afterward.

And all through breakfast, Cassie smiled like a devoted goof, working in "I love you" whenever she could—meaning it half of the time, in spite of herself. And the other half of the time, she was speaking *to* herself, to her decision to handle things, once and for all. She'd been seduced by suicide, intoxicated by the decision that looked like a solution. It wasn't the act itself, it was the weird pride and joy she got out of having decided something that put a cap on everything else, that wrestled away all other decisions—the illusion that it would put her in a place beyond the petty concerns of the day, but that this was a place she could look back from. She kept imagining the world after her suicide as a place in which she was still involved, just with less pressure, fewer problems.

She bit into her bacon and waited for Becky to leave for class, knowing, but not really believing she'd never see her again.

Cassie got as far as getting the belt around her neck, and kicking backward off the chair. That's when *they* took over. Her wings began flapping all on their own and wouldn't let her drop. At first, they flapped just enough to counteract gravity (and knock books off the shelves, lamps off tables, knickknacks through windows). Cassie hung there, underneath them, a bean-bag person. Then they got sarcastic, lifting her headfirst into the ceiling, banging her into the plaster hard enough to leave a grease mark behind. They did it again and again, leaving blurry ellipses across the ceiling.

She began shouting at them. "Okay!" she said. "Okay, already," she repeated. "I get the point . . ." With her arms darting between her flapping wings, Cassie hurriedly loosened the belt from around her neck. Once the belt slipped away, and as suddenly as they had started, her wings stopped, dropping her to the floor.

Sitting there, rubbing her head, her wings making a feathered prayer behind her, Cassie looked around at her ex-lover's apartment, at her life. She looked at the shards of glass where a ceramic horse had gone through a window, at the gauzy drapes blown through the hole in the pane. She looked at the splayed wings of *Gray's Anatomy,* tumbled onto Anaïs Nin, and Audubon. A spray of game tiles from some game they never played together littered the floor. And Cassie—the winged dope in the middle of it all—Cassie realized a few things.

One was that her life was no longer in her hands.

Two was that she needed to report her credit card stolen, and get to Becky's department before the mail did.

And three was the fact that breaking things—breaking *Becky's* things—felt good, and was probably better for her general health.

Afterward, Cassie was scared shitless. *What* had she been thinking? Killing herself? Jeezus! She must have been nuts. Must have been some kind of crazy to go and pull a stunt like that, to even have it cross her mind . . .

Mind.

Cassie started thinking about her mind, and how it thought, and how it got her into a mess like the Becky Affair. And that's how she thought of it—as the "Becky Affair," reserving for it the same sort of intonation she'd use with the phrase, "A case of the clap."

The Becky Affair became for her a sort of emotional cavity—the place her emotional tongue went probing whenever it could, despite the pain, or maybe because of it. And every fresh poke, every twinge of the raw nerve brought forth another theory about why it had happened in the first place.

Like: The Jack Affair created the Becky Affair by introducing her to the dark extreme of heterosexuality, making a homosexual fling seem inviting, a safe vacation, a cooling-down time for reevaluation.

Like: Cassie was a control freak and having an affair with a woman without being a lesbian too was safe and assured her that she was the better-loved one in the relationship, meaning she could drive the car, take it where she wanted, and ditch it when it got old.

Like: Becky was a mother-father substitute.

Like: Becky was Cassie before Cassie got wings, that part of herself she'd not loved enough—before—and to which she would now make amends.

And: Why did her acts of revenge always involve some form of self-destruction?

And: All of the above.

And: None of it.

And. And. And . . .

Cassie had started thinking too much on a pretty much regular basis. It was when she started thinking about what thinking too much might mean about her future that Cassie decided to go into therapy. Not as a cure, per se, but as a career. It seemed the least bloody of her alternatives, kept her away from sharp objects, and still had something to do with getting rid of pain.

And this decision focused her at least as much as the decision to commit suicide. This one felt more hopeful, though, healthy, and right, and was motivated not so much by getting even, as getting better. That night, after signing the forms and changing her degree program, Cassie took herself out flying for the first time since leaving the Coop, since losing her mother, since . . . so damn much.

Up there, in the wild blue, her more mundane blues faded. She flew fast and low, her shadow skimming over the tops of buildings, over the sidewalks of Ann Arbor, making people look up, making them point. She flew through a parking structure, a hand out for the main pylon, spinning herself around, and laughing, and laughing more as her laugh bounced off the concrete walls. She'd be embarrassed about this all, later, her making a public spectacle of herself, but for now she was celebrating—celebrating what was clearly a turning point in her life . . .

. . . and the fact of her having survived it.

12

Cassie blames her first client for getting her hooked on easy answers. Her case is at the heart of *The Angel Blues,* where she shows up as Christine J. Cassie remembers the visit vividly.

"There's been a mistake," Christine J. said, entering Cassie's office all a-flutter. Ms. J. was clearly agitated, first taking a perch, getting up, and pacing, patting herself down for a pack of gum, finding it, and chewing angrily. Otherwise, she seemed a perfectly healthy female Angel, in her mid-twenties. Cassie made note of it on her pad, before looking up.

"Mistake?" Cassie said, flipping closed her notebook, capping her pen.

"Yes."

"What sort of mistake?"

"A *big* one," Christine said.

"Namely?"

She turned around, displaying her wings. She pointed backward and down with both thumbs. "Dum and Dee, here. The Tweedle twins."

"Your wings?" Cassie said, inflection rising.

"Yeah," she said. " 'Cept for one thing."

"And that is?"

"They ain't mine."

Cassie flopped open the notebook again, scribbled "Penguin," and then immediately crossed it out. Penguins couldn't move like Christine. Penguins crawled; you could make them roll on their backs like turtles, just by calling "Hey!" and distracting them from the concentration that even crawling took. Christine, on the other hand, was exceedingly frenetic, found it seemingly impossible to sit in one place for very long, pacing to the window to have a look, opening the closet door, fingering the globe and dictionary, adjusting the wick of Cassie's hurricane lamp. Her eyes were everywhere but where they'd be if she were a Penguin—namely, her feet—which, at the moment, were busily pacing her about Cassie's office, and making the fledgling therapist feel like a judge in a Ping-Pong match.

"Would you care for a perch, Ms. J.?" Cassie managed, and was waved off.

"Nope," she said. "Think better this way. Just don't ask me to chew gum." She laughed, or rather, *brayed*. It made a frightful din. She began chewing more furiously.

"Whose . . . ," Cassie tried, returning to the original subject.

"Huh?"

"Whose wings are they?"

"My brother's, of course," she said, unwrapping another stick of gum. "The genius, the brainiac. Everything's for him. He went to college, got the car, was the pony mom and dad bet on. He's the one that's supposed to go places. I go home with these puppies on my back, and they'll say I stole 'em or something."

Ah, Cassie thought to herself, she's a lottery winner. The I'm-not-worthy syndrome. "Christine," she said. "Do you believe in random acts of violence?"

"Huh?"

"A good man, crossing the street, is mowed down by another good man in a car whose brakes have just failed. Two exemplary people, one kills the other because of a fluke. Do you believe that happens?"

"Of course," she said. "What else would the papers print, if it weren't for—what did you call 'em?—random acts of violence?"

"So why can't you accept a random act of kindness?"

"Lost me, Doc."

"Your wings," Cassie said. "You got lucky. Enjoy! Nobody knows who gets them and who doesn't. It's not a good person, bad person sort of thing. And it's not like you're taking away anything from your brother. It's just that *you* finally got something. I repeat: *Enjoy!*"

"You done?" Christine asked, still for once, and looking right at Cassie.

"More or less."

"That's the real world you're talking about," she said. "*I'm* talking about my family."

"I see," Cassie said, and sadly she did. Many Angels are rejected by their families in a variety of ways. Some treat the new Angel like a foreigner, feeling compelled to explain things that don't need explaining, the message being clear: "You are somebody else, an other." Others just don't let the new Angel join in their reindeer games. The worst is when they break a person into the Old You and the New You. "The *old* Christine would have *never* said a thing like that," for example. Cassie looked at Christine, this bright newcomer to the Angel community, this sad exile. "I see," Cassie repeated with a sigh.

"You do?"

"I do."

"So what do *I* do?" she asked, young enough, Cassie supposed, to expect an easy answer.

So Cassie did her best, and started down the road toward *Oprah* and fraudhood. She took out her prescription pad and scribbled down the only appropriate medication she could think of. She folded it over and slid it across her desk. "Try this," she said.

Christine J. eagerly accepted the script and unfolded it. "Fuck them" it said. Her eyes widened, and then brightened.

"How often daily?" she asked.

Cassie gestured for her to return the scrip.

"As needed," she added.

.   .   .

After that, Cassie felt like God. She felt almost as high as when she flew. She'd taken a person in pain and just by saying the first thing that popped into her head, she made her feel better. This was magic; this was very heady stuff. Cassie took herself out for a big dinner, had two glasses of wine, toddled off to the top of a local parking structure, and dove into the night. She circled the quad, laughing. She told Tree Town that she loved it, and loved being a therapist, and loved being an Angel.

She loved the world—thank you, very much—and it loved her right back.

She flew along Plymouth Road, following it into farm country, wondering if it was lonely enough and dark enough to do what she really felt like doing, namely flying naked, with nothing between her skin and feathers, her sex and soul, and the wind. The stars were out, scattered above her like spilled salt across a dark tablecloth; fireflies blinked in the trees and tall grass below. Lights—tiny lights—above and below, and, for a moment, Cassie imagined herself in outer space, floating, free of the earth and the spaceship and yes . . . it was dark enough.

Cassie unbuttoned her blouse and let the wind blow its wings open, and aside, and off, a flag sailing back to earth where they needed such things to enforce things like boundaries and other things that didn't count up here, with Cassie, the stars, and God.

She was really enjoying herself, and should have realized that the menu of options for enjoying yourself as an Angel meant pretty much something like this. Which is why she shouldn't have been surprised to see Christine J. flying toward her, with some boy Angel already, playing strip Angel tag, it seemed. The boy Angel seemed to be losing—or winning.

"Dr. O'Connor?" Christine said, pulling up short and hovering. Her blouse was untucked, but still buttoned.

"Hello," Cassie said, naked to the waist and blushing all over. She didn't know what else to say. There was client confidentiality to consider. There was a whole minefield of issues to avoid. And there was her blouse, twisted in the branches of a tree about a mile back.

"Dr. O'Connor," Christine continued. "This is Jeff. Jeff, Dr. O'Connor . . ."

"Howdy," Jeff said, beating his wings, hovering and extending a hand to shake. He wasn't wearing any pants, and parts of him greatly appreciated this fact.

"Jeff's helping me fill that prescription," Christine added.

"That's good," Cassie said, wondering if it were true, what she'd read about people spontaneously combusting. It seemed definitely doable at the moment.

"Pleased to meet you," Jeff tried again, his hand and erection still looking to be acknowledged.

"Likewise," Cassie said, lying, realizing that she'd need to avoid such accidental run-ins with patients in the future, and wondering where she might go to ensure that.

Still, the high from her first success lingered, and Cassie's next patient just nailed her coffin tighter.

Henry P. was an Actor! It is what he had planned to be all his life, putting on skits with friends in the backyard, "doing" his teachers during recess for the amusement of his fellow classmates. In college, he majored in theater, became a tree, a rock, and "the best damn end table" his drama coach had ever seen. When he mimed "man walking against the wind," some claimed to see his hair actually blowing back. And when he graduated, and entered the "real" fake world of auditions, he'd do anything for a part. He liked to think of his body as modeling clay, sculpting it according to the demands of the role. For one part, he gained fifty pounds, grew a mustache, and bleached his hair; for another, he dropped the fifty and another ten, shaved his head, and lived on the streets of Ypsilanti in a cardboard box from a Maytag washer.

And then, he was "struck down!"

"By a lightning bolt," he added, grabbing either edge of Cassie's desk, striking an urgent pose. "By the Ultimate Heckler himself!"

"Namely?"

"God, the Director, the Big Cheese," Henry said. "*Mr.* Front-Row-Center."

"Oh," Cassie said, only thinly veiling a smirk. She couldn't help herself. This ham amused her.

"I assume you're talking about your wings."

"Of course!" he said, craning suddenly forward, invading her personal space.

Cassie pushed him back with the eraser end of a pencil, placed carefully but persuasively against his forehead, just between and above his eyes.

"Sorry," he said, and he seemed sincere. "It's just . . . Hell, Doc, the world's not ready for a Willy Loman with wings." He paused. "All these things are good for is a friggin' Christmas pageant!"

"Why don't you look for serious *Angel* roles?" Cassie suggested.

He looked at her, and this time it was his turn to smirk. "Get real," he said. "I could count the number of roles for Angels . . . hell, on my wings here. *And* still have at least one wing left over!"

"So what do you want me to do?" Cassie asked.

"You, nothing," he said. "They made me come here when I asked to have these boys clipped. So, it's what . . . like a sex change, right? You gotta make sure I really mean it. Warn me about post-op trauma and all that doo-dah."

Cassie cleared her throat. "Mr. P.," she began. "It seems as if you are a buck that's being passed, and I'm the place where the buck stops."

"Come again?"

"They're having me do the dirty work."

"Meaning?"

"There's no such thing as a wing amputation," Cassie said. "The AMA has ruled them as unethical, a type of vivisection. Plus, they're too dangerous. Can I see one?" Cassie gestured toward his wing.

He presented it with a flourish and she poked it, quickly, with a lancet.

"Ouch!" he said, a drop of blood welling up and running into his feathers, turning them pink. "What did you do that for?" he asked, looking at the spreading stain.

"Expediency," Cassie said. "That's the quickest therapy session I can give you. Blood—that means veins, arteries, the possibility of bleeding to death. Pain—that means nerves and potential nerve damage. There are also muscles attached to the wings that will have nowhere to go with the wings gone."

"I see," he said, rising, preparing to make his exit. "It's a tragedy. The blessing-curse that destroys life or makes it meaningless." He turned toward the door. "Christmas and Easter shall be boon seasons, I daresay . . ."

Cassie waved him *adieu*. " 'Parting,' as they say . . ."

" 'Parting,' as indeed they do."

He left, apparently, to come to grips with the inevitable, which Cassie trusted he would do.

Henry P., of course, was only acting.

Cassie found out later from a colleague in Mexico City that Henry had apparently gone south of the border in search of surgeons willing to amputate the wings. Given the rather elaborate musculature, circulatory, and nervous-system adjustments necessary for such an operation to render the patient anything other than dead or crippled, however—as well as the negative publicity such an operation was sure to attract—none of the physicians consulted agreed even to attempt the procedure. The news made Cassie sad, as did all the cases of reluctant Angelism.

On bad days, she sometimes wished that transplants were possible, so she could take what one didn't want, and give it to someone who did. Maybe someday in the future, she thought, we'll be able to pick and choose. Maybe in the future, there will be more Angel roles for people like Henry.

In Henry's case, like Christine's, Cassie got lucky. Reading the newspaper, she noticed an announcement, a casting call for an all-the-way-to-the-Midwest-it's-so-far-off-Broadway production of a play called *Hunch!*, a musical adaptation of *The Hunchback of Notre Dame*. It occurred to her that a hump was a perfect place to hide a pair of unwanted wings, and she sent the notice to Henry, who tried out and landed the lead. The reviews for Henry's performance were glowing, speaking of the authenticity of his portrayal of this blighted, hobbled soul. Cassie has seen it several times, and occasionally prescribes it to her other reluctant Angels. Cassie still can't watch the closing number—"Stone, Like You"—sung among the gargoyles of Notre Dame, without losing a tear or two.

When she's feeling like a fraud, sometimes, Cassie consoles herself by thinking about this other part of her—the part that still cries for all the Quasimodos.

. . .

Everything went sour with Mr. F. Mr. F.—that chapter her agent took out—who was really not so much a Mister as a boy, a teenager. Unlike her first patients, Mr. F. was a Pedestrian, one suffering from pteronophobia—a fear of feathers—and Cassie was the deep end of the pool he was being thrown into. Reading his chart the day before she was to begin his treatment, Cassie decided that Mr. F.'s was a silly complaint, one that should be reasoned away in an afternoon. She'd let him touch her wings, let him see that they couldn't hurt him, explain their parts and how they worked, how feathers were put together, the whole "Wonder of Nature" routine. She'd let a bit of her human side leak out, make up something about being afraid of spiders and how she got over it after buying a pet tarantula and naming it Spot. She'd pluck one of her harmless, offending feathers and tickle him with it. He'd laugh—that would be the breakthrough. And, with the half hour that remained, she'd explain how phobias develop, how they're really very human in nature, deriving from our desire to put cause to effect, the same sort of thinking that drives our sciences, but which, when misplaced, leads to things like rituals, superstition, and, yes, phobias. Leaving, he'd shake Cassie's hand and maybe even pet one of her wings. He'd go away feeling a little silly after it all, but decidedly better.

That was the plan.

Of course, when Mr. F. entered her office and got a look at Cassie and her wings, he was less than inclined to play into her tidy little scenario. Instead, he seemed inclined to run to the door his escorts had locked behind him. Cassie offered him a seat, stepping around from behind her desk, and Mr. F. began tugging and twisting at the doorknob, desperately, launching into curses and, as she came closer, open weeping.

"Mr. F.," she said, "please. You're almost a grown man. They're just feathers. They can't hurt you . . ." She prattled on, feeling more and more like a rank amateur.

Mr. F., of course, heard nothing. He was too busy beating his head against the door and sobbing.

When Cassie noticed a spot of blood developing on the door where

Mr. F. continued banging, she panicked, fearing she'd lose a patient to a coma or worse. That's when it occurred to her to crawl under her desk.

"Mr. F.," she said. "They're gone."

He stopped banging his head and turned around, to find himself alone in the room. Cassie gathered her wings in as tightly as she could, so nothing would show underneath the desk.

"They're gone?" he said in a voice that made "them" sound like all the evil the world had to offer. "They're really gone?" The relief in his voice was heartbreaking.

"Yes," Cassie said from under her desk. "Would you take a seat, please?"

She heard the springs of the chair squeak, noticed the pale stalks of his legs and the squiggly black hairs plastered against his skin where the socks inched down. His shoes, really army boots, were newly polished, probably for this visit, for this cruel practical joke the referring doctor had played on him. Mr. F. was a good boy, Cassie decided, looking at his polished boots, and she was an idiot who was being paid too much to be as stupid as she'd been.

"Would you like to talk about what just happened, Mr. F.?" she asked.

"No," he said, and she respected him for that.

"Would you like to talk about . . . anything?" Cassie tried.

"Yes," he said, and paused.

Cassie paused, too. An airplane roared by outside. Traffic noises.

"Ask me what," he said.

"What?" Cassie said. "Oh, you mean . . . What do you want to talk about, Mr. F.?"

"The weather," he said, his voice full of triumph. "The weather is what I'd like to talk about. I have a lot of opinions about the weather."

Mr. F. saw Cassie twice a week for six months. She bought an inflatable donut to take some of the chill and edge off the tiled floor. And then, after five months of talking about all the worst storms he could remember, those experienced personally and those heard about, Mr. F. told her about something that had happened to him as a very young boy. His father had been laid off from the automobile factory where he worked. When unemployment compensation ran out and there was still no job in sight, Mr. F.'s father had a nervous breakdown, which was discovered only after Mr. F. senior tried suffocating his son with a goose feather pillow. Gagging, the boy bit down as hard as he could and managed to rip a hole in the pillow with his teeth. White feathers blew out of the hole as the father continued to press down. Suddenly, noticing the feathers swirling about him, Mr. F. senior froze. He looked at his hands bunching the edges of the pillow and finally felt his son's fists hammering at his back. Stepping away, Mr. F. senior growled—it was a hollow, animal sound—and pulled the pillow apart. And then he just stood there, the two halves of the pillowcase limp at his sides, a snow of white feathers drifting down, and a puddle of urine growing at his feet.

"It was like a Christmas globe," Mr. F. said, like being inside some stupid scene in some ugly, snowing Christmas ornament.

Mr. F. paused after the story. "Do you think . . . ," he began.

"Yes, I do," Cassie said, relieved at the breakthrough.

". . . that's why I'm so hung up on the weather?"

Unfortunately, after a month of no additional progress, Mr. F., the good boy who was afraid of feathers, just stopped showing up. No one called to cancel; no bodies turned up at the hospitals Cassie called. He vanished—*poof!*—off the face of the planet, and Cassie felt betrayed—not a very professional way to feel, but it was honest, and it was how she felt.

In retrospect, now, she wishes he really would have disappeared—into thin air, and forever. In retrospect, she wishes she could edit him out of her life as easily as her agent axed his chapter. In retrospect, of course, she'd still be God, and none of this would matter.

13

There were others, of course, in between, during, and after Mr. F.—
some who got chapters, some who didn't—and then there was Andrew
M. Andrew came to Cassie's hospital suffering from a severe loss of
blood, and in a state of shock. He had, apparently, tried amputating his
own wings with a butcher's knife. He was discovered in his apartment by
his landlady, who had phoned for the ambulance. The butcher's knife had
to be pried from his fingers in the emergency room.

After he was sewed back together, he was transferred to Cassie for
therapy. She suspected Penguinism, but, as was the case with Christine
J., he showed none of the ambulatory impairments normally associated
with that syndrome.

Cassie steeled herself against a sudden flash of anger as Andrew was
brought before her, in his modified wheelchair, hospital gown, and with
an absurd number of bandages wrapped around his wings. She'd grown
accustomed to the fact that many Pedestrian physicians seemed to
overtreat Angel complaints such as sprained or broken wings. Where
lightweight braces and a simple dressing would suffice, they gummed

everything up with crude splints, plaster casts, miles of surgical tape, impairing function much more than was strictly necessary. Before Andrew, she wrote this off as an oddly touching sort of overprotection; after Andrew, however, she would recognize it as cryptomobilism, a (perhaps unconscious) form of castration. Her anger at the moment, though, was not over her colleagues' particular reaction to wing envy. Instead, it was focused on Andrew himself—though she couldn't entirely say why.

"Can you flap?" she asked, to set the diagnostic ball rolling.

"Not so good anymore," Andrew managed.

"Show me," Cassie said, blunt, professional—cold.

He raised his wings slightly, wincing. She had him continue, longer and higher than was necessary to dismiss her diagnosis of Penguinism. Her anger flared again, directed inward this time, aimed at the Cassie with the bruised neck, and head, and soul. She blamed that Cassie and this boy for their respective pains. Perhaps immersion in it would dissuade this particular self-victimizer from such foolishness in the future. Such thinking excused her cruelty, even as she committed it.

After beads of sweat had broken out along his forehead, and, it seemed, he was nearly ready to bite off his own tongue to prevent himself from screaming, Cassie said: "Okay. That's enough."

Andrew stopped trying to raise his wings, but held them where they were, demonstrating remarkable control, and equally remarkable gullibility in the face of authority.

"At ease," she said. He blinked, naïvely. "Drop 'em," she added.

Andrew let his wings fall to his sides with a sigh of relief and a small hurricane gust of air. The papers from Cassie's desk flurried about them, and she thought, for a moment, of Mr. F. and his father.

"I'm sorry," Andrew apologized. And then, as Cassie bent behind his wheelchair to pick up a memo, he flinched. "Don't hit me!" he whined.

A nurse passing by the doorway poked her head in to see what was the matter. Cassie shrugged her shoulders and wings, her hands full of the loosened lives of her patients for the week. She returned to her desk. "I'm not going to hit you," she said, surprised to realize that she was not at all confident that she could keep that promise.

His hands seemed frozen over his head, guarding. "I don't like being hit," he said.

"Well, nobody does," Cassie said, wondering if the boy was actually beyond naïve—perhaps marginally retarded. She looked at the boy, willing to concede a little—very little—sympathy.

"Andrew," she said. "Who's been hitting you?"

"Them," he said.

"Them who?"

"Them everybody," he said. "Them, those Pedestrians."

"Andrew, the only marks on you when you came to this hospital were those you had caused yourself." She showed him his chart. "There—that describes the mess you made out of your wings. And here—where it says 'Contusions/abrasions,' those were all from the fall you took, passing out from loss of blood." She paused, knitting and then unknitting her fingers, making of them an idling set of butterfly wings. She continued, the soul of objectivity. "Andrew, where are the bruises these Pedestrians left?"

He thought, his eyes welling with tears, winning nothing from Cassie except more antagonism cloaked in professional distance.

"Andrew?" she prodded.

"They don't always *hit me,* hit me," he said.

"How else *can* they hit you, Andrew?"

"They mutter things," he said. "They bump me when they don't have to. I can see it in their eyes. They're waiting, but they'll get me. They'll . . ."

"Andrew," Cassie said. "I'm a therapist, and in my considered opinion, I can assure you that the only thing in people's eyes—"

"Yes?"

"—are pupils." Pause. "Anything else that you might happen to see there, you've *put* there."

To say that Cassie was *practicing* therapy back then is to mean she was far from having gotten it right. God help her—she now thinks—she continued.

"Now, about this self-mutilation," she said. "Would you care to explain that to me? And leave out people's eyes; they're really not the problem here."

Of course, Andrew couldn't explain his kitchen surgery without talking about people's eyes. Paranoia—the diagnosis Cassie arrived at—isn't paranoia if it's justified. Which Andrew's was. Cassie, for her part, had simply assumed that Angels who already had their wings could fly above the pettiness of jealous Pedestrians. "Fuck 'em"—it was old advice and good advice and advice she'd taken herself, once she'd started thinking clearly again, after the Becky Affair. When the shit gets too deep, just fly above it. She did—she did it just about every chance she got. In her considered opinion, there were very few Angel problems flying couldn't solve—some just took a little more flapping than others.

Andrew stuttered and grew red, frustrated, as Cassie grew calm, already mentally flying off her lapse into the bad old days. She smiled at Andrew at the end of their hour, prescribing a mild sedative and fewer movies. She took an early lunch, figuring she'd earned it.

When Andrew was released from the hospital, he found he had no apartment to go back to, and no job with which to pay for a new one. He roamed the streets by day, trying to beg, but begging Angels don't do very well. Pedestrians think that Angels have it made with their wings and all, and find charity difficult. Angels generally don't like to see other Angels dragging down the community, and, likewise, find charity difficult.

One day out of the hospital, "cured" and sedated, Andrew went to bed hungry and homeless. It was February, and cold, and his bed was a park bench, out in the open, exposed to the elements, and all those eyes.

There were three boys in all, enough to overcome even a strong Angel, and plenty to keep down one on tranquilizers. They were part of a mobilist hate gang; Mr. F. was one of their members. They had cured him where Cassie failed, teaching him how to fight his fear of feathers by converting it into hatred for those who had them. Finding Andrew on his park bench, they forced a tennis ball into his mouth to keep him from screaming, and stretched duct tape over it to keep it in place. They bound his arms, legs, and wings with a series of three belts from a nearby Big-and-Tall men's shop. These were to be a major link in convicting the culprits, one of whom had charged the belts on his mother's MasterCard.

Andrew was taken to the roof of a downtown apartment building. It is widely believed that they had the complicity of the building's doorman, but such charges have not stuck. The three boys apparently carried the bound and struggling Andrew three city blocks, in through the front door, got him into an elevator, rode it to the twentieth floor, and carried him from there to the roof—all with no eyes anywhere to witness any of it. In this, Cassie was right; people's eyes weren't watching Andrew—or, apparently, watching out for him, either.

One of the boys had brought a length of rope, which he anchored to a ventilation shaft rising from the roof of the building. The rope ended in a noose, which was slipped over Andrew's head and tightened about his throat. He was taken to the edge of the roof. During their trial, Mr. F. was identified as the boy who had unleashed the belt around Andrew's wings, spinning him, and then pushed him off the edge, his hands and feet still bound.

Angels generally don't fly during the winter months. They can hop and float back down, like Cassie's patients did while skating, but full-out flight took a special kind of fool. For one thing, the clothing necessary to keep the rest of the body warm also weighs it down and makes movement difficult. Not only that, but ice crystals in the wings complicate the aerodynamics, and usually end in frostbite. Pushing Andrew off the edge of the building was therefore like tossing someone into ice water with lead weights tied to his hands and feet, and making him swim in place, and for his life.

Andrew flapped as best he could, hovering in midair in what ornithologists call the "Holy Ghost posture." The rope was still somewhat slack, but Andrew could not make it back to the roof, where one of the boys trained a pistol on him, waiting, perhaps eager for the opportunity to shoot. Andrew hovered for about an hour, during which time the skin of his wings froze, and cracked, staining the feathers first pink, then deeper and deeper shades of red. Eventually, his wings and spirit gave up; he dropped and the noose cracked his neck. By the time his body came crashing through an apartment window on the seventeenth floor, he was already dead, a victim of unrandom, mobilist violence . . .

. . . and a therapist who believed in wings and the "Fuck them" more than she believed in eyes.

. . .

Cassie had seen a lot of dead Angels in her time, but Andrew's was the first real Angel funeral she'd ever attended. The decision was not easy, feeling responsible as she did for his death. Add to that the fact that Cassie was not a big fan of Angel functions, and the decision became more difficult still. Ever since she entered practice, in fact, Cassie had made it a habit to avoid large gatherings of Angels.

She skipped the first North American Society of Angels Conference in Anaheim—billed at the time as the Angels' Woodstock, the seminal event of a generation and, as far as anyone knew, a new species. She stayed out of the local Angel bars, belonged to no Angel organizations, and didn't even go to the local Aviary, which was one of a chain of theaters that catered to Angels, with roof entrances, perch-style seating, and old silent movies, shown using hand-cranked, kerosene-lit, Angel-friendly projectors.

It was, she maintained, professional distance she was keeping; she didn't want to seem like an ambulance-chaser at the scene of an accident, drumming up business. She was one of the few Angel therapists in the country; those who needed her would find her. She also needed to avoid the possibility of running into current and former clients in the real world. Beyond the possibility of their wanting their money back, it just wasn't fair to her patients. Therapy was a private matter, and she didn't want to bungle it by putting her patients in the position of introducing her, and her relationship to them. She also didn't want to be in the position of having to ignore patients in public, and all the contradictory messages that sent.

The result, of course, was that Cassie was an Angel with essentially no Angel friends, and no real ties to the Angel community—or to the Pedestrian community, for that matter. All the Pedestrians she knew were jealous, openly or secretly; all the Angels she knew were troubled, messed-up. Without really meaning to, she came to see wings as a symptom, the smoke that meant emotional immolation. No wings, of course, meant the same thing. Her solution, finally, rested in secret places where Angels and Pedestrians didn't go, but where she did. It was a lonely life, yes, but at least she could fly. That's what Bob had always said to whatever new thing the wings drove away. Cassie understood what he'd meant.

Completely.

She also understood—now that it was too late—that the last thing in the world a therapist should specialize in is her own kind.

Andrew's funeral was one of those functions of obligation, Cassie finally decided. After all, how could she *not* attend, especially after that pathetic gesture his parents made by inviting her? Blackmail, most likely, but it worked. They probably knew about their son's inadequate treatment anyway and wanted her there to serve her with a malpractice suit. So be it. Maybe she deserved it. Hell, of course she did. Maybe they'd sue her for all the profits she'd made from *The Angel Blues.* Maybe they'd have her license. Maybe she'd have to start all over again. Maybe she'd get to start out clean.

Maybe the universe would get even for the mistake of giving her wings.

Another reason for not going to many Angel funerals was the fact that, until recently, dead Angels were too precious to stick in the ground. Things had changed, however, as the numbers grew. Gone were the days of Max, where an Angel's death touched off a bidding war for the remains. Nowadays, there were more than enough dead Angels to go around; it was a buyer's market and research facilities went back to getting their bodies the old-fashioned ways, and usually for free.

Of course, Andrew's funeral wasn't going to be just *any* old Angel funeral. Andrew was more than a victim—he was a hero. And, more than that, he was a symbol! Yes, yes—he was his parents' son, but there are some things too big for private mourning. That's what the Angels told Andrew's parents, the ones who stepped in to help out—"financially, and et cetera." And, of course, since they were picking up the tab, the Angels had the right—hell, duty!—to set the agenda. Andrew's funeral, therefore, was to be a public gesture of Angel solidarity. It was going to be a wake-up call to the Feathered Nation, and proof positive that hate was alive and well—and cocked, and aimed.

Cassie debated which was worse—having one's body claimed for science, for love, or for politics—and decided it was probably a draw. She also decided to brave the funeral, regardless of the circus it promised to be, regardless of his parents and whatever papers they might have to serve, regardless even of the fact that her going struck her, professionally, as self-destructive. Cassie needed closure, as they said in her field, and funerals were certainly good for that—if nothing else.

The weather on the day of Andrew's funeral was decidedly funereal; dark clouds rolled in a seaweed-green sky, and a steady rain dripped on all the living and the dead. A crowd stood outside the funeral parlor, jockeying to get under the canopy, while others accepted their bystander status and stood on the outskirts, rain rolling down the black skin of their umbrellas, beading up on the oil of their wings. Vendors set up shop, taking advantage of the predictable crowd. Among their wares was everything from bumper stickers—I ♥ FLYING, THE ONLY FUCK THAT'S WORTH A FUCK IS A *FLYING* FUCK, GRABBIN' SKY, FUCK GRAVITY, WINGS HAPPEN—to under-wing deodorants and assorted wing shampoos, mousses, sprays, and protein conditioners (each promising in its way to make you more Aero-*dynamic!*).

The rain, not playing favorites, fell on the vendors, too—something that was not lost on Cassie. "Thank you," she said, looking up at her old pal, the sky.

In the street, the funeral procession was already lined up alongside the curb, blue and white flags snapping from their aerials.

The crowd parted before Cassie, making her feel even more biblical than usual. She was known and was granted special privilege here, having been the only one in attendance besides Andrew's parents who actually knew the deceased while he was still alive. Cassie, for her part, would have preferred being anonymous, and dreaded the hushed, falsely respectful questions of reporters after the service. How did she feel and what did she think? "I am sad and he is dead, and I think you should leave us alone," she'd say. Or rather, she'd wished she'd have said, later, going over it, beating herself up for playing into the planners' plan.

The real question, of course, was why she was here in the first place. If the reporters had asked her that, they would have gotten something too cold for the dinnertime news. "Curiosity," she would have said. And, as crude as it may seem, the one thing she wondered about, driving to the funeral parlor, was what it was they were going to do with Andrew's wings. For those Angels who didn't end up in the lab, cremation was the interment du jour. In Andrew's case, however, the group sponsoring this shindig claimed that cremation was against his religion. When Cassie treated him, Andrew had responded negatively to her questions about religious background, and she suspected that the real objection to cremation was that it made a less effective photo opportunity. After all, it's not like you have to let out the sides of the urn for an Angel's ashes.

Cassie examined her motivations, and was sure this objective curiosity was just her way of handling, of masking the very great sense of guilt she felt over losing Andrew. So be it. Whatever works is what works in these sorts of situations, she figured, and really didn't feel like going deeper. So yes, when she entered the parlor, she went up to the casket—the *open* casket—and looked in. She looked at Andrew's face, at his (for once) untroubled brow, and realized how really young this boy was. He wasn't older than twenty, Cassie's age when she'd first grown wings. She stared at that face for a moment, looking for . . . she wasn't sure what. And yes, Andrew was on his back, and the wings rose up on either side of him, a tight fit, but a good one, framing his dead face in feathers, like ferns filling space around the roses of a bouquet. It was beautiful in its way, and completely wrong.

Wrong because Cassie was an Angel and she knew—like the other Angels there knew, but wouldn't say—that Andrew's pose was just slightly impossible, just a bit . . . unnatural. But Cassie, she was the one who was curious, so she found the mortician, got him aside, and asked.

"I'm a doctor," she began, lying, wanting to establish a professional common ground, so he could get juicy, could share the details the others weren't suited for. And he told her about the trouble they'd had with Andrew—a professional with a tricky nut he'd cracked, and was pretty damn proud of, thank you.

"Those wings," he said, shaking his head. "They were all froze up when they carted him in here. Tight," he said, demonstrating with his fist, the knuckles going marbly white. "Tight like that. Almost no good for anything. Like boards, you know?"

Cassie nodded her head. All of a sudden, she thought of Bob back at the Coop, and about the last time she'd been touched in anything like an intimate way as a Pedestrian. She blushed.

"So we go to these people who are paying for this and we go, 'You sure you don't want to cremate?' and they go, 'No.' 'Closed casket, maybe, then?' I tried, and they go, 'No,' again. 'Open casket.' So we cut 'em off."

"What?" Cassie asked, wanting to make sure she had heard correctly.

"We cut 'em off, trimmed 'em down, and tucked 'em back in, on the sides," he said. "Kind of like one of these," he said, pulling off his necktie, revealing nothing behind it but a knot and a clipping mechanism. "Kind of clever," he said. "No?" The tie dangled in his hand like something dead.

"Kind of clever," Cassie repeated, numbly, as the room spun around her. She thought of Andrew when he first came in, and how in death he'd finally been relieved of the things that got him killed. She thought of some trendy fashion shop with rows of wings with metal clips on their backs—clip-on wings, wing dickies. She saw men in pith helmets sitting on the carcass of an Angel, smoking elephant guns at their sides and bowie knives at the ready, preparing to harvest a set of wild wings.

And all of a sudden, the thing she'd chosen to help her cope wasn't working anymore. The grief and guilt and old-fashioned horror she'd left back at the office was here, in her pocket—fancy that.

"Ms. O'Connor, are you alright?" a voice asked Cassie as she walked away, dazed. It came from a female Angel, maybe twenty-five, wearing an olive green army jacket and a black armband. She introduced herself, using her Angel name, Akrasiel, which was the name of a sort of heavenly overseer from "one of those old religion books." She belonged to a militant faction of Angel activists and iconoclasts known as the Zuzu Brigade, after Zuzu's petals.

Despite a different hairstyle and some weathering about the eyes, Cassie recognized Akrasiel for who she really was: Christine J., Chapter One.

"Christine?" Cassie said.

"Akrasiel," she corrected. "I read your book," she added. "Heard about *Oprah*."

"And?" Cassie asked, having dreaded moments like this, and stayed an outsider to the Angel community because of it.

"Sucked," Akrasiel said. "You write like a Pedestrian. You're still caught up in that whole bipedal-dominated mindset, all that 'Pull yourself up by your own bootstraps' bullshit. How 'bout this? How 'bout 'Fly high and piss on their heads'?"

Cassie looked at her little militant, wondering how responsible she was for her. Take two fuck-thems and call me in the morning? Brother! She should be in jail; they should yank her license and she should do time.

"Chris, I mean, Akrasiel," Cassie tried.

"My Angel friends call me Crazy for short," Crazy said.

"Craze," Cassie started, and stopped. "Can I just call you Chris?" she asked. "That's who I knew you as . . ."

"I figured you'd have a hard time calling me Crazy," Chris said. "Bad vibes, and all."

"So," Cassie said, forcedly casual. "How are things with the family?"

"I fucked 'em, like you said," Chris said. "And they fucked back. Kicked me out. I was kinda homeless for a while."

"I'm sorry . . ."

"Oh, it's okay," Chris said. "The Zuzu people found me. They're a trip. They told me what I'm—*we're*—all about."

"Namely?"

"Armageddon," she said.

"What?"

"Armageddon," she repeated, underlining the point with a blunt finger to one of the softer parts of Cassie's chest.

"Ouch," Cassie said. "That hurts," as Crazy kept her finger dug in, and twisted it.

"Good," she said. "The truth's supposed to. And that's what Armageddon's gonna be about. Good, evil . . . the big showdown. Us Angels are the chosen ones. And the Peds—boy, do they got a trip coming! In about a year, they're gonna start growing things, only it's gonna be horns and tails, and then there's gonna be this big ape-shit war . . ."

"Crazy," Cassie said, finding the nickname easier this time. "Who's telling you this stuff?"

"Bob," she said. "I mean, Gabriel. He's over here someplace. Hey, Gabe—over here," she shouted.

Gabriel approached—Gabriel being Bob from Cassie's Coop days. He was decidedly heavier than when she'd last known him, and now sported the same sort of getup as Crazy.

"Bob?" Cassie said.

"Cassandra!" Bob said, wrapping his arms around her and giving her a big bear hug, Angel-style.

"What kind of shit are you telling these kids?" Cassie asked in a whisper as their cheeks pressed together.

"Fire and brimstone," Bob whispered back. "It's a great scam. I'm doing it to get laid."

Cassie disengaged herself and gave him the once-over. This was not the Bob she'd known. He'd put on at least a hundred pounds, which couldn't bode well for his flying career. "What happened?"

Bob patted his stomach. "The love of assorted good women," he said. "By the way, have you heard about Angel TV?"

"Huh?"

"Angel TV," Bob repeated. "It's this new thing they've got. Sony makes it. It's Angel-friendly. You wear this thing that looks like a blood pressure cuff around your arm and plug it into the TV. It makes something they call antistatic. I can't tell you how good it is to see *Matlock* again."

"Bob," Cassie said, dumbfounded. "You're dating *and* watching TV? Whatever happened to flying?"

Bob tensed. "Different topic, please."

"Don't tell me you don't fly anymore," Cassie said, incredulous.

"Different subject," Bob repeated.

Cassie turned to Akrasiel, who'd tucked herself under Bob's wing. "Crazy, is he telling me . . . ?"

"He's saving himself up for Armageddon," Crazy said. "He's not gonna fly again until God needs him."

"That's right," Bob said, patting Crazy's head, and searching for something like understanding in Cassie's eyes. "When hell gets icy, I'll be there."

"There you are!" a pair of voices called from behind Cassie. She turned to see a middle-aged Pedestrian couple—Andrew's parents. Cassie offered her hand, dreading whatever legal paperwork might be slipped into it. Instead, she got slightly aging flesh—first the father's hand, then the mother's.

"We really want to thank you for coming, Dr. O'Connor," the father said.

"We've seen your book," the mother said.

"And *Oprah,*" the father added, nudging.

"Yes," the mother agreed. "And *Oprah.* And when Andy said that you'd been his doctor—he called us, you see. He hated phones but he called us. He needed money. He was always needing money."

"That's right," the father continued. "We didn't know that famous doctors could have patients that weren't anybody special. I mean, he had the wings, but so many people have them now."

Cassie waded into the stream. "Your son wasn't not anybody spec—" she began, and stumbled. She righted herself, "I mean, your son *was* somebody special."

"Well, to us, of course," the father said.

"And now that he's gone, to all these other people," the mother added.

"I mean . . . ," Cassie began, and she realized that she didn't know what else to say.

"Yes, dear?" the mother asked.

"Go on," the father added.

Cassie looked about the room, hoping for an excuse. "I think the service has started," she said. "I have to get my seat."

"Oh, sit with us," the mother said. "We'd be honored." Andy's father took Cassie by the elbow, almost as if he were leading his own daughter down the aisle. He escorted her to the front, his wife trailing behind. The row of folding chairs faced away from the coffin, Angel-style, except for two that faced it. Andrew's parents took the two facing chairs and offered the backward chair next to them to Cassie.

"Andy taught us that about the chairs," the father said.

"He was a good boy," Cassie said, straddling the chair, wrapping her arms around the front. The comment surprised her; it was sincere and came easily enough, by itself.

Both parents nodded, and smiled as best they could, their own years-old judgment confirmed now by somebody famous.

The rest of the funeral was one long proselytizing session, aimed, it seemed, at making those Angels who still fed into the whole "bipedal-dominated thing" see what the rest of the Angel world had been living with for years. Eulogists mentioned Andrew the person for a minute, a minute and a half, before launching into Andrew the cause, borrowing the oratory and dreams of this or that pioneer for this or that liberation movement. A spokes-Angel for the Zuzu Brigade defended their practice of breaking into churches and museums to vandalize the host of angelry there by comparing these to black lawn jockeys, to the managers and fans of professional sports teams who saw nothing wrong in ridiculing the cultures of Native Americans. Yes, they broke into houses on Christmas and dragged out the trees and burned them on the lawns, but what would you do with a holiday that saw itself as an excuse to shove a pine branch up your ass?

And so it went, all assembled harking to these herald Angels' rants. Tears were shed, some of them real. Fists were aimed skyward, at the fictional Old Country of the Angels' kind. And Cassie steeled herself against it all, feeling like she was on trial, part of the problem instead of the solution, the author of Angel books that became Pedestrian best-sellers—in short, a traitor to her people.

Then Crazy—Akrasiel—took the lectern, a sad crumpled wad of paper in her hand, ripped from a spiral notebook. She read Andrew's name aloud, and the date that he died. She read another name and another date. And another and another. She said nothing of these names, these dates, beyond putting them there before the group, raw as the reality behind them. Name after name they came, relentless, each a nail, each a bullet, each a blunt finger, pointing, digging, hurting.

Like the truth's supposed to.

After the service, Cassie looked about for Crazy, to tell her how her speech had moved her. The room, though, was a sea of turned heads and feathers, none particularly familiar, none particularly strange. Cassie regretted that she was not taller, went up on tiptoes, and finally stood on her chair, trying to get a better view.

What she saw made her get down from her chair and sent a panic through her. In the back of the crowd, moving its way toward her, was a cellophane-covered New Year's Eve party hat.

"Shit," Cassie muttered, wondering what to do.

"Excuse me, dear," Andrew's mother said, searching through her purse for a dry handkerchief.

Cassie placed a hand on the woman's shoulder, patted it distractedly, and said, "I've got to go."

"So soon?" the father said. "We're having the wake in the back hall."

"I've got an appointment," Cassie lied. She looked up and the hat was getting closer. She realized that she was having trouble breathing.

"It's an emergency," Cassie added, and pushed her way into the crowd.

How? she wondered, assuming many things, among them that the person wearing the hat had died well over a year ago. She hadn't always thought that, of course. In fact, she thought that he'd end up as one of her clients, but when one week, and then another went by, she assumed that his injuries were worse than she'd thought, that the suicide attempt had actually been a success. And now this—not only does the jumper live, but he's apparently taken up stalking.

"Excuse me, pardon, watch it, sorry . . ."

Cassie forged on but seemed to have hit a head wind on her outbound flight. And still the hat drew closer.

Oh, this was absurd, Cassie thought. I'm a grown woman and a professional and famous, by all accounts and—why am *I* running? Because of John Lennon, the answer came back—and Cassie admitted, she had to agree.

Finally, at the door, Cassie paused to catch her breath and . . .

A hand grabbed the sleeve of her suit coat. She shrieked, looked at the sleeve and hand, and noticed that it was younger and smaller than she had expected. When she looked to see to whom it was connected, she found a teenage boy, perhaps fourteen, and a Pedestrian. On his head sat the hat that had been stalking her, nearly as festive as when she'd first tried it on well over a year ago.

"Are you Cassandra O'Connor?" the boy asked.

"Yes?" Cassie said, looking at the boy somewhat bemused, wondering about the seriousness of his expression, a regular junior G-man.

"Can I see some ID?" he asked.

"Why yes, Officer," Cassie laughed, fishing out her hospital identification card. "I only had one gin-and-tonic . . ."

The boy looked at the badge and back at Cassie. He seemed satisfied and returned the badge. He stuck out his hand for her to shake. She did.

"Pleased to meet you, ma'am," he said, and then, "We were impressed with your performance on *Oprah*." Cassie noticed the boy stuff a scrap of paper—his script—into his pocket. His other hand was still pumping away at hers.

"Can I have my hand back, Officer?" Cassie asked.

"Yes, ma'am," the boy said. "Good day, ma'am." And with that, the boy, and hat, disappeared.

It was when Cassie fished her ID out of her suit-coat pocket to return it to her wallet that she found the thousand-dollar bill. Across the dead president's face was written a date nearly two months into the future, followed by a time and a downriver address. On the back of the bill, someone had scribbled, "Thanks in advance."

He signed it "Zander Wiles."

Part Four

Seagull Tag

14

*N*ot that it was the world's business, but when Zander Wiles disappeared the place he disappeared to was a Detroit suburb known as Riverton. A one-time feeder community for an auto industry that stopped needing it, Riverton was pretty close to the last place you'd expect to find Angels of either the earthly *or* the heavenly variety. Bars, tattoo parlors, backyard repair shops, resale, gun, and liquor stores—all these things you could find. Easily. Unlike the center of town, which was lost in the noise of fast-food drive-thrus, 7-Elevens, and a string of greasy spoons that closed and reopened with new names, new menus, but with the same old baseball bat under the register, duct-taped and just out of sight.

Of course, as any Angel can tell you, first impressions can be deceiving. Riverton had its woody parts, too—parts where the streets stopped and the mud roads began, where the skeletons of barns replaced the neon of bars, and where century-old cemeteries gave equal time to pines and one-word headstones, reading MOM, DAD, and ME. It was this other Riverton that Zander had chosen as his home, and, when he was still going out, these cemeteries were the places he went, late at night. They struck him as the proper sort of place for an Angel to go, to collect his thoughts, to be alone, the sort of place it was easy to just . . . *be,* and where the sighing pines took all the words out of his mouth.

To Cassie, Riverton was just a spot on the map she passed through on her way to the Detroit River—back when she still allowed herself such treats. It was a couple of exits off I-94, somewhere near the airport. She couldn't recall anything in particular to recommend the place, as she looked down at the thousand-dollar bill with its Riverton address and that name—the one she thought she should know, but couldn't quite place.

"Zander Wiles?" she mused, out loud and on purpose, within earshot of Bob.

"You mean Judas," he said.

"What?"

"Benedict Arnold," Bob added, spooning egg salad onto his buffet plate. "Pandora. The Antichrist . . ."

"What the hell are you talking about?"

"Alexander Wiles was the one who spilled the beans about Angelism," Bob explained, tastelessly skewering a chicken wing at the same time.

Cassie missed the point and said so.

"He's the guy we blame for getting the whole Vampire thing started," Bob clarified, adding a dollop of mashed potatoes to his already crowded plate.

"We?" Cassie said, tagging along behind, her plate empty. "Who's this *we?*"

"The Angel community," Bob said, reaching for the Jell-O. "The Feathered Nation." He paused.

"Us," he concluded, with an unflattering, toothy smile.

Cassie's feathers bristled; Bob's "us" didn't include her and they both knew it.

"Jesus Christ, Bob," she said, deciding that holding back her anger wasn't worth the ulcer. "What gives you the right to speak for everybody, like some right-wing Nazi wacko who—"

"Watch the wing stuff, Cass," Bob whispered back, icily, cutting her off. "It's considered a mobilist slur." He looked around for who might be listening. "We're the worst with our own kind."

"Meaning?"

"Meaning," Bob said, "rumors spread. Clients come . . . and clients go."

Cassie looked at Bob, at the arrogant balloon he'd become. He was actually threatening her. All she did was mention Zander's name, and a black curtain dropped, forcing everybody to choose sides. She handed Bob her empty plate and stepped out of line.

"Whatever you say, Bob," she said, turning to leave, and then turning back again. She reached a hand toward Bob's oversized shoulder, intending a pat, a squeeze, something good-natured, in parting. But she couldn't quite manage it. Stopping, she pulled back. "See ya," she said, finally, the lie being as much as she could muster out of nostalgia for her old Coopmate.

Originally, she had planned to ask his opinion about Zander's peculiar invitation, and whether paying him a visit was a good idea. Now she realized it wasn't worth the bother. His answer would be no. No, because Zander wasn't "Angelically correct," wasn't part of the club, and wouldn't join one that would have him as a member.

Cassie paused, realizing with a smile that she liked that idea. It reminded her of not being from Cedar Run, and she liked it a lot.

Stepping outside to where her old buddy the sky was back to being blue, Cassie closed the door on all those self-righteous featherdusters. She wouldn't be bullied; she wouldn't be peer-pressured. She'd see whomever she wanted to see, starting with Zander, the Antichrist. Maybe she'd even join that club of his—the one you joined by not joining.

The "nonmembers only" club.

As her car left the pavement and started pulling through the mud of Kresge Road, Cassie remembered the first time she flew over water. God, she loved that feeling. The sudden slip from fighting turbulence into that ecstatic, frictionless glide! That better-than-sex feeling of total release. This shift was just like that shift.

Well, almost.

Just like it, but in reverse.

And she wondered about that. Was this—what she was doing—was it going forward or backward? Given the success of her career, the fraud it was built on, and the guilt she felt for its being that way, Cassie decided that it really didn't matter. Maybe she should just concentrate on the client this time, and screw the career. That'd be nice, she thought, for a change.

Pulling into the drive, Cassie's wheels crunched through gravel in low gear as she wound through a stand of pines that circled the property, closing it off from the road. The driveway stopped just behind the farmhouse and in front of the skewed remains of a barn, weather-bleached and sagging, only a cough shy of collapse.

Cassie slammed the car door and three pigeons exploded through a hole in the barn's roof. Not meaning it to—willing it *not to*—Cassie's heart rose with the three as they pumped their way earnestly across the sky, over the tops of the pines, away and gone.

Fuck, she thought. Fuck me for having an appointment, and driving instead of flying. She looked at the sky. Fuck it, too, for being blue—and so calm while her heart raced in spite of herself.

Of course, Cassie couldn't have chosen otherwise. Flying a long-distance hop like the thirty-plus miles from Ann Arbor to Riverton would have meant full flying togs—meaning a headband and tennis shoes, a water bottle, those Claude-Rains-as-the-Invisible-Man sunglasses (with that dorky security strap), salt pills, a mentholated cough drop in her mouth all the way to prevent dry throat, a Tums to nix the acid indigestion from all that swallowed air, earplugs to prevent whistling, jogging pants, and sweatshirt. Flying would have also meant flight sweat, spreading in moons under her armpits, at her crotch, running like tear tracks under her wings, and glistening up every string and vein in her neck—not a very pretty sight. And definitely not the sort of first impression you wanted to make when you were . . . what was she supposed to be doing again?

Oh yeah . . . meeting a patient.

Or, maybe a patient.

She hadn't decided, and Zander hadn't asked. They hadn't been formally introduced as of yet. As of yet, Cassie was still standing in his driveway, dressed in her suit jacket from the office, holding a briefcase in one hand and shielding her eyes with the other.

"It's just a patient," she scolded herself.

"It's just a house call," she added. "Nothing out of the ordinary . . ."

Except that I don't *do* house calls, she thought, looking back at her car and wondering what excuse she might make for just getting in it now and driving away. This wasn't just any ordinary consult, she knew. And she knew, too, that it was about more than Zander's reputation. She was panicking; her palms were sweating. And it was all because of that hat, and that night, and the high likelihood that Cassie and Zander *had* already met. Of all the suicide attempts she'd treated, this was the only one she'd seen, firsthand.

Other than her own, of course.

And here she was, doing it again—that thinking-too-much thing. Cassie shook her head and knocked on the front door.

She waited. Nothing.

She knocked again. Checked the time, date, and address on her thousand-dollar note. She looked back at the car. She took off one of her high heels, raised it like a hammer, and prepared to knock one more time when she stopped short. From inside, tennis shoes squeaked across a varnished floor; the handle turned; the door opened; and Cassie was face to face with . . .

. . . the kid from the funeral parlor. Again.

This time, however, he wasn't wearing the party hat or Sunday-school suit. Instead, he wore an AC-DC T-shirt, stained with grass, a pair of cut-off jeans, and tennis shoes without the socks. He was sweating and had grass clippings sticking to his bare legs. He considered her for a moment through the screen door and mopped his forehead with the back of his arm. Turning toward the hallway behind him, he called: "Hey, Mom! She's here. Tell Mr. Z. that lady from *Oprah*'s here!" He pushed open the screen door and stepped aside. "Come on in," he said. "Take a load off."

Cassie stepped inside, wondering about the relationship between Zander and the boy. A son wouldn't call his dad Mr. Z., which meant he was probably just some neighbor kid who did odd jobs, like cutting the lawn or shoveling snow off the porch, or wearing party hats to funeral parlors and handing out thousand-dollar bills. Cassie respected that, his not pocketing the money for himself. She smiled, and he looked back at her like teenagers generally will at smiling adults—like they're crazy.

"Mom," he called again. "Didja hear me?"

The woman called Mom approached from behind, wearing an apron that read WELCOME TO DETROIT . . . WHERE THE WEAK ARE KILLED AND EATEN. She noticed Cassie noticing the apron. "From him," she said, scrambling her son's hair. "For Mother's Day. He thinks it's funny." The woman wasn't much taller than her son, and was somewhere between thirty and thirty-five, Cassie judged. She wore single-vision wire-rims and short hair that curled in the heat.

Both mother and son were wingless.

"Well it sure beats 'Supper's On,' " Cassie said, finally, trying to make conversation.

"My name's Delores, by the way," Delores said. "You can call me Del."

"Okay," Cassie said. "Del. I'm Cassandra. Cassie."

"Okay."

And for a moment, the two women just stood there in the doorway, uncomfortably silent, sizing each other up. Del broke the ice.

"You look just like you did on *Oprah,*" she said. "Only prettier."

Cassie blinked. She hadn't been called pretty in . . . she couldn't remember the last time. For her patients, her relative prettiness or nonprettiness was not an appropriate issue for discussion. To her agent, publisher, and publicist, as long as she made a pretty penny, she was doing her job. And as far as other folks—well, there weren't a whole lot of other folks. Or *any,* to be more precise. She wasn't part of the Angel scene; she wasn't part of the Pedestrian scene; and she wasn't part of that scene that liked to mix scenes. What Cassie did was patients, book signings, and *Oprah.* Other than that, she flew; and other than that . . . there was no other than that.

So: "You think so?" Cassie said, blushing almost immediately.

"Oh yeah," Del said. "You're a looker. But you don't need to worry. Mr. Z. ain't looking, if you know what I mean. He ain't doing much of anything, which is why I 'spect he asked you here."

"Mr. Z.," Cassie said. "You mean Zander?"

"Yeah, Mr. Wiles," Del said. "He owns this dump and I clean it, cook his meals, and Jason—my son—he keeps the city off Mr. Z.'s back by keeping the yard up."

"And Mr. Z.—Zander," Cassie said. "What does he do?"

"Lies around in the kitchen, mainly," Del said. "C'mon, I'll introduce you guys."

Del showed Cassie to the kitchen, where they found Zander, lying on his back in a hammock, his wings poking through two holes cut in the bottom. He wore pajamas and was feigning sleep as Cassie entered; the New Year's hat was perched over his face, and echoed his barely credible snore. The hammock was slung a bit low, and Cassie noticed that his dangling wings had buffed a shiny spot on the linoleum.

"Mr. Z.," Del said. "Quit playing. Your guest's here."

Zander roused himself and removed the hat, but otherwise did nothing in the way of sitting up. He stared at the ceiling, and raised his arms, halfway. He cleared his throat, while Del and Jason stepped to, each grabbing an arm with one hand and with the other extricating a wing, being careful not to snag any feathers. After a minute of this, during which he did absolutely nothing to aid the process, Zander was sitting on the edge of the hammock as if it were a park swing, his bare feet stretched in front of him and crossed at the ankles.

"Good evening," he said.

"It's barely noon," Cassie said.

"Doesn't matter, really. Day, night. It's all the same. All needs killing."

Cassie studied his face. It was leaner than she remembered, the eyes darker and the stubble that covered his chin now a respectable beard. Still, Cassie knew it was him—the man from Wyandotte Steel.

"It's you, isn't it," Cassie said, bluntly.

Zander waved the housekeeper and her son out. "It depends on what you mean by 'me,' " he said. "I've been a lot of different people. Where'd you say we met again? Paris, was it?"

"Wyandotte Steel," Cassie said, again bluntly.

"Oh, *that,*" Zander said, dismissing it. "I guess I fucked that one up, eh? Live and learn . . ."

"That's a pretty casual attitude about suicide, Mr. Wiles," Cassie said, floating a test balloon.

Zander's eyes flashed, and his voice went up two clicks. "Who said *anything* about suicide?"

"I was there," Cassie said, professional, calm. She knew this territory. "I saw," she said. "You jumped."

"Yeah?" Zander said, rising to his feet. "Well, I was there, too. I think I get to decide what it was."

"So," Cassie said, "what was it?"

"You like simple answers, don't you?" Zander said, beginning to pace. "I read that book of yours. Total crap! A bunch of no-brainer head cases, individually wrapped for our protection. Yes-no, good-bad, heads-or-tails . . ." He stopped pacing and stared at Cassie. "Well, what do you do when it's not that simple?" he asked. "What do you do when there's no single right answer?" He waited, arms folded, foot tapping impatiently, while—belying it all—his wings hung off his back, dragging on the floor like the ears of a sad dog.

Cassie shrugged. "Fuck it?" she asked, wincing slightly.

It was a total long shot.

It worked.

"Oh yeah," Zander smiled, his wings pricking up. "I *did* like Chapter One."

"So," Cassie said, pushing forward, "about Wyandotte Steel . . ."

Zander still chuckled over Chapter One and acted like he hadn't heard her. "Hey," he said, suddenly, and with great urgency, "are you mooned?" He made it sound like he was asking if she was going steady.

"What?" Cassie asked.

"Are you mooned?" he repeated, angrier now. "M-O-O . . ."

"I heard you," Cassie said. "I just don't understand."

"*Mooned,*" Zander said once more, grabbing her by the arm and forcing back the sleeve. He looked at the unbroken skin of her arm. Birthmarks. A vaccination scar.

"What are you looking for?" Cassie asked, once he released her arm and she'd rolled down the sleeve.

"This," Zander said, rolling up his own sleeve, revealing a series of crescent-shaped scars. "Do you have any of these?"

Cassie shook her head no, meaning not so you'd notice.

"They're called moons," he said, rolling his sleeve back down. "Makes 'em sound almost cute." He paused. "I don't trust mooned Angels. They're . . . touchy."

"I see," Cassie said, meaning she was starting to.

Throughout the rest of that first session, Cassie tried to get Zander to return to the subject of Wyandotte Steel, and whether or not he had tried to kill himself. The nearest she got was a story about what happened after she left, and why she hadn't seen him as a patient earlier.

"I came to in the ambulance," Zander said, "and one of the first things I see is that—*this*—stupid hat. I'm lying on my stomach, and my wing hurts, and some guy's got his hand on my head like he's taking my temperature. I can hear the rain pounding on the roof and the tires tearing up the pavement, and all of a sudden it dawns on me what I'm *not* hearing.

" 'Ah, shouldn't there be a siren or something?' I ask, and the guy holding my head goes, 'Oops,' and 'Hey, Mike, you forgot again . . .'

"Now, I know what they do to Angels in hospitals, so I go, 'Hey, Mike, wait a sec,' and then I explain my proposition. See, I had some money on me, and it beat going out the back way and rolling down West Jeff on a busted wing, so . . ."

"You *bribed* the ambulance people?" Cassie interrupted.

"Yeah," Zander said. "It didn't take much. We went to Dunkin' Donuts and had some coffee. Mike got this big-ass bear claw and I had some cinnamon thingy, and Pete—"

"It doesn't matter what you had," Cassie said.

"Well, see, that's where you're wrong, Doc," Zander said. "I had to concentrate on everything that *wasn't* my wing—you know, to get outside the pain? And I had to drink that coffee and eat that donut and chat it up with Mike and Pete so they'd feel okay about taking the money, and like I was good to go."

"I see."

"I should have had them take me home. Shit, I was paying enough. But no. No, I just had them leave me in the parking lot, like a stud. And it's a good thing it's raining, too. That way, they can't see my tears when Mike claps me on my bad wing and says, 'Take it easy, man.' Then they just split and I walk to the corner and . . ." He paused. "You ever try to hail a cab in the middle of Detroit with wings on your back?"

"I've got a car," Cassie said.

"Sweet," Zander said, smirking.

"Well, anyway," he said, returning to the story, "it seems the cab guys figure that Angels should just *fly* wherever they need to go. Which means an Angel flagging down a cab is looking for something other than a ride, if you know what I mean."

Cassie nodded her head.

"So, flash on this: Me. Wings, one bad. Rain coming down to beat the band. West Jefferson and I'm walking down it, and these things will only bead up so much water before they start taking it on and boy, do they get heavy. So I got these waterlogged wings hanging off me, my hair's plastered down like shit, I'm crying nonstop now from the pain, can't hardly see nothing, and every cabby this side of Beirut is zipping by me, sending up these tidal waves like West Jeff is one of them thunderboat races. And I end up walking like that for five miles through Detroit's finest until this bus finally comes by and I almost get bounced off because I don't have exact change. I gotta let the asshole driver keep a whole twenty, and it's just me and him, and he's suddenly all smiles. I'm looking at the back of the guy's turban, and he's looking at my hat in the mirror, and he says, 'Are we having a nice New Year's, Mister?' And I say, 'No. Not so far. Not by a fucking long shot.' "

"And your wing?" Cassie asked. "Who set your wing?"

"I sent Jason out with one of those three-zero notes," Zander said. "He rustled up this plaster-happy quack and . . ." He stopped.

"And?" Cassie prodded, though she had a pretty good idea what plaster-happy meant.

"And nothing," Zander said. "Do Wednesdays work for you? I'm free, like, always, but . . . you've got other patients and it's a long haul from Ann Arbor, so . . ."

"But we haven't discussed what you want . . ."

"Cool," Zander said, ignoring her. "Next Wednesday, then." He whistled for Delores to show Cassie out.

"I'm in no hurry," Cassie protested, as Del took her arm. "Really."

"But *he* is," Del whispered. "He's already blown a whole week's charm, just on you," she added, pushing Cassie through the door, and then closing it.

Maybe it was the birds flying out of Zander's barn, but ever since she'd left the Wiles place, Cassie had this incredible urge—this *need*—to fly. It was a nice summery day in the middle of the week, and it was an incredibly irresponsible thing to do, but as she approached the exit for 23 off I-94—her exit—Cassie swerved into the center lane and kept going, deciding then and there to take the interstate all the way up to Lake Michigan. She'd get a room for the evening and, first thing in the morning, before anyone else got up, she'd fly as far as she could out over the lake. She'd ride those glass-steady thermals up and up; she'd let the morning air clear her head like a cup of strong coffee, and . . . she'd think about things. Finally. For once.

So much had happened lately, there'd been no time to just take stock and relax. She deserved to, she decided; she owed it not only to herself, but to her clients. She wasn't doing them any good, being all stressed out. She'd get recharged, put this Andrew thing behind her and start over fresh. She realized with a start that she hadn't flown anywhere since Andrew's death.

Punishment behavior—that's what it was. And she knew what she'd tell a patient in that position: Don't. It wasn't your fault. Take a break. Go flying.

Cassie smiled at herself in the rearview mirror—a little ironically, a little seriously—thinking: I'm good at this therapy business. Damn good.

Still smiling, she hit the gas, to see whether or not she could make time go faster.

The beach was perfect. The sand was perfect. Cassie's bare feet and rolled pants were perfect. And the dawn—the dawn was especially perfect, with the dark blue of night still hanging on, the sky cloudless, the breeze warm and clean, the moon just a sliver and hanging there, rippling on the surface of the lake, while slices of violet, then red, then orange broke along the horizon. And Cassie was the only member of the audience—it being the middle of the week, after all, and practically the middle of the night, still, by vacationers' standards.

She'd picked her launch site after arriving the day before—a water tower in the middle of the tourist trap where she was staying. And her pockets were full of Wonder bread balls, trimmed and squashed from the loaf she bought last night. Everything on her, in fact, she'd bought last night—the sweatshirt and sweatpants, even the socks and shoes she was busy slipping back into. Heading toward the water tower, she noticed a seagull hovering overhead. She smiled and fished a bread ball from her pocket, launching it straight up. The bird caught it with a jerk, in flight, tipping its head back and pumping as it worked the morsel down and kept flying.

"There's more where that came from," Cassie shouted after the bird. "Tell your gullfriends," she added, and laughed—another thing she hadn't done in an awfully long time.

It was while flying over the lake, working on her altitude, that Cassie came to a few big decisions. She'd been thinking about Andrew, and all the things she'd stopped doing to punish herself for a crime nobody believed in but her. She decided that Zander, the Angels' Antichrist, was going to be her ticket back to serious therapy. With him, she'd give up easy answers; she'd get this one right. She'd clean the slate as blank as this brittle blue sky, and Zander's redemption would be her redemption.

But for the moment, she'd stop thinking and play in earnest.

For the no one watching in the half light of dawn, Cassie made her figure eights and arabesques, tumbled for fun, and broke into a glide. Hearing their baby cries overhead, she improvised a game of tag with the seagulls, letting out luscious cries of her own. Finally, catching up to one, she stretched out her fingers to pet the feathers of its fantastic head. And it let her, trusting her like a family dog would. On the ground, the same bird would have broken into flight at anything like the same gesture. Here, though, it was different. She'd earned something by breaking free of the dirt. Here, the birds trusted her, and that had to be a good thing.

She scratched the gull behind where she imagined its ears might be, while the great bird stretched back its neck muscles with more luxury than Cassie thought possible. And when the bird took a bread ball from the palm of her hand, it felt right. It felt like . . . forgiveness, and was perfect, too.

15

"You've got a car," Zander said, not giving Cassie a chance to "get professional" first.

"What?"

"You said it last time," Zander said, already up and sitting on the edge of his hammock. "You said you didn't take cabs, you have a car."

"It's a Honda," Cassie said. She popped open her briefcase, which contained her lunch, a pair of folded sweats, and the legal pad she was looking for. "So?"

"I'll bet it's red."

"No, blue," Cassie said, making a mental note always to get the first word in during sessions with this one. He was into control and liked diverting her. "But I don't see—" she began, trying to steer the conversation in a more therapeutic direction.

"I'd like to see it," Zander cut in. "I'd like to see how they customize it for an Angel."

"It's not," Cassie said, a bit too quickly, thrown off guard by Zander's use of the word "customize." Regaining her balance, she continued. "I mean, it's not like it's got mag wheels or anything. The front seat's just a little different. They're buckets, except the driver's side—well, I guess you could order both, but mine's just the driver's side—it's got this padded pole instead of a full back. The pole rides between your wings—"

"Sounds kinda kinky," Zander said.

"Well, it's not too comfortable, and they say it'll be the first thing to kill me in a crash, so I drive carefully," Cassie lied. "I'm getting soaked for insurance, of course."

"I'd like to see it," Zander said.

"Well, it's just outside. C'mon."

Zander froze. "No thanks," he said. He went to the kitchen cabinet and pulled out a Polaroid camera. "Here," he said. "Shoot the roll and we'll watch 'em develop in here."

"Oh," Cassie said, accepting the camera and realizing, finally, what it was she'd be treating Zander for. She couldn't believe she'd missed the clues the last time.

"Agoraphobia," she said, heading to her car. "That's what it's called."

"What is?"

"What you've got," Cassie said, hefting the camera with one hand, as if she were checking for a hernia. "Fear of open spaces. It's called agora-phobia."

Zander—summed up so neatly—smiled as artificially as he could manage. "Sounds like a fear of sweaters," he said, before adding: "Friend-o-phobia."

"What?"

"That's what you've got," he said. "The fear of having another Angel ride in your car." He paused.

"It costs more to have both seats changed," Cassie said, defensively.

"Yep," Zander said, as Cassie left to take his pictures. "Serious case."

"Agoraphobia is also known as the 'calamity syndrome,' " Cassie ex-plained during her third visit, a Saturday. After a brief power struggle, she and Zander had agreed to weekend sessions, Cassie explaining that it was less jarring to her schedule that way. The reality was she'd taken to using her Tuesdays and Wednesdays for middle-of-the-week jaunts to Lake Michigan. Weekends were a bad time for such trips, with the beaches filled with tourists and no small number of her fellow Angels. Early mornings in the middle of the week were the only way to get the privacy Cassie needed.

"The panic attacks normally associated with the syndrome can come as a delayed response to some crisis, such as the loss of a loved one, a long hospitalization, et cetera," she explained. "Or they can be the result of a less focused, but nonetheless pernicious accumulation of stress and anxiety. The attacks are just your nervous system going through a test of its emergency broadcast system; the body and mind are stressed, the nervous system senses this and goes on full alert, which is why your palms begin to sweat, your heart races, and your breathing accelerates. It might feel like a heart attack, like you're dying, but you're not."

"And your practical experience in this area is?" Zander asked.

"Do you mean, have I ever had a panic attack before?" Cassie asked.

"Yes."

"No," she lied. A therapist should be a symbol of strength, after all.

"So, your practical experience is zilch," Zander said. "What we're discussing here is . . . *theory.*"

"There are hundreds of thousands of agoraphobics in this country alone," Cassie said, resting her chin on the back of a kitchen chair, while her wings held themselves uncomfortably, just inches from the floor. "It's one of the most common phobias there is. I've read the case studies. I'm . . ." She paused. She wanted to say that she wasn't a hack, that she had no intention of screwing up, this time. But she couldn't get into *that* discussion; if there's one thing clients shouldn't know about their therapists, it's whatever personal agenda they may have, above and beyond helping their clients.

"So," she said, beginning again, "can you think of any recent sources of stress in your life?" She looked up from her notepad.

Zander, sitting at the kitchen table opposite her, smiled slightly. The smile deepened, cracked, and then exploded into a full-out rolling laugh. He slapped the table, once, twice. He tapped out a drumroll and rimshot. He kept laughing. Finally, wheezing, he said:

"Are you *kidding* me?"

Cassie's face stiffened; she sat straight up. "It's a standard question," she said, realizing that the only word for how she felt at the moment was "miffed"—and that she *hated* that word.

Zander kept on laughing, ignoring Cassie's miffedness.

She forged on. "I'm also supposed to ask you what you'd most like to do," she said, "if you weren't cooped up in the house all the time."

Zander laughed so hard tears came to his eyes. He dabbed them away with the tips of his wings.

"I'll take 'What I'd Most Like to Do' for a hundred, Alex," he said, fighting toward a straight face. "Ah . . . What is fly?" Zander paused and tapped a finger to his lips, humming the *Jeopardy!* waiting theme. "Judges? Bing-bing-bing. Of course, the answer is flying. Show her what she gets . . ."

The not-amused look Cassie'd arranged on her face seemed to have gotten stuck. Time passed, while the laughing Zander wound down.

"Are you through?" she asked, finally. "And how much TV *do* you watch, anyway?" She'd noticed the Angel-friendly TV on the kitchen counter, the blood pressure cuff dangling at its side, just as Bob had described. She found the sight scared her. Drew her, but scared her. Of the two TV watchers she knew—Bob and Zander—both, apparently, no longer flew, and she wondered if TV was somehow at fault. She was surprised and disgusted by how easily she could see herself falling back into that habit—vegging out and glassing up in front of the tube.

"Oh, not much," Zander said. "Nine, ten hours a day. It's good company."

Cassie found herself shuddering and had to fight to stop. She returned to her original question: "Sources of stress?" she said. "And no laughing."

"Okay," Zander said. He thought. "You know," he said, "I guess I'd have to say that I've got more reasons for staying inside than anybody else I know. I mean, half the state of Georgia hates me, my mother hates me, the Angels hate me, most of the American TV-viewing audience thinks I'm scum, the DEA would like a heart-to-heart, the Vampires would love to have me for lunch, and as far as long hospitalizations go, I was wrapped up here tighter than a mummy not too long after . . . you know . . . the accident."

"Full body cast?" Cassie asked, thinking again of Andrew's over-wrapped flipper. Plaster-happy, indeed.

"Yeah," Zander said. "I don't know why. It was just my wing that was busted, but you can't argue with a doctor who does house calls, no matter how much you're paying him. I was like that for a month and a half, eating and peeing through tubes. It reminded me of when I went green and hard—you know—only this time, I got to be awake. I nearly went out of my mind. After that, I couldn't even go out at night. Then it was only certain rooms. And now, I pretty much just stay in the kitchen."

"You said, 'After that, I couldn't even go out at night,' " Cassie quoted from her notes. "Can you explain that?"

Zander began, then paused. He looked embarrassed. Suddenly, he went red and exploded: "I'm not stupid, you know! I didn't go to college, but I can read. I got plenty of time. Ask Delores—I'm always sending her to the library." He paused, and then smiled, evilly. "You know, Angels can get free books. You just rub 'em up and down your chest a few times and it clears that metal strip they sneak in there."

Cassie looked at Zander, trying to catch his eyes, so that he could register the purposefully stricken look she'd fixed there. "Zander," she said. "Look at me. What do you see?"

"You look dumb," he said and paused. "Founded, I mean. You look dumbfounded."

"Good," Cassie said. "I am. I'm dumbfounded because I never—*never*—said anything about your being stupid, or dumb, or anything."

"You implied it," Zander said. " 'Agoraphobia is an irrational fear.' *Irrational*. Unreasonable." He paused. "Dumb."

Cassie put a hand to her head, and placed the other on Zander's wing.

"Ouch!" he yelped.

"Sorry," Cassie said, backing off immediately. "I forgot . . ."

"It's been over a year," Zander said, deadpan. "It's healed." He smiled and Cassie frowned.

"Now who's dumb?" he asked.

"Founded," he added.

.   .   .

More jousting; more jockeying for position, after which Zander came up with a story to explain why he distinguished his loss of the night from his other losses.

"It goes way back," Zander said. "First, I stayed in all the time, to avoid the press and Vampires. I could go out, I just couldn't *go out*. Then that kind of blew over, and I started going out again, but in disguise. There were other Angels by then, and so I was able to blend in, kinda. But then it happened—the curse!"

"Molting?" Cassie said.

"Yeah, easy to just say that now, but when it's never happened to you before and that means it's never happened to *anyone* before . . . ," Zander said. "Well, just put yourself in my position."

"I can imagine," Cassie said. She wrote the words "molting" and "trauma" on her notepad, and drew an equal sign between them.

"I doubt it," Zander said. "When it happened to me, *I* was what passed for an authority on Angels, and there was nobody to tell me that this sort of thing just naturally happened with wings. There were no pamphlets saying not to worry, that it was cyclical and, most important, *not* fatal. I'd been an Angel for a little over a year and I thought all the changing had finally stopped, that things had settled down." Zander paused.

"Go on," Cassie said.

"I just wanted to shower a little dust and grease out of my feathers. I'd taken showers since becoming an Angel, no sweat. I liked 'em. I had one of those shower massagers, which are really great for Angels. You know, especially with all the muscle knots and shit we get."

Cassie nodded.

"The head was set to a single jet, and when it hit my wings, I exploded feathers. Black feathers plastered to the tiled walls, the plastic shower curtains, spinning around my feet and headed for the drain. I freaked totally, pushing against the water jet, trying to turn it down, only it gets jammed in power massage. And each blast of water is like something from a machine gun, ripping through my wings like bullets raking the palm trees in some jungle war flick. So I jump my ass out of the shower and end up pulling the curtains down with me. I look at the mirror on the bathroom door and my wings are Swiss cheese, with great big patches of skin showing through.

"I started puking almost immediately. My gut went nuts and I was sure this was it. I was dying. I'd worried about it in the first couple of months there, but when nothing happened, I figured it was cool. But now this. Shit! Instant cancer. Instant AIDS. Fuck, if I made it through breakfast, it'd be a miracle."

"But you didn't," Cassie said. "Die, that is."

"Matter of opinion, I guess," Zander said. "You know, there are two types of molters—droppers and thinners. The thinners are the lucky ones, losing an equal number on each wing year-round, so there's never this time when they're completely plucked . . ."

"That's the way I am," Cassie offered.

"Figures," Zander said, giving the professional his working-class smirk. "Needless to say," he continued, "I wasn't that lucky."

"I'm sorry," Cassie apologized, and Zander let her.

"You ever see what a plucked Angel looks like?"

"No."

"Trust me, you don't want to," Zander said. "All that's left are the arches. They're wrinkly and flesh-colored, with veins and knuckles. They kinda look like really long dicks, but with hinges." He paused, looking for a reaction, got nothing, and continued. "After that, I stopped going out during the day. Even after they came back, I'd get to the front door and . . . I couldn't get out. I read about that ozone hole and wondered if it had something to do with me losing my feathers. Nighttime was okay, because there was no sun and nobody to see me. I used to wander around this cemetery just down the road a bit. It's a nice place, trees and all, and quiet. Then I had my accident and . . ." He paused again.

"Go on," Cassie said. "Let's talk about the accident."

Zander closed his eyes and rested his head on the kitchen table. "I'm tired," he said in a little boy's voice. "You go home."

"Zander," Cassie tried. He began snoring. "Zander," she repeated, shaking.

"Won't do any good," Delores said, entering the kitchen. "He wants you to go now."

"Oh yeah," Cassie said, marshaling a few choice words, although the only ones to get out were: "Sez who?"

"It's almost three o'clock," Delores said, picking up the portable TV from the counter and placing it in front of Zander on the kitchen table. She rolled up his sleeve and wrapped the cuff around his arm. "It's time for *Jeopardy!*" she said, switching on the set.

Giving up, Cassie went for the door, but then forced herself to look back. Zander had lifted his head and was smiling at the set. The blue light had an embalming effect on his face, washing it out, gargoyling its features. It was a cold tableau, and it made Cassie feel cold, too.

She felt cold all the way to the front porch, in fact, right up until she stepped down. That's when she found the sun again, beaming down on her, not an ozone hole in sight.

Back at the Medical Center, Cassie had taken to spending her lunch hour loitering around the maternity ward. Angels gave birth to Angels maybe 30 percent of the time, though it was anyone's guess whether the dice would come up wings in any particular case. High-tech diagnostics were out of the question, of course, for fear of scrambling whatever fetal magnets might be growing in the mother Angel's tummy. The Wing wing of the maternity ward was therefore very nineteenth century, gaslit and hissing, and resorting to medical instruments like a paper clip dangling from the end of a thread. Cassie thought of the practice as "dowsing for Angels," and she liked it more than seemed rational.

It was the nursery that drew her the most, however. She'd eat her sandwich with her head pressed to the glass, watching the premature cupids, sleeping or squalling. They were so pathetic—part turkey, part lizard, their wings unfeathered and bunched up so tight, like little angry fists. They seemed more human than the regular human babies, and they helped Cassie understand her own rebirth a little better.

That was one theory for why she went.

Another was that the maternity ward felt like Lake Michigan—it had that kind of recharging effect. The most obvious theory she dismissed out of hand. She had a cat at home and didn't want a baby; after the trauma of her own change, she couldn't imagine getting pregnant. So no, her visits were more symbolic than maternal longing. The ward—the Wing wing—was about hope. That was the best theory. And hope was a good thing, like petting seagulls. So she saved it up, one lunch hour at a time.

And God knows, Cassie needed hope—Zander being the way he was. Take those faces he made, for example. Cassie ignored them—or tried to—as she went through her list, but there are limits to even an Angel's patience.

"Desensitization, flooding, modeling, group therapy," she said, during their next session. "These are the behavior-mod options. There's also more traditional analysis, which takes longer to work—*if* it works—but the results usually have more sticking power."

"Sticking power?" Zander asked, screwing up his face, skeptically.

Cassie looked at him. Was he challenging her? He was wearing pajamas in the kitchen in the middle of the afternoon! Who did he think he was?

"Yes, sticking power," she snapped.

Zander blinked, exaggeratedly, and smiled. He'd won a point. She saw that in his eyes.

"Meaning," she said, drawing it out, returning to the topic at hand, "the results from behavior modification don't always last. They're pretty dramatic because they aim at getting rid of the symptoms, but sometimes the symptoms come back," she explained. "My guess is we'll end up somewhere in between—a quick fix of the presenting complaint with behavior modification, and then traditional analysis to see what's underneath."

"Sounds very much like a plan," Zander said, examining his fingernails.

"Indeed," Cassie said, watching him. She made a church of her hands, and tapped the steeple against her lips, thinking. She waited.

The kitchen clock ticked, and with each tick, Cassie imagined a fresh needle tapping into a voodoo likeness of Zander. She noticed the way he held himself, always a bit fetal, always tight and guarded even in his feigned nonchalance.

"So?" Zander said, finally, abandoning his fingernails and breaking the uncomfortable silence.

"So," Cassie said. "First things first." Pause. "We need to get you relaxed."

"Relaxed?" Zander laughed. "I'm already wearing pajamas." He stretched luxuriously, and then cracked his knuckles to underline the point.

"*You're* the one wearing high heels," he added, and then flinched, as Cassie cracked her own knuckles, suddenly, and all at once.

"We need to get you relaxed," she repeated, smiling, "in both body and mind." The score was one to one.

"Close your eyes," she said.

Zander did as he was told, albeit smirking.

"Now I want you to let your body relax totally," Cassie said. "Start with your face. Feel all the muscles—the ones keeping your eyes closed, the ones keeping that smirk in place . . ."

Zander held back a laugh.

"Those muscles are working too hard. Ease up. You don't have to clench your eyes shut. This isn't a holdup. Just relax."

Zander let the muscles of his face go slack. He felt like Richard Nixon—all jowls and gravity—but he also felt better.

"And now your left foot," Cassie continued. "Clench it as tight as you can. Not the leg; that comes next. Just the foot. Tight. Tighter. And then . . . let go. Feel that tingling? Let it spread . . ."

Cassie continued, working her way through Zander's various extremities, saving his wings for last. Remembering the Angel babies in the nursery, she compared his wings to fists, holding on to, and then letting go of "that thing you love most." And she only lost her temper once, when Zander began quibbling about what—exactly—that most-loved thing might be.

"Anything," she said, in a stern whisper. "Flying."

"Can it be a person?" Zander asked, his eyes closed, his puppet limbs splayed to either side, only his wings hitched up tight, clutching their undecided love.

"Yes."

"Can the person be dead?"

Cassie opened her mouth and found it suddenly dry. She swallowed. "Yes," she said, hurriedly, trying not to lose the momentum.

"Thanks," Zander said, sincerely, as his wings let go and dissolved into the same warm pool as the rest of his body.

It was a strange thing for him to say—"Thanks"—and he hadn't said it to her before. Cassie made a note of it, and pushed on.

The next step was to suggest a tranquil image for contemplation, something for Zander to fix on, to draw out and deepen the relaxing effect of the meditation. "Imagine yourself in a boat on a lake," Cassie said, in a hushed, lullaby voice. "Imagine the sound of waves, lapping against the sides of the boat, ebbing, flowing, rocking you gently to sleep . . ."

Zander's left eye twitched.

"Imagine the dawn breaking over the water," Cassie said, "reflecting in the waves, all the colors of the rainbow . . ."

Zander's breathing changed, became shorter, faster.

"Imagine seagulls wheeling in the sky," Cassie said, "the sunlight splashing on their wings . . ."

"This isn't working," Zander said, his wings clenching back into fists.

"Imagine lying back in the boat, dangling your feet in the warm water, all your cares drifting away . . ."

"Quit . . . please . . ."

"Imagine . . ."

"I can't breathe," Zander said, panting now, his chest heaving.

"Imagine . . ."

"I . . . can't . . . *stop* . . . breathing . . . ," Zander gasped, pounding on the table with his fist to get his therapist's attention.

Cassie stopped. She'd closed her own eyes and drifted off to Lake Michigan. Opening them now, she shot back—back to the kitchen and Zander, whose face had gone paper white, whose hair hung down in sweaty spikes plastered to his forehead.

"Zander?" she said, carefully, pushing down the voice inside yelling that she'd fucked up, that she'd fucked up again.

"Zander, are you okay?"

Zander gestured for her to come closer and wheezed: "Get . . . Del . . ."

"Delores!" Cassie shouted, and the housekeeper walked in as if she'd been waiting for a cue.

"Excuse me," she said, brushing past Cassie. "Doctor," she added, gratuitously, before shaking out an empty Wonder bread bag, and then holding it over Zander's nose and mouth. The bag went tight, and then slack, in keeping with Zander's frenzied breathing.

"Hyperventilation," Del announced, once the crisis had passed and Zander was breathing normally again.

"I know that," Cassie said, defensively. "But why?"

"I thought that was *your* job," Del said, wiping Zander's face with her own handkerchief. "You're the therapist."

"I know, I . . . ," Cassie began, strangely distracted by the sight of Del's ministrations. She touched Zander's shoulder lightly, wordlessly, and he tilted his chin up so she could dry his throat. She brushed his hair back from his forehead. She . . . The woman had her whole hand inside Zander's pajama collar, her bare fingers on the skin of his chest—checking his heartbeat, no doubt. At least that'd be the excuse.

Cassie blinked self-consciously and tried again. "Does this happen often?" she asked.

"Often enough," Del said. She didn't elaborate, nor did she need to. The message was clear: Zander needed Del more than he needed Cassie—as far as Del was concerned.

Cassie watched as the housekeeper rolled up Zander's sleeve, preparing him for more TV, the cue that this week's session was over. She watched the small woman's fingers as they snapped the cuff closed, her body so close to Zander's that the metal crucifix she wore began tugging in the direction of his heart.

Feeling superfluous and suddenly embarrassed by the clunky largeness of her own wings, Cassie ducked through the doorway and left.

Weeks passed and Cassie worked her way through the various strategies, with little success. She tried reverse psychology, for example, thinking that maybe if Zander was locked in a closet with no room to spare, he'd welcome the opportunity to go outside. She gave up and unlocked the door after Zander had fallen comfortably asleep and begun snoring.

Maybe she could get him to just imagine going outside, first describing the steps, waiting for his breathing to subside, and then reinforcing with helpful, encouraging comments like, "Now that wasn't so bad, was it?" The only problem with this approach was that Zander disagreed, saying that, actually, it *was* that bad, and then threatening to hyperventilate again if she didn't stop.

"The mouth's a dangerous weapon," he told her, folding his moon-scarred arms. "Or hadn't you heard?"

So maybe it was sensory overload. Maybe if she put a paper bag over his head, or gave him earplugs and a blindfold, she could lead him about, not telling him where they were going. Maybe it would be outside, maybe it would be just some other room, maybe they'd even stay in the kitchen, maybe . . . Maybe Zander would just start screaming after the first couple of steps, to cover all the possible phobic bases.

Okay, then, modeling.

"See, I'm going out the door," Cassie said. "No harm done. Now I'm going around to the side. Everything's fine. You can do this, too. No ozone holes. No reporters, gawkers, Vampires. Just fresh air and sunshine. Now I'm standing next to my car . . ."

"Now I see you getting in and driving home for the day," Zander said. "Session's over. Time for *Jeopardy!*"

"No!" Cassie shouted this time, storming back into the kitchen, grabbing the portable TV, and throwing it to the floor.

"That's coming out of your fee, I hope you know," Zander said, looking at the shattered remains of his one constant companion.

"I don't care," Cassie said, and she didn't. At least she'd made her point.

Until, that is, Zander called for Delores. Smiling, her hands wrapped around the grips of a mover's dolly, Del entered the kitchen, wheeling a large-screen TV in front of her.

"Welcome to the big leagues," Zander said, smiling, chalking up another point.

. . .

Cassie promised herself that she'd think of something by their next session, but the week went faster than she meant it to. It was Friday and noon and she still had no idea what she'd do during her visit on Saturday. She had to plan these things, had to have an outline to stick to, to keep the game-playing and distractions to a minimum. She needed to do something to shave all those points off of Zander's score, or at least pick up a few of her own.

Shit. So much for redemption. So much for getting this one right. Cassie leaned her head against the nursery window, feeling the coolness of the glass, chewing bits of her sandwich and her own ego. And then, all of a sudden, God smiled—as She sometimes will.

The Wing wing's pediatrics section was just down the hall from maternity and they shared the same waiting area. Which explained the sirening toddler who broke Cassie's concentration, and his bewinged and bedraggled mother. The child, winged too, was on a tether and was busily mounting and then diving from the arms and backs of chairs in the waiting area. He was nowhere near flying yet, but could glide a few feet, depending upon how high he'd jumped from, and whether or not the tether's spool went that far.

Cassie's immediate reaction was to the cruelty of the restraint. How symbolic it seemed of adulthood, and its cynical repression of youthful exuberance.

But then the kid kept doing it, shrieking all the while. Over and over and over, until he was finally distracted by another waiting mother, who foolishly decided to eat a candy bar she'd brought. That's when the new game started. The one called "Mine!"

"Mine!" the boy Angel yelled, diving for the accidental bait.

"No!" his mother scolded, trying to reel him in. But he was a big boy for his age, and powerful as even young Angels are. Desperate, the mother Angel with the leashed child fished into her purse and came up with a set of keys.

"Orion," she said, jingling the keys. "Orion, lookit . . ."

Cassie watched as Orion's head pivoted; his arms shot out and his hands opened like twin starfish. "Mine!" he yelled, running for the shiny, jangly whatever-it-was his mother held.

"Prid-dee," he said, drawing out the word, as his mother petted his wings. She apologized to the other mothers, who waved it off with weak, knowing smiles. They'd been there, after all; they'd done that.

Cassie, on the other hand, got an idea.

Zander needed to leave the house and Cassie needed bait. But what could she use to compel him to get out of his hammock, leave the kitchen, push past all the fear and baggage, and actually risk stepping outside? Setting fire to the house—a thought that crossed her mind— seemed a bit drastic, at least for the time being. Food, drugs, sex—these would lure most men out, but Zander wasn't just a man, he was an Angel. That was an important difference. After all, he had the ecstasy of flight waiting for him, and still he sat on his ass, wings gathering dust, watching that goddamn TV . . .

Cassie paused. She smiled.

Bingo.

Of course, she'd need help, given the size of the thing and her reluctance to touch it. Since Delores couldn't be trusted, Cassie had Jason run an extension cord from inside the house to a tree about fifteen yards from the kitchen window, telling him to say, "Doctor's orders," when Zander asked him what the hell he was doing. Once the extension cord was set up, Cassie unfolded a lawn chair under the tree, its back facing the trunk, while Jason ran into the kitchen with the dolly. Tipping the huge TV forward and then back, Jason wheeled the cumbersome appliance out the door, while Zander yelled assorted colorful things like "Hey!" and "Goddammit!" and "I know people who kill for money." Plugging the TV in next to the tree, Jason switched it on and then straddled the lawn chair, wrapping his arms around the back, Angel-style.

"When I give you the signal," Cassie called to the boy, "start laughing your head off."

Zander came to the window to see what the two were up to, while Cassie signaled to Jason, who began laughing and pointing at the set, holding his stomach and laughing some more.

Zander's face registered no emotion. He looked down to where Cassie stood under the window. She looked up. He shrugged his shoulders, sighed visibly, and pulled down the blind.

Point, Wiles. She could just imagine him thinking that. And it pissed her off. He wasn't even trying. This was all a big game, and he . . .

Well, she could . . .

And in a gesture with more dramatic than therapeutic impact, Cassie O'Connor—celebrity, Angel, healer of minds—took a rock from the garden and smashed the window.

Jason stopped laughing, while Cassie fished her hand through the shattered window and pulled the guts of the blind through it.

"Keep this up and you'll start owing me," Zander said, moving away from the window and unplugging the extension cord. He fed it through the hole, adding, "Tell Jason his laughing lacks sincerity."

So much for not fucking up, the voice said in Cassie's head. She looked up, to God or whomever, and noticed Zander's hand poking through the window, still feeding out cord. Grab it, the voice suggested, and so Cassie did. She was desperate, after all, and didn't appreciate being made to feel that way in front of a teenage boy.

"There!" she shouted, pulling his arm the rest of the way through the jagged hole. "A sixteenth of Zander Wiles is outside and doing fine."

Zander wrestled his arm free and showed it to her from the safe side of the glass. "Zander Wiles is bleeding," he said, in rebuttal. "Your point?"

All the way home, Cassie fumed. Zander was a bastard, a prick, a son of a bitch. He was playing with her, making an ass out of her. She'd read the case studies. These things worked with other patients. He wasn't helping at all, even seemed gleeful at each new failure, building up his confidence by running hers down. Fuck him! For all she knew, he might even be faking. Maybe this was how rich Angel recluses were getting their kicks nowadays. Mess with the therapist. Drive her off the deep end and score ten extra points.

Well, *fuck* him . . .

Cassie sped past 23 and kept going. She was halfway to Lake Michigan before she even realized that was where she was headed. It was a Saturday and the place would be crowded, but so what? She'd wait until midnight if she had to.

It was, and she did.

This time, however, things were a little less perfect than her previous trips to the lake. This time, she flew out of spite, and too far, shooting past her safe point just like she'd sped past the exit to 23. This time, her guts turned to steel, her breathing turned to gasping, and she almost didn't make it back to land . . .

But even with all that, there was still a silver lining.

After all, it was as she perched on the sand of that hard-fought-for beach, hugging her knees, catching her breath, that Cassie knew what she had to do with Zander. Watching the bloated moon drop without a splash into the lake that had almost claimed her, Cassie remembered the one strategy she hadn't tried yet.

Flooding.

It was a gorgeous morning, the morning they did it. The sky was almost painfully blue, the trees thrumming loudly with cicadas. Birds were trilling everywhere and Cassie was busy in Zander's driveway, absolving Jason.

"If anything goes wrong this time," she said, "I'll take all the blame."

"What about Mom?" Jason asked. "I'm still grounded from last time."

"I'll tell her I forced you," Cassie said.

He wasn't satisfied. "I'm almost as big as you are," he said.

It wasn't true, but Cassie understood his need for an excuse that made him look better. She reached into her wallet and pulled out a fifty-dollar bill. "I'll say I bribed you," she said. "You tell her you did it to buy her a present. Think of a good one in the meantime."

Jason smiled and saluted. "Will do," he said.

"Now, you made sure he took the pill I gave you, right?" Cassie asked.

"Yeah," Jason said. "I crushed it and put it in his milk last night, just like you told me."

"And he drank it?" she asked. "All of it?"

"Yeah," Jason said. "I think it creeped him out a little, me just standing there and watching."

"Mr. Wiles can stand to be creeped out a little," Cassie said, regretting the obviousness of her hostility even as she said it. "And anyway, that's not important," she continued, righting herself. "What matters is that he should sleep through just about anything." She paused, before adding, "That doesn't mean we don't need to be careful, of course."

"Understood," Jason said.

It was early Saturday morning—much earlier than Cassie's normally scheduled time—and Delores was in town, buying groceries. Entering through the back door, Jason and Cassie stepped quietly into the kitchen where Zander slept in his hammock.

"Now don't get upset," Cassie said. "No matter what happens."

"Aye-aye," Jason said.

"It could get ugly."

"Ugly's my middle name," Jason said, and then thought the better of it. "I mean . . ."

"Understood," Cassie said. "C'mon, Igor."

Cassie took one end of the hammock and Jason took the other. On the whispered count of three, they unhooked their ends and proceeded to carry Zander outside, his dead weight sunk between them as if they were moving a roll of carpet.

After they restrung the hammock between two trees, Cassie stepped back and looked at her sleeping patient. Sunlight bled through the leaves fanning overhead and dappled Zander's face and wings—the first natural light either had seen in quite some time. Cassie tried to imagine being grounded for that long, and reassured herself that she was doing the right thing. And Zander would thank her. Eventually.

Cassie popped open her briefcase and withdrew three large belts. Fastening them—one each about Zander's ankles, waist, and mid-torso—she flashed on an image of Andrew, similarly lashed, struggling to keep aloft while another of her patients trained a gun on him. She closed her eyes and took a deep breath, willing the picture away.

"What next?" Jason asked eagerly, hands at his hips. A part of him, at least, seemed to be enjoying this.

Cassie unfolded a lawn chair and sat down, hugging its back. "Next," she said. "Go watch for your mom and don't let her come back here."

Jason saluted, a little disappointed, and left.

Settling in for the long wait, Cassie gave the hammock a push, setting it rocking gently back and forth. As the birds chirped and the hammock tick-tocked, she watched the steady rise and fall of Zander's chest, her chin cradled now in her upturned palms. One of these days, she told herself, she'd have to ask him about his pajamas, and why they always seemed to have ducks on them.

"Now what?" Delores said, returning early from her shopping trip and noticing Cassie's car in the gravel drive.

Jason blew the two-whistled signal he and Cassie had worked out. He rushed around to his mother's door. "Pop the hatch, Ma, and I'll get the—"

"What is she doing here?" Delores asked, rolling down her window.

"Nothing," Jason said. "Did you get toilet paper?"

Delores got out of the car and started heading toward the backyard.

"You're not supposed to go back there," Jason shouted suddenly.

It was all Delores needed to hear.

"Get out of the way, Jason Douglas," she snapped, brushing past her son, carrying a bag of groceries she promptly dropped when she saw Cassie, sitting next to the trussed-up and still unconscious Zander.

"What the hell's going on here?" she shouted, as Cassie ssshhhhed and gestured for her to be quiet.

"Are you crazy?" she asked, her volume and pitch both steadily rising. "What are you trying to do, kill him?"

Cassie responded by pulling rank: "It's part of the treatment," she said. "Get the hell out of here."

"I will not!" Delores shouted, going to Zander and trying to work a buckle free. "This isn't treatment; this is torture!"

"Get away from him!" Cassie shouted back, leaping to her feet and grabbing Delores's arm. "Leave him alone or I'll . . ."

Cassie stopped shouting.

Delores stopped shouting.

Zander, however, was just getting started . . .

He awoke as the two were squabbling, took one look at the sun, the unceilinged sky, and began screaming loud enough to tinge the air around them a different color. The cicadas shut up; the birds took a hike. And Zander kept on screaming. He screamed until his vocal cords frayed and his lung sacs collapsed. He screamed about any number of things, most involving his imminent death and/or the rather graphic deaths of those who had done this to him. And all the while he struggled in his hammock, pushing against the belts, swinging and bucking, bucking and swinging—an absolute model of helplessness.

All the points were Cassie's now and she realized she didn't have any use for them. She realized, too, that she felt like shit, and a monster, and worse.

Zander, meanwhile, had grown light-headed and begun singing "Row, Row, Row Your Boat," quietly, desperately, as if he were praying for his life. And though he struggled mightily with them, he only got out three of the merrilies before finally passing out.

With Zander in a headlock, Cassie was prepared for the thrashing that would no doubt begin again, once Jason did as he was told and opened the bottle of smelling salts. She was prepared, too, for the revived threats and accusations, the premature wills and testaments, the desperate pleading and ad hoc self-diagnoses of imminent demise. She was ready to feel like a shit again and was even ready for more rowing, if it came to that, but what she wasn't prepared for was being bitten. Which she was—by Zander—hard, and on the left hand.

"God *damn* it!" she yelped, jumping away from Zander and looking down at the crescent of puncture wounds. Blood began welling up almost immediately, and Cassie fished out a handkerchief from her jacket pocket, wrapping it once, twice, three times around the wound.

In the background, Zander was trying out his lungs again.

"I'M DYING!" he shouted. "SHE'S KILLING ME! SOMEBODY STOP HER! I'M DYING! I'M DYING, AND SHE'S KILLING ME! I'M—"

"So *die* already!" Cassie snapped back, nearly ready to help.

And just like that, Zander went quiet—so quiet Cassie turned, wondering if he'd actually made good on his threat. What she saw was a contemplative Zander, one who realized he'd been challenged—dared—and was screwing up his face, trying to rise to meet it and . . . falling short. The harder Zander tried to die to spite her, to prove what a bitch she'd been and how incompetent a therapist, the steadier his breathing became. Try though he might, he couldn't even faint.

He lost.

He'd lost, and been cured.

"I can't," he finally said, softly, and a little sad.

"I guess that means we're stuck with you, then," Cassie said.

"I guess," Zander sighed.

Cassie waved Jason and Delores away. She toyed with Zander's damp hair with her good hand, and looked down casually at the one he'd bitten. A bright red moon had risen to the surface of the handkerchief. She wondered if that made her touchy now.

Oh well . . .

The cicadas, meanwhile, had taken up shimmering again. The sun went back to shining. And the sky even had the nerve to be blue.

"Nice day for it," Zander said, weakly.

"Yes," Cassie agreed. "Kind of summery."

Offering him a chair next to her after she'd let him out of his cocoon, Cassie decided to ask Zander about something that had been on her mind lately. Namely, Delores.

"Are you two . . . ?" she began.

"You mean me and the harpy?" Zander asked, resting his chin on the back of the lawn chair. His wings drooped, and the way he hugged the back of the chair, it seemed like the only thing holding him up. "Hardly. I think she might have a thing for me, though," he confided.

"Oh yeah?" Cassie said, mirroring his posture, a bit undone by the struggle herself. They both seemed focused on something off in the distance, at the edge of Zander's property.

"Yeah," Zander said, smiling weakly. "I think it's called employment."

It was the first time Zander had made a joke at his own expense in her presence, Cassie noted. She also noted, against her better judgment, that she found it charming.

"Why, Mr. Wiles," she said, "you do have a way with the ladies."

"Oh, I *used* to," Zander said. "I was a real Casanova, in second grade."

"Oh yeah?"

"Well, that's the first time I got kissed, 'for real,'" he said. "I'd been kissed by my mother, of course, and aunts and whatnot, but the first real kiss from a real girl was in second grade."

"A *real* girl, as opposed to . . ."

"You know what I mean," Zander said, not in a jousting mood. "Her name was Katy Adler, a real heartbreaker, and I had strep throat. My mom sent me to school anyway, because she couldn't get a sitter. Our teacher, Mrs. Ferguson, told all the other kids to steer clear of me—the little plague boy—and made some smartass comments about responsibility, thoughtfulness for others, and civic duty.

"Most of the kids treated me like the leper Ferguson made me out to be, but not Katy. No, Katy runs right up to me and kisses me on the lips. Not only that, but I swear to God she stuck her tongue in my mouth. She says it's something her older sister said boys like. And me, being a boy, I did. Of course, being a boy in second grade, and girls being the enemy, I had to push her away . . . but not real hard.

"Katy didn't really like me or anything. What she liked was the fact that I was sick. You see, Katy was a real popular kid, had a ton of friends that I wasn't part of, and her dad ends up getting a job in Montreal. Naturally, Katy doesn't want to go. Naturally, me and my strep throat look like a way out. It didn't work, of course. Katy got sick and got moved anyway. Her sister called my mother to tell her to tell me that Katy said she hated me. And that was the last I ever heard from the Adlers."

Cassie turned her chin to face Zander. This was a weird—and pleasant—surprise, coming long after she thought she knew him, this ability to break her heart. "That's a very sad story, Mr. Wiles," she said, looking at him suddenly in a new light, not as a client, but . . .

And why not? She'd shied away from relationships in the past because . . . well, who the hell knew what they were based on? Her? Her celebrity? Her wings? There were just too many not-really-her aspects to her that got dumped into the mix, that complicated things at the beginning. But Zander . . . he was an outcast, too. He wasn't just famous, but infamous. He had his own wings, and money, and a lot of not-really-him aspects to him, too. And now that they'd turned the corner, well . . .

"Are you okay?" she asked, suddenly, noticing that Zander had begun crying.

Zander shook his head no. His shoulders rose and sank and rose again, as great sobs broke through. Tipping his head back, he fought for breath.

Cassie placed a hand between his wings, trying to untie the knots his muscles were in. "Zander," she said. "Calm down. Tell me what's wrong."

Zander covered his face with his hands.

"So many people *died,*" he said, still sobbing.

"What?"

"I should have known better," he said. He began slapping his moon-scarred arm, striping it red, repeating, "I should have known, I should have known," rocking back and forth, and slapping himself again.

"It's not your fault," Cassie lied, suddenly understanding the depth of the water she had stumbled into.

"I should have known there are some things people *want* to catch," he said. "I fucked up . . ."

Cassie tried to imagine what hundreds of Andrews would do to her soul; she couldn't. The magnitude of the grief was stunning; it wouldn't fit in her heart, her brain . . . it wouldn't fit anywhere inside. But she admired it, admired anyone's surviving it. This was something she'd stopped hoping to find in anyone—Angel or Pedestrian—and it drew her.

"I can't undo it," he said. "I can't . . ."

Cassie couldn't speak. She wanted to, wanted to tell him that she was an outcast, too, that she understood about the things people wanted to catch, that she didn't blame him like the others, and how she knew, first-hand, how sometimes, throwing it all away seems like an answer. She wanted to tell him she understood about Wyandotte Steel, and why he lied when he said he didn't know what he hoped to accomplish by jumping. She knew. She wanted to tell him that. She wanted him to know all the things they had in common.

Cassie looked at Zander, at the strained muscles of his hunched shoulders, at the fists of his wings, beating him for not being a better human . . . and she wondered whether this was how other people managed it, this strange business of falling in love.

16

To celebrate his breakthrough, Cassie invited Zander to go flying with her during one of her jaunts to Lake Michigan. It was a date, her first self-conscious attempt at such a thing since the Becky Affair, a lifetime ago. She couldn't believe it had been so long, and couldn't believe she was letting herself take this kind of risk again.

Zander declined. He didn't know what type of exception Cassie was making in his case, but even if he had, he'd still have said no.

"Oh, come on," Cassie prodded. "You owe it to yourself. Don't tell me you've got something to watch on TV. You tell me that, and I'll—"

"I don't want to go flying," he said, flatly.

"Come again?" Cassie said. You could have knocked her over with the proverbial feather.

"I don't want to fly," Zander repeated.

"Bullshit," she said, unable to come up with a more therapeutic term. "I asked you what you most wanted to do once you got out of the house and you said, 'Fly.' If I recall correctly, you even got a hundred points for it."

Zander blushed. "I lied," he said.

Cassie'd read that the responses to the question "What do you most want to do?" were often inverted by agoraphobics, that what they claimed they most wanted to do was actually the thing that their agoraphobia was saving them from, helping them to avoid. Cassie just couldn't imagine it in this case; she simply assumed he was telling the truth. It would have been true for her. It would have been true for just about any Angel she knew.

With all appropriate dread mounting, she ventured out onto the ice. "Have you ever flown before?" she asked.

"Hell yes," Zander said. He paused. "In a plane," he added, almost too quiet to be heard.

"Otherwise?" Cassie asked.

"Otherwise," he said. He cleared his throat. "Um . . ." He looked away and lowered his voice even further. "No."

"What?" Cassie snapped. "Speak up."

"No," Zander said, louder, but just barely.

"You don't know how?"

He scratched the back of his neck. "I don't know how," he admitted, to the floor, his feet, the dust balls in the corner.

Cassie stood there, her hands out, and empty, her mouth open, no sound. Her wings shrugged, shivered—embarrassed for that other, unused set, hanging there on Zander's back, as useless as a joke without a punchline. Angel equaled flying. Form equaled function. Sure, she'd heard that the early Angels hadn't, at first, because of fear, and the contradictory statements of scientists concerning the adequacy of Angel wings for flight, but . . .

"Have you ever tried?" she asked.

"Yes," Zander said, surprised that she hadn't made the connection already.

"You were there," he said. "Wyandotte Steel," he added.

"Oh my God!" Cassie blurted. "Oh my God . . . ," she repeated.

And when she finally had to sit down, still saying it, a third and a fourth time, gasping a little with each repetition, Zander reached for the Wonder bread bag, just in case.

.   .   .

Flying over Lake Michigan, still solo, Cassie decided that Zander hadn't learned to fly because he was afraid to, and that this fear of flight was actually a fear of commitment and intimacy. During their next visit, she began by insinuating that his fear of intimacy, his manipulativeness, his knee-jerk insults and jokes—in short, the core of his personality—all of it constituted the baggage that was keeping him earthbound. Eventually, though, what began as insinuation grew to be rather blunt.

"You're being a jerk," she said. "A typical male jerk." She paused, surprised that Zander wasn't disagreeing. She continued.

"Flying is about commitment and trust," she said. "You trust that the air will hold you up. You commit to the flight, knowing that once you've started it, you can't just stop in the middle and take a breather. You stop, you drop—end of story. Now, I know you know about dropping; I've seen you do it."

Zander took this in, all the words of it, pretty sure he knew what Cassie was getting at. She was coming on to him; that was pretty clear. Plus, she was daring him to make a move, this Ms. Angel-car with only one seat. Ms. Friend-o-phobic. Talk about projecting! Naturally, Zander responded to the dare the way he normally did—by taking it.

And so he kissed her. From behind. On the neck.

And . . .

She *didn't* pull back. Instead, she pulled her hair aside, tilted her head back and kissed *him*, full on the lips.

"Really?" he said, pleasantly stunned. "I guessed right?"

"Really," she said, a little stunned to admit it. "You guessed right."

They headed toward the bedroom, unbuttoning, unzipping, and then, pausing.

Where, and how, and what to do about the wings?

The hammock wouldn't do. More likely than not, whoever was on top would be pitched to the floor for a mild concussion. And standing . . . well, their height difference nixed any thought of that kind of geometry. The chairs in the room? They all had backs. And as for the other options, well, neither knew the other anywhere near well enough to hazard suggesting such things. So what was left?

Suddenly: "Stay right there," Zander said, holding up a hand like a stop sign and bolting from the room. Cassie could hear the sound of casters rolling across the hardwood floor, just before Zander reappeared, smiling. "Ta-da!" he said.

"A footstool?" Cassie said.

"Best I could come up with on short notice," Zander said.

"Oh well," Cassie said, as they both finished undressing.

They were rushing this; both of them knew that, but neither seemed to care. It had been an awful long time for both, and so they pushed it— until it started pushing back, of course.

Neither noticed anything wrong until after Zander turned down the wick of the hurricane lamp, sat on the footstool in the dark, and helped Cassie as she straddled his lap.

"Why are you pushing me away?" she asked.

"I was just going to ask *you* that," Zander said.

"Goddammit! I knew this would happen," Cassie snapped, wondering, Did I *hope* this would happen? before shaking her head and continuing. "I'm right. You're terrified of this kind of thing."

"I am not," Zander protested. "I love this kind of thing. I mean, *you*." He stumbled and tried to right himself. "I love *you,* Cassie O'Connor."

"Nice try, Wiles," Cassie said. And then she noticed something odd. She noticed that while she could feel him moving closer, could feel his breath on her neck and *both* his hands on the small of her back, she could also feel a *third* hand, pressed against her chest and pushing her away.

"Wait a second," she said. "This is getting weird."

"Getting?" Zander said. "It's arrived. It's claiming squatter's rights."

"Shut up," Cassie said, getting up from his lap and stumbling toward the nightstand. "Come over here and help me get this damn thing going again."

Zander produced a lighter from his abandoned pants' pocket. The wick sputtered and came back to life.

"Come here," she said. "Stand facing me. Closer. Bring your chest level with mine."

Both watched as the skin of their chests rippled. They both jumped back.

"Jesus!" Zander said.

"Shit," Cassie said. "Did you feel that?" she added. "Like invisible fingers, pushing us apart."

They stood that way for a moment—quiet, naked, thinking.

Cassie slapped her forehead, opened her mouth to speak.

"I'm way ahead of you," Zander said, cutting her off.

"The Halo Effect," they said together.

"We've got fucking magnets in our chests," Zander said.

"And, apparently," she added, "their poles are oriented the same way. And like repels like."

"So, regardless of whatever chemistry we might have going here . . ."

"Right," she said. "We're screwed by the physics," she added, reaching for her shirt and closing the subject, at least for the time being.

Afterward, flying over Lake Michigan, clearing her head, recharging her battery, Cassie decided their not getting together was probably for the best. Zander was a client; sex was not a good idea. If anything happened, she could be sued for malpractice and it wouldn't matter if she claimed he initiated it. It was about power, and, in the therapist-client relationship, the assumption of power went with the therapist, regardless of extenuating circumstances.

Plus, Cassie knew herself and knew she'd put way too much pressure on the sex for it to be any good. It would have to compete with flight, first. It would have to make up for all the things that had gone wrong in her life up to that point, second. And it would have to unify her with another in body and spirit, offering total satisfaction, complete fulfillment, etc. Come to think of it, Cassie wasn't looking for sex, really, but a form of demonic possession—one where she could play the demon. Problem was, she knew, Zander fancied that role for himself. It was a matter of his manhood, and other such nonsense. Why did men always think that anything involving penetration, no matter how rarefied, was *their* territory? Freud, Cassie thought, it's his fault. A man, of course.

"Mine!"

Cassie smiled, remembering the boy Angel on a leash, thinking, They never change, do they?

Of course, who needed to compromise their ethics for sex when they could fly? Cassie wondered, sailing out over the great lake, the sand, water, sky as perfect as always.

Well, for the most part.

There was only one nonperfect thing about Cassie's latest trip to the lake—the fact that she'd come even closer to death than the last time.

"You're making too much of this, Lee," she told her agent, after she'd made the mistake of telling him. "I pushed it a little too far, that's all. You know how it is—the adrenaline starts pumping, you hit the wall, you push beyond it, there's the rush, and you feel like God and keep going."

Lee was a Pedestrian, and he reminded Cassie of this fact.

"Christ, Lee," she said. "You jog. You can't tell me you don't know what I'm talking about. No pain, no gain. Pushing the envelope. You know the drill."

"Yes," Lee said. "But if I go too far when I'm jogging, I can stop and call a cab. You get tired in the middle of a Great Lake, and it's bye-bye Icarus."

"I'll never do it again, Dad," she said, knowing even as she said it that it was a lie. The almost-dying thing had been a whole separate rush in itself; she'd had an orgasm—several—which is something she decided *not* to mention to Lee.

It had started innocently enough. Cassie had been playing tag with the gulls, tossing them bread balls, trying to see if she could pet one. That was something that had changed, she'd noticed. The gulls wouldn't let her pet them anymore. And now that she thought about it, she was overwhelmed by the impossibility of what she'd done. All the things that had to be just right, just to pull it off. The same speed, height, forward momentum, to say nothing of the bird's cooperation and trust. The whole operation . . . it was like trying to shake hands between two cars, speeding over the edge of a cliff. Those few times it had happened, they were miracles. It was probably horrible of her to want the miracle to keep happening, but that didn't stop her from missing it.

She was also thinking about Zander, the bullet she had just dodged. Talk about two cars going over a cliff! She must be living right.

And then she spotted one particularly fat gull that looked especially in need of chasing. He—she just assumed it was a he—was huge, and fast, and up for the game. He knew maneuvers she didn't, seemed able to freeze himself in the air, make impossible turns, and go from zero to sixty in nothing flat. He even had a sense of humor—speeding for all he was worth, looking back to make sure Cassie was closing on him, and then stopping, just stopping, as Cassie overshot him, after which he'd pursue her, darting after strands of her fantastic red hair.

They kept it up for about an hour, after which Cassie started noticing the steel-band feeling in her stomach. Her gullfriend had disappeared. She looked down and saw water; she looked up and saw sky. She looked left, right, behind, and in front and judged—correctly—that water and sky were pretty much it, for the moment.

And Cassie realized, almost casually, that she wasn't sure she could get very far in any particular direction before her wings simply conked out. She pictured herself in a coffin like Andrew's; she pictured Bob helping the mortician to get her into position, and arranging her detached wings like ferns in a bouquet. From the magnetic tugging in her chest and the position of the sun, she made an educated guess as to the direction of land and headed that way.

When her wings finally *did* conk out, she was less than a hundred yards from land. Her wings helped her float and the waves took her in.

The vacationers were out by then, cluttering the beach, milling about as the lifeguard gave Cassie mouth-to-mouth. They saw what he did with his hand, and heard him ask her if kissing an Angel was good luck. She came to, coughed, and threw up on the sand.

Once she abandoned the hope that she could ridicule or otherwise goad Zander into flying to spite her, Cassie realized that she was going to have one big problem as a teacher—the fact that she'd never "learned" to fly herself. She just did it. The books said you weren't supposed to dream during the hibernation, but she had. She dreamed of flying; the secret folded itself into all her new cells. And when she hatched and woke, she went to the roof of the Coop, first thing. She dried her wings on her first flight, hit a home run, first time at bat. She was—both Bob and Sharon agreed—a natural.

The problem with naturals, though, is that they generally can't say how it is they do what they do so well. Naturals, as a rule, make the worst teachers. The second worst were the enthusiasts—something Cassie also happened to be.

Being at a total loss, Cassie decided to just wing it, smiling at the wholly intended pun.

She began the first lesson by asking Zander two questions up front: Where was the longest stretch of untraveled asphalt in Riverton, and what size was he? Zander said it depended upon what time of the week and day you were talking about. After business hours and on weekends, there was always Enterprise Drive, a couple of miles worth of dead-ending delivery road running through the industrial park, flanked on either side by sheet-metal hangar-style warehouses and one-story brick buildings, most bearing company names including the words "Tool," "Die," or "Screw." In more polite days, kids used to do their drag racing on Enterprise Drive. Now, of course, they did it through residential areas, in front of schools, and through hospital quiet zones. And . . .

"What was the other question?" Zander asked.

"You look like a size eleven," Cassie said, walking with Zander from the porch toward her car.

"Depends on what department we're talking about," Zander said.

"Foot," Cassie said, trying to recall if Zander had any cause for implying what he was implying.

"Oh, well then, yeah," Zander said. "I'm an eleven."

"Good," Cassie said. "I guessed right. Now, close your eyes," she said. "I've got a surprise for you."

Zander closed his eyes and Cassie opened up the passenger door. A box rested on the non-Angel-friendly seat, wrapped and bowed. "Ta-da!" she announced.

"What is it?" Zander asked. "A time bomb?"

"Open it and see," Cassie said, ignoring Zander's tendency to put a negative spin on everything.

Zander took the box and shook it. "No ticking," he announced. "Which means no Rolex, I guess."

"OPEN THE GODDAMN BOX!" Cassie snapped, and Zander complied, albeit slowly.

First, he loosened the ribbon, carefully spooling it around his hand, and then tucking the roll into his back pocket. With the same care, he undid the taped seams and removed the wrapping, trying not to tear it. As he was folding the sheet into neat quarters, Cassie spoke up.

"How poor *were* your parents?" she asked.

Zander looked up. "Huh?"

Cassie gestured toward the folded wrapping paper. "Oh," Zander said, realizing suddenly that not everyone saved such things. "Bad habit," he said. He paused. "Money was an issue when I was a little kid." He refused to discuss it further.

"Well?" Cassie finally said. "What do you think?"

Zander remembered the present in his hands. He looked down. "In-line skates?" he said.

"Size eleven," Cassie said. She opened the driver's door and rolled open the sunroof. "Hop in," she said.

Zander ducked under the door well and then poked his head and wings through the sunroof. He rested his butt on the headrest and his feet on the seat. "Where we going, boss?" he asked, drumming "Shave and a haircut" on the roof of the car, but saving the "two bits."

"Enterprise Drive," Cassie said, beeping out the missing quarter on her horn.

Along the way, Cassie tried explaining Beaufort's scale of wind strength, meaning it to be a tender time of sharing between Zander and herself. It was developed in the eighteen-hundreds by Sir Francis Beaufort, ran from zero to twelve, from weakest to strongest wind, and always struck Cassie as almost poetic and something every Angel should know. Bob had taught it to her in the Coop. It had been an unusually warm moment and out of character for both, sitting in front of the fireplace, with blankets and just the two of them, Bob toasting marshmallows, staring at the flames, and talking in an almost whisper. Cassie was getting greener and weaker by the day, couldn't shake the feeling of death, even though she knew better, and needed something just like that.

Bob had started on the other end of the planet, like he usually did. "Before I changed," he began, "I remember sitting in a jazz club in D.C., a neighborhood place out among the three-syllable street names in the northwest part of the district. It was a dive, really, but it was dark, the music was good, and they had candles on all the tables. The girl I was with was busy breaking up with me, telling me she just wanted to be friends, and I'd been down that road before, so I just stared at the candle. That's when I noticed that the flame was keeping time with the music. The drummer would beat his drum and the flame would take it like a punch in the gut. All the candles on all the tables were doing the same thing. It blew me away, and I started thinking about how much there is to know about this stuff we live in, this air, and how it moves and is moved."

And then he told her about the Beaufort scale, about how zero was less than a mile an hour, how zero lets smoke rise vertically. At one, smoke could show wind direction, but wind vanes couldn't. At two, you could feel it on your face and leaves began rustling, showing their bright green backs. Three caused leaves and twigs to move constantly, and raised small flags. Four could raise dust and paper, and make large branches move. At five, small trees with leaves bent, and whitecaps formed on lakes. Six—six meant telegraph lines would whistle, and umbrellas turned inside out. It was hard to walk in seven, and eight ripped twigs off trees. Nine sent slate sailing from rooftops, and ten uprooted trees. Eleven—eleven hardly ever happened, but when it did, it exploded windows. And twelve—twelve . . .

"What happens at twelve?" Cassie had asked Bob.

Bob still looked at the fire, still kept his voice at a whisper. "The scale has just two words for twelve," he said, and paused.

" 'Devastation occurs.' "

The moment Bob gave Cassie was the moment Cassie wanted to give Zander, but it didn't quite work out that way. For one thing, there was no fireplace along Telegraph Road, and Cassie found herself shouting, just so Zander could hear from his position above her, sticking halfway out her sunroof. Bob had competed with the warm fluttering of flames, the occasional collapsing cinders, while Cassie had to break through the traffic, and wind, and Zander's preoccupation with what the latter was doing to his feathers.

"They're all pointing straight back," Zander called down. "Like my hair when it's long and I'm swimming . . . just cutting straight through the water."

He shouted this at roughly the same time Cassie was shouting up about what six meant. They both shouted "What?" back at the other.

After a few more stabs, Cassie stopped shouting and just drove, deciding that Zander was probably learning more about wind by just playing in it like he was. For him, Cassie realized, one "Fucking shit!" shouted happily into the pelting breeze as she floored it was probably worth more than all the science and found poetry the nineteenth century had to offer.

"You like flying kites?" Cassie asked, after turning the car around at the dead end of Enterprise Drive and facing out.

"As a kid, yeah," Zander said, crawling the rest of the way through the sunroof and sliding off the side of the car to the asphalt.

"Good enough," Cassie said, walking around to the trunk and popping it open. "Put on your present."

Zander looked puzzled. "What?"

"Put on your present," she said. "The skates."

"Oh," Zander said. "I thought you were using some kind of pop-psyche buzz-phrase, like 'Take it one day at a time.'"

"Nope," she said, fishing the towline out from the trunk and fastening it to her bumper. "I was being literal."

"What's that?" Zander asked, looking up from tying his skates.

"A tow rope," Cassie said.

"It looks like something you'd use for water skiing," Zander said.

"Good," she said. "'Cause it is, and you are."

Zander stopped tying.

"Think of it like flying a kite," she said, slamming the trunk closed and then starting the car up again. "Only this time, you get to be the kite."

Zander looked at her, his brain bubbling with smartass things to say, most having to do with his real-life experiences with kites, and trees, and power lines. Problem was, they all needed him to be standing to carry their full, bad-ass weight—something he was having a hard time doing just then, with the skates and all. "You've got to be kidding," was the best he could manage, delivered pathetically while trying to stop his legs from drifting out from under him in either direction. "Shit!" he said, grabbing the door handle for support.

"Don't worry," Cassie said. "You'll catch on."

And was that a smirk? Was she smirking at him? Maybe she didn't know he could see her face in her rearview mirror, but he could, and that was definitely a smirk.

So he stood up—*willed* himself erect, like the first male Neanderthal, goaded toward bipedalism and civilization by a Neanderthal wife who was light-years ahead of him, and taunting. Cassie had included knee and elbow pads, as well as a helmet along with the skates, but Zander was too cool for any of that. So he stood, locked his knees, and asked, "Now what?"

"Grab the towline and let me know when it goes tight," she said, revving the engine and then grinding slowly across the asphalt, picking up the slack.

"Tight!" Zander shouted.

Cassie stuck her head out the window and called back, "First I'll take it slow, so you can get used to the feel, and then I'll speed up." She paused, and then added, "Remember: Think kite. Think altitude. Let the wind take you."

A little unsteadily at first, but then with greater confidence, Zander rolled behind Cassie's car, feeling the wind tug at his wings. On a signal from Zander, Cassie took the car from simulating a four on the Beaufort scale through five, six, seven . . .

The wind blew Zander's smirk into a smile, peeled back the lips and showed teeth. He could do this. He could make this work. The wind howled and what words he shouted blew apart, blasted into random consonants and vowels. His wings and hair flagged backward, thwipping as Cassie gave it more and more gas.

Getting airborne would mean getting on top of the air, Zander knew, which meant bringing his wings around it and . . .

He spread his wings like a wall, and regretted it immediately. Inside the car, Cassie felt the sudden tug backward caused by the braking effect of Zander's spread wings. The car swerved and then stopped. Zander tried to drop his wings, but the damage was done. He shot past Cassie's stopped car, the towline going first slack, and then tightening again. Zander's body popped off the ground for a second, like a Doberman surprised by his leash, and then, like all good, gravity-bound things, he came down.

Hard.

On his wing.

The one that snapped, just like a twig in a Beaufort eight gale.

Zander looked like a dead deer, strapped to the hood of Cassie's car, stomach down, all trussed up and no place to go. It couldn't be helped, of course. She couldn't risk making matters worse by trying to maneuver his only periodically conscious body under the door well and up through the keyhole of her sunroof. Of course, dead deer don't shout. Zander, when he was conscious, did—shouting, among other things, for Cassie to not let them make him a mummy again, to not call the doctors, to call an Angel doctor . . . did she *know* any Angel doctors . . . could she . . . did she . . . et cetera. And Cassie shouting back that she wouldn't, she didn't, she would try.

Spraying gravel like water, Cassie bounced into Zander's driveway and almost skidded through the gap-toothed door of the barn. Delores and Jason ran out to see what was the matter, Delores adding, gratuitously, "Now what?"

"We've had a little accident," Cassie said, teeth clenched, damming up the things she'd say if she had the luxury. "Get some scissors, something to use as splints, some peroxide, gauze, and . . . some duct tape."

Jason ran to fetch the supplies while Delores demanded more information, and Zander faded in and out. Cassie would be needing Delores's help to hold him down when it came time to set Zander's wing, and so continued to curb her responses in the direction of simple, impersonal data.

"It's his humerus-P," Cassie explained. "It's broken."

"Humorous pee?" Delores asked. "What's so funny about—"

"No," Cassie continued. "Humerus. It's a bone, like in the arm, only it's in his wing. The P stands for *Homo pterylae,* which is the scientific name for Angels." She thought of Max the cadaver, of Becky, and the pain that had led her down the road to this, to all this shouting, and pain, and blood.

Delores grew silent, not wanting to give Cassie any more opportunities to make her feel stupid.

Meanwhile, the birds made their bird noises, and Zander moaned, delirious by now. Cassie'd given him three Tylenol-3s that she had left over from a little Lake Michigan mishap. They seemed to be taking effect.

When Jason returned with the supplies, Cassie directed Delores to hold Zander still while she trimmed the feathers away from the spot nearest the fracture. A splinter of bone poked through the skin, making the job of locating the break unfortunately easy. As Cassie dribbled peroxide over the wound, the blood frothed, looking like some Vampire's milkshake. She kept pouring until the peroxide ran clear, and then placed a hand to either side of the fracture. She commanded Delores to hold on tight, and for Jason to grab the tip of the damaged wing. On the count of three, he was to pull the wing out straight, once, quickly, and with all his strength.

The sound of the bones popping back into place chilled them all.

When Cassie looked at her again, Delores had gone frighteningly pale, and tears dampened her face. And there was something else there—a smile three shades subtler than Mona Lisa's. Cassie ripped off a long stretch of duct tape and began wrapping it over the gauze on Zander's wing. She recognized the expression and named it:

Relief.

During their next session, Cassie brought Zander books on hang gliding. He read them and shrugged his wings—the good one, and the bandaged one. "So?" he said.

She followed with books on wind and the weather, books on ornithology, books on small aircraft aviation. May became June became July, and still Zander said: "So?"

In between the recommended readings, Zander confided that he wanted to, but didn't think he'd be *allowed* to fly.

"Allowed?" Cassie asked. "By whom?"

"God," Zander said. "The universe. The dealer-out of karmic justice."

"Don't be silly," Cassie said. "You've got the equipment, you just need practice."

"Two tries," Zander said. "Two broken wings."

Zander told Cassie about seeing the pictures of Lizzy, and how he couldn't get them out of his head. She'd tried flying, he said, he knew her and he knew that. "And she died, and they cut her open." Maybe she and he got a weaker dose of whatever it was. And it was so much like his luck to get wings that didn't work. If he were God, he couldn't see himself resisting a joke like that. And he kinda deserved it, you know? Payback.

Cassie noticed him staring at one of his moons. "That's not what this is about," she said, feeling him drifting back to the kitchen and his hammock.

"Whatever," Zander said in a pouty voice, flipping through the pages of his latest book. He didn't bother looking up.

Day, night—it all needed killing. But once the cast came off, Cassie decided that the book approach was all wrong. Knowledge—*book* knowledge—was what was weighing him down. So, three months after she'd given up on the intimacy theory, Cassie announced:

"Flying is about denial."

Zander smirked. He'd given up on the intimacy theory, too. And gone back to making faces.

"You deny everything you know about what should happen to a body that jumps," Cassie continued, having gone back to ignoring Zander's faces. "You step off the ledge, denying that you'll plummet to the concrete, denying what all the scientists have said about your wings, denying the impossibility of doing what you're doing now."

"De Nile is a river in Egypt," Zander said.

"Don't joke," Cassie said. "People from screwed-up backgrounds, from dysfunctional families and so forth—they're the ones who fly like they're born to it. Denial is in their blood."

"Hugs, not drugs," Zander said. "One day at a time."

"No kidding, Zander," Cassie said. "From what you've told me about your family, flying should be a skate."

"Don't mention skates," Zander said, his wings hugging closer to his body, retracting on their own with something like fear.

He went to Cassie's office window. Now that he could leave the house, she preferred treating him here, on neutral territory. It seemed safest for all concerned. Delores, for her part, was playing chauffeur, having removed the backseats of her minivan so Zander could ride more comfortably. She went to coffeehouses or shopped at Borders while Zander had his sessions. She didn't mind. *Really.* She didn't. She said so all the time.

Outside the office window, some of Cassie's other patients played in the courtyard with members of the hospital's Pedestrian staff. It was Angel Slaughter Ball this time, only instead of a ball, a Frisbee was used. Foul for the Angels was any resting place—the ground, a tree branch, a building ledge—that let them stop flapping. That's how their strength was handicapped, to even up the odds. If a player was hit with a Frisbee, he or she was out; if they caught the Frisbee, the thrower lost.

Zander stared out the window, feeling like Rudolph, barred from the reindeer games, except that even Rudolph could fly.

Cassie said nothing, letting him mope and long and feel sorry for himself. When she judged the time right, she moved silently behind him. "Wuss," she whispered.

"What?"

"Wuss," Cassie said. "Chicken."

"Am not."

"Are so."

"Fuck you."

"Fuck you back."

Zander turned back to the window. "I know what you're doing," he said. "And it won't work."

"Will too," Cassie said. She brocked like a chicken and flapped her arms, fully intending the irony. When Zander didn't react, she cackled some more—though only halfheartedly, to tell the truth.

A few days later, it occurred to Cassie that Zander's problem was that he was too in love with feeling sorry for himself. He didn't fly, or he bungled each attempt, just so he could feel like a martyr. What she needed was a bigger and better martyr to shame him with. A simple case of "I cried because I had no shoes, but then I saw a guy who had no feet" should do the trick.

Maybe one of her group sessions would do it? No, he'd fit right in with the other whiners; they'd make him king and she wouldn't have accomplished anything. That it should be another patient seemed obvious; that it should be someone much worse off than Zander was imperative.

The problem was, her other patients were doing okay, relatively speaking. Oh well, she thought, I'll just have to keep my eyes open. Maybe I could drag in one of those homeless Angels who camp out on the quad, she thought. Or maybe I could dig up Andrew and wheel his moldy corpse in . . .

Cassie covered her mouth. Oh God, had she actually thought that? It was exactly the sort of crass, knee-jerk thing Zander would have said. She rolled a pencil between her palms. They were cold.

She wondered—as she'd started to, lately—whether she was influencing Zander, or if it might be working the other way around. It was a thought she took with her to Lake Michigan, which was starting to be the only place she could think about such things. The nursery—she'd done it and it got old. It was just a bunch of fat women with wings, and whiny kids on leashes. It was like everything else, just another variety of down time—that whole category of time spent *not* flying. Somehow, it all felt less real, kind of foggy and gummed up . . .

Zander was the only one she took flying with her—even if he was all in her head. She'd remember something he'd said, some stupid riff on something, and envy his easy immaturity. It was his primary coping mechanism, she knew, one he'd elevated into a personal style. When he did it, she found it almost cute, though she had to be careful not to let *him* know that.

Cassie knew she couldn't be that immature without a lot of practice. The closest she came to it was doing what she was doing now—flying, trying to play tag with a bunch of seagulls treating her like she had the plague.

She thought some more about Zander and her, in some scandalously nontherapeutic situations. She shook her head and flew—past the wall, into and out of orgasms. She continued flying. She'd already turned back. Hadn't she? She looked down, and up. No clues. No points of reference. Had she turned already? Was she headed in the right direction? She couldn't remember.

She flew in a panic, heart racing.

She *knew* this would happen some day.

(Did she?)

If she did, then why did she . . . ?

She didn't want to think about it.

By the time she blacked out, still nowhere near shore, she'd tripled her distance above the water, flying at a steady incline, registering unconsciously the fear of death by drowning, rising to ensure something else, something quicker.

What she got, though, was a broken arm, and fished out by some preppie yachtsmen who recognized her from *Oprah*. She woke to an argument between two of the boatmen—a medical student and a law student—about whether they should attempt to set her arm. Shivering and in pain, needing whatever help they could offer, Cassie decided *not* to say what Zander would say under similar circumstances.

17

Their next session promised to be hell, and it delivered. The first thing Zander did, entering her office, the cast and sling registering, was laugh—a surprised, spluttering, hand-to-the-mouth-oops-it-came-out-anyway laugh. Tears came to his eyes. Cassie went red and scowled. Normally, she would have folded her arms in a harrumph to underline how pissed she was. She realized, though, how silly that would look with the cast. Unfortunately, this realization didn't come until she'd already started in that direction, and there she was, stuck, not knowing what to do with these stupid, unfeathered sprouts, suddenly out there in front of her, caught in midsomething and looking dumb. And all the while, Zander kept going, "Oh man . . ." and "Sorry . . ." and laughing again until he started wheezing.

"Christ," he finally said. "What happened to you?"

"Do you care?" Cassie asked. "Are you done laughing?"

"I'm sorry," he said. "I'm . . . I'm a jerk. It's just, you know, ironic. I'm done laughing. I swear." He paused, to make sure he wouldn't start laughing again. It really all depended on her answer to the next question.

"How did you say it happened?" he asked.

"I didn't," Cassie said. "I was busy trying to figure out how a bone broken in two places is funny."

"I said I was sorry, already," Zander said. "So?"

Cassie looked at him. The truth would just bring more laughter and I-told-you-so's, and only strengthen his resolve against flying. Though lying usually wasn't, in *this* case, it seemed best for the patient—and the therapist, too, yes, as a fringe benefit, but mainly, she was doing this for the patient. And so:

"I slipped in the shower," Cassie said.

"Don't you use a bath mat?"

"Bath mats promote mold. They get all gunky underneath."

"What about those rubber stick-on thingies," Zander said. "Those no-skid flower deals?"

"What does this have to do with anything?" Cassie said, shrugging her broken arm without thinking—and recoiling in pain. "Ouch," she said.

"Careful," Zander advised.

"Too late for that," Cassie said, meaning the obvious things, and the not-so-obvious things—like the fact that she'd drifted off for a second there, during the Bath Mat Debate, and saw Zander and her as an elderly Angel couple, sitting at a sidewalk café, their chairs backward, having a fond, old-people's argument over nothing, the whole thing being in the code of a shared lifetime . . .

She shook her head, letting the BBs roll back into the clown's eyes. She knew what Zander's chitchat was all about, and why he laughed so delightedly; he was happy. Not happy that the broken bone was *hers,* necessarily, though an outsider might think so, but happy for the fact of a broken bone, period—one that would get him off the hook for the next couple of months, which would bring them into winter, which would get him out of flying for several months more. It was like Delores, realizing she'd gotten her invalid back; the smile of secret relief.

"So, about these," Zander started up again, "I think they're called appliqués."

"So," Cassie said, ignoring him, "about the next couple of months, and your flying . . ."

"Understood," Zander said. "Under the circumstances, it's on hold. These things happen."

"I think that maybe you should see somebody else," Cassie said, not knowing she would, until she had. It struck her as the logical solution, the only fair thing for the client . . . until she started wondering what the problem was. Both courses of action, either getting Zander to fly or getting Zander to somebody else who could teach him, achieved the same thing—namely making Zander-the-patient into Zander-the-ex-patient, making Zander-the-ethics-problem into Zander-fair-game. Was *that* what was going on? She tried not to think about it, while Zander, for his part, reacted rather violently to her original suggestion.

"No," he blurted, a bit too suddenly, a bit too desperately. Righting himself, he said, "I mean, I'm in no hurry. I've gotten used to waiting for bones to heal. It's no bother, really."

"It wouldn't be fair to you," Cassie continued. "I'm sure you can find a flying coach someplace in the yellow pages. It's—"

"I'm not Mr. Popularity with birds of a feather," Zander said. "In case you'd forgotten."

"So what do you propose we do, for however many months this takes?"

"Talk," Zander said, shrugging his shoulders, his wings.

"Talk?" Cassie said. "Just chitchat, about bath mats and such and . . . Don't even think about it!"

Zander froze. While she spoke, he'd stretched his arms out, knit his fingers together, and was preparing to crack his knuckles when she stopped him short. "Sorry," he said, slowly unlacing his fingers. "It wouldn't have to be bath mats," he continued, offhandedly. "It could be about cheese or sensible shoes. We could maybe not talk, sometimes, walk around Ann Arbor, grab lunch at Zingerman's . . ."

"Zander," Cassie said. "I can't charge you for walking in the park and doing lunch at Zingerman's."

"I don't mind," Zander said. "I like the conversation." He paused, and went a bit quieter. "I like . . . I like watching your pretty face get so red . . ." He'd said this last bit to the floor, his long hair hanging down, hiding his eyes.

"Zander," Cassie began, ready to add, "let's not do this," when Zander bolted up.

"Time," he announced. He stood to leave.

"Wait," Cassie called, but Zander just put a finger to his lips.

"Next week," he said, and closed the door.

The idea, Cassie didn't mind saying, was a stroke of genius. After their last session—the Bath Mat Session, as she came to think of it—she realized there was no way she could let the rest of the summer go like that. He'd be back in his kitchen watching TV in no time. She had to get back on track. It was the sort of problem she'd have solved while flying, before. She'd have chased the answer while chasing seagulls, mulling over what he'd said and she'd thought, and what the next course of action might be. Grounded, she had to find something else.

And she had to do it without much sleep. She had too much energy; too many unorganized thoughts. She took to pacing like she had during her sleepless time in the Coop. She paced all of a couple of nights, and then the answer just came to her. While pacing, and gritting her teeth, rubbing the spot just below her ear where the jaw was hooked, and wondering if it were possible for teeth to itch, which hers *seemed* to be doing, just faintly, just a bit . . . God smiled on Cassie again.

The problem was this: How do you teach an Angel to fly when you can't? What do you do when you can't stand by, ready to scoop him out of an unfortunate plummet? How do you teach someone to fly, indoors, under circumstances controlled enough to ensure at least some margin of safety, while also nailing down the basics? The answer paced into Cassie's overworked brain: Trampoline. Of course.

Cassie, thinking more like Zander every day, bribed the janitorial staff with two bottles of Finlandia. That, and a couple of twenties, got her inside the university gym and ensured that the trampoline was set up when she needed it. Given Zander's lack of enthusiasm for the plan, however, she could have saved herself the trouble.

"You're kidding," he said. "We spent a quarter of my hour driving for this?" Zander was in a bad mood already. It was raining, and he couldn't ride poking through Cassie's sunroof, instead having to spend the whole trip to the gym hunched over and kneeling backward on Cassie's Angel-unfriendly passenger seat, his ass resting uncomfortably on the dash just above the glove compartment.

"You know, the Flying Wallendas . . . they don't *really* fly," he said.

"It's to get a sense for how air feels under your wings," Cassie said, excited. She did a little hop across the gym floor, hung in the air for a second under the canopy of her wings, her good arm cradling her bad arm, and gently drifted down. "Like so," she said, smiling.

"You like torturing me, don't you," Zander said. "Ever since I bit you, you've been . . . touchy."

"Just try it," Cassie said, smiling, patting the edge of the trampoline, setting it bouncing. "I bet you like it."

"I bet I land on my ass," Zander said. "If we're betting, that's what I bet."

"You know," Cassie said, "normally I find bullshit pessimism *incredibly* attractive, but . . ." She paused. "JUST GET ON THE GODDAMN TRAMPOLINE!" she shouted.

Zander raised his hands and wings in surrender. He crawled up onto the trampoline and jumped as high as he could, trying to cup air under his spread wings. Timing, generally, was a problem. He jumped up with his wings at his side and tried to open them on the drop, causing them to ruffle and splutter, but not much else.

"At the apex," Cassie shouted. "At the zenith."

"What?" Zander said, walking, bouncing clumsily to the edge of the trampoline.

"Open your wings like a flower," she said. "At the top of your rise, before you start coming back down. Hold them straight up like this," she said, holding the backs of her wings pressed against each other. "Like you're praying backward, palms out. And then, at the top, move them apart and down."

Zander did as he was told. He jumped with his wings praying backward, he bloomed like a flower, he . . .

Spun.

Corkscrewed, actually—his wings acting like the veined plume on a falling maple seed, the ones he used to call "helicopter seeds" when he was little. The spinning caused him to travel perhaps a yard from where he'd originally leaped, which was just about six inches shy of the trampo-line.

Fortunately he was wearing socks, otherwise when he hit the pol-ished floor, still spinning, the friction between his bare feet and the fresh wax would have likely sprained or even broken his ankles. As it was, his socked feet skidded out from under him and he landed squarely on his ass—as predicted—his ill-fated flying practice breaking nothing but his pride. This time.

Still, on the drive back to the office, Cassie was enthusiastic. "You kind of flew," she said. "You came down slower than you would have nor-mally."

"I spun like a top," Zander said, brooding. "Crashed. Burned. End of story."

"You're being pessimistic," Cassie said, pulling into her spot.

"I'm being realistic," Zander said. Facing the back window where she couldn't see his expression, though, he smiled. In his head, he was a little kid, riding a buffer down the halls of Wyandotte Steel.

I flew, he thought. I flew! I flew . . .

I *kinda* flew.

"You're too heavy," Cassie announced during Zander's next session.

"Excuse me?"

"I mean, you're too heavy to fly," Cassie corrected. "In your head." She tapped her own to underline the point.

"So," Zander said. "It's not that I'm fat, I've just got a fat head?"

Cassie shook her head. "You're being difficult," like this was some-thing new. "In your head," she said, adopting the tone she used with her younger—or slower—patients, "you're not doing what it is Angels do to make themselves . . . *light*. You read about the Cincinnati experiment, didn't you?"

Zander had heard about the experiment, and about why it was Angels could fly, even though traditional science had them needing wings the size of small aircraft. It was a simple enough experiment, performed with a budget of next to nothing in the basement of a university profes-sor's home in Ohio. Take a mix of Angels and Pedestrians, tie them up, put them on bathroom scales, and see what happens to the needles when you hypnotized them into thinking they're flying.

"Yes," Zander said, his throat dry, too quiet to be heard. The problem was, the needles had gone backward for some of the Pedestrians, too. And the papers reported it, and Zander kept seeing them, those Pedestrians who'd heard, climbing out onto their balconies, rooftops, building ledges, and fire escapes, betting their lives on a few network sound bites. It took a whole goddamn week for the official correction, the fact that the Pedestrians who levitated were actually incomplete Angels, that they'd turned green and everything, but just hadn't sprouted wings.

"Excuse me?" Cassie said, having missed his answer.

"Yes," Zander repeated, feeling embarrassed yet again for lacking the courage of those Pedestrians who jumped with nothing more on their backs than hope. "Yes, I know about the Cincinnati experiment," he said, as if she'd asked whether he'd heard of World War II.

"Good," Cassie said. "The point of the Cincinnati experiment is that aerodynamics is only *part* of flying. If it were the whole thing, then those scientists comparing our wingspans and body weights to Canadian snow geese, they'd be right. We shouldn't be able to fly. But there's the other thing, that thing our minds do when we jump that makes us lighter. You need to learn that."

"And . . . "

"I want to hypnotize you," Cassie said.

"Is *that* what they're calling it nowadays?" Zander said, smirking, trying to break out of the heavy mood that had descended upon him ever since Cassie started talking about being light.

Cassie, for her part, saw the smirk and couldn't make herself mind. It'd make as much sense as getting angry at a zebra for being striped. Smirking was what a Zander did; sarcasm was the call it made under stress, or when the rhinos stampeded. It's also what passed for a smile from his kind, and Cassie'd grown less picky.

"I'm serious," she said, unruffled.

"I'm sure you are," Zander said. "But I don't want you going into my subconscious without a search warrant."

Zander, Zander, Zander . . .

"It's the only way," Cassie said. "If you're serious about flying," she added, a little ashamed that she was yet again resorting to the therapeutic dare.

Unfortunately, Zander was also getting better at letting things pass. "You learned without being hypnotized," he said. "Find another way."

Cassie looked at the hourglass on her desk. There wasn't much sand left, the sand reminding her, like it had lately, of Lake Michigan, and what she wasn't doing. She sighed and gave in.

"I bought some tub appliqués at the hardware," she said. "They're little angels. Halos, the works."

"Very retro," Zander said, brightening. "*Très* P un-C."

"I was sure you'd approve," Cassie said.

An attendant knocked on Cassie's office door. "You ready for a present?"

"What?" she said, looking up from her desk. She had no patients scheduled for the next hour, and she'd begun reading through the latest issue of *In Flight,* an Angel magazine. She was reading an article on snowbirds—Angels who keep two homes, one for the summer and another for the winter, so they can fly year-round. She was thinking how she and Zander might benefit from a change of scenery, and how they could get back on schedule with their flying practice even after winter set in, when the attendant knocked.

"Hope you're not too busy," the attendant said, tossing a patient folder onto her desk. "He calls himself William," the attendant said, "but he's got no ID to prove it. We like to call him Chilly Willy."

"Why?" Cassie asked.

"Oh, you'll figure it out," the attendant said, returning to the corridor and walking away, whistling.

As the whistling died, Cassie noticed another sound, coming from the opposite end of the corridor. It was a familiar sound and Cassie tried to place it. Oh my God! she suddenly thought, recognizing the sound. She saw Zander clearly before her, naked and smiling, wheeling in the footstool.

That was the sound. Casters, squeaking.

The squeaking grew steadily louder, and suddenly, a hand clamped itself around the frame of Cassie's door, near the bottom. The hand wore a brown leather driving glove. The hand pulled the rest of a body in, winged and kneeling on a wheeled platform.

"You must be William," Cassie said. "Can I call you Bill?"

"Ah," William rasped. "I have been foretold. And yes, Bill is fine."

William, or Bill, or Chilly Willy—Cassie noticed—was a Penguin. And for once, the diagnosis was correct.

Standing to get a better look at her new patient, Cassie knocked over a pencil she'd been using to jot down an address from her magazine. She regretted it immediately, for when William looked up at the sound, it was as if Cassie had pulled off a leg from a three-legged stool. His head tilted back, and he tipped over.

"Shit!" he said, his arms working and his legs pedaling like a turtle flipped on its back. "Can you give me a hand here?" he asked. He was humiliated, and this wasn't the first time.

With her good arm, Cassie helped him into a sitting position on his platform; she didn't even bother offering him the use of the perch. Instead, she handed him the pencil she'd dropped, and asked him just to focus on the eraser, to ignore whatever his body might be telling him about falling.

It was as he reached for the pencil that Cassie noticed the stitches lacing up his wrist.

"Thank you," he said.

Cassie took her perch and looked at William, wondering what to say, what to do, what course the treatment might take, and what they were to hope for as a cure. One object, of course, was to make sure that he didn't try suicide again. Cassie wasn't sure she was up to it. In his position, even she might . . . well, she had, hadn't she? And over much less. Next to breathing, flying was one of the most important things in her life; she couldn't see herself living without it.

And, of course, that wasn't the worst of it. She tried to imagine living William's Tilt-A-Whirl life, never knowing when the floor would pitch up at you, when the walls or trees would suddenly go slant. A sermon about the goodness of life coming from someone like Cassie wasn't going to convince someone like William.

"Bill," she said.

"Yes?" he said, staring at the head of the eraser.

"If you were me," Cassie said, "and I were you, what would you do to help me?"

"I'd give you a gun, I'd help you aim it, and I'd pull the trigger for you."

"And when you went to jail," Cassie said, "what then?"

"I'd say to myself, 'Damn, so this is what that poor bastard's life was like.' "

Cassie didn't know what to say. Bill filled in.

"I used to be a lawyer," he said. "I used to have a wife. I used to call myself happy, and believed it, and was." Pause. "The old me wants to sue the motherfucker who did this to me, except I can't find him." He paused. "You know, I was really looking forward to the change. Not just personally, but professionally. I figured, shit—can you imagine an Angel lawyer, spreading those Word-of-God wings during a closing argument?"

Bill started crying, and Cassie realized that she did know what to say, but didn't want to admit it. There was nothing she could do.

"Bill," she said, finally, "I can't imagine what your life is like, and I don't honestly know what I can do to help you."

"I figured as much," he said. "I told them that when they said I had to see you. Rules, you know? Every attempted suicide has to see a shrink." He paused. "I like the fact that you're not bullshitting me, though. That's good."

"So," Cassie said, "what do we do?"

"How many times do I have to see you?" he asked. "I mean, what's the legal minimum?"

She told him.

"Hmmm," he said. "That's a lot of time. No chance I could get out early for good behavior?"

Cassie shook her head. Policy was policy.

And then, suddenly: "Do you like chess?" he asked.

Cassie admitted that she did, but wasn't very good.

"Good," he said. "Bring a game next time. As long as I'm staring at the game, I'm okay. It's when the world gets any bigger that I get into trouble."

Cassie looked at him as he sat on his platform, too awkward even for the decency of a wheelchair, kneeling there, staring at—praying to—a pencil's eraser. She agreed to bring in a chess set for their next session. Maybe it would be therapeutic. Maybe he'd get it right, once he was through with their obligatory sessions. In any event, it would kill time—their mutual enemy.

It was only after Bill had rolled away, back to wherever they were keeping him, that Cassie realized she'd finally found her man with no feet.

The Angel world is small, literally, and full of coincidences. Which is why what happened next was really not too extraordinary.

Cassie had decided that Bill and Zander could be good for each other. With any luck, Bill would make Zander stop feeling sorry for himself, and Zander could—who knows?—maybe he'd be good for Bill. They were both guys; maybe they could do some guy stuff—bonding, and whatnot. Even at his worst, Zander couldn't offer Bill any less than what Cassie had planned—namely playing chess until the clock ran out. It was worth a shot, at least.

And so Cassie brought the chessboard as promised, and she and Bill played two games for their next session. Cassie was careful to let the last game run long, and a few minutes into the next session—the one she had rearranged to be Zander's.

Bill had just begun complaining about Cassie's strategy of moving her queen one space forward, and then one space back, turn after turn, when Zander walked into the office.

"Oops," she said.

"Oops is right," Zander said, finding the two of them on the floor, lying on their stomachs in front of the board. Bill propped his head up by resting his chin in his upturned palms, his elbows on the floor. "She never plays games with me," Zander said, nudging his fellow patient amiably with the toe of his shoe. "At least not board ones," he added.

Bill, caught off guard, lost his concentration and rolled over onto his back. Zander looked down at Bill's face; Bill looked up at Zander's.

"Thom?" Zander said, shocked.

"Wiles?" Thom said, equally so.

"No," Cassie said. "His name's Bill."

"His name's *Thom,*" Zander corrected.

"We're old spelunking buddies," Thom said, as Zander scooped him up from the floor and hugged him.

"God, it's good to see you, Thom," Zander said.

"Good to see you right back," Thom said. "Watch where you drop me."

Zander looked at Cassie as she mouthed the word "Penguin." "Christ," Zander mouthed back, hugging Thom a little tighter, noticing, finally, the deadness of his weight, and wings.

Cassie let it go on for a few seconds. She scratched the back of her neck, looked away, and then finally cleared her throat. Loudly.

"You told me that your name was Bill and that you were a lawyer," she said.

"Thom's a pathological liar," Zander said.

"So's Bill," Thom said. "Though in his line of work it's no drawback."

Zander stood there with Thom in his arms, looking uncomfortable. It didn't seem right to be holding on to a person who was having conversations with others. Cassie pushed his platform over with her shoe, and Zander carefully placed his ex-friend upon it.

"You know," Zander said, the shock gradually wearing off, reality setting in, "I seem to recall things getting a little ugly between us there, toward the end."

"You know," Thom said, "I seem to remember you hitting me in the head with a . . . what was it?"

"A bookend," Zander said, the old wounds as fresh as ever. "A brass bookend of a monkey holding a skull," he added. "And you deserved it, leaning over that woman's dead husband and—"

"Whine, whine, whine," Thom said, the passing years gone. "Cry me a fucking river."

Zander tensed, his fingers curling into a fist. Cassie, noticing, forced eye contact with him. And then she looked down, toward Thom's platform, toward his wrist, baseball-stitched and straining to hold on.

"Jesus Christ, Thom," Zander said, staring at his ex-partner's wrist as all the steam went out of him. "Christ," he said again, though mainly to himself, thinking: Why'd you have to choose my dad's way?

Thom, noticing what was being noticed, twisted himself to give them all a better view. "Cut myself shaving," he said. "Gotta go electric one of these days."

"What . . . ?" Zander began, as his hands sifted the air for the rest of the question.

". . . happened?" Thom supplied.

Zander nodded his head. Cassie nodded hers, too.

"Well," Thom began, "it happened a couple years after we parted company. High-risk activity being *de rigueur,* what with the possible all-or-nothing payoffs at stake, I basically stuck to the game plan I always had, shooting up now and then with pals and associates. You know . . ."

Zander nodded again and Cassie tried to place him in that world, which she knew about vaguely, but couldn't quite believe. Zander-the-hood would be a make-believe bad guy, doing it to seem tough, and on a dare. He'd have fooled Thom, but not her.

"And, well, one of the ugly crew musta had that wing-germ you had, Wiles, and sucked it into the gimmick I was using. Of course, by then, you'd shot your mouth off to the world and so gonna-be Angel blood was a marketable commodity."

"You didn't," Zander said, wanting to believe, vainly, that there were some things too low, even for his ex-partner.

"I'm a businessman," Thom said, grinning at the euphemism. "And what I had to sell was the real thing. Beauty part was, I didn't need any in-between folks. I was making the shit by being me. Trouble was, I ran into a little problem with supply and demand."

"You . . . ," Cassie began.

"I kinda overdid it," Thom said. "Next thing I know, I'm in a hospital and they're telling me I almost died. Seems I was better than a quart low and burning my rings."

"You're supposed to bulk up during the change," Cassie said.

"*Now* you tell me," Thom said. "The first sign of trouble was when I went green. See, I didn't, quite. Instead, I went this pissy sort of yellow. It never even got hard, just sort of leathery. And . . . well, I guess I fucked up. I broke the first rule of dealing."

" 'Cut everything,' " Zander said.

"Right," Thom said. "I coulda cut it with beef blood or catsup or something, but no. I sold off the good stuff, straight, and got left with the backwash."

"Thom," Zander said and stopped. He didn't know what else to say. He hadn't read anything about a connection between anemia and Penguinism, which wasn't to say there wasn't one, but . . . Should he let him off the hook, or should he say "Typical" or "Serves you right" or "When will you ever learn"? Just saying "Thom" seemed to say all of that.

Zander looked at Cassie for a hint, a clue, a safety line, but she just stood there, hugging herself as if she were cold.

"Thom?" he said.

"Present," Thom said.

"You got a place to crash, after they spring you?"

"I got nothing *but* places to crash," Thom said. "What do you think I've been trying to tell ya?"

Thom and Zander shared the former's sessions for the next several weeks, playing chess and catching up. Sometimes Cassie sat in; more often she used the time to do errands. She justified the arrangement as a mini, unmoderated version of group therapy. And anyway, she'd run out of ideas for Zander, and this was as good a way to kill time as any. They'd get back to flying practice once her bones had a chance to heal.

The arrangement also gave Cassie a breather, which she needed, now that she was temporarily grounded. Temporarily—she had to remind herself of that. This *wasn't* permanent, although it sometimes felt as though it were. Once they cut her out of this thing—this fucking sarcophagus—she'd be free to fly until her heart said, "When." Of course, it'd be snowing by then. Well, let it! She'd shoot out to Metro and hop a plane to someplace warm and southern and grab herself a piece of what the Angel magazines called "prime sky." That'd do it. That'd hit the spot.

But what about her other patients? Well, she'd been kind of losing her patience with those whiners anyway. Every time she looked at one of them, she wanted to scream. They were emotional wimps—every one of them—and if they ever got a dose of real pain instead of the shit they were whining about, it'd kill them. All they wanted, really, was a cookie, a gold star on the forehead, and a mother they paid by the hour to say,

"There, there . . ." So she took their money as a kind of revenge and tuned them out during their sessions. "Interesting," she'd say occasionally, while in her head, she was wheeling in a blue-blue sky, somewhere over the cliffs of Maui. "What does that suggest to you?"

"Tell me more about . . ."

"Hmmmm."

And they seemed to do as well or as badly as they had when she'd actually paid attention. She was on full autopilot, and it didn't matter.

Or, really, it probably saved her a lawsuit. After all, when Cassie ignored her patients, she felt less like punching them—something that seemed to be getting more and more tempting.

It was during her last session with Zander that Cassie made the mistake of confiding her feelings about Thom.

"I think he had the right idea all along," she said. "I'd talk him out of his depression, or medicate it away, if it were irrational, but it's *not*." She paced about the office, more animated and agitated than Zander had ever seen her.

"Thom's got a wholly justifiable case of depression, and I don't think there's a way out," she said, staring at her reflection in the office window, giving Zander her back, her wings.

Zander was unimpressed—not to mention worried. There was something not right with Cassie; he'd been sensing it for the last few weeks. When he was able to catch them, he'd noticed something wrong with her eyes. And it was getting worse.

"You just think a life without flying isn't worth living," he said, finally placing the look. She was a junkie, a day too long into needing a fix. "You're hooked," he said, feeling like he was talking to one of his old clients. "You're hooked and you think *everybody* should be hooked." He paused and then rolled out the latest spin:

"You just don't *respect* the nonflight life-style," he said.

Cassie looked at Zander and didn't know whether to laugh or scream—laughing or screaming being the extent of her repertoire, lately.

"Zander," she said, stopping to face him. "Do you know what the worst thing you can give a person is?"

"What?" Zander said, waiting for the punchline.

"A loaded excuse," Cassie said. She began pacing again, as if constant movement were the only way to get the sentences out.

"Don't dress up your fear as some freedom-of-choice issue," she continued. "Don't try to pass yourself off as some martyr, abstaining because you don't want to make your little buddy feel bad." She paused, too angry for this discussion, trying to force herself to calm down, despite the chemicals inside, telling her to hit something—anything.

"An albatross is an albatross," she concluded.

"And a Penguin's a Penguin," Zander said, folding his arms and rocking back on his perch. "So we just chuck it, send him out on an ice floe, let 'im—"

"Listen," Cassie said, giving him her retreating back—the theme, apparently, of this session. "Thom's a tragedy—but you don't have to join him in it. *He* doesn't have a choice, but *you* do. And you can't claim to be making an informed life-style choice when you don't know what you're giving up."

"Which is why priests check into brothels before they get ordained—"

"Stop it," Cassie snapped, turning around suddenly.

"You're not a very good therapist, are you," Zander said, looking Cassie in—and just a bit *through*—the eyes.

"Okay," Cassie said, staring him down. "Quit. Leave." It wasn't a very professional suggestion, but she hadn't been feeling very professional lately.

"Oh, *that* was easy," Zander laughed. "Dropped ya with one shot." He blew across the top of his smoking finger.

"I'm serious," Cassie said, through her clenched—and itching— teeth. "Get out of here."

"You're kidding," Zander said. "You can't just—"

"I can and I am," Cassie said, panicking inside like she had, lost over Lake Michigan, but knowing she'd have to do this quickly, or not at all. "Leave, or I'll call security."

"Oh, now I *know* it's a joke," Zander said, grabbing Cassie by her good arm. "C'mon. Fess up."

Pulling away violently, Cassie slapped Zander across the face, hard enough to leave stripes.

"Jesus," Zander said, and because he didn't know what else to say, "Jesus Christ," he said, again. This was too much. It was too fast. His heart—Jesus!—his heart was doing that thing it used to do that stopped him going outside.

"Cass," he tried. He wanted to say he was sorry, to beg forgiveness for whatever he'd done, to . . . but he couldn't do it to her back, to those damn wings.

Cassie had turned around, yet again, and was staring out the window. Beyond it, the season's first snowflakes swirled. Zander stood, looking at both; he even thought about telling Cassie he loved her—which he thought he might, given the chance. Her wings shifted, rising higher on her back, echoing, he knew, her stern and awkwardly folded arms on the other side. He sighed, and walked out the door.

Cassie watched his reflection in the window, the transparent Zander a receding ghost, shrinking, fading. When he had disappeared, when even his footsteps in the corridor were gone, Cassie turned around and closed her office door. She turned the lock with a click, and lowered herself to the floor.

Hugging her knees to her chest with her good arm and the other one, Cassie began rocking back and forth slowly, looking at her office, at the two perch chairs, her desk, the bookshelf with copies of Freud, Jung, and, so vain, *O'Connor*—the candy dish and notepad, the appointment calendar, the hourglass, the stupid shells from Lake Michigan, the flat stones from the same place, the ones so smooth, so thin they were born for skipping, the ones she'd picked up for that reason, yet brought back here, anyway, to be saved, maybe, for the perfect time . . .

The New Year's Eve party hat Zander'd given her after his first visit to her office, thanking her for saving his life a second time. He'd placed the hat on top of her globe, and she'd left it there. It had seemed as good a place as any.

Now, however, it seemed a much too hopeful commentary, under the circumstances.

Part Five

One of Those Earth-Going-Around-the-Sun Things

18

$\smile$

What day is it? Cassie wondered, sitting in her apartment, in her bathrobe, listening to a 78 playing on the hand-cranked gramophone she'd paid too much for at the antique store. It was worth it, though. It gave her music, which gave her something to do with her days now that she'd been put on indefinite leave.

It also helped cover that noise coming from the street outside her apartment window. It was winter, but a freak warm spell had settled in—apparently to torture Cassie. Outside, teenaged boy Angels were shagging cars. She could hear their laughing and whooping, the grinding of their inline skates down the pavement, the beeps of angry motorists. She refused to look. She'd made that mistake before, and it always made her so angry, their stupid, reckless joy.

They were getting stoned on the exhaust; she'd seen it happen. They'd grab a fender for a free ride, their faces in the tailpipe plume. They'd launch when the car stopped, and then go flying off, all zigzaggy and laughing, like wasps high on Raid. As if they needed that! As if flying wasn't good enough! God, it made her mad.

God, it reminded her of Zander, and all the other things she wasn't doing.

Even with the recent mild weather, it was proving a rough winter for all of them—Cassie, Zander, and Thom. As for Zander and Thom, Cassie could only guess. They'd disappeared from her schedule and her life, right around the time it had decided to fall apart. And as for Cassie . . . well, she knew damn well about that. Bathrobe, and bunny slippers, and unemployed.

It started when she decided to stop waiting for the cast to come off. No arm, she figured, no cast. No cast, less drag—aerodynamically speaking. *That* was the general thought process.

She wasn't thinking very clearly at the time.

Originally, she just wanted something to make her teeth stop itching, and then something to help her sleep. The sleep thing worked too well, and she found she needed another something to wake her up. The wake-up thing was pretty good, too, and she noticed it made her heart go like it went when she was flying—which she still wasn't, yet, a fact that had led to all the trouble in the first place. So she took more of the wake-up thing to feel like she felt when she was flying, and more go-to-sleep stuff to stop her teeth from itching, which they'd started to do, again.

As circles go, it was a vicious one, and in the middle of it, Cassie noticed how goddamn heavy her arms were—the one with the cast, of course, but the other one, too. The one in the cast was taking longer than expected to heal. Looking at its X-ray—the electric field from which had made her nauseous for the rest of the day—Cassie began wondering how bad her arm would have to be for it to be amputated completely. That'd speed things up, she thought. And then she thought some more.

The legs, she knew, had to stay; they were necessary for landing and steering, acting as an Angel's tail feathers. But those other, gratuitous sprouts, her arms and hands . . .

The justifying comparisons were obvious. To her. She'd . . . she'd be like a . . . a *swimmer,* shaving off her body hair before a big meet. Actresses got breasts enlarged or reduced and liposuction was an office visit. There'd come a time when Angel babies would have their arms tied off along with the umbilical cord, so all three could wither and drop off together. Birds managed perfectly well with just wings and feet, and she'd do the same. She'd learn to do things with her feet, like those noble cripples.

Looking back now, she realizes that her toes definitely could have used a better grip on things. Things like the ground. Reality. Her sanity.

In between her decision to cut off her arms and her decision not to, Cassie was fired—something the hospital felt compelled to do, once she'd started slugging patients.

Well, *a* patient.

His name was Steven, a big Adam's-appled boy with acne, mysteriously cocky, given his appearance, and not much older than . . . than Jack, when Cassie'd known him—in the biblical sense, and against her will. This had nothing to do with her slugging him, though. The slugging was brought on by Steven's fantasy, the one he told Cassie about, the one that involved flying over Depot Town in downtown Ypsilanti with three dollars in penny rolls. He'd fly to several thousand feet and begin unwrapping his pennies like rolls of Life Savers, letting them spill out. Steven was a physics student at Eastern Michigan, and had been thinking about this a lot. The pennies would accelerate at a constant rate of thirty-two feet per second per second, and even after accounting for terminal velocity and the braking effect of friction and resistance against the air through which they passed, by the time the pennies reached ground level, they'd be traveling with the velocity of bullets—*three hundred* bullets, splintering the pavement, ricocheting off the rails of the train tracks, shattering the windows, piercing the hoods of cars—and wounding and killing innocent bystanders.

He'd be an instant celebrity and at his trial—he'd give himself right in—at his trial, he'd not answer the prosecutor's questions. No, he'd sing a few rounds of "Pennies from Heaven" and then go on to live rent free, courtesy of the state of Michigan. Cassie asked him if he wasn't worried about being raped in prison and he said, with his teenage cockiness, big Adam's apple, his acne-constellated face: "These bad boys," meaning his wings, "will keep the other bad boys at a distance."

After which, Cassie slugged him, sending a few teeth hurtling to her office floor at a constant rate of thirty-two feet per second per second.

It was while punching Steven that Cassie started thinking about keeping her arms. As her fist hit his face, she thought: There's something they're good for. They—meaning her arms, her hands—were also good for pounding on her supervisor's desk, protesting her termination. And when she broke down in the women's room, humiliated and terrified, a great sob wracking her chest and big stupid tears dampening her face— they were there again, pulling off reams of toilet paper for her. They were there to hold the seat up and the edge of the rim as she retched into the bowl, realizing, finally, how close to the edge she'd come, how casually she'd considered cutting this last thread binding her to humanity and the whole rest of the world.

A thing with wings: that's what she was becoming. She got lucky. She shot out of herself at that moment and got a good look. As she knelt there, the tips of her wings splaying across the dirty tiled floor, inching under the toilet stalls to either side, she felt like a monster, and a fool. She checked for feet—yes, of course. Whose, she didn't know. Maybe they even belonged to a patient, or some higher-ranking colleague. Whose ever they were, though, their owner knew exactly who Cassie was, going on and on, sniffling and crying her heart out. She couldn't stop, even as embarrassed as she was, the need to pull herself together only drove the wedge in farther, splitting her apart.

And through all the racket of her crumbling life, the questions came: What had become of her? Were hugging and touching such small things to the thing she was becoming?

19

Meanwhile, Thom had moved in with Zander, and was proving to be something other than the world's best houseguest. To him, everything was "a dump," or "shit," or "lame." His casters scratched the hardwood floor in the living room, and the linoleum in the kitchen. He had to be lifted to go to the toilet, and couldn't be relied upon to always confess the need. He complained about Delores's cooking, used his condition as an excuse to look up her dress, which was also just an excuse to piss her off, and, occasionally, he threw himself down the steps to the basement. During his recuperation from this or that accidental-on-purpose fall, of course, he'd while away the hours by telling Jason stories about the "real" Zander and their outlaw days.

Zander, who'd read what self-help books he could get his hands on concerning depression, gradually came to the same conclusion that Cassie had—Thom was justifiably depressed and untreatable. It killed him, giving up like that—killed him, because of Henry. He'd taken Thom in, hoping to . . . he didn't know what. Fix things, he guessed. And he'd talked to Thom more in the last few weeks than he had throughout their entire friendship. He'd talked to Thom more than anyone else he knew. They discussed parents, childhoods, relationships, fears, first memories, last wishes, attitudes about men, women, sex, religion, politics, and junk food. The only problem was that none of it—sex, religion, junk food—none of it had anything to do with those lines on his wrists.

Thom was beyond therapy and there was only one answer for it. Cassie and Thom already knew it, and Zander had finally worked his way around to it. He wondered if Thom was being such a prick just to make it easier to come to the inevitable conclusion.

Of course, with Thom, it could also be that it was just naturally easier, being a prick.

The morning of the day Zander conceded started out bright and sunny, but changed. Around midafternoon, the snow began—a light dusting at first, just enough to outline the world's cracks, its fingerprints. By five, it was coming down pretty heavy—big goosedown flakes, piling up on the ground like crumpled love poems. By the time Zander and Thom set out on their mission, the weather had changed yet again—a freezing drizzle this time, which came and went, leaving the blue-white snow glistening with a skin of ice.

Jason had cleaned out a wheelbarrow from behind the barn, lined it with a thick towel, and brought it around to the kitchen exit, per Zander's instructions. He then helped Zander load their houseguest into the wheelbarrow, along with a fifth of Smirnoff vodka. Zander and his friend were off to the cemetery to get drunk at midnight and look at the snow. Jason knew it was something the high school kids did on weekends, and wasn't worth questioning.

The gun—the just-in-case gun from a lifetime ago—contained a single clip, sported a new silencer, and rested in the left-hand pocket of Zander's parka.

"You're sure this is what you want?" Zander asked, pushing the wheelbarrow through the crackling snow along Kresge Road.

Thom mumbled, finished his swig of vodka, and said: "Yes." He passed the bottle to Zander.

"Beautiful night for it," Zander said, accepting the bottle. Looking back, he noticed three jagged furrows where his feet and the wheelbar-row's tire had cut through the ice-coated snow. They reminded Zander of stitches—Thom's, Henry's—though he didn't say so. Instead, he took a swig and passed the bottle back and forth with Thom, the world gone silent, save for the faint splintering of thin ice.

By the time they reached the cemetery, Zander began thinking about how he'd have to hide their trail on the way back, hoping he wouldn't forget, or get stupid, afterward.

"So this is where you used to come to think," Thom said, craning up at the speared gate of the cemetery.

"Yeah," Zander said, parking the wheelbarrow by the low stone wall, and helping Thom out.

"Morbid fuck," Thom said, wrapping both arms around Zander's neck for support.

"Look who's talking," Zander said. He paused, and they both thought about what they were trying not to think about.

"Step on my boots," Zander said. "We only want to leave one set of footprints."

Thom did as he was told, and the two entered the cemetery, like clumsy waltzers. Working against Thom's dead weight as best he could, Zander was still unable to stop his friend's sagging wing tips from drag-ging in the snow. "Sorry," Zander said.

"About what?" Thom said. "I asked you to do this."

"No," Zander said. He lifted his chin, jutting slightly, indicating that Thom should look behind him.

Letting his head loll back like a baby's, Thom looked down at his wings. "No problem," he said. "No nerves. *That's* the problem."

Laboring under the weight of his friend, Zander roamed about the cemetery grounds, panting out puffs of steam, offering Thom his choice of resting place.

"Nope," Thom said of the first. "Dump."

The next was "shit," followed by "lame."

"It's not like you're going to be looking at it long," Zander said, exas-perated.

"Quality," Thom said, not missing a beat. "Not quantity."

Continuing their search, their clumsy waltz, the two finally came to a weeping willow at the north end of the cemetery. Its leaves were gone and its spindly branches were glazed with a fine sheet of ice.

"Stop," Thom said. "Here."

"It looks like a fucking ballroom chandelier," Zander said.

"So?" Thom said. "It's sparkly and I like it and fuck you."

"You're the boss, boss," Zander said, unclenching Thom's arms from around his neck and lowering him to the ground. "You comfy?" he asked, leaning his friend up against the tree.

"Fuck," Thom said, focusing on his surroundings.

"Now what?"

"That," Thom said.

Zander followed Thom's line of sight and noticed a stone angel, perching on a nearby headstone.

"Oops," Zander said. He took a swig of vodka and then pulled out the gun from his pocket. "For every problem, a solution," he said, drawing a bead on the angel's left wing. He pulled the trigger. The bullet made a muffled thwipping sound as it cut through the cold air, and pinged as it hit the granite. The sheared-off wing sliced into the snow, tip first.

Zander amputated the other wing in the same way. Surprised by how good it made him feel, he'd begun wondering how much of it was really the vodka taking hold when Thom called out.

"Hey, Wyatt Earp . . ."

"Yeah?" Zander said, turning and noticing the stone angels to Thom's left and right.

"You got me in the middle of Angel Grand fucking Central," he said.

"Done," Zander said, pulling the trigger and reducing one of the angels to a set of hand-capped knees and nothing else.

"Let me try that goddamn thing," Thom said, as Zander aimed at the last remaining angel.

"Oh," Zander said. "Okay." He placed the gun in Thom's hand and helped him draw level with the angel. "Now, on the count of—"

The gun fired and Thom rocked back from the force, glanced off the slickened tree trunk, and lay sprawled in the snow. His breath chugged out in bursts like a toy choo-choo train, and it took Zander a moment to realize that his friend was laughing.

"You missed, you know," Zander said.

"I figured as much," Thom laughed, looking up at the clear night sky. "Hey," he said. "Did you order all these stars?"

Zander looked up as he knelt by his friend's side, prying the gun loose. "Yes," he said. "I thought it'd be a nice touch."

"A touching touch, yes," Thom said. "Consider me moved."

Suddenly, Thom, who'd been giggling since he hit the ground, broke into a long, loud, rolling laugh. He began working his arms and legs opened and closed. "Hey," he said.

"What?"

"You know what I am?" Thom asked.

"An asshole?"

"Bingo!" Thom shouted, still laughing. "Right on the first guess!"

He laughed like there was no tomorrow.

The two killed two hours, three angels, and a fifth of vodka before getting down to serious business.

"We've got one left," Zander said. "You sure you want . . ."

Thom waved away the rest of the question. "I've got to tell you something," he said. He paused, weighing whether he was drunk enough. "I . . . ," he began, and stopped. He moved his hands in a "fill in the blank" gesture. "You know . . . ," he said.

Zander leaned his head against the tree's icy trunk and decided to let his friend off the hook. He filled in the blank.

"You love me," Zander said. "Kinda, sorta. Yadda, yadda . . ."

"Yeah," Thom said, relieved. "Something like that."

"I knew that already," Zander said, looking at the gun, its simple, well-turned parts. "I knew that even when you were being a prick."

Thom bristled suddenly at the bald characterization, the vodka making him, if not sensitive, at least touchier.

"You know, I didn't start out to be a bad guy," Thom said. "My parents fucked me up."

"Oh, yeah?" Zander said, drawing in a sharp, cold breath and holding it. He'd been secretly dreading this—the deathbed confession, the last-ditch plea for understanding. He didn't want to hear it. He appreciated Thom as a joyously evil son-of-a-bitch prick. He didn't want Thom's loaded excuses. He didn't want to know about the beatings, the sexual torture, the verbal abuse, the alcoholism, or bestiality. He didn't want to be connived into pity, especially if it was justified.

"So they, like, what, beat you or something?" he tried, a foot testing the ice, ready to bolt in the opposite direction.

"Huh?" Thom said, looking at Zander strangely. "Beat me? Shit, no. My parents were perfect. What made you think . . ."

Zander shrugged his shoulders.

"Naw, my parents were good," Thom said. "Too good for their own good. They . . . Have you ever met a true believer?"

"I think we ripped off a few," Zander said. He looked up. Geez, there was a shitload of stars out tonight. "Georgia," he added, sighing. "A million years ago . . ."

"No," Thom said. "That was a bunch of dabblers staring point-blank at the Grim Reaper. I'm talking about faith. *Real* faith. The sort of faith that makes you walk on broken glass and hot coals."

"Oh," Zander said. "Put that way, I guess I'd have to say no, then."

"You see, that's what my parents were," Thom said. "True believers. I mean, I found it in their *bed*, for Christ sake!"

"Found what?" Zander asked.

"Broken glass," Thom said, in his lying, "of course" tone of voice.

"Like fuck you did," Zander said, faking the anger to hide his relief. This was more like it. The old Thom. Lying all the way to the bitter end.

"They were chumps," Thom continued. "Holy, ecstatic, true-believing, speaking-in-tongues *chumps*. And I loved them and I wanted to be like them, but . . . it just didn't work out.

"It was hard work not taking advantage of them," he said. "I mean, Jesus, what's a kid s'pose to do with parents who actually buy it when you tell 'em the fish sticks you got busted with at the Winn-Dixie were placed in your pocket—by *God*, no less?"

Zander looked at Thom, at the curlicues and wisps of his glorious bullshit fading in the cold night air. He almost butted in, almost told Thom he was taking it too far, but finally settled on leaving it alone. He blew into his hands for warmth, instead, and Thom went on.

"I loved my parents," he said. "I loved them so much, I had to go away. Sometimes you just know these things. I knew I'd be a disappointment, that I'd never pull off anything holy. I tried. I let a snake bite me and al-most died. I stuck my hand into a campfire and got rushed to a hospital. After that, I gave up on holy and tried . . . something else."

"Hmmph," Zander hmmphed, not knowing how else to respond. He was a little confused now as to whether this was a lie Thom wanted be-lieved true, or something true he was telling like a lie. Thom had dropped into a tone Zander hadn't heard before, something low, and se-rious—something that felt like eavesdropping, just listening to it.

"You ever have this thing with your brain where it just kind of dares you?" Thom asked. "Mine used to do that shit to me all the time. It'd get me thinking things that scared the shit out of me, and then it'd dare me to do 'em. And I did 'em, got the fear behind me, and each one became a step farther away."

"From?" Zander said.

"Shut up," Thom said. "You know . . ."

And he did. They both did. Knew how whole lives can sometimes just "get gone," just a step—just a dare—at a time.

Neither said too much after that, taking turns, instead—separately, silently—making sure the vodka was really all gone.

Not too much later, Thom announced: "I'm ready." He turned his head away from Zander and looked up at the stars through the shiny branches of the chandelier tree.

"Sure?"

"Sure," Thom said. "Just do it. Quick."

Zander worked the last bullet into the chamber and cocked the gun. He aimed the barrel at the back of his friend's head, closed his eyes, and began silently counting to ten.

Around four, Thom said:

"Tell me about the rabbits, George . . ."

Zander dropped the gun to his side, said, "Fuck you," and discharged the last bullet into the trunk of the tree, sending shards of ice raining down on the two of them in one swift whoosh, followed by . . .

Silence.

Zander said, "Thom?"

No answer.

Zander opened his eyes slowly, not wanting to know, not wanting to see.

Sprawled at Zander's feet, Thom lay unconscious—blacked out from fear or alcohol, but still alive.

"Asshole," Zander muttered, slipping the empty gun back into his pocket and pulling Thom up by his arms. He headed back toward the wheelbarrow, not worrying about tracks, or evidence, or anything of the kind.

Nothing happened here.

Two friends got drunk.

Zander balanced the empty vodka bottle on the lap of the torsoless angel, saluted, and headed home. Struggling under Thom's dead weight, Zander thought about maybe leaving him behind, to wake up in the middle of the cemetery, in the middle of the night. By the time his friend crawled home, his hands and knees frostbitten and bleeding, Zander would open the door, his unloaded excuse ready.

"Aversion therapy," he'd say, to the curses, questions, and bleeding.

"Step One," he'd say.

20

Cassie had stopped flying, and stopped going out. There seemed to be a connection. It wasn't like Zander, though; it wasn't fear. She was kicking a habit that had gotten destructive. She was kicking it cold turkey. And the not-going-outside part . . . well, she'd lost her job, which dried up most of her excuses for venturing out. Plus, there was wind out there—cloying, and clawing, and trying to get her to spread her wings, to blow her resolve. And Angels—they were out there, too. Flying in the morning, out on the horizon, gangs of them, *flocks* of them, the sun lighting up the undersides of their wings with gold, and Cassie really didn't need that. She also didn't need their shadows passing over her, or their voices calling down about how weird it was, and how warm it was, and how it was great flying weather. Damn the jet stream or whatever the hell it was. It was supposed to be snowing. The paper said snow for later this week. Where the fuck was it?

"Where the fuck is it?" she asked Sid, her cat. She was washing dishes, and talking to Sid, damning the sky she'd parted from on such bad terms, when a knock came at her door. A glass slid from her soapy fingers and shattered on the floor; Sid split to find someplace that wasn't being bombed.

Another knock thudded, and Cassie panicked. She was in her bathrobe and slippers; she had belts lashed across her chest, holding her wings down. Her hair was a mess, the house was a mess, and there was all this broken glass now, between her and the door.

And who the fuck was it, anyway? She was at home. Home, where people don't just come knocking. It was her private nest. There were strict rules in her subdivision barring solicitors, and other than that, well . . . there was what Zander had diagnosed as her friend-o-phobia problem.

Another knock—an impatient, angry one it seemed to Cassie. She tip-toed around the broken glass, checked the peephole, and braced herself. There was an Angel woman standing on her stoop, wearing sunglasses and smiling—her mouth a whole gate of teeth jumping out at Cassie through the fish-eye lens. She opened the door a crack, leaving the chain on.

"Yes?" she asked.

"Is that little Cassie O'Connor?" the visitor proclaimed with unbridled delight, like a long-lost aunt.

The gears in Cassie's head whirred and clicked; she knew the voice, but from where? She wasn't a patient . . . or at least hadn't been, back when Cassie still had such things.

"The head of her Coop class and everything," the woman continued. "Let me get a look at you, Miss Talk-Show celebrity . . ."

"*Sharon?*" Cassie shouted, her heart lifting for the first time in weeks. "Is that you?" She slid off the chain and threw open the door. "Come in. My *God* . . ."

Sharon stepped inside and gave Cassie a big, Angel-style hug. "It's official business, I'm afraid," she said.

"Come again?"

"Sort of a recall, actually," Sharon said.

"You've lost me."

"Oh, I think it's a little premature to give up hope," Sharon said, smiling the smile of someone who's found God, or something better. She flipped the tongue of one of Cassie's belts. "Nice evening wear, though. Very S-and-M-y."

Cassie grew flustered. "Um . . . I . . . can . . . explain . . . ," she tried, closing it with a circling gesture, including the belts, her wings, her heart.

"So can I," Sharon said. "You've been having a little flying trouble lately, haven't you? A blown gyroscope in the moderation department?"

"Look, Sharon," Cassie began. "If this is about AA, I'm going to save you some time." She started to fold her arms, mainly to stop her hands from shaking and to create the illusion of control; she stopped, noticing how it only drew even more attention to the leather straps crisscrossing her heart.

"The short version: I've quit. Cold turkey. I'll never fly again, I swear." She paused. "I mean, unless I'm diagnosed with *cancer* or something, and then, you know . . . what the hell, right?"

Sharon looked at Cassie and tried to catch her eyes, no easy trick, given the fact that Cassie's eyes were trying desperately *not* to be caught, looking at the floor, the ceiling, out the window. "Angels Anonymous isn't about abstinence," Sharon said. "It's about moderation."

"So, I only never fly sometimes, forever?" Cassie cut in, sarcastically. She was going to explain how she was a therapist, had studied shit like this, and . . . but Sharon continued.

"Total abstinence is a chicken route and it usually breaks down," she explained. "Plus it leads to health problems. The atrophied muscles. The weight gain. The shallow breathing. It's a whole domino thing."

"Moderation, eh?" Cassie continued on the defensive. "And how *is* Bob, anyway? Is he still . . ."

"Fat and preaching Armageddon? Fat, yes," Sharon said. "Armageddon, no. He blew that scam when he decided to set a time and date, which came and went, along with his followers. Now he's claiming that he did it on purpose, but who can tell with Bob?" She paused. "He was a prodigy, too, you know."

Cassie began gearing up to ask Sharon to leave, when Sid entered and rubbed himself quite happily against this novelty, a stranger's legs. Sharon scooped him up and began stroking his chin, while Sid purred like a Model T.

"I'm not a joiner, you know," Cassie said. "I'm a therapist. How would it look, me going to one of your meetings and running into a client?"

"You're still in active practice?" Sharon asked, doubtfully.

"THAT'S NOT THE FUCKING POINT!" Cassie shouted, surprising not only herself but Sid, who bolted from Sharon's arms and hid behind Cassie's new, Angel-friendly TV—the one she'd been working up the nerve to unpack.

Sharon—the recaller of Angels—was apparently no stranger to being yelled at; she continued.

"So," she said, "to answer the original question: You go to a meeting where that probably won't happen. We hold 'em all over the place. You don't have to stick to Ann Arbor."

Cassie looked at Sharon, saw some flicker of Mercy run across her face . . . and realized she was stuck. There was no way she could ask her to leave now and—truth was—she didn't really want to. Instead, if she could just get Sharon off this stupid subject, she'd like to have her stay and chat, to keep her company. She could show her things, photos and things, clippings from her book tour, thank-you letters from patients; she could vindicate the life she'd lived, document a whole unfucked-up, pre-belt-bound Cassie O'Connor who was someone Mercy could be proud of.

"Would you like some coffee, or something?" Cassie asked, realizing that Sid, with his cat's intuition, had been right all along.

"Yes," Sharon said.

"Cream?" Cassie called from the kitchen, being careful about the broken glass that was still everywhere.

"No thanks."

"Sugar?" she tried.

"Is it real?" Sharon asked.

"Yes . . ."

"Then six would be lovely," Sharon said.

Getting Sharon off the subject proved difficult—especially with a cup of fresh fuel cradled in her hands. "AA is not about giving up flying," she said. "It's about changing direction. You've got to stop flying *away* from things, and start flying *toward* them—things like other people, for instance. Flying isn't a friend or a lover or a substitute for either; it's just a way—a really *fun* way—of getting from point A to point B. In AA, we help you renegotiate your relationship with flight."

Cassie didn't want to admit it, but what Sharon said made some sense. She hoped so much for it to be true; she wanted so much for her and the sky to still be friends. It was a thin thread, but better than none at all.

"I still don't know," Cassie said. "I don't want to have to deal with any of this God or Higher Power stuff. I don't believe and I can't pretend."

"You don't have to," Sharon assured. "God, as you might imagine, is a sore spot with most recovering Angels. Lots of pressure from the old image; lots of flying in the face of the stereotype and getting burnt. Mostly, we tell war stories and drink coffee." She smiled. "Lots and lots of coffee. And then we hug and tell each other to 'Fly straight.' It's a good time, really."

"It sounds too touchy-feely for me," Cassie said.

"That's part of your problem," Sharon said. "You refuse to risk the pain of being separated from others, and so you never get attached in the first place, choosing instead the controlled security of flight."

Cassie gave Sharon the sort of look she deserved. "You sound like a book," she said.

"I am," Sharon said. "I mean, that comes from one." She reached into her pocket and handed a paperback to Cassie. "Hazelden puts it out. That's your copy to keep."

Cassie turned the book over in her hands and read the title: *With Both Feet on the Ground: A Book of Daily Meditations for Recovering Angels.*

Sharon continued: "Read it. Sleep on it. If it makes sense, try a meeting." She paused. "Listen, I'll make you a deal. If you don't like it, I'll refund your misery, no questions asked."

"Cute," Cassie said, flipping through the thin book, noticing lots of white space and exclamation points.

"They sure do like bold ital, don't they?" she said, finally, looking up.

Sharon sipped her coffee and smiled. "Honey," she said, "the truth comes in all type styles."

When Cassie went to bed that night, alone and belted in, she had no real intention of sleeping on any of Sharon's prepackaged suggestions—

whether they be bold, or ital, or underlined and starred. She wasn't a group-hug kind of person; she'd get by on belts and willpower. Plus, she was no stranger to giving things up; this was just the latest in a series. It was a character-building thing. She'd do just fine on her own, thank you.

Cassie's subconscious, however, had a different agenda entirely, and that night, she dreamed.

In the dream, Cassie saw herself walking down a rain-slickened street in downtown Ann Arbor. The sun was out again and steam rose from the sidewalk as the rain evaporated. The street was deserted and as Cassie noticed this, she stepped on a wad of gum. She looked down at her stuck shoe and her lips mouthed the word, "Fuck." She couldn't hear herself say the word, though; her voice was drowned out by a great, blasting noise that split the sky.

And then things started falling.

Up.

First scraps of paper started swirling at her feet, screwing themselves upward, higher and higher in a little cyclone. Then pebbles lifted up, casting small shadows underneath for a moment, and then firing off, and up, like bullets. Leaves rustled and then stripped themselves off the trees; branches worked themselves back and forth, broke off and shot up. Sharon approached Cassie from the opposite end of the street, walking a poodle she introduced as "Cassie." The poodle began floating upward, and yelped when it hit the end of its leash. Sharon let go, and then started swimming through the air, after her dog.

Elsewhere, a mailbox vomited a flutter of bills and birthday cards, before yanking its feet out of the concrete, the long bolts squeaking out and zinging upward along with the box itself. And soon, everything went—the topsoil and grass, the sidewalk in chunks, Indian tools and dinosaur bone splinters—the whole world now, leaving behind just Cassie, her shoe, and a wad of gum. She looked at the sky, at all the receding specks of everything and thought, Now what?

Then her wings themselves unhooked and joined the wash of things, beating their hasty retreat away from wherever it was Cassie was.

And in the morning, waking in a cold sweat, Cassie decided that an AA meeting or two wasn't going to kill anyone.

. . .

Cassie felt like an idiot, standing outside St. Antoine's with her wings lashed down, looking like she was into some weird Angel bondage scene. Of course, Sharon would have to choose a meeting here. It was Cassie's own fault, asking for a meeting as far away from Ann Arbor as she could get. And still, she showed up a half hour early, and staked out a spot in the bushes, with her hands curled around a large to-go decaf from the Dunkin' Donuts down the way. From here, she could watch the cars pulling in, and note whether any of her patients—ex-patients—were among them.

God, she hated this. Hated the fact of her being here and the innumerable weaknesses that had led this way. Hated being nervous, and afraid, and worried, and anxious, and angst-ridden, and . . .

Cassie wondered if she should tell Sharon about Wyandotte Steel, and how this area had once been one of her secret places, during her glory, lone Angel days. She figured probably not; Sharon would just say something about how recovering alcoholics have to go to parties where drinks are served, and that almost anyplace they might meet was bound to have some little bit of sky, and a bird or two.

Of course, Cassie didn't buy Sharon's claim that Angels Anonymous had anything other than total abstinence as its goal. It was just a come-on to get her involved, to get her hooked on meetings instead of flying, which was how these twelve-step deals generally worked, replacing one addiction with another. Cassie was no rube, after all. She read the journals; she was a mental health professional; she knew the lines, the scams, the placebos that impressed and kept 'em coming back, but didn't— thank God—*cure* anything. So no, Sharon's Pollyanna promises about moderation didn't fool her. AA was going to be a replay of the cold turkey she'd already settled on—with a little bit of that company misery supposedly loves.

Of course, Sharon hadn't lied about the coffee. The first thing Cassie noticed upon entering the meeting room was the coffee-urn-per-chair ratio. There was one four-gallon urn for every ten seats, and a couple dozen donuts per urn. In the front was a lectern, and rows of tables set up and marked Step One through Twelve. Cassie noticed an Angel walking up and down the rows, turning the chairs to face out.

"No matter how often you tell 'em," he muttered to himself. Somehow, though, Cassie sensed that he found this little ritual settling. That's what the world is for Angels, after all—a place where the chairs are forever backward.

Sharon led Cassie to a Step One table. Cassie pulled out a chair for her, too, and Sharon asked what she thought she was doing.

"Being noble," Cassie said. "Chivalrous."

"I'm not at Step One, Cass," she said. She flipped the tail of one of Cassie's belts. "I've gotten a few steps beyond needing a leash," she added.

Cassie bristled at the characterization. "But . . . ," she protested, feeling betrayed, abandoned. It didn't matter. Sharon was already seated at a table on the other end of the hall. She had a cup of coffee in front of her and raised it when she saw Cassie staring back, helpless. Sharon smiled. She knew Cassie'd figure out what to do for herself. It was just Cassie who wasn't so sure.

Gradually, the basement filled up and Cassie was shocked by the assortment of Angels. They looked like perfectly normal people, with wings—not the skid-row types Cassie had imagined. They wore suits and blue jeans. They hung out by the coffee table and talked about sports and the weather and who was banging whom. They laughed. Cassie'd forgotten how long it had been since she'd laughed.

After a while, an Angel approached the lectern and cleared his throat. His face was long and creviced, his chin stubbly; he wore a pure white suit, a tie, and a tie tack; and he looked like a Steinbeck Okie crossed with Tom Wolfe. His name was John. Cassie learned this when he finished clearing his throat and said: "Hi, my name's John, and I'm an avia-holic."

"Hi, John," everyone said.

"Hi, John," Cassie said, a second too late.

"Hi right back atcha," John said. "Everybody got enough coffee?"

The people around Cassie laughed. It was an inside joke. Cassie let her shoulders shake, trying to fit in.

"How many first-timers we got tonight?" he asked, looking at the Step One table. A girl, maybe sixteen, sat opposite Cassie; she wore braces and had circles under her eyes. She raised her hand.

"Only one?" John said, and Cassie felt a hand on her wrist, gently but persistently pulling her arm into the air. "Oops, my mistake. Two."

Cassie shot a death-stare at the Angel sitting next to her, a fiftysomething guy in a Detroit Tigers baseball cap. "Sharon told me to help you out," the man said. He stuck out his hand. "Name's Simon."

"Cassandra," Cassie said.

"Is Cassie okay?" Simon asked. "Sharon told me you preferred that."

"What else did Sharon tell you?" Cassie asked, looking past him to the table where Sharon sat. A woman in a lime green windbreaker eclipsed Cassie's view of her sponsor.

"Well, she said you're a little squirrelly, but a nice girl."

"She did, did she?"

"Well, she said the nice girl stuff," Simon said. "And I figured out the squirrelly part from how you keep looking away from people when they talk to you."

"Sorry," Cassie said, turning to look him in the eye.

"No problem," he said, turning away, scratching the back of his neck distractedly. "I'm a little squirrelly, too."

Simon, it turned out, was an alcoholic before he ever became an Angel, and he'd exchanged one addiction for another. He was a good guy and, true to his word, a little squirrelly. He'd plucked his wings in his crusade to stay grounded.

The girl in the braces and nervous-breakdown face was named Tanya; she wore belts like Cassie. She was still a virgin, technically, but in no other way. She'd started flying to keep her mind off sex and then, wouldn't you know it, she got hooked. She was a good Catholic kid and was trying really hard, you know, to keep it that way, but these things kept happening inside her, and she could swear God had it in for her. And she really didn't mean that, because God she knew was love, and so this must be a test. "You know," she said, "like the Emergency Broadcast System. This is only a test . . ." And she proceeded to shrill like an air-raid siren until the table leader patted her on the shoulder and thanked her for sharing.

Next to Tanya was Bill, who sat rapt throughout Tanya's talk, nodding, empathizing, looking at her breasts with something like a laser's intensity. He'd done nothing to his wings, and seemed out of place. When it was his turn, he said, "You know, I can really relate, Tanya. You know, the trying to be good stuff when it's really against your nature, and you got all these chemicals saying, you know, go for it, man . . . just, you know, go for it." The others at the table looked at one another, skeptically. Apparently, they'd heard Bill "relating" to other first-timers of Tanya's weight class before.

Nancy wanted everybody at the table to know that she liked flying and intended to keep on flying and the only goddamn reason she was there with a bunch of whiny losers in the first place was because she got busted on a goddamn FUI—Flying Under the Influence—like that wasn't redundant already. "Who the fuck flies straight?" she asked. And frankly, none of them (the fuck) knew.

Frank wept. He just wept. Frank weighed over three hundred pounds and he started saying something about how he loved everybody at the table and loved AA, and how, dammit, he promised himself he wasn't going to do this, and then did. Tanya looked at him and tears began welling up in her eyes. Bill looked at both of them, and cursed himself for not having thought about crying.

The table leader, Patrick, was barrel-chested, even by Angelic standards, and he talked about training for the Olympics. He was going to snag a gold for the USA in the last Olympics, except word got out about how the sponsoring government was secretly rounding up Angels and gassing them. As it turned out, the rumor was started by the local Angels themselves, the only ones who *didn't* boycott the Olympics that year. It was when Patrick decided to cut back on his training and found out he couldn't that he realized he needed to renegotiate his relationship with flight. His left wing was bandaged, and Cassie wondered if he'd chosen Andrew's route.

When Cassie's turn came, she said she'd come because a friend brought her, and was just trying to figure out if this was the sort of place for her. She thanked them, and passed to the next person, which was something Sharon promised she could do.

Then came Devlin, the theorist. "You know," he said, "I've been to AA—the alcohol one—and this one, and Overeaters Anonymous, and Gamblers and Shoppers, and Sexaholics, and I'm gonna tell you, man, it's the last one that's talking straight about all this stuff. It's all sex. Flying is sex. Food is sex. Drugs are sex. Booze is sex in a bottle, and sex is . . . well, you know, *sex*. And I was reading how they've started calling this whole wing deal—'this period in history'—the Rapture, and I looked it up and you know what I found? Sex. Rapture, raptor, and rape *all* come from the same root. And when you think back on how you changed and what flying has done to your life—ain't it like being raped? I mean, you're minding your own business and, boom, these wings just grab on to you and you got no vote and—"

Cassie broke in. "SHUT UP!" she shouted, in bold, in ital, underlined, and with exclamation points.

The background noise in the church basement stopped. Heads turned. It was going to be a show.

Devlin looked at Patrick. "Hey man," he said.

"No cross-talking," Patrick said. "That's one of the rules."

"I'm not cross-talking; I'm unskipping," Cassie said. "I'm taking back my turn."

"Let Devlin finish first," Patrick said.

"I would if he wasn't talking *complete shit,*" Cassie snapped, realizing as she said it that she had no plan of ever coming back, and realizing, too, that this afforded her untold freedom.

"He shouldn't talk about things he doesn't understand," she continued. "He has no right." She looked at Devlin, who shrank back in his chair. "Have you been *raped,* Devlin?"

Devlin shrugged his shoulders.

"That's no answer," Cassie snapped.

"No," Devlin said.

"SEE!" Cassie shouted, suddenly—finally—aware that the entire meeting had gone quiet, and not caring. "See, Devlin's never been raped. So, when Devlin says that something is like being raped . . . well, he's full of shit, isn't he?" She paused; a few heads bobbed around the table.

"Now *me,*" she continued, clapping a hand to her chest, "*I've* been raped, and I've grown wings, and you know, Devlin, they're totally different things." She paused, suddenly feeling the silence as a heavy, downward-pushing thing.

"And that's all I have to say," Cassie said, quieter now, embarrassed, noticing that she was standing, and unable to remember having risen. She noticed, too, that the anger was still rippling through her like electricity. She'd never told anyone in the world the secret she'd just confessed at the top of her lungs to a room full of strangers. And it felt *great,* she realized. Fantastic, really, like the good kind of tired after flying almost too far.

And then she wondered about the room. It was *still* quiet, in the slowed-down time of her rush. She looked around, expecting some AA goons to come charging up to drag her out. She looked at the tables, filled with Angels, and noticed that it was only her table—the *first* one—where the Angels bound, or plucked, or weighed themselves down. The others seemed . . . *normal* and . . .

Why were they smiling?

And Sharon, all the way over there in the back, at the Step Twelve table, why was she standing? Why was she beating her wings together like that?

Cassie noticed other Angels standing. They smiled in slow motion, and moved their wings like Sharon had. They were clapping. This was how Angels clapped. They were clapping for her, stupid ol' Cassie O'Connor, who couldn't remember now when it was she'd started to cry. She blamed the noise, of course. The noise of Angels clapping would make anyone cry, so strangely warm, so soft, the thump-thumping steady, steady, like the beating of some great, inexplicable heart.

After that first meeting, Cassie decided she was cured. Sharon, of course, had a different opinion.

"We've all gone through it," she said, sitting opposite Cassie in a booth at a Big Boy a few blocks from St. Antoine's. "It's like going to the dentist; the pain miraculously disappears in the waiting room. AA's like that. You have some showy breakthrough first time out and leave all jazzed because you don't *really* need to do all the hard work of recovery."

Cassie sat, too excited to eat. She toyed with her pie and left her coffee untouched. She smiled and nodded, not listening. Her head was a Christmas tree and the Fourth of July. She'd get her job back tomorrow, and take a drive up to Lake Michigan, maybe that weekend.

Sharon raised two fingers while sipping her coffee.

Cassie, mistaking the gesture for either Peace or Victory, said, "Yeah?"

"Give me two more meetings," Sharon said, "before you start hitting the wild blue. Let's see if that tooth acts up again."

Cassie agreed to two more meetings, not because she needed them, but to get Sharon off her back.

At meeting two, the Becky Affair was the topic of tearful confession. Meeting three was about Cassie's mom, Mercy, while Andrew hung around for meetings four, five, and six. Which was okay, by that time, seeing as Cassie was doing meetings once or twice daily. Meanwhile, the refund offer on her misery went unclaimed.

Cassie became as obsessed with her recovery as she had been with flying, moving from Step One to Step Twelve in almost no time. She discovered what Sharon had promised, that moderation, and not abstinence, was the key. There was no reason not to enjoy flying; it sparked off the same chemicals as chocolate cake and a good hug. Deep down inside, she knew she'd turned flying into an act of glorified masturbation. Deep down inside, she knew life should be big enough to include loved ones other than the sky. Still, it helped, hearing it said out loud.

Eventually, as she started hugging more, Cassie found she needed flying less, which, in the double-reverse world of human psychology, made flying okay, again. Slowly, Cassie herself became okay, again. She returned to work, and, with her supervisor's support, began diversifying her patient load to include non-wing-related complaints. And when the warm weather returned in earnest, she started flying again, on the buddy system, this time, because two wills are stronger than one.

Sharon came with her that first time back, and Cassie showed her how to pet seagulls. It was the damnedest thing she'd ever seen an Angel do, Sharon said, and couldn't stop laughing when she did it herself.

"You kids," Sharon said, drawing her fingers down the back of a gull. "You gonna show this shit to that guy of yours?"

Cassie said she didn't want to jinx it by talking, wondering if she'd really said anything out loud. She'd been thinking about him more and more lately. Wherever Zander was, she hoped he was okay. Or at least working on getting that way.

21

Waltzing in the cemetery with his unconscious friend, Zander had a breakthrough.

"You don't need a therapist," he announced to Thom in the morning. "You need a mechanic."

Thom—a disgruntled, still-alive Penguin with the sniffles now, and a headstone-sized hangover—said, "Shut up."

"It's an issue of balance," Zander continued, undeterred—excited, even. He sat on the floor of the kitchen, filling two large tubs with cement as he explained. "Not spiritual, psychic, or emotional balance," he said. "No. Just stupid, dumb, physical *balance*," he added, placing the legs of a walker into the cement. "And counterbalance. We just need to tip you forward to the same degree your wings want to tip you back."

"There's more to it than that," Thom said.

"Oh, I'm sure there is," Zander said, almost gleeful, now that he had a handle on a problem that didn't involve him personally. "Atrophied muscles, probably some inner-ear stuff, but . . ."

And so the project began. Jason and Zander worked on massaging

Thom's legs while the cement set. Thom's legs had become pale, almost blue, withered stalks from months of inactivity. Zander began slapping them to bring color to the surface, and instructed Jason to do likewise, despite Thom's complaints that unlike his wings, his legs had their full complement of nerves.

"I learned this from my stepdad," Zander explained. "We had this sick tree that had stopped growing, and he got it going again by beating it with a rubber hose. He whipped the trunk with it so hard, it wrapped all the way around, then he whipped it back off, and gave it another whack. He said the tree would send too much sap, trying to fix the damaged bark, and the extra sap would wind up as extra growth . . ."

"I'm not a tree," Thom protested, "but I'm starting to feel like a sap . . ."

"Humor's good," Zander said, working at Thom's legs and practically glowing. "Keeps the spirits up." He reached a hand toward one of the cement-filled tubs, tapping the surface. "Looks like we're good to go," he announced.

On the count of three, Jason helped Zander stand Thom up, each wrapping one of Thom's hands around the walker's rubberized grips. "This is one small step for Penguins," Zander said, patting his friend's shoulder. He counted to three again, and the two let go.

"It looks retarded," Thom said, teetering, but remaining upright.

"I'm sure it does," Zander said, placing a pair of side-shielded glasses on Thom's face. "But you're standing."

"Standing," Thom said. "And that's all."

"Give it time," Zander said, patting his friend on the shoulder and walking away. "Give it till dinnertime," he added, closing the door.

Thom stood where the two had propped him. He looked at Jason, who sat eating an apple. "Give me a bite of that," he said.

"Get it yourself," Jason said, leaving the half-eaten apple on the kitchen sink opposite Thom, and exiting.

At noon on that first day, Zander entered the kitchen to find Thom moved approximately one and a half feet from where they had left him. The apple on the kitchen counter had gone brown, and a puddle of urine spread at Thom's feet, making more progress across the floor than he had. Thom's head was angled back and he stared at the kitchen ceiling, opened-mouthed, but still standing.

"I've got something for you," Zander said, producing two Tupperware bowls, one flat-bottomed, the other domed, with the first nested inside the second. A marble was locked inside, between the two.

"What is it?" Thom asked, still staring at the ceiling.

"A hat," Zander said, forcing Thom's head straight and placing the bowls on top. Using a belt left over from his own reintroduction to the world, Zander strapped the ad hoc affair to his friend's head.

"And a stylish one," Thom said, bitterly. "What's it supposed to do?"

"Feedback," Zander said. "It gives you feedback so you can work on reorienting your sense of balance." He smiled. "Neat, huh?"

"I look like an idiot," Thom said.

"No," Zander said. "You look like a moron. An idiot wouldn't be caught dead in something like this."

Thom tilted his head to one side, listening to the marble roll. "Are you sure you used all the bullets?" he asked.

Thom went without food that first day, but hit the table in time for breakfast the next. Gradually, he got good enough with the walker to get anywhere in the house that didn't involve going up or down stairs. He also made it something of a mission in life to internalize Zander's damn marble hat and blinders, and consigned both to a closet after a month.

During this time, Zander noticed a distinct change in his friend. Things were no longer dumps, or shit, or lame. He stopped talking about or attempting suicide. Words like "tomorrow" started reentering his vocabulary. He also began asking Delores to make special meals for him, and stopped complaining about her cooking.

And Delores, for her part, stopped complaining about Thom. She laughed when he made a joke, and occasionally joked back. Zander noticed that she was actually a rather striking woman—it was something about her eyes—and hardly the harpy he'd pegged her. Halfheartedly trying to regain her attention, he realized it had shifted away from himself and toward Thom. She did the thing with brushing the hair out of his eyes; she lit his cigarette. Thom's plate was filled first, and with the best slices of whatever they were having. And she smiled like a goof when he was around.

Thom, meanwhile, taught Jason how to make a fake ID, and gave him a few pointers on shoplifting. Delores scolded them when she found out, but was actually relieved, and thanked Thom later, privately, in her own way. She'd grown worried that Jason was becoming too much of a wimp. So, while it was not generally the case with most boys, she figured Jason could benefit from a few bad influences. "He doesn't have any thug friends," she confided. "That's not healthy, is it?" It was a fairly pervasive though unspoken opinion downriver that you needed friends on both sides of the law—for balance, and to qualify as a well-rounded individual. Thom, for his part, was happy to be of service. Delores, for hers, realized she wouldn't mind having a thug friend of her own. Neither told Zander, of course, though the fact of Delores's unrumpled bed, morning after morning, spoke volumes.

Another thing Thom didn't tell Zander was thank you for getting him back on his feet. Zander, for his part, considered the project only half-done as long as Thom still needed the walker.

So Zander read books about Penguinism and other cases of partial transformation. He read books about physical therapy, meditation, mind-over-matter, and faith healing. He asked himself what Cassie would do now, if she'd gotten this far.

In his dreams, Zander worked on the problem. Weight was the problem. And balance. And falling. And gravity. And in the answer dream, Zander and Thom were astronauts, living on the moon. For some reason, there were headstones on the moon, and Zander and Thom didn't need space suits, and they were dancing in slow motion. Cassie was there, too, shaking her head at the two of them. She was made of stone, with one wing cracked off and wedged into the lunar soil.

Zander woke up from this dream in a cold sweat, thinking first to make an appointment with Cassie, but then pushing beyond it, to the eureka.

And when he finally announced to Thom that the two of them needed to break into the local high school, Zander left out mentioning the dream altogether.

. . .

"You know," Thom said, holding on to the grips of his walker, "when I busted out of this place a hundred years ago, I never figured on busting back in."

Zander wedged his crowbar under the padlocked latch, the only thing standing between Thom and him and the high school's indoor pool. He twisted, jammed the point in as far as he could, and then ripped the latch out of the door. One of its four screws hit the concrete—*pink!*

"Things change," Zander said, pushing open the door. The warm, humid air poured out as steam, billows and wisps through which Thom shuffled and Zander walked.

"I don't like the looks of this, boss," Thom said.

"Get closer to the edge."

"I see where this is going," Thom said. "I think I'd rather not . . ."

"GET TO THE FUCKING EDGE," Zander shouted, remembering with a piercing feel Cassie and the trampoline.

"Right-o, boss," Thom said, resigning himself to it and dragging his walker and his body to the edge of the pool.

"I ever tell you about how Cassie cured me of agoraphobia?" Zander asked.

"Nope."

"She called it flooding," Zander said. "Total immersion." He stepped around to the side of his friend and pulled the walker out from under him. Catching Thom as he tilted back, Zander pushed with all his strength in the opposite direction, knocking his friend into the pool.

"Sink or swim," Zander said, "in other words."

Thom thrashed about in the water for a moment, rolling under and then gasping to the surface once again.

"What do you call a paraplegic in a pool?" Zander shouted, over Thom's racket.

Thom shook his head, pleaded with his eyes.

"Bob," Zander said. "Christ, that's an old one. I figured—"

"I'm drowning!" Thom screamed.

"Oh," Zander said. "You should have said so sooner." And with that, Zander jumped in after Thom, found his hands, and held on.

"Calm down," he said. "Relax. Float. Bob . . ."

"Fuck you, Wiles," Thom shouted. "Fuck you. Fuck you. FUCK YOU!"

Zander said nothing. He just held on to Thom's hands and tried to catch his eyes.

Gradually, once he stopped sinking, Thom stopped struggling, stopped screaming, and started looking Zander in the eye. His wings had risen to the surface and floated behind him like life preservers; his feet rested firmly on the bottom. Something very weird was happening behind their eyes. Thom saw it. Zander saw it.

They smiled.

"Did you feel that?" Thom asked Zander.

"Yes."

"Kind of like a bubble," Thom said, "only inside, around the stomach and rising and popping in your head. What's it feel like? It's like . . ."

"A coffee maker," Zander said. "Percolating."

"Yes!" Thom shouted. "Christ . . . ," he added.

Zander let go of Thom's hands and moved away. "Walk toward me," he said.

Slowly at first, and then with greater confidence, Thom walked toward Zander. "It feels . . ."

"Yes," Zander said.

". . . like I'm floating."

"I know."

"I could do this on land," Thom said, excitedly. "I *know* I could do this on land. I just have to get the coffee maker going inside my head and . . ." He stopped.

"Hey," Thom said, suddenly, pointing at Zander's feet, which were themselves resting firmly—six inches *above* the bottom of the pool.

"I know," Zander said, blushing for a million stupid reasons he couldn't name.

22

The downriver area has more resale shops than Ann Arbor. There's the Salvation Army, Value Village, Bargain Barn, St. Vincent de Paul, Cinderella's Attic, Riverton Rummage, the Penny Pincher, Memory Lane, and the Little Sisters of the Blind. Cassie loved resale shops; they made her nostalgic for her Coop days, and gave her a weird sense of hope, knowing that somebody's castoff was another person's treasure. And anyway, downriver wasn't that far from St. Antoine's, a place that had become her second home, so . . .

So what? she'd tell Zander if she happened to run into him. It's not like she made a special trip or anything. That she'd worked her way through the shops one by one like a detective on a case, asking if they had any other Angel customers and what they might look like . . . well, Zander didn't need to know that. He also didn't need to know about her scanning the obituaries for either his or Thom's name, or that she had looked up Delores's number and called it, once, twice, from a pay phone—hanging up each time before saying anything, humiliated by the sound of her heart's static. And he especially didn't need to know that coincidences like the one she was currently engineering . . . well, he didn't need to know how much work they take.

So, when Cassie ran into Zander at the Bargain Barn off Telegraph that Friday afternoon in early May, her surprise was semipracticed. The part that wasn't was the part that came at seeing Thom alongside him, walking.

"Why, Zand—" she began. "Oh shit," she ended.

"Nice to see you, too," Thom said. Despite his initial hopes at the pool, Thom had not quite abandoned external aids. Instead of the walker, however, he wore weighted, Frankenstein-style boots and a vest with lead bricks sewn into the front hem. A cane finished off the ensemble— not exactly fashionable, but light-years better than the walker and the marble hat. Next to him stood Zander, dressed the same way, save for the weights, but including the cane.

"What happened?" Cassie asked, realizing that she meant the question for both of them.

"Zander cured me," Thom said. He looked at Cassie, stuck out his tongue, and then smiled. "So there . . ."

Cassie looked at Zander. Her face said, How? though her mouth couldn't make it come out.

Zander shrugged his shoulders and wings. "First-timer's luck," he said. "Turns out he didn't need a therapist; he needed a mechanic."

Cassie was about to say that *that* made a lot of sense, capping it with something bitter and sarcastic, when Zander touched her shoulder so lightly the words, again, went away.

"I'll explain it to you later," he said.

"So, what kind of boys' club is this, anyway?" Cassie asked, indicating the matching outfits.

"We're going to go spelunking," Thom said. "Any idiot could see that."

"That's a long story, too," Zander said. "What we're really doing is looking for something to get this asshole married in."

"*Thom?*" Cassie said.

"And Delores," Zander said. "It's a totally codependent thing and sick from the get-go, but . . ."

"Codependent," Thom said. "Simpatico. Split hairs. All I know is . . ."

He paused, running out of sarcasm. "She makes life seem like a good idea," he said, a little embarrassed at the sentiment, but serious.

"Well," Cassie began, and realized she didn't know where to go with it. "Well, well," she concluded.

"A 'Congratulations' would be nice," Zander whispered, leaning next to her ear.

"Oh, yeah," Cassie said. "Congratulations." She stuck her hand out, and then withdrew it. "Is it okay to shake hands?" she asked.

"As long as you don't do any of that martial arts stuff on me," Thom said. "I'm cantilevered."

Thom and Cassie looked at each other silently for a moment, trying to figure out which of them was the official third wheel. Zander cast the tie-breaking vote.

"Hey, Thom?" he said.

"Yeah?"

"Killer suit coats in aisle six."

"Fuck you very much, too," Thom muttered, limping away and giving the two their privacy.

"I figured out what you were doing with me and Thom," Zander said, now touching Cassie with both hands, one on each shoulder.

"I—" she began, but before she could finish, Zander slipped his arms between her wings, and, pushing against the invisible fingers, hugged her, Angel-style.

"Thanks," he said.

"Thanks for what?" Cassie asked.

"You know . . ."

"Know what?" Cassie demanded.

Zander turned toward the rack next to him and slid some hangers around, clattering, and changed the subject. "The weather's getting nice again," Zander said.

"It's called spring," Cassie said. "It's one of those earth-going-around-the-sun things that happens every year or so."

"Uh-huh," Zander said, clicking his way through more used clothing. "What are you doing after work on Thursday?"

. . .

It was the second full week in May, and the evening was warm and windy. During the day, Zander visited Cassie in Ann Arbor, several hours ahead of schedule. He left the agenda ambiguous, a sort of maybe-date, maybe-friends thing. By then, Zander had his own car, with *two* Angel seats, and so he'd be driving that evening. To her question about where, he said only, "Downriver." Cassie wore lipstick, and made sure she had money for a bus. At his request, she made sure to bring the New Year's Eve hat in a shopping bag.

Sitting in the quad, waiting for Cassie to clock out, Zander looked at the sky, the almost painful blueness of it, and watched the high, stretched-out clouds blowing by. It was the warmest day so far that year; shorts and sundresses made their first appearances on the quad. And the possibility of flight was everywhere Zander looked—in birds chirping here, the Frisbees flung there, and the kites. Christ, the kites! The sky was lousy with them, darting, colorful, mad. How Zander longed to be up there among them! He closed his eyes and imagined himself snagging kites one by one and running with them, like a fish snatching a worm in an upside-down version of the sport. The line would zing out from the kite-flyers' spools, slicing or burning careless hands. Drops of blood would fall to the grass; they'd curse Zander like they cursed foul weather, and he'd just laugh back at them. He'd laugh back at them like God!

When Cassie finally came out and found where Zander had parked himself, she commented on the weather. "It certainly is blustery, isn't it?" she said.

"It sure is," Zander agreed. "Good kite-flying weather." He touched her knee in a gentle, familiar way. "Let's go," he said.

Along the way to wherever they were going, Cassie decided to tell Zander about the rape. It was forcing intimacy, she knew, and could scotch her hopes for the evening, which could be why she was doing it, for all she knew. It was a leap into the unknown, like jumping from the roof of the Coop that first time. She didn't know how Zander would react. Would he make light of it? Would he go silent or treat her like a Fabergé egg?

As she told him her story, she watched his hands on the steering wheel, the whitening knuckles. Then she went into the details she hadn't even told her AA friends. She told Zander about what happened *after* the bike lock.

"It was a message," Cassie said. "He was supposed to understand how he hurt me." She paused. "Both things didn't have to be wrecked. He could have cut his car and freed my bike. Or . . ."

"He cut the bike," Zander said, his teeth tight.

"Yes," Cassie said. "He cut the bike, and then he got a locksmith to drill out the core. If he was going to use a locksmith anyway, you think he could have at least saved my bike. But he couldn't do that. Everybody knew whose bike that was." She paused. "I suppose it could have been worse," she said. "He could have claimed it was the act of a woman scorned, or something."

"Christ, Cass," Zander said. "I'm sorry." He paused. "Do you know where this guy lives?"

"Why?"

"I've . . . ," he began and stopped. "I've kind of got connections, from the old days, and . . ."

Cassie looked at Zander and smiled, her eyes shiny and just short of tears. How sweet, she thought. He was offering to arrange a hit, to have Jack—what did they call it?—whacked. In the idiom they were slowly coming to share, it was as close to a profession of love as he'd ever made.

"Thank you," Cassie said. And though she couldn't think of anyone she'd like to have whacked more, she politely declined the offer, patting the back of Zander's hand to let him know she appreciated the gesture all the same.

Zander took Southfield all the way down to the river, and hopped onto West Jefferson. "Oh no, Zander," Cassie said, recognizing the route. "Not there."

"Why not?" Zander said. "I've got to get back on the horse."

"It's creepy," Cassie said. "It makes me nervous."

"All the more reason," Zander said. "You told me once that this used to be your favorite, secret place." He paused. "I've got enough on my shoulders—wings included. I don't want to be responsible for taking away your special place."

And with that, they pulled up alongside Wyandotte Steel, a bit rustier, a few more broken windows, but otherwise no worse for wear.

"Please, Zander," Cassie said. "It's too soon."

"I almost flew when we did the trampoline," he said. "I've got to give you that."

"But almost isn't enough," Cassie said. "You can be almost alive after you break your neck."

"I've got a secret," Zander said. "I've been weighing myself."

"And?" Cassie said, looking at Zander, wondering if he'd taught himself the trick on his own.

"And I'm getting lighter," Zander said, smiling.

"You can levitate?" Cassie cried, throwing her arms around his neck. "That's fantastic!"

"Well, in water," Zander said. "Land, not so much. But I'm definitely down to what the books say is a good flying weight for my span."

"Okay," Cassie said, getting out of the car, heading for the fence. "We'll try this, but promise me one thing."

"Shoot."

"If you have any trouble, try to get yourself to the water," Cassie said. "I'll get you out like before."

"Ms. O'Connor," Zander said, "as far as I'm concerned, 'before' is history."

"Well, yes, technically," Cassie said, smirking before Zander got the chance.

Facing themselves as they had before, more than two years earlier, the story changed. Zander looked pale in the light reflecting off the river. Even from where she perched, Cassie could see that he was holding on with all his might, and that it might not be enough.

"You don't have to do it," Cassie shouted, something that Zander would have been willing to concede, until she said it was okay. Then it became a dare not to back down, and he was stuck.

"Nobody will think anything less of you," Cassie added, and Zander thought, Why don't you just push me off now, and get it over with?

"You don't have to *prove* anything . . ."

"Will you please stop talking," Zander said. "For once," he added. It was not the tone of a patient talking to his therapist, or even the old Zander talking to Cassie. There was something stronger, yet more desperate in it, and Cassie didn't know whether to be happy, or afraid.

"I just need to think," Zander said and Cassie prepared to shout that not thinking was the best strategy, but then decided that the same could be said for not talking.

But she couldn't help thinking herself—couldn't stop thinking how like before this current silence, this current waiting was. Her hat was on tighter, this time; that seemed, perhaps, the only difference.

Meanwhile, Zander—his *brain*—was a wild salad of thoughts about all the last times he'd already been through if this didn't work. The chili cheeseburger he'd eaten on the quad, waiting for Cassie, would be his last supper. The piss he'd taken in the Rackham Auditorium john afterward would be his last. He'd never know whether Thom and Delores worked, and he wouldn't be around to be a best man, Angel, or whatever. And was he crazy, or did Cassie still seem to have a thing for him? Was that just another thing he'd never find out? Was tomorrow going to be sunny like today? Would they outline his wings with their chalk?

At some point, Zander began crying quietly to himself. Or maybe it was just flop sweat. He could taste the salt of whatever it was in his mouth, and he thought, Man, this is stupid. I don't have to do this, he thought. I have taste buds. I eat, shit, and sleep, he thought. People who eat, shit, and sleep don't fly. People with taste *buds* don't fly. Get serious.

And then the police helicopter stopped by for a look at the two lovebirds, guilty of misdemeanor breaking and entering. Or was it trespassing? Split hairs. It was a law they were breaking—of nature, and the state of Michigan.

"Stop where you are," the bullhorn crackled. "Raise your arms—and your wings—in the air."

Zander did as he was told. He prayed backward with his wings. The searchlight hit him full force, bleaching his body—and even his black wings—a blinding white.

Man, Zander thought, how'd the world get so heavy all of a sudden? He thought about Jimmy Cagney in *White Heat,* thought about shouting, "Top of the world, Ma! Top of the world!" but figured it'd get lost in the translation—and the chopping of the helicopter blades.

"Don't make any funny moves," the bullhorn sputtered again.

Funny? Zander thought. How's this, he added, stepping out into space and falling . . .

Cassie shut her eyes as Zander leaped. She heard the sound of his body whistling through the air, and waited for the splash, or worse. Instead, she heard the slight cough of his wings opening; the warm *harrumph* of air gliding over and under their canopy. The bones in his wings creaked and cracked, like stiff knuckles. But they worked! She opened her eyes. They worked just fine.

The helicopter took off, with more important matters to attend to than a pair of miscreant Angels.

Zander, meanwhile, had stopped his rapid descent, had slowed, and slowed again, until he finally reached some balance point. He felt like he felt when he first learned to swim, learned that he really could trust the water to hold him up. He tried a circle. It was easy. First he dipped his left wing, then his right, riding the thin skin of the air, its direction telegraphed to him down the quills of his flight feathers, into the skin from which they sprouted, and up the main cables of his nervous system.

He flew over the city of Detroit, which didn't get many Angels. He headed toward the Arts Institute, and Wayne State, flew past the student apartments. He could see the students gathering slowly on their balconies. He could hear the distant ringing of telephones, followed by dark apartments going bright, the drapes spreading, and more students, and more fingers, pointing. There were catcalls and whistles; there was some applause.

He wanted to say something to the gathering crowd, but could come up with nothing more profound than "Wow!" or "Jesus," knowing that the wind would blast his meaningless words anyway, scattering their letters like dandelion seeds.

Cassie, watching from her perch with binoculars, smiled, thinking things like, Go, Zander! Go! and other rah-rah silliness. And then an unsilly thought poked its way into her brain: He didn't know how to land.

Landing was subtle; you didn't do it on concrete on your first flight. Cassie herself, a flying whiz kid, had trouble her first time, finally grabbing the top of a pine tree and whipping back once, twice, nearly spraining both wrists, and then clinging there, not knowing how to get down. Bob finally had to come after her with an extension ladder and a "Ho-ho-ho, merry Christmas," to fetch down this Angel, stuck at the top of a pine tree.

There were no pine trees here, no safety nets, and what Cassie knew of Zander told her he wouldn't think to head back to the river for a splashdown. He'd try a running three-pointer right onto West Jefferson, in between lights. He'd jam his tibias into his femurs and blow out his kneecaps. And they'd be doing the recuperation rag all over again.

Shit.

Holding down the party hat with one hand, Cassie jumped from her perch and headed for Zander. Seeing her, he smiled, and blushed and shrugged his shoulders. There was something just slightly embarrassing, being caught having so much fun.

He tried to talk and she tried to talk, but the blood rushing in their heads made conversation pointless. Seeing no other way around it, Cassie grabbed Zander's arms, just above the wrists, like a trapeze artist catching her partner.

Zander, for his part, didn't have the faintest idea what was going on. Did she want to dance? Was there something else they could do while flying? Certainly not in front of these kids on their balconies! Not to mention that Zander was nowhere near that coordinated. Hell, he wasn't even sure how he was going to . . .

Oh.

He got it. He watched Cassie's eyes, doing what she did. Big, slow flaps, followed by short, quick, quick, quick ones, just before reaching the sidewalk and . . .

"So?" Cassie said, after they'd touched down safely.

"So what?" Zander said.

"Sew buttons," Cassie said. "How was it?"

"Oh," Zander said, smiling, *"that . . ."* He paused, as if giving it some thought. "Not half bad," he said.

Cassie glared at him. He was messing with her, pushing her buttons, and this . . . *this* was what she was thinking of getting messed up with?

She looked at Zander—objectively—at his smiling, sweaty face, his heaving chest, his tight little excited nipples pressing against the fabric of his work shirt, its tail out and flapping in the breeze like some ten-year-old playing full-out during recess.

She looked at Zander, and answered her own question:

Hell, yes!

Grabbing his shoulders in both her hands, she pulled Zander toward her, stronger now than the dumb physics of repelling electrons, stronger even than the fear of who needed who more. She kissed him with all her neediness, and all her might.

And, like Katy Adler before her, she used her tongue.

A funny thing happened on the way to Zander and Cassie making love. The Halo Effect that had driven them apart with no little bit of relief on either side during that first attempt wasn't such a big deal, this time. Sure, the element of surprise was blown; sure, the mutual, unspoken, but real desire to flee, to use whatever happened by as an excuse for not doing what they'd hastily dared themselves into doing—that, too, shot, blown, likewise. But there was something else, a wonderful surprise you had to push to find and that, pushing, they found. Who knew—who would have suspected—that the polarity of an Angel's halo was a mood thing? Who knew—or could have guessed—that it could flip if an Angel wanted it to, that it could be *adjusted* to fit the situation, or that the process of adjustment could do such glorious things to the heart?

"Did you . . . ?" they asked each other.

And they had. It was a flutter through their bodies, like ripples on a sunlit pond, followed by something like melting, something like sex, but bigger and better. A moment's resistance, like two bodies meeting at the barrier of their skin, and then a shimmer and resistance became attraction, the skin dissolving as the two entered a common space, and not just a few inches' worth, "down there," but all over, full-bodied penetration, followed by full-bodied orgasm, the sort of thing that could give heroin or even flying a run for its money.

"Did you . . . ?"

"Would you . . . ?"

Oh yes. They did and would. They did and would until they were done, and then did and would some more. They did and would each others' brains out . . .

And it was about damn time.

About the Author

DAVID SOSNOWSKI has lived in Fairbanks, Alaska, and Washington, D.C., and now lives in Taylor, Michigan. He has worked as a teacher, gagwriter, and part-time fireworks salesman. He won the 1994 Thomas Wolfe Fiction Prize for his short story "Useless Things," which is now a part of *Rapture,* his first novel.